PRAISE FOR

THE UNSPEAKABLE ACTS OF ZINA PAVLOU

'Eleni Kyriacou has drawn such a rich cast in this enthralling
and wholly original novel. Utterly compelling.'
Clare Mackintosh

'Impressive… [Kyriacou's] evocation of postwar
London and the benighted attitudes of its
citizens is worthy of Sarah Waters.'
The Times

'Immersive, gripping, authentic: the kind of historical fiction that
has the reader lookingup from the page, astonished
to find themselves in the 21st Century.'
Erin Kelly

'A complex and fascinating portrait
of the immigrant experience in postwar Britain,
and a tragic and compelling tale.'
Guardian

'Poignant.'
Sunday Times

'A hugely powerful book… Easily one of the
best books you'll read this year.'
Emma Christie

'Tense. Moving. Morally complex. Zina Pavlou
is part monster, part victim and wholly unforgettable.'

THE
Unspeakable
ACTS OF
Zina Pavlou

ALSO BY ELENI KYRIACOU

She Came to Stay

THE
Unspeakable
ACTS OF
Zina Pavlou

ELENI KYRIACOU

An Aries Book

9 7 5 3 1 2 4 6 8

A catalogue record for this book is available from the British Library.

ISBN (PB): 9781837930364
ISBN (E): 9781837930326

Cover design: Ben Prior | Head of Zeus

Printed and bound in Great Britain by
CPI Group (UK) Ltd, Croydon CR0 4YY

MIX
Paper | Supporting
responsible forestry
FSC® C171272

Head of Zeus
5–8 Hardwick Street
London EC1R 4RG

WWW.HEADOFZEUS.COM

*This work of fiction is inspired by true events,
and dedicated to the memory of Hella Christofis and
Styllou Christofi.*

PROLOGUE

They have told so many lies about me.

It's a terrible thing to be accused of a crime so dreadful. To be told every day that you're lying, when you are almost certain that you're not.

Their stories spin above my head, their words snagging in my hair. I dig my fingers in to pull them out. This morning I found black strands on my pillow. I must have tried to untangle the lies as I slept.

I don't speak their language and they look at me wary-eyed. Everything they ask me is kneaded into Greek through an interpreter and whatever I reply she twists back into English. She's young and I can tell by the set of her shoulders and the pull of her mouth that she regrets taking this work.

Today, again, she asked me if perhaps I'd committed this crime when I wasn't in my right mind. And I repeated what I'd told the doctor. I did not do this unspeakable thing. I may be uneducated, I may be poor, but I'm not mad. I'm a respected woman in my village. And, yes, it's true I didn't like the deceased, but it is also true that her disregard for me was well known. Even my son – who has abandoned me, but I'll save that for another time – even he will tell you that.

During her visit, the interpreter girl caught me off guard. She said she'd come to see how I was, but I keep forgetting she works for them and now I'm worried sick because I said too much. Before I could stop myself, I mentioned the first time, years ago, when they said I'd killed the other one.

Her face went white and I knew I'd made a terrible mistake. But if she asks again I'll press my lips together to stop the story slipping out.

I'd like to see Anna but they say I can't. What have they told her? Does she wonder where her *yiayia* is? Or worse, does she believe what they say about me? She may be eight, but she's clever, that granddaughter of mine. She's here, always. A pebble of joy, held tight in my pocket, her imprint on my palm.

All I do now is wait – for their questions to stop, for the visitors who never arrive, for the officials to decide when I'll go to court. And then, once the jury's heard everything, I'll wait for their decision: will they set me free or will I be hanged?

The verdict will be translated through the girl. She'll know everything before I do. At times she cannot look me in the face. I don't think she can bear it.

CHAPTER ONE

London, July 1954

Eva had just slipped into sleep when the thud made her jump. Had the baby fallen from her cot? Had she forgotten to pull up the railing? She sat up quickly, searching the room in the milky light. Nothing. There was no railing, because there was no cot and no baby.

Another thump – it was the door.

'Mrs Georgiou, you up?' A man's voice, outside their bedsit, his London accent all colliding vowels. 'It's the police.'

Jimmy shuffled further down the bed and pulled the sheet over his head. Sighing, she swung her legs round and placed her feet on the cool, cracked lino. She tiptoed towards the door and turned the key, cursing the way it always stuck. She opened it a crack and recognised the face in the hallway.

'Sorry, miss – I mean madam.' It was the same young constable they'd sent last time. Roberts? Robinson? Their names all sounded the same. He looked twenty, if that. 'Can you come?'

'*Now?* I've been working late. Can't it wait?'

A lock of hair fell into her eyes and, as she pushed it away, she felt her thin nightdress pull across her chest. She stood back a little, letting the door shield her.

'Who's there?' called Jimmy.

'PC Robertson,' he said, trying to poke his head around the door. 'Sorry for the disturbance, sir. We need your wife's services.'

Jimmy turned over and grunted an obscenity in Greek, something about the man's mother. It was always about the mothers, thought Eva. Of course, Robertson didn't understand.

'Serious case,' he continued, speaking past her into the room, as if Jimmy cared. 'Need to get things straight. But the suspect doesn't speak a word.' Then he looked at Eva. 'You'll come? Sarge will have my guts for garters if I go back without you.'

Eva sighed. 'Give me five minutes.'

She shut the door on him and went to the sink where she ran a trickle of water. Jimmy's plate was on the draining board, unwashed, a few beans still clinging to the edge. She'd started taking more shifts at the Café de Paris and he'd had dinner alone again. She splashed some water over her eyes, patted her face dry and wiped her hands down her hips.

'You really going?' asked Jimmy. 'You haven't been back long.'

She shrugged in the dark but didn't say anything. She walked past him to get her clothes and he reached out his hand to touch her leg but she moved away.

He sighed. 'They've got you on a string, Evie.'

It was money, wasn't it? They'd agreed the plan months ago. Step one, save up and move somewhere bigger. They'd made a start but it wasn't nearly enough. Step two, try to get pregnant again. Step three, hold on to the baby. Tight this time. Last week she'd turned twenty-nine.

She rummaged past her uniform and found the dress she'd been wearing earlier that day. Luckily she hadn't bothered to rinse out her stockings when she'd returned from the Café, so she pulled them on again and stepped into her shoes.

Grabbing her bag from the chair, she turned to leave.

'See you later?' Jimmy said, half sitting up. 'Before I go to the bakery?'

'I'm not sure – it might take a while.'

He nodded. 'Bye then.'

She started for the door, walked back and leaned down to give him a quick kiss on the cheek, not waiting for him to return it.

In the hallway, PC Robertson was leaning against the bannister.

'Careful,' she said. 'It's rickety.' Nothing in this dump felt safe or sure. He stood back and looked down the stairwell. She had often wondered what that fall would feel like; she'd pictured surrendering to it last Christmas when things had unravelled.

'I'm just out front,' he said. 'We'll be there in a jiffy.'

While the car lurched towards the station, Eva watched the empty Camden streets glide by. Before she'd lost the baby, she and Jimmy had loved walking at night, especially by the canal. If you knew where the trouble was and where it wasn't, you were safe on these streets. During their long walks, they would talk about their plans, what they hoped to squeeze from life. There was none of that now, of course. They still ate a meal together once a week in a café, but the conversation between them had dwindled and she suspected these dinner dates might fall away soon, too.

The constable was prattling on and she made herself pay attention: 'You're the only Greek interpreter we can rely on,' he said, taking a corner with gusto. 'You know Harry C, right? Harry Christos? He got done for forgery last week so he's resting at Her Majesty's Pleasure.' He laughed. 'And old man Whatshisname-opoulos, he must've moved out or died because we can't get an answer from him.'

She felt out of sorts, not ready. She hated not having time to do her face. She quickly ran her fingers over her hair, checking it wasn't sticking up at the back, then pulled her compact from her bag, turning slightly because she didn't like applying lipstick in front of anyone.

'What can you tell me?' she asked, as she Max Factored her bottom lip. 'About the case?'

'Well, Sarge took down her statement.'

'*Her?*' Eva jolted in her seat and just missed getting lipstick all over her chin.

'Yes – didn't I say? Not sure we've had a Greek woman in before. You ever translated for a woman?'

'Once or twice, a robbery, that kind of thing.' She blotted her lips on a handkerchief then dropped everything back in her bag. 'But it's rare.' Despite the muggy evening, she felt cold and realised she'd come out without her mac. She recognised the street and could see the sapphire-blue beacon of the station ahead.

'Well, there are plenty of women arrested,' he continued. 'But she's not the usual type – you know, pickpockets and prosti— well. Working girls, if you get my meaning.' He coughed and swung into a parking space.

'So how did the sergeant get a statement? If she doesn't speak English?'

'Well, she's got a few words, but *very* few.' He yanked up the handbrake and turned off the engine. 'We got her son to question her and translate her answers. He's been here years, so his English is pretty good. But we have to get it all checked, of course. So it's above board.'

He jumped out of the car, ran around the front and opened the door for her. 'It's a big case, so assuming Harry C doesn't get out on good behaviour, you never know... You might get a lot of work out of this.' He tapped the side of his nose twice as though he were doing her a favour and she should keep it quiet, although of course he had no say in the matter.

Eva pictured the money she could earn. Last time it had been five shillings an hour. That was twice as much as she got checking coats at the Café de Paris.

He sprinted up the stairs and held the door open for her, and she hurried through.

'So what's she done?' Eva asked, as he signed her in. 'The suspect – what's she accused of?'

The constable leaned in a little too close and a sickly floral smell hit her nostrils. Then his mouth moved and she saw some crunched sweets inside.

'Murder,' he said, and slipped his hand into his pocket.

'You're joking?'

He shook his head, and one corner of his mouth tugged up, pleased at the effect he'd had.

'Wish I was,' he said. 'Terrible crime scene.'

Eva took a deep quiet breath and tried to get hold of herself. *It's a job, that's all.* She'd been on the Met's books for five years now and she'd translated for dozens of London's thieves, thugs and swindlers. But she'd never been hired to speak up for a murderer.

Robertson pulled out a small lilac box and rattled the Parma Violets at her.

'Want one?'

She declined.

'Shall we?' He motioned towards the corridor.

Her heels click-clacked on the tiled floor as they walked towards the holding cells.

'Who?' she asked, her voice quieter now.

'What?'

'Who's she killed – or meant to have?'

'Daughter-in-law,' he said. Eva slowed down. 'Gruesome,' he continued. 'Looks like she was strangled and set alight. There was some blood as well, so she was probably bashed about a bit, too.'

Eva stood still.

'You alright? Mrs Georgiou?'

Her mouth filled with saliva and she forced herself to swallow hard. She couldn't be sick, not right there in the corridor. *Breathe. Just breathe.* She put her hand to her forehead as though trying to shield her eyes.

'You alright?' he asked again. Then he laughed. 'You're not going to faint on me, are you?'

She shook her head.

'I'm fine.'

'It's shocking, I know, but best you hear it now before you go in. And she's a tiny thing – you won't believe it when you see her.'

Eva looked down the corridor. She could turn and walk out

and never have to face the accused, hear the details of the case, sit and listen to her tell her side then translate it all.

'*Who* did you say was the interpreter at the scene?' she asked.

'Her son.'

'You think she killed her daughter-in-law and you asked her *son* to be an interpreter?'

There was a silence.

'The dead woman's *husband*?'

Robertson nodded then gave a little shrug. 'Nobody else around, and he'd got back from work an hour or so after we got there. We needed someone – she was talking gibberish. We had no choice.'

He waved her forward. 'Come on,' he said, pointing to a door. 'She's in here.'

CHAPTER TWO

The woman was sitting in the corner of the cell, her back to the room, head swathed in a cloud of cigarette smoke. As the door scraped open, she glanced over her shoulder and watched Eva hesitate before stepping inside.

She shifted in her seat but didn't get up.

'Who are you?' she asked, her English soaked in a heavy Greek accent. She took a final drag of her cigarette and squashed it into a tin plate on the floor. 'What you want?'

An officer who'd been leaning against a wall stepped forward.

'She's your trans-la-tor, Mrs Pavlou.' He spoke loudly and slowly, as if she was stupid rather than foreign. 'The one we told you about.' Then to Eva, 'Sarge knows you're here. Won't be a moment. This is the accused, Zina Pavlou.'

Eva faltered, took a deep breath and nodded. She held out her hand.

'Hello, Mrs Pavlou,' she said in Greek, her voice louder than she'd intended. 'I'm Eva – Eva Georgiou.'

The woman shot up, grabbed Eva's hand and clasped it to her chest, making Eva jump.

'You're Cypriot?' she gasped in Greek.

'Let go, Mrs Pavlou,' said the officer as he stepped forward.

'That's alright,' said Eva, trying to take control of the situation.

She offered a small smile, while firmly pulling away her hand. Robertson had been right when he'd said the accused was tiny – she was barely five foot. It took a few seconds before the woman realised what she was trying to do and loosened her grip.

'Thank you.' Eva stood up straight and felt a slick of sweat collect along the nape of her neck. 'I'm here to explain what's going on, Mrs Pavlou.'

Zina let her head drop to one side as she took her in, top to toe. 'Can you get me out?'

'No. That's not up to me.'

'But... but I want to go home.' She spoke quietly, her voice rising and falling on waves of emotion. 'They won't let me see him – my son. They *have* to let me see him.'

Eva could feel the surge of nervous energy coming off the woman, and she braced herself against it.

'*Kyriah* Pavlou,' she said, calmly addressing her with respect. 'I'm here to translate, so you know what's happening. I'm sure they'll let your son visit if...' How could she put this? '...if he wants to.'

Eva watched as Zina grabbed a pack of Player's cigarettes from the bed and counted them to herself, before putting them back. She was thin, as if she hadn't eaten for a while. Could she really have committed such a violent crime? Eva was only a few inches taller than her but suddenly felt huge, and once again was conscious of her sturdy, hollow body. The woman looked up and smiled with such tenderness, the warmth Eva felt was quite unexpected.

'But look at you, *gori mou*,' Zina said. 'What are you, my girl? Twenty-five? Thirty?'

'I'm... I'm twenty-nine.'

'And you're just a woman,' she said. Then the smile dropped and her dark eyes emptied. 'What good are you to me? Eh?'

'Well, I—'

'It's the men who say what happens here,' she continued, stepping closer. Eva instinctively took a tiny step back. 'You know that. Cyprus, London – it's the same everywhere. I need to get out. Don't you understand?'

'Well, I'm going to—'

She lurched forward and grabbed Eva's arm tightly. The police officer was there in a second.

'Let her go right now!'

She quickly released her grip.

'Sorry, sorry,' Zina said to him in English, though didn't bother to apologise to Eva.

Her heart raced in her chest at how fast it had happened, and the sheer strength of her. She could feel Zina's grasp on her skin and resisted the urge to rub at it; there'd be a bruise tomorrow.

'What was that all about?' asked the officer.

'Nothing, we're just saying hello,' said Eva. 'She's just upset.'

'Well, you know you have to report everything she says, don't you?' he replied. 'Anything in Greek has to be translated and handed in.'

'It's nothing, honestly.'

The truth was they didn't really care about the detail. She'd made that mistake years ago when she'd first started translating for the police – you didn't get paid more for being meticulous. She would give them the gist of what was said, as she usually did. Unless it seemed important, of course. But she wasn't going to waste her time with all the ins and outs of it, creating more work, writing it all down in Greek then translating it into English. For what? For it to pile up on some Chief Something-or-other's desk and eventually be discarded?

'Shall we sit, *Kyriah* Pavlou?' she said.

Zina ignored her and held herself tight, looking around the cell as if for the first time. She seemed lost.

Eva pulled out a chair and tried again. Perhaps she'd respond to less formality.

'Can I call you Zina?' she asked.

All she got was a shrug, so she sat at the small table and Zina hesitated then did the same. Eva placed her handbag on the floor by her feet. It was her good brown one, which she'd grabbed in a hurry, and she felt foolish placing such a lovely thing on the damp, dirty lino.

Zina reached across the table but this time didn't touch her, just let her arms lie there, palms up as if waiting for something.

'Can you really help me?' she asked, in Greek. 'My son told so many lies about me and now they think I did this terrible thing.'

Her head was bent over and she stared at her palms, then turned her hands over and started picking at her nails. Looking up, she pointed to the Player's on the bed, and said in English: 'Cigarette? Please?'

'Not now,' said the officer. 'You'll have to ask Sergeant Parks. He might mind.'

She looked at Eva for an explanation.

'Just wait a moment,' she said.

Zina's mouth tightened. 'Tell him I've counted them, and if he tries stealing one I'll know.'

'I'm sure he won't,' said Eva. 'Just wait and you can have one later.'

'What did she say?' he asked.

'She said she really needs a cigarette.'

He snorted in response.

Zina leaned across the table. 'You'll tell them I'm a good woman, won't you? I need to get home to Anna, my granddaughter. They won't look after her properly. But you'll help, won't you?'

Eva glanced away and picked up her handbag from the floor. She opened it and started rummaging inside, unsure what she was looking for.

She spoke into the bag. 'The sergeant will probably want me to read your statement to you,' she said, ignoring the question.

She decided a handkerchief would do, pulled it out and dabbed her temples. Despite the chill that permeated these brick walls, she was warm.

Zina stared at her as she patted her forehead and she suddenly felt self-conscious. She hadn't had time to apply her usual careful face – foundation, powder, a little rouge on her cheekbones – and she was sure she looked pallid and unkempt, but she could hardly take out her compact here. Why hadn't she gone to the Ladies' and fixed herself up a little? Why did it even matter?

An unease that had descended when she'd walked in now felt palpable – a stale taste in her mouth, like a stagnant river filling up her insides. She couldn't get one of her heads, not now. She wiped at her forehead again and saw Zina follow her hand with her eyes, noticing her ring.

'You're married?'

Eva nodded. Greeks always wanted to know everything – why would a woman accused of murder be any different?

'Children?'

Always this. She hated the question and gave a small shake of her head.

'Don't wait too long.' Then in the next breath, 'How old do you think I am?'

Eva shrugged.

'Just say what you're thinking. I don't mind,' Zina said. 'I'm not one of those vain ones. Not like *her*.'

She put a hand up to smooth down her thick black hair that was caught at the nape of her neck in a bun. Eva tried to take in her features without staring. Her skin was a sallow, faded brown, with a hint of yellow under it – she'd been nut-brown at some point, but hadn't seen the sun for months. Her brow protruded a little, and the deep lines that ran down either side of her mouth to her chin revealed a face more used to frowning than laughing. And there was a determination there. It was the face of a survivor. She could have been fifty or seventy.

Zina leaned forward and said in a whisper, 'They don't like foreigners you know.' She might be a murderer but there was plenty of truth in that. 'They'll say I did it because they hate us.'

'What's going on?' asked the officer. 'No whispering allowed.'

'Nothing,' said Eva. 'She's just asking what's going to happen.'

'Can you get me some biscuits?' asked Zina. 'I want something sweet.'

At that moment, the door clanked open and Sergeant Parks walked in.

'Good morning, Mrs Georgiou,' he said. 'If I remember rightly it's Eva, isn't it?' He pronounced it with a long 'e'.

Relieved to see him, she stood to shake his hand. 'Morning, Sergeant. Yes, it's Eva,' she corrected him, rhyming it with 'clever'.

Another chair was brought in and he sat at the table.

'Thank you for coming in at such an early hour, but there's some urgency.'

'That's alright, sir.' He always made her nervous. It wasn't just the uniform – she was used to that. Perhaps it was the way the others straightened up when he walked in.

'You've been filled in, I take it?' he asked her.

'Briefly.'

'Shocking case,' he said. Then he leaned across to Zina. 'So, Mrs Pavlou, are you ready to answer some more questions?'

Zina lifted her head a little and nodded.

'You can understand some English, can't you?' he said. Then he turned and muttered, 'More than she's letting on, I think.'

Eva shifted in her chair. She'd never met an English person yet who spoke Greek, but here it was again – the idea that all foreigners who said they didn't speak English were lying. As if the thought itself was ridiculous.

Someone placed three glasses of water on the table.

'Right then,' said Parks. 'We'll get you to read her statement to her first – she doesn't read or write Greek either, if you can believe that. See if she agrees it's correct, then we'll continue with the questioning.'

Eva explained all of this to Zina.

'I've told them everything,' she replied. 'But if they want to waste their time, go ahead.'

'She said alright,' said Eva, 'but you know everything already.'

'I doubt that,' he said. 'Here.'

Eva took the sheaf of paper, read each paragraph to herself then translated it for Zina. It took longer than usual; she stumbled over some of the words – not because she didn't understand what was written down, but because, as she read, she couldn't help but picture the scene.

> I came here from Cyprus in July 1953 to live with my son, Michalis, his wife, Hedy, their daughter, Anna, and baby boy. I wanted to work, to make money and pay off a debt I had. But they asked me to help them, so I stayed home and looked after the house instead. I had to leave for a few weeks, owing to some difficulty with my daughter-in-law, but when I went back, before Easter, we got on much better.

She stopped to check Zina was in agreement, but also to take a steadying breath for what she was about to read. The woman nodded.

> At 7.45 p.m. on Wednesday, 28th July, my son left for work as usual. He works in a bar in the evenings. I tidied up and Hedy was washing some clothes. So I decided to go to bed. Every night she takes everything off and washes herself at the sink, too.
>
> She bolted the door that leads to the yard and put the garden fork under the handle inside, as usual. The lock is broken, so we do this to make sure nobody can get in.
>
> Around 1 a.m., I woke to go to the lavatory, which is outside. From the top of the stairs I could see that the street door was open and smoke was coming from downstairs.

Eva faltered, took a sip of water then continued.

> I went downstairs and saw that there was a bonfire in the garden and – and Hedy was lying there... on top of the fire.

She was determined her voice wouldn't break. Whatever she read next would stay with her, but what choice did she have now?

At once, I ran to get a bucket of water. I threw it over her to save her. I tried to put out the fire but I couldn't. I threw more water but it made no difference. The fire was so strong.

She paused.

'Yes,' said Zina in English. 'I try stop fire.'

'When you're ready, Mrs Georgiou,' said Sergeant Parks.

Eva shifted slightly and tried to sit up straight.

The children were upstairs – Anna, my granddaughter. and the baby. I was worried because the house was filling with smoke. So I ran into the road for help. There was a car coming so I waved my hands to make them stop. I shouted, but the man and woman inside couldn't understand me. Then when I said, 'Fire! Children sleeping!' they realised what I meant.

I ran to the house and they drove up and followed me. The woman wanted to call the fire brigade and asked me for the address. I didn't know how to say it so I found a letter and showed her the address on the envelope. That's when she rang them and they rang the police.

Eva stared at her. Perhaps it had happened like this? Why did they think she'd had a hand in it? There was nothing to suggest she'd done it. Yes, she'd said herself that she didn't get on with her daughter-in-law, but wasn't that the case with most Greek mothers? Greek mothers who were besotted with their sons and resented another woman taking him away from them? Running a house when they thought they knew better?

'Is that what you said?' asked Eva. 'Is it correct?'

'Yes,' said Zina.

'Is this your mark, your signature at the bottom?' She pointed to the X in lieu of Zina's name.

Zina nodded. 'Tell them I tried to save her.'

'It's in here.'

'Tell them again.'

'She says it's an accurate statement,' she said to the sergeant. 'And wants me to tell you again that she tried to save her.'

Parks scribbled something in his notepad, giving nothing away.

'I have questions,' he said. 'But let's take a moment.'

He stood and motioned for Eva to leave the cell. She quickly bent down to pick up her bag.

Zina jolted. 'Where are you going?' she shouted. 'Don't leave me with them.'

'It's okay,' said Eva, trying to keep her voice calm. 'I'll be back.' She turned at the door. 'I promise.' She was relieved to step outside, even if just for a minute.

The sergeant followed her. He sighed as they slowly walked away from the holding cell towards reception.

'It's a particularly violent case,' he said. 'Are you up to more questions or do you want a break? I realise we got you out of your bed.'

'I'm alright,' Eva said. 'But has she slept?'

'Oh, don't worry about her. But if you need half an hour we can wait a bit – she's not going far if you want some air. You will continue with the interview, won't you?'

She wanted to say no. She glanced at her watch. It was seven in the morning now. If she hurried, she'd see Jimmy before he left for work. She knew she should go, she'd seen so little of him lately. How could they mend everything between them if they were never together? And she did still want to mend it, she really did. But soon one of them would give up, and it would be too late.

'You'll stay?' he asked.

'Can I have ten minutes? I just need to powder my nose.' So, listening to this dreadful case was preferable to going home. That's how bad things were. She started to walk away then turned back.

'Sir?'

'Yes?'

'Do you think she did it? I mean – *strangling*? A *fire*? She's tiny, and she looks quite old and...'

He laughed.

'That's not the half of it,' he said. 'I've been doing this long enough to know some things are rarely what they seem while others are *exactly* as they seem. She's not that old, she just looks it – she's fifty-three. And if you ask me, she's as strong as an ox. One of those uneducated peasant types, used to hard manual labour.'

Eva clenched her jaw.

'She had the opportunity – apart from the children sleeping, they were alone. And the motive seems to be there, too. She's admitted herself that there was no love lost between them. So yes, I think she's more than capable. But it's not up to me. That's for the jury to decide.'

But you've already made up your mind, thought Eva. She turned and walked into the Ladies', where she quickly slid into a cubicle and locked the door behind her.

Placing her hands over the tiny cracked sink, she let her head drop and took in a couple of deep breaths. It wasn't unusual for fleeting thoughts of her mother, Katerina, to come to mind when she saw an older Cypriot woman. But this time felt different. This time she was shaken, and not just because of the awful details of the case. Something about Zina had stirred Eva's memories, bringing back those terrible days before her mother's death.

She turned on the tap and let the cold water run over her fingers, then put them to her temples. Zina looked nothing like Katerina, who'd been much younger when she'd died. But her panic and vulnerability had hit a nerve deep within Eva. Like her mother, Zina was a desperate woman in a strange country where she couldn't make herself understood.

She placed her hands at her neck to cool the skin around her throat. Her mother hadn't spoken English either. Neither had Eva – she was eleven at the time, and they'd only arrived weeks earlier.

She patted her neck dry with a paper towel. That one simple fact – their lack of language – had been their undoing. Because if you couldn't speak English here, you just didn't matter. And when you did learn it, and tried to fit in, well. Then you couldn't help but feel you were giving away a small part of yourself.

Which was a price she'd been happy to pay, as she'd slipped into London life over the years, making this place her home. But it was different for Jimmy. He'd arrived just a few years ago, and had struggled with the weather and customs and missing his brothers back home. Learning the language when you're older is much harder, he often said. But still he persevered, ploughing through the English newspaper every day as he battled to learn new words.

She turned off the tap and noticed the shadow of a bruise blossoming just above her wrist. Had Zina Pavlou killed her daughter-in-law in cold blood? And simply because she didn't *like* her? Who in their right mind kills someone because they don't *like* them?

I ran to get a bucket of water. I threw it over her to save her.

She had to stop this. She had to be professional. She was here to translate, that's all. She owed them nothing and could walk away from it right now. With Jimmy's wages, the two of them made enough to put food on the table. This was just a bit extra. To save for rent on a bigger flat, and the baby. If there was a baby. But as she tried to calm herself, a splinter of fear scratched at her stomach. She dried her hands, opened the door and stepped outside.

On her right was the cell where Zina was held. On her left, the exit. She could go home and creep back into bed. Jimmy would still be there, warm, sleep-addled. He'd open his arms, and this time she'd slide inside them, instead of turning over. They'd wake an hour later and start afresh.

'Ready?' The sergeant was in front of her.

She set back her shoulders a little and nodded, then slowly walked towards the cell.

CHAPTER THREE

'I tell everything,' said Zina in English. 'I go home now?'

Parks shook his head. 'No, Mrs Pavlou, you're not going home. I have more questions.'

'Everything true,' she said. A police officer shifted near the door. Then in Greek to Eva, 'Tell him it's true.'

'There's no point pleading with Mrs Georgiou,' Parks said to Zina. 'I'm the one in charge.' Then to Eva, 'Shall we begin?'

She nodded. 'I'm ready.'

As he asked questions, Eva translated.

'Can you tell me why your daughter-in-law's wedding ring was found wrapped in a piece of paper behind the china clock in your bedroom?'

Zina didn't respond.

'Ask her if she removed it from Hedy's finger,' he said.

'He asks if you—'

'I found it when I was cleaning,' Zina interrupted. 'I thought it was a curtain ring so I put it there for safe keeping.' Her mouth pulled into a tight little smile.

'A curtain ring? I see.' He wrote it down. 'PC Watkins?'

The constable by the door bustled over. 'Yes, sir.'

'Call Davies – he's at the crime scene now. Ask him to check the curtain rings in the property and if there are any missing, then report back immediately. Get him to take one off so we can see what they look like. Straight away. Tell him we'll wait for his response.'

'Yes, sir.' The constable rushed out and the determined smack of his footsteps could be heard fading along the corridor.

'Where's he going?' asked Zina. Eva looked at Parks but he shot her a warning glance, so she didn't respond.

'Next question. I want to ask her about this,' he said, and opened a large paper folder. Inside lay a long piece of red cotton fabric – a scarf. It had a faded gold floral pattern on it and had been ripped.

There was only one reason he could be showing this to Zina. Eva's throat tightened.

'Don't touch,' he said, putting out his hand. 'Ask her what this is.'

She took a gulp of water and relayed the question.

Zina shrugged.

'Do you recognise it?' Eva asked. Her head was thumping now. Was it too late to leave?

Zina said in English: 'No.'

'Tell her it was lying on the ground next to her daughter-in-law, Hedy. Tell her we believe it was used to strangle her.'

Eva turned and stared at him.

'After she was bludgeoned with an ash pan and before she was set alight.'

Eva's mouth hung open. Dear God.

'Whoever did this,' he said, 'wasn't taking any chances.'

Eva coughed, the sergeant pushed the glass of water towards her, and she took another gulp.

'He…' she began, '… he believes it was used to strangle Hedy.' She couldn't look at it, so stared at Zina. She couldn't say the next bit.

'Say all of it. I want to see what she does.' •

'He says it was used to strangle Hedy, after she was hit on the head with the ash pan and before—'

Zina's hand flew down onto the table as she leaped up. 'They want to say I would do this thing? I'm a grandmother, a respectable woman!' An officer came over and she sat back in her chair, her cheeks red.

Eva took a deep juddering breath, not caring now if she showed her distress. 'She says she wouldn't do such a thing. She's a respectable woman, a grandmother.'

A weary look crossed Parks' face. 'It's all very well protesting, Mrs Pavlou, but the evidence says otherwise. How did you not see it on the night your daughter-in-law died? Ask her.'

Zina didn't respond.

'It was next to her head,' he continued. 'Your daughter-in-law was lying on the ground face up, her head just a couple of feet from the back door. Only the bottom part of her was on top of the bonfire. You said you threw water over her. It was next to her, but you're telling me that you didn't see it?'

Eva repeated it all, her voice flat. When would this end?

Zina's eyes filled with tears. 'No, no – I no see,' she said in English, then turned to Eva and spoke in Greek. 'I'm telling the truth. I want to go home to see my son. Why don't they believe me?' Her hands were fists now and she started hitting her own chest.

She seemed so helpless. Eva was surprised at the wave of pity that rose inside her. She stared hard at Zina's shoulder rather than her face. Whoever heard of an interpreter crying? She'd look ridiculous. They'd never hire her again.

'My son,' said Zina in English. 'Please.'

Parks stood up and leaned over the table.

'Your son, Mrs Pavlou, doesn't... want... to see you. And you can stop that chest-beating or whatever it is *right now*.'

She stopped, letting her hands fall into her lap. She'd understood either his words or his tone.

'This scarf, Mrs Pavlou,' he pushed it slightly towards her, 'belongs to your granddaughter, Anna. I think you know that, because your son told us you often pick it up from the chair where Anna leaves it after school and hang it on the back of the kitchen door.'

Eva paused for a moment then translated.

'Anna,' said Zina, but nothing else.

He closed the folder on the scarf and put it away. 'Ask her this word for word: did she step into the garden last night when she saw Hedy's body was on fire?'

'No, I was too scared,' she responded. 'I stood near her. I filled the bucket with water and threw it over her to put out the flames. But I didn't go in the garden.'

Eva was careful to relay the answer exactly.

'Are you certain? It's a small garden, barely ten-foot square. Where did you stand?'

'On the step that leads from the kitchen to the garden.'

'You're certain? You didn't step into the garden at all?'

'Of course I'm sure. Why would I go near a fire? I'm not stupid. I threw water over her twice, but from the doorstep.'

Parks sat back, then turned to Eva. 'Ask her to take off her shoes.'

Eva frowned. 'Excuse me?'

'Her shoes. Could you please ask her to take them off and hand them to me?'

She had no idea where this line of questioning was going but was resigned now.

'What is it?' Zina asked.

'He wants you to take off your shoes.'

'Why? They're mine. They can't take them from me.'

'He's not going to take them away, but you have to do as he says.'

'*Sta anathema*, to hell with all of them,' said Zina under her breath. 'Making an old woman take off her shoes.'

She bent over, unlaced her heavy brown shoes and slipped them off. She handed them to Parks begrudgingly.

He took them, held them up and turned them over. The

creased leather had seen years of wear. He looked at the soles and then held one up to the accused.

'Ask her what she can smell on the sole,' he said.

Before Eva was able to translate, Zina shook her head.

'Ask her.'

'What does he want?'

'You have to take the shoe,' said Eva, embarrassed for the woman. She knew what was coming. 'And smell the sole. Tell him what you can smell.'

Zina tentatively reached out, took her shoe back and sniffed the sole. She shrugged.

'Well?' he asked.

She didn't reply.

'Mrs Pavlou,' he began. 'I can smell paraffin from here. I could smell it as I walked in. Mrs Georgiou can certainly smell it, and I think the desk sergeant down the corridor can too. Don't tell me you can't.'

Zina didn't say anything.

'There was also a very strong smell of paraffin in the kitchen,' he said. 'And yet the floor was very clean. Can you tell me why that might be?'

'No,' said Zina.

'Did you spill paraffin and mop it up?' he asked.

'No.'

He leaned in. 'Did you stand next to the deceased while she was burning?'

'No!' She shook her head. 'I was on the step, throwing water on her.'

'Then how did paraffin get onto your shoes?' he persisted.

Eva translated and Zina pulled her face into a tight frown.

Parks scribbled on his notes. 'Tell her she's not helping herself by not speaking. She's making it much worse.'

'If there's something you want to say,' said Eva, 'you must say it. If there's anything you think he needs to know. That you haven't told him.'

Zina's gaze slid across to her.

'You're just like them,' she said, with a brittle stare. 'I thought you were here to help me, but you're here for them. You lied to me.'

Eva blinked several times to stop her eyes welling up. She was trying to do her job. And now this. And she was so tired. And she should have gone home to Jimmy.

'What?' he asked.

'She says I'm on your side, not hers. Says I'm here to help you, not her.'

'Mrs Georgiou is here to make sure you understand everything. So you get a fair hearing.'

Then Zina spoke and it came out in a torrent of Greek.

'Yes, I've just remembered, I spilled it days ago – the paraffin – when I was filling the heater. I must have stepped in it without realising. It's not anything. Just an accident.'

The sergeant, one eyebrow raised, wrote it all down.

'I see. In the middle of July, she was filling a paraffin heater.'

Just then the door opened and the constable who'd been sent on the mission walked in. He handed a piece of paper to Parks and took up his previous position, back against the wall.

'So… let's see.' The sergeant read the words on the paper then slid the sheet across and showed Eva what was written there. 'Please translate,' he said.

Eva sat up. 'It's about the ring,' she said to Zina. 'Which was found behind the clock in your room. The constable reports that there are no curtain rings missing in your son's house.'

'But I didn't know that. It looked like a curtain ring. So I kept it, in case.'

Eva shook her head. 'Let me finish. There are no curtain rings missing, and in fact there are no curtain rings used at all in the house.'

There was a silence.

'Tell her there is an inscription on the inside of the ring, clearly showing that it is from her son to the deceased, with the date that they married,' he said. 'Then you can tell her I think she's lying.'

'No!' shouted Zina. 'I'm no liar! You liar! My son liar!'

'Please tell Mrs Pavlou that she is being charged with the murder of her daughter-in-law. I will now read out the charge.'

Eva placed her hands under the table to hide the shaking as she translated.

'Mrs Pavlou, you're being charged with the murder of—'

Zina started howling.

'Please let me finish,' said Eva. 'With the murder of your daughter-in-law – please – please – I will now read out the charge.'

Zina clasped her hands behind her head and started rocking back and forth, wailing. The sergeant ploughed on, so Eva had to, too.

'You are charged that on the night of 28th July 1954,' repeated Eva, 'in London, you murdered Hedy Pavlou, contrary to common law. I have to make sure you understand. Do you wish to say anything?'

Zina's cries continued as she rocked back and forth, back and forth. Her arms clamped over her ears.

'What will happen to her now?' asked Eva, as she walked along the corridor with Parks.

'The usual. She stays overnight, then first thing tomorrow goes up in front of the magistrates' court.'

'Then on remand till her trial date?'

He nodded. 'In Holloway. Can you see this through to the end? It's better to have the same interpreter for the whole case.'

'No, I don't think so,' said Eva, already feeling the weight of responsibility tugging at her neck. 'I mean, I don't think she wants me.'

'She doesn't get a choice, does she? We've only got three Greek interpreters including yourself. And frankly with the way this is stacking up against her, she'd do well to cooperate.'

'Who's her solicitor? Is he Greek?'

'A Welshman, Ellis, but he's lived in Cyprus, so he speaks it well enough. We've used him before – not exactly fluent but gets by. So he probably wouldn't need you.'

'Isn't there a Cypriot solicitor who can represent her?' asked Eva. 'So he can explain things properly?'

He laughed. 'Not unless she's willing to pay for someone to come over. Ellis is quite competent. Let's hope he can talk some sense into her, because her trial won't be easy.'

Eva paused. 'What do you mean?'

'A coarse, peasant woman who can't even read and write her own language – let alone English – accused of killing her pretty young daughter-in-law? No prizes for guessing which way the jury will go.'

'But she'll still get a fair trial, won't she?' asked Eva. 'I mean, she's innocent till proven guilty, surely?'

'Juries are unpredictable, Mrs Georgiou. And she doesn't make it easy to like her. You saw what she's like. Anyway, she'll be under lock and key till it goes to court. Will you do it? See it through?'

She pictured Zina Pavlou in the cell, rocking back and forth. How angry she'd looked, then how lost. Confused at what was happening around her. An image came to Eva's mind: a framed photo of herself as a child, sitting on her mother's lap, that she kept on her bedside table.

'Alright.'

'Good girl. I'll make sure you're on the whole case from beginning to end. And there shouldn't be any more early mornings like this. What do we usually pay you?'

She hesitated. It was going to be an awful few months. She may as well get what she could.

'I know Harry C is paid fifteen shillings an hour,' she said. 'Sir.'

Parks pulled a face. 'How do you know that?'

'He told me. He was boasting he gets much more than me.'

'I wish people wouldn't discuss money like that. Alright, how about ten shillings an hour but no expenses? As you've promised to see it through. I know that's probably double what you usually get.'

There was no chance he'd give her the same as Harry, she knew that. And none of the better-paid clerical positions were open to married women like her anyway.

'How about a shilling on top of that if I work two hours or more? So it's ten shillings for the first hour in the day, but eleven after that? It's exhausting work and there's a lot of it, as you said. And it *would* be better for everyone if she didn't keep changing translators.'

He looked at her through narrowed eyes as if only now seeing her for the first time.

'No expenses,' he said.

'Of course. Thank you, sir.' She'd be making more in an hour on this job than she did in a four-hour evening shift at the Café de P. And she wasn't on her feet.

'This'll earn you a pretty packet. Worked at Holloway before?'

She nodded. She'd translated for a Cypriot woman accused of stealing a pair of gloves from Selfridges and a pair of sisters who'd worked as prostitutes.

'A couple of times,' she said.

'Good,' he said, 'then you won't be daunted by it all. Let's see what our Mrs Pavlou makes of it, shall we?'

'What do you mean?'

'Well, it's hardly the most welcoming of places, is it?' he said. 'Once locked up inside, she might change her tune. Maybe she'll tell us what really happened last night.'

CHAPTER FOUR

July 1953, one year before the murder

Zina knocked on her son's front door and straightened her coat. She was about to see Michalis for the first time in years. So when the door swung open, she was surprised to find a woman in front of her. But there she was, all rounded edges, her mouth half open as though she'd been interrupted mid-laugh.

'Yes?' she asked, brightly, then immediately raised her eyebrows as she realised who her visitor was. '*Zina?*'

A young girl with the blackest hair, perhaps seven or eight years old, peeped out from behind her skirts.

'Is it really you?' asked the woman.

Zina smiled at the mention of her name.

'Mi–Michalis?' she said. She put her hand on her chest, to indicate herself: 'Mamma.'

The woman turned. 'Mick! She's here!'

'Daddy!' The girl ran down the corridor.

'We thought you weren't coming for another hour or so,' said the woman, 'but it's lovely to finally meet you. I've been telling Mick to get you over for ages.'

Zina stared as she spoke; after a few seconds they both laughed as they realised they couldn't understand each other.

She was prettier than Zina had expected, plumper too. Her short coppery hair was set just so, her eyebrows arched, and she was wearing plenty of red lipstick.

'Hedy,' she said, putting out her hand. She gave Zina a warm smile. 'So pleased to meet you.'

Zina took it in a firm grip.

'*Herredeh*,' she replied, knowing the *Englessa* wouldn't understand her hello but hoping that the small nod and shy smile would be enough.

'Well, do come in,' said Hedy, 'please.' She was about to make space when there was a rush of footsteps and Michalis barged towards the door, practically knocking her over.

'Mamma! You really came!' he shouted in Greek.

He hugged Zina, then picked her up off the floor, making her laugh like a *goritsi* – a young girl – at the village fair. The little girl laughed, clapping by their side. He put her down and she immediately hugged him close, then held him at arm's length.

'My son, look at you,' she responded, tears in her eyes. 'You've filled out!'

Hedy stood awkwardly, looking from one to the other, waiting for a translation.

'I was a kid – what, twenty-two? – when I left. It's been twelve years. You look the same, Mamma.'

Zina laughed. 'I've got old.' She swept a hand over her face. 'It's been so many years I've been asking you to let me come, and finally I'm here.'

He shifted his feet. 'It wasn't that we didn't want you, Mamma. We just weren't ready before. You're always welcome in our house.'

She smiled and nodded and they both knew this wasn't true.

Hedy grabbed his arm. 'Well introduce us properly, Mick.'

'Mamma, this is Hedy,' he said in English. He put his arm around his wife's shoulders, and she pulled it down a little so he hugged her tighter, keeping hold of his hand. 'Your daughter-in-law.'

His wife smiled broadly now, showing all her teeth, and spoke loud and slow.

'Hed-dee.'

'Hed-dee,' said Zina and smiled. Then she held out her arms to the little girl, who came to her immediately.

'Anna?' she asked her. The girl beamed that her grandmother should know her name.

'I'm your *yiayia*,' Zina said to her in Greek.

'*Yiayia!*' the girl responded.

Michalis pulled away from his wife and crouched down to the girl.

'We taught her that word, didn't we, Anna?'

'*Yiayia* has come all the way from Cyprus to stay with us for a while,' said Hedy. 'We've done a little tea party for you,' she said to Zina. 'Mick, tell her we've made some cakes.'

Mick translated and Zina looked pleased. She gave Anna a kiss and stroked her thick, dark hair, then Michalis led her into the house.

'You must be shattered, Mamma,' he said. Then in English he called, 'Hed, would you grab her case, love, and bring it in?' As he passed the staircase he pointed upstairs. 'Georgie's sleeping, so I'll show you around later.'

In the kitchen, Zina sat down with the girl on her lap and took in her surroundings: a grubby little stove with a pot bubbling on top, windowsills that were smudged grey from the fog, and washing hung up haphazardly in the corner. You'd think they didn't know she was coming.

'This is how you live?' she asked Michalis, astonished.

'What's wrong with it?'

'But it's no better than home.'

He laughed. 'Oh come on, Mamma, it's a hundred times better.' Then he slapped the wall. 'Look! Brick, not mud. And see this?' He gestured towards the cooker. 'In the last place we rented we had to take turns on the landing, but here we have a stove to ourselves. We can cook a meal any time we want.'

Zina shrugged a little.

'We have our own oven back home,' she said.

'What is it?' asked Hedy, depositing the suitcase in a corner and carrying over a tray of tea things. 'Is something the matter?'

Michalis smiled. 'She's not as taken by the stove as we are.'

'Really?' said Hedy. 'What's wrong with it?'

'Nothing. I just told her life's better here than Cyprus, and we have our own cooker. She says she has one back home, too.'

'Like this?' she asked Zina.

'That's just it,' he said. 'She's got an outdoor clay oven, and the whole village uses it.'

There was a second's pause, then both he and Hedy laughed. He translated for Zina and she nodded, not understanding why that was funny.

Hedy placed the tray on the table and Anna wriggled off Zina's lap and hurriedly laid out four cups and saucers, plates and forks.

Zina listened as her son prattled on in Greek about how good life was in London, and a twinge of sadness snapped at her heart. She'd expected more. Much more. She'd heard about the opportunities here, the money that could be made. And while she never thought Michalis would be rich, his letters had led her to think that they were doing well for themselves. Twelve years he'd been here, in this big dirty city, and this was as far as he'd got?

'Look, *Yiayia*,' said Anna, as she slowly carried a plate of misshapen cakes to the table and placed them in the middle.

'They got up early and made them this morning,' said Michalis.

The girl then took a vase from the kitchen windowsill that had a few green sprigs in it and put it next to Zina's plate. Zina nodded and stroked Anna's arms in thanks as she casually glanced around at all the things she'd have to get to work on. That rug needed a beating, and Anna's clothes hadn't seen an iron in a while. Her hair looked tangled too. She should plait it.

'Would you like a cup of tea, Mrs Pavlou?' asked Hedy.

Zina turned and looked at her. That milk-white skin had a transparent quality about it. If you held her up to the light you'd probably see right through her.

Hedy held the teapot up to Zina's face.

'Tea?' she asked again. 'You must be parched.'

'Mamma,' said Zina. 'No Mrs Pavlou. Me Mamma.'

'Oh,' the girl laughed. 'I've got a Mamma, but alright. Want a cuppa, Mamma?'

'*Chai*,' said Zina. And nodded. '*Evharisto…*' She frowned as she tried to recall the words she'd learned on the boat. 'Taink you?' she asked, unsure it was right.

'You'll have to learn some Greek now, Hed,' said Michalis. 'She doesn't speak any English really – just a few words here and there.'

Hedy picked up the kettle, walked to the sink in the corner and turned on the tap. There was a terrible noise in the pipe but eventually the water burst out in spurts.

'Well, if she's here for a few months,' she said, turning her back and setting the kettle on the stove, 'she could learn some English, eh, Mamma? I mean she really should try. How will she get by?'

Zina picked up the word 'English' and 'Mamma' and thought they must be talking about her lack of language. They were probably right. It *would* help her to learn a little.

But there was something about her daughter-in-law's tone. The way she'd turned her back on her, her mother-in-law, who she'd only met minutes before. And how she kept it turned as she lit the flame and watched the kettle kick into a slow boil. If Zina had to put her finger on the exact moment that a spark of unkindly feeling towards the *Englessa* had ignited, it would have been then, as Hedy brewed her a cup of tea for the first time.

Perhaps the *Englessa* didn't know it was disrespectful to turn your back to a guest, let alone your mother-in-law. But then you had to ask yourself, what kind of a family had she come from not to know such a thing? And what kind of standards did her son keep in his house?

After they'd had their weak English tea and nibbled on the dry cakes (Hedy removed the plate once everyone had taken one, so she couldn't eat another had she wanted), Zina opened her handbag. She pulled out a small cloth doll, with a hand-sewn face and yellow wool for hair.

'A gift for Anna,' she said, and handed the rag doll to the girl. 'I made it for her.'

Anna gasped, took the doll and immediately started stroking her woollen hair.

'Say thank you,' said Michalis.

'Thank you, *Yiayia*. I'm going to call her Maria.'

Zina grinned and delved into her bag again. This time, she pulled out a cotton drawstring bag, the size of her palm.

'What's that?' asked Hedy.

Zina tugged the ribbons apart and took out two small wooden icons that opened up like tiny books, then stood and surveyed the room. She walked to a corner where a pot plant, bent over in its death throes, hung over a shelf. She moved it to the floor, then placed her icons there.

'Mick?'

'It's okay, Hed.'

Zina crossed herself, kissed one icon, did the same with the second, then knelt right there on the worn lino to pray in front of them. She could feel them watching as she whispered the words. When she got up, knees cracking, she motioned to Michalis and Hedy to come over.

'Come, pray,' she said in Greek.

Michalis shook his head.

'What's wrong with you?' Zina asked.

Hedy got up and started clattering the plates.

'Mick. Tell her it's fine if she wants to pray,' she said, over her shoulder. 'I mean, that's up to her. But not here, in the kitchen. Can't she keep it to her room?'

Zina knew from the tightness of the girl's voice that she wasn't happy. She glanced at her son for a response but saw none was coming.

'What is it?' she asked in Greek. 'Don't you pray in this house?'

He shifted his feet.

'Not really, Mamma,' he said. He walked to the sink on the pretext of needing a glass of water, and drained it quickly. 'You see, it's not that Hedy doesn't believe, but not in the same way.'

'And what about you?' she asked. 'God is God. There's only one.'

Hedy started running hot water into the sink, again turning her back.

'Well,' said Michalis. 'Hedy's German, so she doesn't go in for all these icons and things. It's not their way.'

'But they're holy,' said Zina. 'You need an icon in the house, to protect you.'

'No, not in the kitchen, Mamma. Put them in your room, alright?'

Zina looked at the floor and wondered what to do. This wasn't the boy she'd brought up. What had happened to him? It was clear the girl hadn't been a good influence, but it *was* their house after all, even if it was a godless one. And she was a guest.

She took a deep breath and resolved to make it right. She walked to Hedy, who was busying herself with soap suds and a ragged dishcloth, and gently put her hand on her shoulder.

Hedy jumped and turned around. Her face was pink now, and she looked a little startled. Well, she scared easy.

'Is okay, Hedy, is okay,' said Zina in English, patting her shoulder kindly. 'Okay' was another word she'd learned on the boat. She knew it was gentle and meant the same as *entaxi*. That everything would be alright.

While they watched, she walked to the corner, reached up to the shelf, took the icons down and put them back in the drawstring bag. She slipped it into her pocket. Then she carefully replaced the shrivelling plant on the shelf, turning it just so to make sure its brown leaves were hanging in exactly the position she'd found them.

* * *

Just before bed that evening, Michalis put Zina's suitcase in Anna's room, which she'd be sharing, and gave her a tour of the house. Zina remarked on the musty smell and patted the damp walls.

'It's the fog,' he explained. 'The winters here are terrible, and even though it's summer now, it seeps into the bricks.' He pressed the wall just beneath the kitchen window then showed her his finger, which was smeared grey. 'The patches dry a bit but never properly, then the weather turns and it starts all over again. It's the same wherever you go – what can you do?'

He opened the door to his bedroom.

'Well, this is nice,' said Zina, walking in. The room was filled with light as the fading sun threw shadows on the floral wallpaper. There was no musty smell here, and while the rest of the house felt cramped, here you could breathe. She frowned to see that the bed was unmade – had they been sleeping before she'd arrived, or did they just not bother in the morning? On the floor lay a pair of stockings and she averted her eyes.

'Come and see our Georgie,' said Michalis, and they walked over to look at the pudgy baby sleeping in the cot by the wall. She stroked his cheek then went to the window.

'The windowsills seem good here.' She pointed.

'Other side of the house,' he said, 'gets more sun.' Pulling back the curtain, he showed her the road running along the front. A number 24 bus went by and the frame rattled in its casing. 'Bit noisy,' he laughed.

'Oh, but I wouldn't mind that,' she said. 'I mean better that than damp.'

He dropped the curtain and turned towards her. 'Sorry, Mamma, but you can't sleep in here. This is our room. We need the space for the baby. We can't have little Georgie in the damp.'

'I don't mind the baby staying,' she said. 'It's big enough for me and Anna, too. The damp can't be good for her. And I'd be closer to the stairs. I'll probably be going to the lavatory at night. You don't have one inside, do you?'

Michalis shook his head. 'It's our room,' he said. 'Anyway, we'll get you settled in and you'll see. You'll like it. The back of the house is much better for you. Quieter.'

'I see.' She folded her arms and surveyed the room as she walked slowly around. 'You know, back home we always used to give up our beds for guests. Remember when your uncle—'

'Mamma, please,' he interrupted. 'It's *our* room. Anyway, Hedy wouldn't hear of it even if I wanted to. She spent ages making this room special – choosing the wallpaper, the curtains. She decorated it all herself, you know.'

It was a little showy now she looked at it properly.

'Don't be difficult, eh? Your room is perfectly fine.'

She gave him a tight grin and nodded. She'd been here a few hours and there were already so many things she wanted to say; words piling on top of each other in her head, threatening to tumble over. No, best keep everything tight in place. Wait for a better time. It was her first night, after all.

'I'm sorry.' She smiled. 'You're right. Forget I said anything.'

They left the cheery lightness and walked along the corridor, where he opened the door to her murky room. He shushed her and pointed to the bed in the corner, where Anna was fast asleep. Pushed up next to it was a sagging mattress.

'Make yourself at home,' he said. 'You're family after all.'

CHAPTER FIVE

The following day, Michalis suggested a walk around the neighbourhood, to help Zina get her bearings. They strode along, arm in arm, just the two of them, as he pointed out Pietru's, the Maltese grocery, and the Belgian bakery.

'Did you do as I asked?' she said, as they crossed the square. 'Did you find me some work?'

He stopped, offered her a cigarette and lit one for himself, too. Then he threaded his arm through hers again, taking his time before replying. Eventually, he said, 'I wanted to talk to you about that.'

A thread of anxiety pulled tight in her chest. 'But you've had all that time. I need to save money, I have to pay that debt. I said in my letters – I don't mind what I do.'

'It's alright,' he said.

'Sewing, cleaning,' she continued. 'I can take in washing, too. That debt on the land your father bought – you know it's due.' She paused and took a puff. 'And I have to pay you for the ticket you sent. I'd never have been able to come otherwise.'

'Will you stop worrying about money?' he said, smiling. 'And I told you the ticket was a gift.'

'Only people who have money don't worry about it.' She flicked ash to the ground.

'What I'm trying to say,' he said, 'is that we're doing alright. Me and Hedy. We're both working. We'll make sure you're okay.'

She frowned. 'But why bring me here if I can't work? You know I've wanted to visit you for years, but I need to make money, too. Your brother read out all your letters to me. There's always been a reason, hasn't there, that I couldn't come. Your house was too small, then Hedy was pregnant,' she was marking the excuses off on her fingers, 'then you were looking for work, then she was pregnant again and then—'

'I know, I know,' he said, blowing smoke to the side. 'I'm sorry, but you're here now, aren't you?'

He stopped at a park bench and motioned for her to sit, then did the same.

'I was beginning to think you didn't want me,' she said.

'Stop that, will you?' he said. 'Look, Mamma, all I'm saying is you don't *need* to work. I can give you money to send back for the debt – well, a bit anyway. And you're probably only here for a few months. Why should you work for someone else?'

She shrugged. She'd worked in the fields since she was ten, had sewn clothes for neighbours, baked bread for the village bakery. And brought up five children. Not working was something she'd never considered.

'What will I do all day?'

'Well,' he smiled, 'I knew you'd want to keep busy, so you can help us a bit – you know, look after the house. Hedy has a part-time job in a dress shop, but if you're around to do the cooking and a bit of cleaning, they'd give her more responsibility.'

Zina frowned.

'She could extend her hours and earn so much more,' he said. 'We'd even give you a little bit each week – pocket money – to buy yourself anything you need, or to save. Whatever you want.'

Still she didn't speak. After all these years of fobbing her off, and she thought they'd had a change of heart. But it seemed they'd sent for her now because the timing suited their plans.

'It makes sense to do it this way,' he continued. 'She can earn much more than you can.' He paused, took another drag of his cigarette and let the smoke billow out with his words. 'There's not much work you could get anyway, what with you not speaking the language.'

She knew he was right, but did he have to say it out loud?

'We want a bigger place,' he said, 'that's why we're working more hours. Just need to get the money together for the first few months' rent, then we'll be alright.'

Zina pulled her coat a little closer.

'Then she can go back to part-time, once we've saved a little.'

'So.' She tossed her cigarette away. 'There's no paid work for me but you'd like me to look after your house, cook, clean – and you'll both go out to work.'

He laughed, nervously, and she made him wait a little. She could always say no, but where would that get her?

'Alright.' The look of relief on his face warmed her. 'I'll do it for you.' She reached out, took his chin and brought his face to hers so she could kiss both cheeks.

'Thank you, Mamma.'

'I'll get to spend time with my grandchildren. It's not right hearing about them through letters. Knowing they're here and never setting eyes on them.'

'Oh, no – you don't need to do that,' he said. 'The children are all taken care of. Anna's at school all day and little Georgie is looked after by Rose.'

'But – he's a baby,' she said, frowning. 'Who's Rose?'

'Friend of Hedy's – two streets away. She's got one of her own. Hedy met her in the hospital. She doesn't even charge us anything. Like family, she is.'

'But I'd love to have the children to—'

'No, Mamma, you're not listening. We have all that sorted.'

He dropped his cigarette and killed it with the toe of his brogue.

'Just the house, the cooking, cleaning – you know.'

'But—'

'Just the house.'

Zina nodded. The sun was still out but it had turned cold.

CHAPTER SIX

E va woke in a sweat. Since meeting Zina a few days before, she hadn't managed a night of uninterrupted sleep. Now, as she lay wide awake next to Jimmy, she could see from her watch on the bedside cabinet that it was twenty-past four in the morning. She let out a gentle groan at the thought of staggering through another day.

Every morning was the same: she felt a heavy hand across her chest, pushing her down until her panic woke her. Startled, she'd catch her breath and then a terrible dread unfurled in her stomach like a lazy spider.

She wasn't usually superstitious, but what else could it be but an omen? A sign that she should leave the case immediately.

Last night she'd mentioned to Jimmy she was tired, and he'd snapped: 'You're never here, Evie, it's no wonder you're tired. You need to take care of yourself.'

She'd called him selfish, said he didn't want her to make something of herself. But even as she'd spoken the words, she knew they weren't true.

The hurt that swept his face cut her. 'I'm worried, that's all,' he said. 'I'm trying to look after you.'

'I don't want looking after. Will you stop holding *everything* over my head?'

He knew what she meant; she'd taken to her bed after the

baby had come and gone, and he'd cared for her for weeks. The miscarriage had snagged at the threads of her grief from all those years ago, when she was a child, pulling the tangled mess of it back to the surface.

She could still recall the doctor's office, the warm leather seat sticking to the back of her legs, as she tried to explain that her mother needed more than another tonic. Eva only knew the words she'd picked up in the couple of months since they'd been here.

Despite several visits, he'd dismissed Eva's anxiety about her mum's back pain and exhaustion. But she knew something was very wrong. And when she looked into her mother's eyes, she saw that she knew it, too. Eva had never found the words they needed and, six months later, her mother had died.

And then last year her baby had arrived too early, and the grief had echoed up through her once more.

In the days after the miscarriage, Jimmy washed her and fed her and said that in time they could try again.

But something shifted between them; she resented needing him so completely. Their joint grief seeped into the walls of the flat and the air around them grew thick with sorrow: the way he silently blew on his morning coffee before sipping, the way she lay on her back at night and stared at the ceiling. Living together apart.

Now, months on, and he still handled her like a china doll. She turned and glanced at him across the pillow, watching as his breaths came deep and calm. She wanted to shake him from sleep and tell him she was frightened about this case, appalled at the crimes Zina Pavlou was said to have committed and worried that she might not be able to see it through. What kind of a job was this anyway, speaking for a murderer?

They hadn't discussed anything that mattered for months now. How could she begin with this? She knew he was aware of the details of the murder but only because she'd seen him reading the *Gazette*, following the words with his index finger.

Since taking on Zina's case, he'd sighed at the constant prison calls that came through to the phone on the landing.

'You're at their beck and call now,' he'd said.

And she'd tried to say that Zina had nobody apart from her, but he'd snapped open his paper and buried his head in the pages.

Eva had visited Holloway Prison twice in the past few days: once so Zina could hear her statement again (she was convinced her solicitor had changed it), and the second time because she was demanding something from home, but nobody understood what it was.

'Can't you put the accused on the phone?' she'd asked the warden who'd rung as she was getting dressed for the Café de Paris.

'No, ma'am,' she'd replied. 'The governor says you must come in. She calms down when she sees you.'

It turned out that Zina's request was simple. She'd wanted some biscuits to be sent from home. She missed the taste of sweet things.

The staff door was right around the other side of the Café de Paris and, running late, Eva decided to risk the secret spiral staircase. It wasn't actually secret, because all the staff knew about it, but they were forbidden from using it. If they were caught climbing the metal stairs from Rupert Street straight to the entrance, instead of coming through the staff door, they'd be fined a pound.

The staircase was reserved for royalty but was also favoured by film stars who were having affairs and didn't want to be seen arriving or leaving. The doorman also found it handy for evicting anyone whose jollity had turned ugly.

But it was also a handy short cut when she was late like today, and Eva took a quick look around before running up. At the top, she slipped off her jacket and hid it behind her as she hurried down to the foyer and pushed through the heavy crimson velvet curtains.

All clear. She darted towards the coat-check station, lifted the counter top and slipped into position behind the desk. She flipped the latch on the closet that housed the dustpan and brush, pegged her jacket on the back of the door and quickly shut it again.

'Naughty!'

She jumped, then laughed in relief.

'Oh Elsie – thank God it's you! Did you clock me in?'

The girl stood on the other side of the counter, tugging at the silver chain around her neck that held a large tray of cigarettes in place just under her bosom. She rested it on the counter and smiled.

'Of course. But Charlie keeps an eye on the staff door. If he doesn't see you coming in, he'll figure it out.' They had a pact to help each other out if one of them was running late. Then she leaned in as if about to share a secret. 'He's ugly, but he ain't stupid.'

Eva laughed. 'Oh, I don't know about that.' She turned to make sure the padded hangers were in a neat row, all facing the same way, and checked she had the numbered tags to hand, ready for the rush.

'Did you hear he tried his luck with Vivienne again? Won't take no for an answer.' Elsie pushed back her curls. 'Think they're God's gift, some of 'em. Told you he tried it with me, too, didn't I?'

Eva smiled. 'You've mentioned it… once or twice, or maybe three times.'

Elsie slapped her arm, gently.

'Well, it's nice to be asked even if he is a gorilla. Alright for you, you've got your Jimmy at home.'

Eva turned towards the umbrella stand and readjusted it.

'Jimmy's not too happy with me right now,' she said. 'I've hardly been home, what with all this translation work.'

'You just can't help yourself, can you, Eva?' Elsie laughed. 'All those thieves and gamblers – crying out for your help.'

Eva pictured Zina sitting in her cell and the terrible charges she'd read out. 'Something like that.'

'If I was married to Jimmy,' said Elsie, 'he wouldn't be able to push me out of the door. If you know what I mean.'

'Charlie's coming over,' said Eva, nodding at nothing in the distance. 'You'd better go.'

Eva loved working at the Café de P because it helped her forget. When her shift ended, she'd take her jacket and bag and, before stepping into the street to head home, she'd stand in the shadows at the very edge of the foyer, leaning over the side of the curved balcony. From here she could gaze down on the parquet dance floor. She sometimes spent half an hour like this, unseen behind one of the tall potted plants, drinking it all in, as if the spectacle had been put on especially for her.

Tonight she'd be quick because her feet hurt. She slipped off one of her suede shoes, wriggled her toes and peered around the bend of the balcony and down the twisted double staircase. Some guests propped up the foyer bar for hours, their glasses constantly filled with champagne, but others were here to be seen. They'd take the gold and crimson stairs that swept to the dance floor very slowly, the mirrors and lights bouncing off the women's glittering outfits. A Caribbean four-piece band played on the platform at the bottom of the stairs, and the audience on a Saturday night could be as famous as the entertainers. Just a couple of months ago she'd seen an almost-nude Josephine Baker perform her daring dance in front of Humphrey Bogart and Lauren Bacall. It could be anyone on stage from a risqué cabaret act to a Hollywood star. Real life didn't have a place here and, for four hours every evening, that suited her just fine.

She smiled as she watched two women in long silk dresses

descend arm in arm. One wore emerald, the other sapphire and they slowly floated down and came to a decisive stop at the bottom, jewels settling in a sparkling pool. Two men in immaculate dinner suits followed a few steps behind, taking care not to tread on the trailing gowns.

Eva had worked in the cloakroom for two years, and although at first Jimmy wasn't sure about a job in such a 'high-class establishment' as he put it – kept saying rich people would always take advantage of people like them – the tips alone made it worthwhile. She only got ten shillings a night, but a couple of times a week a customer would toss a pound note into her tip dish. Americans were always the best tippers.

The money meant they could buy some new clothes once in a while, and have a fish-and-chip supper every week at a table in the Golden Plaice, rather than eating from newspaper on the bus home.

She glanced at her watch. Quarter-past midnight. She pulled her jacket tight, slipped her shoe back on and slowly wandered to the staff door. The first year she'd worked here, Jimmy had stayed up most nights, waiting to have a drink with her: a whisky for him, a G&T for her. The one o'clock club, they called it – but they hadn't done that for months. She'd started returning home later and later, knowing he'd be asleep, because she couldn't cope with the look he gave her when, after a few drinks, he moved towards her and she gently pushed him away. Instead, she'd watch his chest rise and fall as he slept, knowing it was just a matter of time before he gave up on her completely.

She suddenly felt the urge to see him, just to kiss him on the cheek and show him that she still cared. As she clocked off and swung out of the staff door, she heard her name being called. Head down, collar up, she walked fast. She liked Elsie but could only take her in small doses. And she wanted to get home now. She really did.

There was the number 29. It took her from Leicester Square all the way to Camden. Eva ran towards the bus stop and jumped on just as it began to pull away. Climbing the stairs, she walked to the front where she liked to sit so she could look out on night-time London. There wasn't much traffic and she let out a sigh of relief as she opened her bag, found her ciggies and lit up. The bus stopped at traffic lights for a while as she gazed out of the window. The West End was eerily quiet. Then, thump-thump – she could hear someone coming up the stairs.

'Oh what luck!' Elsie came and plonked herself next to her. 'I was trying to catch you. Didn't you hear me calling?'

'What? No I didn't, sorry.' Eva offered Elsie a cigarette but was refused.

'Not now. Look at this. You'll never believe it.'

Elsie rummaged in her bag and pulled out a newspaper that had been folded into quarters. It had a glass-ring stain on it and some of the newsprint was smudged.

'One of the waitresses left it behind,' she continued, 'and it's all anyone at work can talk about. I'm surprised you didn't hear.'

'What?'

Her cheeks were flushed pink and she looked as if she might burst.

'Tickets, please.' The conductor was suddenly next to them and Elsie shoved the paper under her bag while she searched out a few pennies. They bought their tickets, and once he'd left, she retrieved the paper.

'I don't want to gloat,' she said, then grabbed Eva's arm. 'But it's the most awful thing ever.'

A shiver ran through Eva, as if an icy hand had stroked her neck. Elsie unfolded the paper and placed it on her lap. She pointed at one corner.

'Look. Read it.'

Grandmother Charged With Killing Daughter-In-Law
Mrs Zina Pavlou, aged 53, was charged at Hampstead,
N.W., yesterday with the murder of her daughter-in-law,
Mrs Hedy Margarethe Pavlou, whose burned body was

*found on Thursday in the garden of the flat where they
lived at Cedar Hill, Hampstead. Mrs Pavlou, who had the
charge repeated to her in Greek by an interpreter, was
remanded in custody.*

Eva didn't speak.

'Well?' asked Elsie.

'Well what? What do you expect me to say? It's an old newspaper, Elsie. This happened days ago.'

'I know, but we've only just put two and two together.' Elsie pointed to the words. 'A Greek interpreter – is that you? Is that what you've been doing?'

The bus lurched, Elsie squashed her a little then righted herself.

What was the point of lying? It was no secret. Eva shrugged then nodded.

'It's just a job, Elsie – nothing more. She's a woman who needs my help. That's all. But please don't tell everyone I'm on this case. I don't want them asking questions. It's none of their business and I don't want to lose it. It's good money.'

'What? Oh, I wouldn't. I mean, I know you do that on the side but I didn't tell anyone the "Greek interpreter" is you.'

'Then what did you mean?' asked Eva. 'You said everyone had put two and two together?'

'Not about you, silly. You don't recognise the surname?'

Elsie unfolded the newspaper and there, below the story, was Zina's face staring out at her. There was a smudge of newsprint on her cheek.

'It's him, isn't it?'

'What?'

Elsie jabbed at the paper. Beneath the photo of Zina was a picture of a smiling couple. She had happy eyes, was young, carefully made-up. He grinned, wore his black hair slicked back, and a jacket and tie. The caption read: *Hedy Pavlou, the victim, and her husband, Michalis.*

He looked familiar. Why did he look familiar?

'I can't believe you didn't realise,' said Elsie. 'It's Michalis.'

Eva shook her head.

'I know that's his name, but who…?'

'It's that moody waiter. The one from work. Look, it says so here.' Elsie ran her finger over the newsprint, blurring it a little. '*A wine waiter at the glamorous Café de Paris.*'

Eva frowned. They hired hundreds of people in that place. That wasn't it – that wasn't why the photo had tugged at her memory. Then she remembered. Her face dropped.

'You okay?' asked Elsie.

She knew him alright. She'd seen him up close. He'd been furious, had frightened her.

'I'm fine.'

'That's how I felt when I saw it,' said Elsie. 'It's shocking, isn't it? To think, we work with him. Well, I know we don't really know him, but still.'

She folded the paper again but this time so his photo faced out.

Elsie sighed. 'Poor thing,' she said, 'coming home to find her like that. And their kids sleeping upstairs.'

Eva closed her eyes as Elsie chattered on, and saw it all again. The night she'd first noticed him had been an extraordinary one. The atmosphere in the Café de P was highly charged, and all the waiters and cigarette girls had asked to work that evening because it was to be Marlene Dietrich's opening night.

Her concert was being recorded and there was great excitement among the staff at the prospect of it all. Noël Coward introduced her with a witty verse he'd written especially, and applause and cheers erupted throughout the building.

Eva had left her post and peered over the balcony just in time to see Miss Dietrich float down the staircase and onto the stage, her long white fur wrapped around her slender body like a python. She wore a luminous rhinestone-studded evening gown and as she launched into her first number, 'La Vie en Rose', the air crackled with electricity.

It had been magical, but completely spoiled for Eva by what followed. She'd been humming that same tune as she left the club that night, and as she stepped from the back door she practically stumbled over Michalis in the alleyway. He was bent over a figure on the ground, hitting someone with terrible force. He looked up, and saw the horror on her face before she thought to hide.

'Go home!' he shouted. 'Don't say a word, or I'll come for you, too.'

And she'd done just that. She'd rushed away, from him and from that poor man who'd been flat on his back, arms outstretched, his face covered in blood.

When she walked into the flat, Jimmy had wanted to know everything. Was Marlene Dietrich as stunning in real life? Did the crowd love her? Who was in the audience? Did she spot any other stars? But all Eva could do was shrug as if she hadn't been much impressed by it all. Of course, the truth was she was still thinking of Michalis punching that man and the brutality in his eyes when he realised she'd seen him.

'Eva?' said Elsie, bringing her back. 'You alright?'

She looked down at the photo of the couple in the newspaper. The evidence seemed to point to Zina, without question. But perhaps the police had got it all wrong.

CHAPTER SEVEN

Holloway Prison, Hospital Ward

Zina slowly steps out of her navy cotton skirt and holds it out. The prison warden, a meaty woman, grabs it, but instead of folding it, bundles the fabric carelessly and drops it on the hospital bed. She points at Zina's blouse.

'And the rest,' she barks.

Zina hesitates. Perhaps she's misunderstood? Surely they can't want it all? The interpreter leans in. She's always perfectly made-up apart from that first time, and Zina catches a whiff of something light and floral.

'Zina,' says the girl in Greek. 'They need you to take everything off.'

A fiery shame sweeps over her and she clenches her teeth. There's that twinge in her jaw again.

'It's alright,' says the girl. What *is* her name? She knew her name but there's so much to remember. Everything's gone now.

'They'll let you have it all back,' she continues.

Zina nods and turns to face the screen that separates her from the others in the ward. She works her fingers down the front, unbuttoning her blouse, taking her time, because why should she hurry? Facing them again, as she stands in her half-slip, brassiere, stockings and worn-down shoes, she hands over the blouse as slowly as she can.

The warden snatches it with her huge hands and says something curt that Zina doesn't understand.

'They'll give you a gown for now,' explains the girl, 'and then you'll get your clothes back once the doctor's examined you. He'll be here in a moment.'

The warden points to her shoes.

'They took the other ones,' says Zina, her voice thin as it hits the damp walls. It's the first thing she's said since walking into the prison's hospital ward. She coughs and speaks a little louder. 'Tell her I need them back. They're my only pair now. I'll get them back, won't I? When I leave?'

The girl hesitates, as if she doesn't want to translate Zina's words, but then she does as she's asked. The warden emits a juicy, raucous laugh. She leans down to Zina's height and puts her mouth near her ear.

'Where you going, love?' she asks. 'Timbuktu?'

Zina fixes her with a stare, slips off her shoes and hands them to her, all the while not blinking. She may not understand all the words, but there's no doubting the sentiment behind them. She knows, for instance, that the twist of a person's mouth can usually show if they mean you harm. When she remembers, she tries to keep her own face still; if they saw inside her head they might never let her out.

'You'll get these ones back,' says Eva, kindly. That's it. *Eva*. 'And if you want, we can get some of your clothes and maybe some slippers from home?' She smiles and Zina feels that perhaps she's on her side after all, rather than just another bystander.

'Knock, knock – we all decent?' The screen is pulled away and the warden throws her a large cloth. Zina realises she's meant to put it on and just manages to slip one arm through before a white-coated man stands before her. Eva helps her quickly adjust the rest.

He's tall, fair, good looking, but not as handsome as her Michalis. She notices him glance at Eva once, twice, before he addresses the warden.

'What's taking so long?' he asks, irritated.

The warden doesn't reply but quickly pushes Eva out of the way. She yanks at the ties on the back of the robe and it pulls tight against Zina's throat. Zina gasps and swears in Greek, then tugs the neck down an inch.

'Steady!' says the doctor. 'Alright, Officer. Thank you.'

As the warden stands back, Zina looks to Eva for guidance. She'll tell her what to do.

'This is the doctor, Mrs Pavlou... Doctor...'

'Garrett,' he says, and smiles at Eva and shakes *her* hand rather than greet Zina. His hair is as bright as sunlight, and Zina's pleased to see the girl isn't fazed by him and keeps her eyes fixed on her instead.

'He's here to check you over,' explains Eva.

Zina steps back.

'Tell him there's nothing wrong with me,' she says to Eva, then thumps her chest and says in English, 'Strong. Work farm.'

He asks her to stand on the weighing scales, then against the wall to see how tall she is. He scribbles it all down in a folder he carries, then gets her to sit on the bed and attaches a stiff cuff to her upper arm, tight, while he squeezes a rubber pump in his hand and reads some numbers. Whatever he learns from all this he writes down again without speaking. Then he listens to her chest through her gown and asks her to stand and open her mouth, so he can look down her throat, searching for goodness knows what.

She thinks they've finished then he reaches behind her neck and for one awful moment she thinks he's going to pull her towards him to kiss her. Zina's hand shoots out and she pushes him in the chest, hard. He says something in a cross voice and Eva explains.

'He needs you to turn around so he can untie it, to listen to your chest. In case there's an infection. He won't pull it down.'

Zina lets him do this, but keeps her hand hovering around her shoulder in case he doesn't keep his word. She can feel the fabric fall off one shoulder and he says something to the girl.

'He just needs to unclip the back of your brassiere,' she says, 'but you don't have to take it off.'

Zina closes her eyes and doesn't know what to say.

'Shall I do it?' asks Eva.

She nods. Eva gently unclips the bra and Zina can feel the metal mouth of the stethoscope sucking her skin in different places – here, across here, now further down on her sides.

'What's that?' he asks, and swipes his finger down the top of her arm, making her shift as fast as a fish. The doctor says something, Eva clips her together and ties the gown again.

'Zina, the doctor asks how you came about that scar – on your arm.'

Zina shrugs.

'He says it looks like a burn,' says Eva. 'Did you have an accident?'

'Tell him I don't recall,' says Zina abruptly, as she rearranges the gown to cover her neck.

The doctor scoffs at this and scribbles something down.

'So, anyway, how are you, Mrs Pavlou?' he says loudly. 'In yourself?' Eva translates and it's the first time he's looked Zina in the face. A wave of self-pity threatens to drown her.

All her aches and pains since it happened have made her feel quite undone, and at last someone has asked how she is. She points out a quick but comprehensive map of everything on her body that distresses her.

'Hurting,' she says, rubbing her shoulders, then lower back and finally her sinewy calves which throb in protest at her inactivity. Then she rubs her tummy. 'Full,' she says. 'Too full,' and motions it expanding. He nods and writes some more. Then she places her palm to her forehead.

'Headaches too?' He smiles. 'Well, it seems you've got a touch of everything, haven't you?'

Zina's not sure if he's laughing at her or being kind. Perhaps the girl is in on the joke. He turns to say something else and Eva steps forward.

'Apart from the pains, the doctor asks how you're feeling?' says Eva. 'Your mood, if you're sleeping, if you have an appetite, whether you're anxious...'

Zina scowls. 'My son has betrayed me – how does he think I'm feeling? He told them lies and now he won't come to see me.' Tears spring to her eyes and she dashes them away.

Eva translates and barely finishes before Zina speaks again.

'Worry, worry,' she tells him in English.

'What do you worry about, Mrs Pavlou?' he asks, pen poised.

She understands the question and nods but hasn't the words to reply in English.

'Tell him I can't sleep for the worry, for worrying what might happen to me. Can he help me? Does he know what will happen?'

Eva asks him and he scribbles it all down, then says something quite carefully to the girl. She nods seriously, takes a breath and speaks, more slowly than usual, to make sure Zina understands. He says one sentence and Eva repeats it, and they alternate till he's done. His voice is matter-of-fact, Eva's has a firm gentleness.

'This is what will happen, Mrs Pavlou,' she begins. 'The case – your case – will go to court.' Her hair falls forward and she pushes it back behind her ear and continues. 'It will be heard in front of a jury and you will get a chance to tell your side of the story and so will the police.'

Zina folds her arms, stares at him and purses her lips impatiently. She's heard it all before.

Eva continues: 'At the end of it all, the jury will then decide if you are guilty or not guilty.'

She starts to shake her head, but the words keep coming.

'If you're not guilty, you'll be released. If you're found guilty the judge will sentence you.'

Eva has barely finished translating when Zina speaks sharply in Greek, her finger in the doctor's face. He pulls back slightly but she continues for a minute or so while Eva listens, reddening.

'What on earth was that?' asks Dr Garrett. 'Tell her I don't appreciate that tone.'

'She's upset...' Eva begins. 'She's doesn't mean to be rude – it's just her way.'

'Well, you can tell her whatever it is she wants, she won't get it by speaking to me like that,' he says. 'Go on – tell her.'

Eva falters, then explains to Zina what he's said.

'It's not how we do things here.' He bristles, then after a moment, 'Anyway, what's so important? What did she say?'

'She...'

'Yes?'

'She says she's sick and tired of hearing about the court and the police. She says nobody will answer her questions about Anna.'

Zina turns round at the mention of her name. She clasps her hands and nods at him, her face soft now as if she's a different person entirely.

'Who's Anna?' he asks, opening the file and looking to find it in there.

'Her granddaughter.'

He makes a note.

'She's eight. Zina – Mrs Pavlou – wants to know what will happen to her, to Anna, while she's here. She says she isn't being brought up properly. She says she needs to get out so she can look after her.'

He looks up at her and lets out a short but scornful laugh. 'She's in no position to make demands.'

'She's not demanding, she's very anxious about it,' continues Eva. 'She mentions Anna constantly.'

He tilts his head. 'She's killed the girl's mother. I doubt she'll be getting a visit any time soon.'

Zina looks from his face to Eva's.

'I can't tell her that,' says Eva. 'It'll break her heart. And anyway, she hasn't been found guilty yet, has she?'

He raises an eyebrow. 'From what I've seen, it's fairly evident,' he says. 'I don't envy you your job.' He briefly places a hand on Eva's arm, then thinks better of it and takes it off. 'But look at her, Mrs Georgiou, she's peasant stock. You shouldn't worry so much about her feelings. She's made of harder stuff than that.'

Zina tugs at the hem of Eva's jacket, like a child needing attention. 'What is it?' she asks in Greek.

'You can tell her from me,' Dr Garrett continues, 'that it's a bit late to be concerned about her granddaughter now. I very much doubt she'll see her again.'

He notices the look on Eva's face. 'Some information is very difficult to impart,' he says. 'But there it is.' He turns back to his file.

Eva slides a glance at him as he carries on writing in his folder. Then she puts her hand on Zina's shoulder.

'You have to be patient,' she tells her. 'Once this is over, if it all goes well, if they find you not guilty, then you can see her. Then you'll see Anna.'

Zina nods, the ghost of a smile on her face, worry etched deep on her forehead.

Dr Garrett closes his folder and walks away.

CHAPTER EIGHT

The squeal of the library cart is coming down the prison corridor. Zina hears it every week and, as it rolls towards her cell, she drops her head to the pillow and quickly turns to the wall. A heavy tread stops outside and the peephole scrapes open.

'Zee-na! You sleeping again?'

She tries to breathe evenly.

It's one of those thick London voices she hates.

There's chatter and laughter from prisoners standing on the balcony.

'She's never awake, that one,' shouts the voice. 'She's not *dead*, is she?'

A warden halfway down the hall says something and there's more laughter.

After calling her name once more, the woman gives up and pushes the library cart to the end of the corridor, where Zina can hear the gate to the next wing being opened for her to pass through.

She stays still and counts to ten in her head: *ena, thio, tria, tesserra, pente, exi, epta, octo, enia, thega*. Then she sits up, swings her legs over the bed with the energy of someone half her age and slides the book from under her pillow. A curl of delight twists inside her. It's the small victories that matter in a place like this.

The cover is tatty but she still takes care, checking her hands front and back for dirt. There's a smear of blood where she's chewed the skin at the base of her thumbnail. She sucks it clean, wipes it on her skirt and opens the book. If you can't read or write in here, they offer you picture books like this. They handed this to her on her first day and now she can't let it go.

It's the faded story of a family day out, drawn for children of course. A simple tale where mothers aren't betrayed, children do as they're told and there's no violence, no recriminations. She knows this book so well now but the deep, warm pleasure she feels every time she looks at it never diminishes. Carefully, she turns the cover and the pages fall open at her favourite place.

The little girl looks seven, maybe eight at the most, but either way very close to Anna's age. She glances up at Zina, her hand frozen in a friendly wave. Zina has examined the drawing on waking every day. She has the same thick, long black hair as her granddaughter and just staring at the very shine of it calms her. She used to love tending to Anna's hair every night with her old wooden brush that she'd brought from Cyprus. It was one of the few times that woman allowed her near the girl, but that's over now.

With her eyes closed, Zina brings her hand up to the top of her head and, as she runs her palm over her scalp and down, she imagines that the wiry, dry mop is Anna's glass-smooth hair. It's the same colour, but that is all.

Today it feels more difficult to pretend. She's worried because soon she'll be going to court. Zina examines the book once more, trying to push away the thought that she may have brushed Anna's hair for the last time. Even if that ungrateful son of hers decides to visit her after all, he'd never bring Anna to a place like this. The only way she'll see her again is if she's released.

Her solicitor, a man who spits like a donkey when he speaks, has told her twice now that the situation is 'not looking good'. His Greek is not as good as he thinks it is and he places his accents in all the wrong places, his voice jerking up and down like a cart with a broken wheel. He keeps asking if she understands how serious this is.

'Do you know what it will mean if you're convicted, Mrs Pavlou?'

'It means I will lose my children.'

She's lost so many children: twenty years ago in Cyprus, ones that were born too early, two who moved to another village and others who left her completely, like Michalis. And now Anna.

She looks at the book again. The little girl is still waving. Zina kisses her fingers and places them on the girl's face.

'I love you, Anna,' she whispers in Greek, and she waves before closing the book and slipping it back under her pillow.

There's a small cough and she turns. That girl, the translator, is standing by the door of her cell, watching. Has she been there all the time? She doesn't even remember her coming in.

CHAPTER NINE

Eva sat at the table in the cold cell and watched as Zina made her bed with meticulous care. Although she didn't understand it, she knew she'd just witnessed something deeply personal. Zina pushed the book further under her pillow, and Eva averted her eyes. She'd definitely heard her whispering to herself, but was that so surprising when nobody else spoke her language? What had really rattled her, though, was that she was sure she'd seen Zina wave at the book. Eva's stomach tightened. Why would she do that? And did it even matter?

She straightened up in her chair, pulled her pencil out from the top of her notepad, and wrote the date on the sheet of paper. She'd think about it later, decide what it meant and whether to report it.

In the month she'd been at Holloway, Zina had dictated several letters to her son Michalis, but had never received one in return. She'd told Eva that today she wanted to write to someone else.

At the top of the sheet, Eva wrote:

To: the Governor
Please find attached a letter translated on behalf of Prisoner 7145, Mrs Zina Pavlou, to her brothers, Vasos and Panayi, in Cyprus.

Signed
E Georgiou
Interpreter/Translator

The governor's secretary kept a list of addresses for each prisoner, detailing friends and family to send correspondence to. Eva just needed to put the person's name on the sheet, attach the English translation and once it was read and approved, the Greek letter would be sent. Zina sat next to her and swigged tea from the battered tin cup she used each day.

'Let's start,' she said.

30 August 1954

My beloved brothers, Vasos and Panayi,

How are you? And your children? You're the first relatives in Cyprus I'm writing to because I think you, of all people, will help me. I'm sure of it. I know you've been told the dreadful news. They've put me in prison and accused me of something so terrible that I can't even say it out loud.

Of course, none of it's true – you both know me and know I couldn't do such a thing. I'm innocent and my soul is clean. But the police suspect me because I was in the house on the night that it happened.

My nephews, who've lived here for years (and whose birthdays I've never forgotten, by the way), have now forgotten me. They don't come to visit. Nobody comes. When our sister, Sophia, needed help in Cyprus, you know that I brought those boys up as if they were my own. And now? They've cast me aside. And what of Sophia herself? I heard she's come to visit them in London but she hasn't come to me to see if I'm dead or alive in this world.

You won't forget me, will you? Please come to see me. I'm sure if you were here you'd be able to help. It's your duty as my brothers to look after your sister. The fare is £23 by boat. I know that's expensive, but how much is my life worth? If you ask our neighbours and friends to help, I think a little here and there and you could afford it. If you come to London, you could tell them what kind of a woman I am, how respected I am in our village. That I could never do such a thing. They'll believe you.

Please tell me when you can come. Tell me what to do. My head is sick with worry.

There's an interpreter here who's written this letter for me. She's been provided by the police. A woman. Can you believe it? A Cypriot girl who came here years ago and never left. I wish I'd never come here, that I'd never set foot in this place.

I'm sending my love and kisses to your children, and wait for your letter.

X (the mark of Zina Pavlou)

P.S. I think the trial will be in October, so please hurry.

CHAPTER TEN

August 1953, eleven months before the murder

It was during the second week of Zina's stay that Hedy first shouted at her.

Now that Zina cleaned the house, Hedy rarely went into Anna's bedroom, so had only noticed the lit oil lamp on the shelf by chance while putting away the sheets.

'For heaven's sake, it's dangerous,' she said. '*Dangerous*. Do you *understand*?'

Zina didn't respond.

'Zina, you can't do this,' she'd admonished, her voice louder now.

Zina understood that she didn't like it but had no idea what the problem was. It was a votive lamp, one she'd made with a dark blue espresso glass she'd brought with her from Cyprus, some oil she'd taken from the kitchen, and a small floating wick. They sold bags of them at the Greek church and she'd bought a supply. She had lit the lamp and placed it in front of the two small icons, on a shelf out of harm's way. It was important that the light didn't go out – it was offered as thanks to Christ.

Just then they heard the front door bang. Michalis was back from his day job, selling cleaning products door-to-door.

'Mick, Mick, have you seen this?' Hedy was on to him straight away, taking his arm and pulling him into the bedroom to see.

'Look! Please explain. She'll set the place alight, Mick.'

Anna was watching from the doorway.

'I won't touch it, Mummy,' she said. 'It's alright.'

'Stay out of it, Anna. It's not alright. It's dangerous.'

'Michalis?' Zina stood in front of him. 'It's just a *kandilli* – a votive lamp. Every home needs one. I put it up there so Anna couldn't reach.'

Michalis looked from his mother to the lamp to his wife.

'It's really alright, Hed,' he said.

Hedy stood with her hands on her hips.

'All the Greeks do it,' he continued. 'The flame's meant to show devotion.'

Perhaps, thought Zina, she didn't want it in the bedroom? She tugged Hedy's sleeve.

'Kitchen,' she said in English.

'No, I don't want it in there.'

'Kitchen, okay,' said Zina.

'No – it most certainly isn't!' Hedy said, raising her voice. 'I don't want it there, or anywhere. I bet she keeps it lit at night, too.'

'Alright, Hed,' said Michalis. 'No need to shout.'

Hedy stared at him, waiting to see what he'd do. Then she walked to the small desk in the corner, took a chair and dragged it under the lamp.

'It's a flame, in my child's bedroom. In *our* house. I'm sorry but I'm not having it.'

She kicked off her heels.

'This might be what she does back in her village, but this is London and we do things differently here.'

She got onto the chair and leaned towards the lamp. When Zina saw what she was about to do she reached out to stop her. Hedy pulled back and for one moment the chair wobbled and it looked as if she might fall. Zina reached out and grabbed her arm, saving her. But as soon as she was steady again, Hedy shook her off in anger.

'Hey, hey, let's all calm down,' said Michalis. 'Hedy, come on – be reasonable.'

Hedy ignored him, leaned over again till she was a couple of inches from the oil lamp, took a deep breath and blew it out.

'No,' she said to the both of them, stepping down. '*You* be reasonable.' Her voice shook and it was clear she was trying to control herself. 'Tell her from me if she lights it again, I'll blow it out again. I don't want to fall out over this, Mick, but I will get rid of it if she doesn't listen.'

Michalis nodded and translated it all, while Zina stood there, her lips pressed together as she summoned all her strength not to say anything.

She'd worked so hard this past month, cleaning and cooking and trying to please them both and now this had happened. Every day she rose early, put the coffee on and made sure Anna was washed and ready for school. Even when Hedy was home, earning extra with that dressmaking she'd taken up, Zina did chores. Yesterday she'd tackled the stove, which judging from the thick grease hadn't seen a good scrubbing for months. But when Hedy had walked in to fetch the scissors, she hadn't taken the scrubbing brush from Zina and told her to sit, Mamma, and rest. She'd allowed her to carry on. Now she was forbidding the *kandilli*, one of the few things she had to remind herself of who she was and where she was from.

Later that day, Zina watched Hedy chatter over dinner as if nothing had happened. There were many Cypriot girls now in London, but for some reason Michalis had decided to choose her, a German. A non-believer with skin so pale and hair so fair she couldn't possibly pass for a Greek. You could tell she'd never spent more than a few minutes in the sun, let alone worked the land. Not with those nails.

As Hedy took a long drink of water, Zina slipped into the conversation.

'So she was here during the war?' she asked Michalis. 'Even though she's German?'

Hedy looked from her husband to Zina. 'What was that?' she asked.

68

'Yes, Mamma, I've told you,' he replied in Greek, ignoring Hedy. 'She's been here for years.' He tore a piece of bread off the loaf and mopped up the tomato sauce from his plate.

'But it can't be easy,' said Zina. 'Being married to a German.' She picked up a forkful of food and asked, 'Didn't people call you Nazis?'

Hedy flinched at the word, and slammed down the water glass she'd been holding.

'No,' said Michalis, reddening. 'Not often.' He chewed and swallowed.

Hedy got up, her chair scraping the floor.

'Of course, some people were ignorant,' he continued. 'But we soon put them straight.' Hedy took the saucepan from the stove and started to wash it noisily. 'Anyway, most people are kinder than that,' he continued. 'They don't blame Hedy for what happened. Everyone suffered in the war.'

Zina placed her knife and fork on her plate. Michalis stretched and reached out to his wife, but she moved away and busied herself near the draining board.

'It doesn't matter where we're from, does it, Hed?' he said in English. 'We're all Londoners now.'

Hedy turned and gave a tight smile, then picked up the plates without offering anyone any more.

Then in Greek, he said, 'Her family have a bit of land in Germany, and... well, you never know. They might leave it to us if we're lucky. We don't want to live there, so we'd sell it. But there are so many chances to make money here too, Mamma, and we want to work hard. So they don't think we're expecting anything.'

'But you are,' said Zina.

'Sorry?' he asked, frowning.

'You are,' repeated Zina. 'Expecting something. You just said if you're lucky they'll leave it to you.'

'Yes, but that's not the point.'

Zina smiled then shrugged. 'If you say so.'

'Anyway,' he continued. 'We like the life here. The English can be really quite welcoming, you know, especially if you make an effort. You can get anywhere in London. Be anything, anyone.'

'What's wrong with who you are?' asked Zina. 'Are you ashamed of where you've come from?'

He let out an exasperated sigh. 'It's about moving forward, Mamma. Getting more. Making more of ourselves. That's why we're working so many jobs. Look.' He pulled one of his English newspapers from down the side of the armchair where it had got wedged. He found the page he was looking for and pointed to an article. Of course, Zina couldn't read a word but above it was a photograph of a bombsite with men in hard hats pointing into a crater.

'It says here,' he said, translating into Greek as he went along, 'that there's a huge regeneration programme in London. What matters now isn't the past, it's building a future from the rubble. Something better.'

Zina nodded. Well it *would* be wonderful, she thought, to make something new from the rubble of her own life. And yet a nagging soreness in her chest reminded her that she'd never be free of the things she'd seen and done over the years. They were embedded deep in her very bones.

CHAPTER ELEVEN

Eva stood behind the coat-check counter, Elsie in front, and they both moved their shoulders from side to side in time with the beat. It was Saturday night and the Café de Paris was in glorious full swing. The band had whipped the crowd into a frenzy and, from her vantage point, Eva could just see an edge of the dance floor below, as the crowd pushed for space. Not for the first time, she wished she was down there with them, dipping and shimmying in a silver evening gown rather than stuck behind this desk in her black cotton cocktail frock.

There was a crash and they both stood on tiptoes to see a pair of legs sticking up from a table of diners. One of the dancers must have taken a tumble. Laughter followed and everyone carried on regardless.

'It's mad tonight!' shouted Elsie, resting her tray of cigarettes on the counter. 'What a crowd. I've had lots of tips – even a pound note.'

'Me too,' said Eva. 'I love it when it's like this. Wish we could be down there, though.'

Elsie grabbed her arm.

'Come with us!' she said. 'A group of us are going to the Mapleton afterwards.'

Eva hesitated.

'No. I can't,' she said. 'I mean, Jimmy would worry.'

'Oh, come on, Eva. Didn't you say he's always asleep when you get back anyway? It's just John and a few of his friends. They're harmless enough.'

John was Elsie's brother, a freelance photographer who worked for the papers and *Picture Post*, snapping the singers and film stars who dropped in. The Café de P gave him a regular table, and one of their famous bacon and egg breakfasts when the night was through, but all on the understanding that he asked permission and only photographed those who craved column inches.

'I really can't, Elsie.' Eva saw her pull a face. 'Sorry – but I wouldn't like it if he went out dancing without me... so...'

'Oh, so nothing. Suit yourself,' Elsie said, shrugging. She rearranged the boxes of ciggies, bringing the expensive gold-tipped Sobranies to the front, and turned to start another circuit of the club, yelling, 'Cigars, cigarettes!' as she went.

Eva watched her walk away, then her eyes slid along to the dance floor again. God, how she loved to dance. It was the only time she felt free and light. She remembered toing and froing and swaying with Jimmy. It had been over a year ago, maybe two, since they'd gone to the Mapleton, leaned into each other as they'd become steadily more tipsy and wandered home to bed. Out of the blue last week he'd suggested they go to a nightclub again, but she'd made some excuse. It was the third time she'd said no in the past month.

She turned to rearrange the hangers and, as she slowly moved them along the rail, she wondered what would happen to the two of them. She'd pulled away from him since the baby had died and she didn't know how to make her way back again. Was scared to. What if she got pregnant again? How could you want something so much and be terrified of it at the same time? Her heart was already chipped around the edges; if she lost another baby it would crack right through.

Someone coughed and she turned around, automatically reaching across the counter to take their coat or fur wrap.

A man stood there, all shoulders and slicked-back hair. He was wearing a waiter's uniform.

'I thought it was you,' he said in Greek. It was him. From the newspaper. Zina's son, Michalis. The man she'd seen pummelling that poor sod just outside. 'That *was* you, wasn't it, at the police station?' He leaned closer. 'The night Hedy was killed.'

He was broad and tall and she wondered if he had any idea how threatening he seemed. Perhaps it was deliberate. Her throat felt dry.

'I'm... I'm so sorry about your wife,' she said. She straightened up and pushed her shoulders back a little, then put her hand out to shake his. 'Yes, that was me. I'm Eva.'

'I know who you are,' he said, ignoring the gesture. She drew it back. 'For days I couldn't place you, but then it clicked where I'd see you before.' He shifted his feet. 'You saw me that night – outside.'

She hesitated and for a moment thought of denying it all. It had been dark, she could pretend she had no idea what he was talking about.

'I know it was you,' he said, as if he could see the thought running through her mind.

'I promise, I didn't tell anyone,' she said. 'About that night. I didn't mention it to a soul.'

He squinted, thinking hard.

'What were you doing there? At the police station the other day?'

She hesitated, then took a cloth from under the counter and started wiping it down. He slammed his huge hand on top of hers, making her jump.

'Get off!' she said, pulling away.

'Are you the *interpreter*?' he asked, incredulous.

'You've got no right to grab me. Don't touch me again.'

He put his hands up, as if to apologise. 'The police said they'd found someone for my mum,' he said. 'It's not you, is it?'

She glanced over his shoulder. Where was Elsie now she needed her?

'It's just a job,' she replied, folding her arms across her chest, 'to earn a bit extra. I've done it for years. I'm sure both of us working here isn't a problem. They must know you work here too?'

'They do but—'

A flushed woman in a silver evening gown practically threw her fur stole at Eva. 'Can you hurry, darling?' she said, waiting for the tag. 'It's my favourite song!'

She rushed away and Michalis leaned in again, more worried now than angry.

'They know I work here, yes,' he said, 'but they don't need to know about the other thing, do they?'

'Of course not.' Whatever he was mixed up in, she had no intention of getting involved. Her job was to translate for Zina – nothing more.

A dinner-suited man passed his raincoat to Eva, and Michalis shifted along again till he was seen to.

'So you won't tell them about the other thing?' he asked.

'I haven't till now, have I?' she replied. 'And anyway – it's not like they're asking *me* questions.'

'Good. I mean, thank you. They've been asking all sorts. Do I have a temper? Did we ever fight? On and on. It's been bloody awful.'

Did the police have doubts? Despite charging Zina?

'I didn't mean to get heavy-handed,' he said. 'Sorry about that – I just needed to check you wouldn't say anything. As long as we're agreed.'

He didn't wait for a response and walked away. It was then she realised he hadn't asked after Zina.

* * *

Hours later, as her shift was coming to an end, Elsie ran up to the coat desk already in her wrap. Behind her stood her brother John and a few of his pals.

'You're sure now?' she asked. 'You won't join us?' Eva nodded.

'Hey, Eva.' John sauntered over. 'You never come out – come on. Just this once.'

'Hey, Eva,' called out one of his friends, his American drawl making her look up. 'Just this once!' He came and stood next to John, leaning heavily on the desk, obviously a bit worse for wear. She'd never seen him before. His bow tie had been loosened and his skin was flushed, telling the tale of a good night. 'What do you say, Eva?' he said, pulling down on the lapels of his dinner jacket, as if to make himself presentable. 'Is it true you never come out? Never Eva... that's a lovely name.'

She smiled.

'Don't mind him,' said John. 'These Yanks can't hold their liquor. And he gets soppy when he's tight, don't you, Bert?'

He stood up straight.

'That's absolutely not true. This man speaks lies.'

Eva laughed. She liked his voice. His face wasn't bad, either. There was something attractive about his carefree confidence. His hair was a light brown with a few blond strands that kept falling over one eye.

'Come on, Never Eva,' he said. 'Do it for Queen and country!' He clicked his heels like a soldier and gave her a salute. 'Better still, do it for *me*.' A cheer went up behind him. 'I'm a guest in your country, after all. What do you say?'

'An unwelcome guest,' laughed John. 'He's been here for years. Won't leave.'

Bert ignored him and turned his full gaze on her instead. 'For me, ma'am?' he repeated. 'Come dancing – come on.'

'Ma'am?' laughed someone behind her.

He ignored the laugh. 'As a favour?'

She smiled. 'Favours are for friends,' she said. 'I don't know you, do I?'

'Ooooh!' John cried. 'Bertie boy, you've been shot down!'

Bert clutched at his chest as if injured. Eva laughed and at the same time felt self-conscious. He wasn't the first tipsy customer to make a pass at her, but she felt awkward now they were all looking at her, so she started rearranging the coat tags.

'Hey, I know you don't know me,' he said, slouching over the counter, 'but isn't that the point? We can *get* to know each other.'

She faltered then held up her left hand, waggling her fingers to show her wedding ring.

Bert took his hand out of his pocket and did the same. 'Snap.'

'Leave her alone if she doesn't fancy it,' said Elsie. 'You always take things too far, Bert.'

'Where's the harm in asking?' he protested.

'But she's got a better fella than you at home,' Elsie replied. 'Why would she want to?'

'That's alright,' said Eva. 'He's just fooling around. Didn't mean anything by it, did you?'

Bert winked. 'Maybe I did, maybe I didn't.'

John came and pulled him away but not before Bert looked over his shoulder and gave her a soft smile. She couldn't help but return it as she watched them head towards the staff exit and tumble into the street.

She opened the cupboard and pulled out her jacket. She should have said yes. Just gone for a few drinks, a few dances. But once that music started she would have danced till her feet throbbed. And how could she, without Jimmy? She put her arms through the sleeves, took her bag and lifted the counter top.

As she walked to the bus stop, she thought of him and knew he trusted her completely. She'd always been the jealous one, not Jimmy. She'd often seen other women looking at him as they'd strolled through Regent's Park. He seemed oblivious to the effect of his floppy dark hair, straight nose and beautiful olive skin. And if he did notice, she'd never once seen him return the stares. No, it wasn't other people that had driven them apart, they'd done that themselves. Though she blamed herself more than him. She'd repeatedly refused to talk about the distance between them, even though he'd tried to meet her halfway, dropping it into the conversation every now and then. He'd eventually given up and now they were stuck on opposite sides of the road, neither of them knowing what to do next or how to make their way towards each other.

The bus arrived and she stepped on, and went upstairs. Her favourite seat was taken so she sat at the back instead and lit up. She put her bag on the seat next to her and pressed a hand on her belly. To think, a year ago a life was there. She took another drag of her ciggie, and stared at the West End lights as the bus chugged along.

She'd been right to go straight home tonight. She'd done it partly because Jimmy would worry if he woke and she wasn't there, but he hadn't been her main concern. She'd been thinking of Zina. She had to be at Holloway early tomorrow, to translate some letters for her.

The truth was, she was apprehensive about this case and what it might bring for her. And she felt afraid of Zina, too. She wasn't sure what that son of hers was mixed up in, but she had a strong feeling that Zina had committed this awful murder. Could they have done it together? The way he'd lost his temper tonight, grabbing her like that. No – what could possibly be their motive? It wasn't like they stood to gain anything.

She was almost certain Zina had been there when Hedy died – her paraffin-soaked shoes were proof enough, surely? And yet Eva still felt an inexplicable urge to help her. Perhaps it was because she knew Zina would be at a loss without her. Not because Eva considered herself excellent at her job (although she did) but because the other translators were men who were either slapdash or lazy or petty criminals. They'd take one look at Zina, read the police report and make up their minds then and there, the way Sergeant Parks had. They'd do the bare minimum for her, and abandon her if a better offer came up anywhere else to make some fast cash. Then she'd have to start all over again with someone else. Eva resolved to see it through and do it well. Of course she had no control over what happened to her in court, but she could be the bridge between the old familiar world Zina knew and this frightening new one. She could make sure that while she waited for her trial and during the proceedings, she understood what was happening. Didn't everyone deserve that, even a murderer?

Eva had tried to be that link once before, when her mother had been ill. Things were different now, weren't they?

'You're just a woman,' Zina had said to her. 'What good are you to me?'

But she was all Zina had. And even if she was guilty of this horrible crime, Eva decided as she sat on the top deck of the number 29 bus that she wouldn't let her down.

CHAPTER TWELVE

September 1953, ten months before the murder

It was Anna's eighth birthday and, after twenty minutes of searching, Hedy had finally found the paper decorations they used for all celebrations. Zina sipped her coffee as she leaned in the doorway and watched. Michalis placed the rickety ladder in one corner of the living room and Hedy climbed it, wobbling as she reached the top. He passed her one end of the yellow crepe-paper garland then held the ladder steady.

'Got it?' he asked.

'Got it.'

She reached as far she could to pin it into the ceiling corner, then she let the rest of the decoration fall onto his head.

As she carefully climbed down the ladder, steadying herself as she went, he reached up and grabbed her all over, his hands going everywhere.

'Mick!' she laughed. 'Stop it!'

'What? I can't see what I'm doing. I'm trying to save you.'

He grabbed her tightly and picked her up off the ladder, then turned and let her fall slowly between his hands. She slapped him playfully on both shoulders as she came down.

'We'll never get this done if you carry on like that,' she said.

Zina took another sip and watched as they pulled the ladder to the middle of the room and set it under the lampshade. She didn't need to understand English to see that they were besotted, and she fleetingly wondered if Hedy would ever cheat on her son. Now she was here, she could keep a close watch on her, for his sake.

Once they'd twisted the garland, Michalis nudged Hedy towards the ladder again.

'Up you go!' he said and she climbed to the top, reached for the decoration and pinned it near the light fitting.

They did this at each corner with four separate decorations, and every time went through the same carry-on with his hands touching her. Hedy stopped twice to catch her breath from all the laughing. They'd seen Zina standing there, drinking her coffee by the door, but it didn't seem to bother them.

Later that day, Hedy hummed a tune as the two women stood side by side making Anna's birthday dinner. It had been Michalis' idea for them to share favourite recipes, probably in an attempt to smooth the waters after the incident with the *kandilli* lamp. Zina had been pleased at the suggestion. After all, they both loved the same people. Why couldn't they get on?

Perhaps they could start over. Despite the weather and the hard work, Zina was enjoying her life here. It had been years since she'd had children around her and she'd forgotten the joy they could bring. Well, Anna at least, who she'd taken to quickly. She had very little to do with the baby.

The plan was that Hedy would prepare the filling for a dessert she was making, then Zina would show her how to make *tavva* – a dish that Michalis loved but hadn't eaten in years.

Zina watched as Hedy stirred the chopped apples and raisins in a saucepan, sprinkling a little cinnamon and smiling as she offered her a taste. Zina pretended to like it and nodded, staring into the pot and thinking about the countless cakes and pastries she'd cooked in her life and how much better they would have tasted. She smiled at the notion that Hedy could teach her something she didn't already know.

But Zina had to admit, she was relishing this afternoon spent with Hedy, standing so close to her, getting a chance to really look at her. She was fascinated by the translucent quality of her skin: no freckles, no scars or burns, no wrinkles. Just smooth like fresh paint. And so thin in texture, delicate as an eggshell. Tap her and she'd crack.

'Smells good, yes?' Hedy smiled.

'Very good,' she replied.

The fabric of the girl's blouse stretched tight across her chest as she reached up for the flour. Under her arm, a sweat patch in full blossom. She turned off the stove, blew at the steam rising off it and went to lift the pan.

'I do,' said Zina and got there before her, picking up the heavy saucepan effortlessly.

'Oh, thank you.'

Zina smiled. Despite Hedy's curves, the fact that she had more meat on her body than was strictly necessary, Zina could tell she wasn't strong, not in the way she herself was. She'd never churned butter with those arms, or climbed mountains till her calves burned just to pick the best of the wild asparagus.

In fact, thought Zina, I'm only up to her shoulder but I bet I could lift her right up if I set my mind to it.

'Pastry later – tonight,' said Hedy.

Zina nodded and started getting her ingredients together to make her dish. It would take a few hours in the oven and there'd be no space if Hedy was putting her strange pie in as well, so she'd better get it cooked.

As she got the onions and potatoes together, the chopping board and the good, sharp knife, Hedy switched her weight from one leg to the other. She didn't seem to be paying careful attention, and started rubbing at her neck and then her lower back. Zina knew what was coming so decided to get the whole charade over and done with.

'You hurt?' she asked Hedy, pointing to her back.

She nodded, put her hands together under her cheek to act out sleeping and then said, 'My back – need to lie down. Anna can help you.'

Zina got the gist, and before she could respond, Hedy had

untied her apron, dropped it on the chair and called Anna to take her place. Well, she could have been offended but it was clear Hedy had made up her mind and, anyway, who wants a student who doesn't want to learn? This way she'd have a little time with Anna by herself – a rare thing.

Within a few seconds, the girl had bounded in, put her mother's pinny over her blue birthday dress and washed her hands rigorously. Then she stood at the chopping board ready to work. She watched carefully as her *yiayia* demonstrated what to do.

It took the girl a long time, but Zina was in no rush. They slept in the same room, but they never spent time together. Her mother seemed strangely possessive about that. And little Georgie? Well, she wasn't allowed anywhere near the precious baby.

After about half an hour of painstaking peeling of potatoes, they made a start on the carrots (there were no tomatoes, so she hoped carrots would add some sweetness, even though she'd never used them in this dish before). She'd found a small amount of lamb, so she'd stretch it out with the vegetables.

Zina stood behind her granddaughter. She placed her hand on top of the girl's and pushed down on a carrot as she helped her chop it into chunks.

'I can do it, look, Granny.' Anna moved her hand away from Zina's and chopped the next chunk by herself, and the next.

Zina took the knife from her hand and placed it on the counter.

'Look, Anna.' The girl looked up at the mention of her name. They didn't share many words but seemed to always know what the other was saying.

'No, too big,' said Zina. To be sure she understood, she showed her the size she wanted with her thumb and index finger.

Anna nodded, picked up the carrot she'd just cut and measured it against her granny's hand. It was twice the size. They both laughed and, on impulse, Zina bent down with her mouth open as if to swallow it whole, including Anna's hand.

'Granny, no!' squealed the girl. She pulled it away but Zina pretended to snap at her hand several times, making an 'Um! Um!' hungry sound and the girl laughed and held the carrot at arm's length.

Anna ran around the table then made swooping sounds, and the carrot became an aeroplane diving down.

'Bomber coming in!' she shouted. 'Watch out!' And her hand swooped down, went towards Zina's mouth and, at the last moment she popped it into her own and crunched down hard. Chewing fast and furiously, she moved away from her granny and opened her mouth to show her it had all gone.

'Oooh, you little *katsaritha*!' laughed Zina, and even though Anna didn't know she'd just been called a cockroach, she was delighted she'd made her laugh.

Zina rummaged in a paper bag and took out a shrivelled brown onion. She sniffed it loudly, made a silly dreamy face and pretended to swoon because it smelled so lovely.

'Eat! Nice!' she said to Anna and pushed it in front of her nose.

'Ah! No! Granny – don't!' Anna moved away from the table. Zina, onion in hand, started to chase her round one way then quickly stopped and changed direction.

'Granny, no!'

'*Fayito* – dinner time!' shouted Zina in Greek, as she lurched towards the girl. She caught her easily and pulled her down onto the cracked lino.

'Hey, hey. What's going on here?' Michalis walked in and stood laughing at the scene in front of him.

'Daddy!' shouted Anna, her arm up in a dramatic plea. 'Daddy! Save me!'

Zina pulled her tighter. She pecked into Anna's neck and her kisses rained down like hailstones on a tin roof. The girl struggled and finally stopped to catch her breath. Just when Zina thought she'd won, Anna started to tickle her.

'No!' laughed Zina.

'Oh clever girl, Anna!' said Michalis, and kneeled down to join in. 'She hates that.'

'Please, please!'

'For heaven's sake!' Suddenly everyone stopped.

Zina looked up and saw the solid shape of her daughter-in-law in the doorway.

'What a mess. Michalis, stop it. And Anna, get up. What are you doing on the floor in your best dress?'

'Sorry, Mummy.' Anna scrambled up and looked down at the pinny which had twisted around her waist and creased her dress. 'We were just playing. It was so funny. Granny was showing me how to make tavvy.'

'*Tavva*,' said Zina, understanding the word and wanting to correct her. 'Onion, potato, carrot, lamb.' She'd learned a few words in the last two months – mostly ingredients. Useful for shopping.

Hedy ignored her mother-in-law.

'For God's sake, Mick, look at this mess.'

Michalis looked down at the floor. There was a piece of carrot by the stool and an onion at his feet. Hardly a mess, but he picked them up.

'Just a bit of fun, Hed.' He put them on the table. 'Nothing to get cross about.'

'I've got a wretched headache,' she said, putting her fingertips to her forehead, 'and all I can hear is screaming and laughing.'

Zina stared at her and said to Michalis, 'I thought it was her back?'

'She says it's a headache,' he said.

Zina got up. 'She should sit down.' She pulled out the stool and motioned to Hedy. 'Make *chai*.'

'I don't want a *chai*,' said Hedy. 'I want some bloody peace.'

She turned and walked out and Michalis followed her. Instead of consoling her, his mother, he went to his wife. There was a tug on her hand and she looked to see Anna by her side.

'Come on, Granny.' She pulled her back towards the table.

Zina kept staring at the doorway.

'Granny, come on,' said Anna. 'Show me how to cut the potatoes.'

Zina looked back at the girl and smiled. '*Patata*,' she said.

'*Patata*,' said Anna.

'Bravo, Anna.'

She gave her granddaughter a tight hug and, as she leaned down to kiss the top of her coal-black hair, she was thrilled to note once again that it was the identical shade to her own.

CHAPTER THIRTEEN

Holloway Prison

To: the Governor
Please find attached a letter translated on behalf of Prisoner 7145, Mrs Zina Pavlou, from her brothers in Cyprus.

Signed
E Georgiou
Interpreter/Translator

21 September 1954

To our dear, never-to-be-forgotten sister, Zina,

We, and the whole village, could hardly believe it when we heard the news. Murder? What a thing to be accused of, and you who've already had more than your share of whispers and troubles.

When we received your letter the family all sat together and cried for the shame of it, both for us and you. We also cried at the thought of you there, in a foreign land, not speaking English and with such an accusation hanging over you. But then we read that you have a good Cypriot interpreter and, even though she's a woman, she must know the ways of the courts and will help you. We're so relieved for you and are sure you'll be acquitted.

Yes, you're right when you say your sister, Sophia, is in

London. She arrived about a month ago. In her letter she said the boat had made her very sick. Perhaps that's why she hasn't visited? She didn't mention your name or coming to visit you. Is it possible she doesn't know? But then again, a friend sent us a page from The Times *with your photograph, so we think the newspapers must be full of this business. Perhaps it's too painful for her.*

If we were in London right now, we'd come to see you every day. We'd bring you your favourite honey cakes, melomacaroona, and tell you stories from the village to distract you from your difficulties. If we could walk across the sea we would without hesitation.

But we can't. It's just too expensive to visit you, and we couldn't possibly ask others to pay. Also the crops need tending and we can't leave Cyprus now or it would ruin us. You know how hard life is.

Have strength, sister. God will watch over you and one day, if He wills it, we'll be drinking kaffé on the veranda again. We pray to St Andrew and all the saints that you'll be released. If you're convicted of murder it would bring such shame on the family.

With love
Vasos and Panayi

CHAPTER FOURTEEN

November 1953, eight months before the murder

Hedy was at Rose's, going through her wardrobe to find something for tomorrow's wedding, and Michalis had fallen asleep in the armchair.

Zina stood in the kitchen and placed the terracotta incense burner on the table. She slipped her hand in her pocket and took a few silver-grey olive leaves from the pack she'd bought at church. Holding them between the index finger of her right hand and her thumb, she crossed them over the bowl of the *kabnistiri* burner several times, top to bottom, right to left, while she said a rushed silent prayer.

She dropped them into the bowl, took the small box of *livani* from her pocket and added one honey-coloured nugget of the frankincense to the pile. Then she carried it all to the baby's cot, where she knelt, set a match to the leaves and *livani* and poked it around with the match until it caught. Once the flames had died and the leaves were smouldering, she stood, picked up the *kabnistiri* and wafted the grey smoke in a circle over baby Georgie's head, once, twice, three times.

She blessed the baby then carried on with the circular movements throughout the room, over Michalis and Hedy's bed, and was about to go into her own room to bless Anna's bed when she turned to find Hedy standing in the doorway, arms full of dresses. She threw the clothes on the bed and put her hands on her hips.

Zina clutched the *kabnistiri* in both hands now and didn't say anything. What was the point? The smoke snaked up between them.

'Mick!' shouted Hedy. 'Mick! Come here right now.'

He was by his wife's side faster than a dog called to its owner.

As Hedy continued to shout, Zina stared at her son, waiting to see what he would do. Eventually, the girl stopped to take a breath. Michalis put a finger between his neck and his shirt collar and tugged, then said in English, 'Mamma, we've spoken about this.'

'Speak Greek,' she replied, 'so I can understand.' She knew she was being admonished. He'd recently started talking to her in English, and she didn't like it. He reckoned speaking Greek wasn't fair to Hedy, as it was leaving her out of the conversation. But what about *her*, his mother? Didn't she count?

'I said,' he started in Greek, 'that you can't do this. We talked about it before.'

'You said I couldn't light the lamp, not this. It's just incense.'

'It's the same thing and you know it,' he said. 'It's still something burning indoors. It's not safe.'

'Greeks have done this for centuries,' she said. 'We do it every day in Cyprus and families here, too – God-fearing families...'

Hedy shifted her feet, her cheeks pink, waiting for a translation.

'Look,' he continued, 'you can do it in the garden but not indoors. Hedy doesn't like it.'

Zina smiled. 'But it's indoors that it's needed – to bless us all, to show God we have faith.'

'Ask her if she was doing it over the baby,' said Hedy. 'Bloody ask her.'

Michalis did as he was told.

Zina lifted her head and stared at Hedy. 'Yes, baby,' she said in English. Then to Michalis, 'Tell her the baby needs to be christened. It's a sin not to christen him. If she'd just let me make the arrangements—'

Michalis put his hand on his mum's arm.

'Just stop, Mamma, alright? We don't want Georgie christened – and if we did, we wouldn't do it in the Greek Orthodox church. You know Hedy's Protestant.'

Hedy said something to him and he gave a small shake of the head. Then she glared at him and said something else and his shoulders dropped and he reached for the *kabnistiri*.

'What?' Zina couldn't believe it. 'What are you—'

'It's not safe. If the ashes fell into Georgie's cot it would go up in seconds. I'll keep it for you and when you want to use it in the garden just ask.'

She held onto it tight but he gently prised her fingers off, careful not to spill any of the ashes onto the floor. He held it away from himself, as if it were alien to him, and as he left the room, Hedy swiftly followed.

The next day, Zina clutched Anna's hand as they walked to the wedding reception. She'd been invited last minute and, while pressing her best navy dress, decided that the invitation meant they were trying to make amends for the day before.

As they walked up Hampstead Hill Gardens, the wind whipped around their legs and Zina wondered why anyone would hold a wedding in November. Then she saw Ivy, the bride, walking towards them, waving and laughing as she tried to hang onto the veil on her head, and she understood. She was at least six months gone. The venue was a tired, small restaurant off the Camden Road, owned by the family of Freddy, the groom. Michalis had met him when he'd first come to London, and he often called round for drinks and late-night card games. He was one of those pink-faced men with a sheen of sweaty excitement about him, always smelling of spirits. Zina had disliked him on sight.

On their poker nights, Hedy didn't leave the men to their whisky and cards, like most wives would. She joined in as they all sat in the kitchen getting steadily louder till the early hours.

Within an hour of the wedding reception starting, it was clear Michalis and Hedy weren't making amends. In fact, they intended to drink and dance all night and leave her with the children. She was deposited in a draughty corner, the droning English music so loud it deafened her, and was ignored for the rest of the day. Every now and then, Anna ran up to give her a kiss or to introduce her to one of her new friends. She even deposited a small piece of dry wedding cake in front of her, but then she ran off again to play.

Zina held baby Georgie in her lap and, despite the noise, he slept. Once, Hedy came over and made a fuss of the way she was holding him, shifting his crocheted blanket a little and showing her that she should be supporting his head with her arm, as if she hadn't held five children of her own. But it was the first time they'd really let her have any contact with the baby so Zina wasn't about to complain. As time wore on she looked down on the child and realised she didn't care much for him at all. She felt very little for this puffy, coppery-haired baby that looked like nobody in her family.

A plate of bland, cold food was handed to her by one of the young people, and she picked at it while sipping at her bottle of Coca-Cola through a straw. Not even a glass to pour it in. She'd forgotten her cigarettes at home and nobody thought to offer her one of theirs, although everyone around her was chain-smoking. She couldn't do anything but sit and wait patiently. Nobody bothered to try and speak to her, just nodded her way occasionally. Her arms were heavy now and the baby was stirring restlessly.

Suddenly she felt exhausted. Surely they would leave soon? Zina changed arms so she could rest her left shoulder a little, then within a few minutes Anna came and sat next to her and promptly fell asleep too, leaning on the arm she'd just freed. The noise had subsided a little and the crowd was thinning out. Michalis had spent all the afternoon laughing loudly, knocking back spirits and talking to everyone in the room, apart from his mother.

A voice rang out that Zina recognised. She turned and saw Hedy holding court in a small group of friends. Standing in a corner, she had a cigarette in one hand, a glass of wine in the other. Two other women with her were in the same pose. She was wearing a green and white floral dress that she'd borrowed from Rose, and she'd cinched it tight at the waist, making it shoot out at the hips. Underneath she wore several layers of stiff petticoat and her skirt took up more space in the group of friends than anything else.

You had to hand it to her, thought Zina, she was an attractive woman, though why she had to make such a display of herself she didn't know. In Cyprus, only the unmarried women took that kind of care over their appearance. She'd noticed how a couple of the men here had given Hedy a second glance, and Freddy seemed particularly attentive tonight. Of course, Hedy didn't stare back, but she knew what she was doing alright.

Opening a stale sandwich on her plate to peer inside, Zina grimaced then shoved her food away. She wondered what to do after yesterday's argument. She was still furious, of course, that they wouldn't allow her to burn incense, but the atmosphere at home had become increasingly frosty lately as both women had given up pretending to like each other. Would they turn her out? It was worth making more of an effort, she thought, if it meant she could stay, even though she was in the right. Even though she wasn't earning the money she would have liked, she enjoyed being with Anna, and having Michalis near her after all these years.

Just then there was a hoot of laughter. Zina turned to see Hedy had put her cigarette in her mouth and passed her drink to Freddy, in order to free her hands. He was watching her with a huge wet grin on his face. She was now extravagantly crossing herself again and again then, clutching her hands in prayer, looked upwards. One of her friends held her stomach, laughing, while the other dabbed at her eyes, trying not to smudge her make-up as the tears coursed down her face. Just then, Freddy leaned in very close and said something in Hedy's ear.

Hedy looked over her shoulder and saw Zina watching. Her face didn't redden, she didn't look appalled that she'd been seen mocking her. Instead, she took her glass, raised it and shouted cheers in Greek: '*Stin eeyeeah sou, Mamma!*' More laughter, and Freddy slung his arm around her shoulder, and joined in.

A familiar flame of humiliation seared through Zina. She'd been demeaned by a woman before and was sick of being ridiculed. The sharper, prettier ones were all the same. She gave Hedy a filthy look and cursed herself for not knowing how to retaliate. Not in words, anyway.

Later that evening, as they all wandered home up Cedar Hill, Zina was still seething. She watched as Hedy stumbled a little and Michalis held her tight. She's just a silly drunk girl, she told herself. It really meant nothing. With one hand she pushed Georgie's pram and with the other held onto Anna's. She squeezed it and was pleased to feel it tighten around hers in return.

CHAPTER FIFTEEN

The following day Zina was making toast when Michalis walked into the kitchen.

'Hello, Mamma.' He kissed her on the forehead and poured a cup of tea from the pot. 'We've had an idea.'

She stopped scraping the burned bits off the toast into the sink and stood still.

'I think we're all tired,' he said, blowing into his cup. 'Hedy's tired, I am too. And that's why we haven't been getting along that well, wouldn't you agree?'

'We're getting along fine,' she said, not giving an inch. These were Hedy's words, not his.

'No we're not, Mamma. I think we need a break.'

He added a splash of milk and stirred his tea again and again, stalling for time.

Using the back of the butter knife, she continued to scrape the black bits from the crust. Once she was done, she turned and lifted her face towards his.

'So you're throwing me out?' she asked. 'Your own mother?'

He laughed. 'Don't be silly! Of course we're not.'

The rush of relief made her sigh. 'Oh, I thought—'

'No, we just need a little break – all of us. Me, Hedy, the kids – and most of all you.'

She sat down and crunched into the dry toast. 'Alright. What do you have in mind?'

Hedy walked in. Her forehead had a slick of sweat on it and she hadn't put on her make-up yet.

'Morning, Mamma,' she said, subdued. Was she a little crestfallen? Was Zina imagining it? This must all be part of her apology, her way of saying she didn't mean the silliness yesterday and to offer her a little treat.

'I was just telling Mamma,' Michalis said, 'that we all need a break.'

'Yes, a breather,' said Hedy. 'That would be lovely, wouldn't it, Mamma?'

Zina shrugged, not sure what she'd said. 'Holiday?' she asked in Greek.

'Exactly, just a weekend – two days,' said Michalis. He sipped at his tea and sat down. 'Brighton. The seaside, Mamma – the sea…'

'But it's freezing,' said Zina. 'It's November.'

'Oh, but we went a couple of years ago and it was so nice – completely empty. You just have to wrap up warm, take a couple of blankets. There are a few places still open. You can have fish and chips on the beach and hot tea.'

Zina grinned. 'Really? Well, when you describe it like that it does sound nice. I've never seen the beach here.'

He stopped, cup half raised to his mouth. 'Oh, no, Mamma, you've misunderstood.'

'What?'

'Not *you* – we want to have a little break ourselves. You can stay here. Look after the house and have a rest. From us.'

Hedy looked from him to her, not understanding what was being said.

Zina glanced at the burned crumbs on her plate.

'So you'll go with Hedy and I'll look after the children?' she asked. 'Alright. It will be nice to have some time—'

'No,' he laughed. 'Mamma, don't you understand? We're going as a family. We're taking the children with us. They could do with a break, too. You can stay – just you in the house. It will be so nice and quiet and you'll have nobody to clean or cook for. Two whole days to yourself. A break for all of us.'

She picked up her bitten toast, looked at them both then dropped it onto the plate. The dry bread had scratched her throat and she got up, took a glass from the draining board and turned on the tap.

'What is it, Mick?' asked Hedy.

He put his hand on her arm to silence her.

'But you're going as a family,' said Zina, wiping her mouth. 'I'm family too, aren't I?'

Michalis stood and said something quietly to Hedy. She could tell from his tone that it was a question. Hedy stared at him and didn't respond, but it was clear that she'd given her answer.

After a moment, he turned back to Zina.

He smiled brightly, trying to make light of it. 'We need a break,' he said.

'From me?'

He let out a long breath.

'I'm caught between the two of you here,' he said. 'Don't make this harder than it already is.'

There was a pause, then Zina said, 'Is Freddy going?'

Michalis pulled back in surprise. 'What?' He laughed at the absurd suggestion, then his face dropped. 'No, of course not. Why would he? I told you, it's family.'

She shrugged. 'I've no idea who's family now and who isn't.'

'What was that about Freddy?' asked Hedy, but nobody answered. Instead, Michalis lifted his chin and gave his mother a cold, hard stare. Then he turned and walked out of the kitchen.

Hedy stood there, twisting the wedding band on her finger, something she did a lot when she was nervous.

'What did you say about Freddy?' she asked again.

Zina took a few steps towards her and stared in her face. Hedy gave a tiny flinch, so small it would have been easy to miss.

'You have nice time, Hedy,' she said.

The following weekend, just after the whole family had left, Zina walked through the silent rooms, staring at the empty beds, wondering what she'd do with herself. She had no paid work, the house was tidy and she didn't like not being needed, not being useful. She sat at Hedy's dressing table and touched the embossed silver flowers on the fancy hairbrush that she'd never seen her use. Just two days, she told herself. She'd be fine. In fact, she'd make the most of it.

The grey swollen clouds looked ready to rip open, so she would get out while she could. Picking up her bag from the kitchen, she walked to Pietru's, where she bought some *lahana* greens and black-eyed beans. An hour later and she was standing over the stove, sleeves rolled up, pinny around her waist, cooking her favourite meal, *louvi*. It was something none of the others liked and she'd craved it for months now.

Later that afternoon, she spooned the steaming beans into her bowl, took the expensive dark green olive oil from the top cupboard and drizzled a generous amount over the dish. Then she squeezed half a lemon over it, peeled an onion, sliced a wedge off it and put it on the side. Michalis turned his nose up at raw onion, now he'd cultivated fancy English ways, but everyone back home ate like this.

Balancing a slice of thickly cut bread on the side, she carried it all to the living room. She never ate in here, but why not? She placed it on the table and was about to settle down to eat but turned at the sound of frantic scratching. What was that? Next door's cat? A mouse?

The rain slapped at the windows but it sounded closer than

that. She wasn't accustomed to a house with no people, and perhaps her mind was playing tricks on her. A heavy unease fell over her like a damp jacket, and she walked to the wireless and twirled the dial. Hedy had said she should never touch it or they wouldn't be able to find their favourite station again.

She spun it one way then the other. Some music would wipe away the loneliness. She couldn't find a Greek station, but there must be one, surely, what with all the Cypriots in London now? How she craved the twang of the bouzouki, or the sparkling soprano of Maria Callas right now. She'd have to settle for something else. Anything to get rid of this terrible scratching that was growing more insistent. She found a station with light, cheery music, all twinkling keyboards like the sounds of spring. It brought to mind the fountain in the middle of the town she'd passed through as a girl. It was music fit for a holiday, a weekend to herself.

She turned it up loud, sat in front of her dinner and began to eat. The rain gained force and slammed even harder against the glass. She ate quickly, one spoonful after another, overwhelmed by the fury outside these walls and inside her head. As the music built to a glorious crescendo, her tears came thick and fast, but she continued to shovel the food in, only stopping to gasp for breath and wipe her face with her sleeve.

CHAPTER SIXTEEN

Holloway Prison

The scratching comes at night. It's not the rhythmic pit-a-pat of Zina's heart, but a frantic scrabble, like someone grappling behind the wall. It peaks, subsides, then starts over. Just like that time they all left her and went to Brighton. Now everyone has gone again but they won't be coming back.

She pulls the itchy blanket up under her chin and tries to ignore it, but the familiar rhythm has stamped itself into her mind. One-two-three, let-me-out. It's so close to her ear now. Perhaps something is crawling inside the iron bars of the bed, trying to escape?

She opens her eyes and it retreats, but when she closes them it returns. She'd give anything for an hour's rest, but daren't succumb. What if it means her harm? She thinks about the letter from her brothers and how easily they dismissed the idea of coming to save her.

There's the clack of footsteps in the long corridor outside, and the whisper of wardens as they talk. All day the distorted sound of the radio ricochets off the staircases and railings from the lower floor. Some of the women sing along, laughing, but for her it's unbearable. No peace anywhere. And it's so dirty here she feels quite sick at times. She has one cloth and they expect her to use it to dry her body and wipe out her tin cup.

It's been two months now, and her solicitor says she'll get a trial date soon. Another hauling in front of men to be accused of unspeakable things.

Trying to damp down the panic in her mind, she takes steady breaths and clenches and unclenches her fists under the covers. She stares up and mouths encouragement to herself: *Stay awake, Zina. Soon it will be day again.*

Finally, hours later, a square of light slides across the wall to announce the morning. The shape is divided into four and, although she knows it's just the day leaching through the windowpanes and not a sign from above, the shadow of a cross that's thrown onto the brick gives her hope.

There's a clatter and the door swings open.

'Morning, Pavlou.'

It's Jenners, the older prison warden. She's told her that her name is Mary and seems kinder than the others. She hands her a plate of undercooked porridge. Zina takes it with a nod and begins to eat. Now there's daylight she feels stronger. Today, she decides, today I will say something.

An hour or so later, Mary opens up again and Eva bustles in with her sad smile and notepad. Mary picks up the scraped plate and is about to leave.

'Mary?' says Zina.

'Yes?'

Then to Eva she says, 'Tell her there are noises at night.'

'Sorry?' says Eva.

'Noises. I can't sleep. I want a different cell. Ask them to move me.'

Eva hesitates, then reaches up and pushes her hair back; Zina's noticed she does this when she doesn't want to translate something.

'Just tell her, please – it's noisy. I don't know the word for it. I can't sleep at all.'

Eva does as she's asked, explains about the noise and how it's disturbing Zina, how she wants to be moved.

'Rats.' Mary nods. 'They run under the skirting and from one cell to the next.'

'She says she hasn't slept for days,' says Eva.

Then the warden says more, much more, and Zina can see her mouth working, the words making the girl cross.

'What is it?' Zina asks.

Eva shakes her head. Reaching out, Zina grabs her arm, startling her. Mary goes to make a move then decides not to bother.

'It's your job to tell me everything,' Zina says, suddenly angry at the thought that she, of all people, would keep a secret.

Eva's cheeks flush red.

'But, I...' she stammers.

Mary watches, a smile on her lips, enjoying the spectacle.

'Tell me,' says Zina, 'tell me what she said or I will complain about you. You'll lose your job.' Then she folds her arms and feels a surge of pride that she's stood her ground. Eva glances at Mary, who's cocked her head to one side and is smirking.

'You're sure you want it all?' she asks Zina.

'Yes – tell me everything.'

Eva's shoulders slump in resignation.

'The noise is because of the rats,' she begins. Then she sits on Zina's bed, unasked, and rubs at her forehead. 'They're in the walls and run between the cells, so there's no point moving.'

But there's still something the girl's not saying.

'All of it,' says Zina. 'Come on. Don't you keep secrets from me.'

Eva takes a breath.

'Very well,' she says. 'What she said is that it's the least of your worries. The noise and the not sleeping.'

'Why's that?'

'If she was you,' continues Eva, 'she says she'd be more concerned about *not* hearing anything.'

Zina looks across the cell at Mary's face. She's staring at Zina, waiting for a reaction.

'But that's what I want,' she says to Eva. 'Silence.'

'No,' Eva says. 'That's not what she means.'

Zina waits but it's as if the girl can't say the words.

'*What?*' she asks. 'Just say it.'

Eva stares at the floor.

'She says,' she begins, 'that if she were you she'd be more worried about never hearing anything again. Once... once they've hanged you.'

Zina's arms fall to her side. Then in a quiet voice she asks, 'They don't hang people here, do they?'

Eva's mouth opens and closes. She swallows hard and her voice breaks. '*You didn't know?*'

Eva watches her, incredulous. It's impossible. Could Zina *really* not know that if she's found guilty of murder it's a mandatory death sentence? Her solicitor *must* have told her. But then she looks at the fear and confusion dancing across the woman's face and knows that in this moment Zina is telling the truth.

'What... what do you mean?' Zina asks. 'They really *hang* people in this country?'

'Someone must have told you,' says Eva. Of course they have. But how could Zina forget a detail like this? Unless her grasp on reality is irretrievably damaged.

Eva softens her voice. 'Zina, listen – although it's written in the law, hanging is *so* unlikely for a woman.' She gives a quick smile. 'It just doesn't happen any more.'

'But it's true?' asks Zina. 'The law lets them do that?'

She has the look of someone who's woken from a deep sleep to find herself in a nightmare.

'Well, yes – but like I said it's very unlikely. *Rare*, in fact.'

'How rare? How unlikely?'

'What?'

'When did they last do it?'

'At Holloway? I can't ever remember it happening, so it mu
have been many years ago. Twenty, maybe thirty. Trust me.'

Zina sits on the bed next to her and Eva squeezes her hand.

'Honestly,' she says. 'The English don't like hanging *anyone*
any more. They think it makes them look uncivilised, to the rest
of the world. And as for hanging women, well that's even more
unpopular.'

Zina frowns. 'Not even foreign ones?' she asks.

Eva doesn't speak for a few moments and then says, 'Look,
take no notice.' She nods towards the warden. 'She's taunting
you because she's bored.'

Mary looks up, aware they're talking about her. 'You know
you're meant to write everything down?' she says. 'Every word.'

'Oh, really?' replies Eva. 'You want to report all of this, do
you? That you were mocking a prisoner?'

She turns back to Zina.

'Let's take this one day at a time, alright?' she continues. 'Let's
get your side of the story across, yes?'

Zina gives a small nod then casts a sidelong glance at the
warden.

'I thought she was the kind one,' she says, 'but look at her.
Stone face. Stone heart. What kind of woman takes a job like
that?'

Eva smooths down her dress and doesn't say anything.
Perhaps people ask the same question about her.

'Cigarette,' says Zina, and reaches for her Player's. She pays
for ten a day in a plain box.

Mary trudges over, resentment in each step, and as she puts
the flame to the tip of the ciggie, Zina blows smoke right into
her face. Mary laughs, knowing she's riled her, which was what
she wanted all along.

Eva picks up her folder and sits at the table.

'Shall we go over a few things?' she says.

'Tell them I don't like those walks in the yard every day,' says
Zina. 'All we do is go round in circles.'

'But it's good to get into the fresh air,' says Eva. 'It's just an hour every day. You must get bored sitting here.'

'I'd rather be here than have them all nudging each other, talking about me.'

'Come on,' says Eva, 'sit down. Yesterday you said you'd remembered something about that night.'

Zina nods.

'I'll make a note and your solicitor will come and see you, do it all officially.'

'I don't want him here. I've told them already. I only want to speak to you.'

'I'm not allowed to take down a statement, I've told you before. He has to come. But tell me now and I'll send it on, then you'll have to tell it to him again anyway.' Eva pulls out her pencil from the top of her pad.

'So, what is it?' she asks. 'Come on – sit down. What do you want to say?'

Zina sits hesitantly. 'I don't want to get anyone into trouble,' she says.

'What? Who would you get into trouble?'

'There was a man,' says Zina.

'Where?'

'On the night, at the house. The smoke made me wake up and when I went to the top of the stairs I saw a man, at the front door.'

Eva scribbles everything down. 'In the *house*? What was he doing?'

'No, he was on the front doorstep that leads to the street. When I came down the stairs he turned and ran away.'

'Where did he go? What did he look like?'

Zina shrugs. 'I didn't see his face, but it could have been one of her men friends. She was always dressing up – I'm sure she had a few. He was wearing a brown coat. That Freddy has a dark coat.'

'Who's Freddy?'

'A friend of Michalis. He ran away before I could get downstairs and that's when I saw the fire and I saw Hedy – she was in the garden. The man must have done that to her, not me.'

Eva writes it all down and wonders if Zina even believes this story herself. This is the first she's heard of Freddy. Owning a dark coat is hardly a reason to accuse someone.

'Is there anything else?'

Zina doesn't answer.

'I'll give all of this to the governor and she'll talk to your solicitor. Can... can I ask you something?' She tries to make her voice casual not accusatory. 'Why didn't you mention it before? They'll ask you that. You were questioned for hours – weren't you? – but I don't think I ever saw anything in your statement about this.'

'I couldn't say before,' Zina says firmly.

'Why not?'

She presses her lips together. 'Just say I forgot. It's easier that way.'

'Zina, you have to tell the truth. They'll question you and they'll get it out of you. Then they'll think you're lying about everything.'

'I,' she says leaning close, 'am lying about *nothing*. Put that in your report.'

Eva lets out a sigh.

'Alright.' She uncrosses her legs, and as she goes to stand, her foot kicks something on the floor. It's Zina's red cardigan, rolled in a ball and filthy with footprints.

'Don't touch it!' says Zina, and kicks it towards the corner, carefully with her shoe, not letting it touch her ankle.

'What's the matter?' Eva asks. 'Let me get it to the laundry for you.'

'She's cracked,' says Mary. 'She's been stamping on that since yesterday.'

Eva stares from Zina to the jumper, which is now filthy with her tread marks.

'Don't touch it,' says Zina. 'I don't want it in here. It's bad luck.'

Eva laughs then realises she's serious.

'It's cursed,' Zina says. 'I want it out of here. *Out of here.*'

'Oi – keep your voice down,' says Mary.

Zina stares at the cardigan and backs away.

Eva reaches out and strokes her arm. 'You've worn it for days now,' she says. 'It's just a cardigan, it's—'

'Please, Sophia,' says Zina, her voice softer now. 'Take it with you. I want my green one. That's the one I need. Can you bring it? Can you get it from the house?'

Eva doesn't say anything. Does she think she's her sister? Several footsteps patter outside the cell as a group of prisoners walk past, and someone lets out a squawk of laughter. It's quickly followed by a stern telling-off.

'Alright,' she says. 'I'll get rid of it if that's what you want.'

She goes to pick up the cardigan, but Zina pushes her out of the way and uses Eva's coat to lift it without touching it. Eva opens her bag and she drops it in.

She glances at the warden.

Mary puts an index finger to her temple, twirls it around and says, 'Told you. Loopy. Cracked. Gone.'

CHAPTER SEVENTEEN

S leeve pulled over wrist, Eva rubbed a circle of condensation from the Golden Plaice window and peered outside. Where was he? He was already a quarter of an hour late and she might not be able to hold the booth much longer. Twice, the same woman with a face like spoiled milk had asked her in a loud voice if she needed the table, and Eva could see her still bristling in the queue, making ready to approach again.

'Sorry!' Jimmy slid into the seat in front of her.

'Oh thank God,' she said. 'I think that woman was about to thump me. She keeps asking for the table.'

Jimmy leaned forward and Eva went to peck him on the cheek but he moved his head to one side and she caught his mouth instead. When had she stopped giving real kisses? She couldn't remember.

'Had to lock up at work,' he said, slipping off his jacket and loosening his tie. 'Bloody customers. This man wanted a birthday cake but just couldn't make up his mind. I've ordered us the usual.'

'Wonderful.' She smiled brightly. They'd missed last week's dinner here because she'd been so busy at Holloway, and now she felt strangely shy. 'I'm starving.'

'You not eaten today?' Jimmy searched in his jacket and

pulled out a packet of Craven 'A's. He offered her one but she shook her head.

'Zina was distressed. It took a while to calm her down.'

Jimmy nodded but didn't say anything. Two teas arrived and he dropped the tiny hill of sugar from his spoon into his cup and stirred. The clatter of the café seemed to fade away and she worried they had little to say to each other. She felt her throat tighten and she turned away to look over her shoulder, relieved to see the waitress already approaching holding two plates above her head.

'Here you go,' she said, sliding them onto the table. 'Cod and chips, twice. Lemon on the side, like you asked.'

'This looks good,' said Jimmy. 'Though I don't think they could cut that lemon smaller if they tried.'

Eva doused her meal in vinegar as he took the lemon segment from her plate, the other from his and squeezed both all over his fish.

He winked. 'Greeking the fish.' He always said that, and it always made her smile.

She started to attack her battered fish. Say something, she thought to herself. Talk about your day. About his. What did you used to chat about for hours? Years ago, when they were courting, they'd been bemused by other couples who sat in silence.

'They've been together so long they've run out of words,' she'd say.

'You've got enough words for a lifetime.'

Then she'd slap him lightly on the arm and he'd hug her. Now she glanced up at him. He was frowning at his fish in concentration, carefully cutting it in equal neat pieces before eating. She'd already forked a couple of chunks into her mouth.

Was this as happy as they'd ever be? Suddenly she was scared at the thought of being trapped in this limbo forever, and seconds later was annoyed with herself. She was having dinner with her husband, what was there to feel apprehensive about? But she realised she couldn't see a way out for them, a way back to how they used to be. Sadness seeped through her as she reached across for the salt.

A hand slapped down on the table and she jumped, dropping her fork.

'What did you tell them?' boomed a voice in Greek.

'Hey!' Jimmy jumped up.

'Did you tell them?' the man demanded. '*Did* you?'

'Who the hell are *you*?' asked Jimmy. He reached for the man's arm, but he pulled away.

'It's okay, Jimmy,' said Eva. 'I know him. Will you sit down, both of you. They'll throw us out.'

The waitress walked over.

'Everything's fine,' said Eva. 'Sorry about that.'

The waitress looked from the man to Jimmy, nodded and walked away.

'Jimmy, this is Michalis Pavlou,' said Eva. 'He's the accused woman's son. You know, the case?'

Jimmy's eyes widened. 'Oh.' He sat down and shoved up a bit. 'Well, don't just stand there,' he said, when Michalis didn't move.

Michalis sat heavily on the bench.

Jimmy went to say something else, stopped himself then blurted, 'I'm… I'm so sorry about your wife. Terrible.' Michalis didn't respond. 'But – well, what do you want?'

Michalis leaned across the table and spoke directly to Eva.

'Did you tell the police?' This time his voice was quieter. 'What you saw, that night?'

'No.'

'What did you see?' asked Jimmy. 'Where?'

'Are you *sure*?' asked Michalis. 'Because they've been sniffing around again and asking more questions. Some neighbour said they'd heard us shouting and now they're asking what we argued about. Did I ever – how did they put it – "knock her about a bit"?'

'I didn't say a word,' she said. She motioned to Jimmy with her head. 'I didn't even say anything to him.'

Jimmy pushed his plate away.

'Will someone tell me what's going on? Did you see something the night she died? His wife?'

Eva shook her head. 'No, of course not. It was a month or so before. He,' she pointed at Michalis, 'he was hitting someone outside the Café de Paris one night, when I was leaving.'

Michalis' mouth twisted. 'That bastard deserved everything he got.'

'He was in a really bad way – the other man,' she continued. 'He had blood all over him. He was flat out cold and he kept lashing out at him. And…'

Jimmy leaned in. 'What?'

She looked from Jimmy to Michalis.

'And then he threatened me. Told me not to tell anyone else or he'd come for me.' It was a relief to finally say it out loud.

'You did what?' said Jimmy, squaring his shoulders as if getting ready for a fight.

'I… I panicked,' said Michalis. 'I didn't mean it. I was scared. I would never hit a woman.'

'You'd better not. You threaten my wife again and you'll have me to deal with.'

'Look, I'm sorry,' said Michalis. 'I wouldn't hurt anyone.'

'Apart from the man you half killed,' said Jimmy. 'Who was he anyway?'

'He worked in the kitchen, he'd been having a go. Someone mentioned that Hedy is… was German. He did a Nazi salute every day as I walked by.' He looked down at his hands and his voice was quieter now. 'He said terrible things about her.'

There was a pause, then Jimmy offered him a cigarette. Michalis accepted it, along with a light, and took a long drag.

'We had so much of that in the early days here,' he said. 'Swastikas through the letterbox. A bottle thrown at us in the street. I'd had enough.'

'How did you keep your job?' asked Jimmy.

Michalis shrugged. 'Sheer luck. Nobody saw, apart from Eva. And I never laid eyes on him again. He just never came back.'

'I promise you I didn't say a word,' said Eva. 'If the police are asking questions that's nothing to do with me.'

He nodded.

'I believe you.' He blew smoke away from the table. 'They started asking me things and I thought, well... I'm sorry.'

'Anyway, you were at work the night Hedy died, so they can't suspect you,' said Eva.

'That's the problem – they checked the records and saw I clocked off a bit early. I had some business to take care of.'

She waited for him to explain but he said nothing.

Jimmy picked up his fork and started eating again. 'What you've been through is terrible,' he said, 'but like I said, you threaten Evie again and we'll come to blows.'

Eva glanced down at the half-eaten food on her plate.

'I meant no disrespect,' Michalis said to Jimmy. 'But I don't understand. Why are you letting her do this?'

Jimmy looked at him bemused. 'Do what?'

'Translating. Working at a prison – hardly a job for a woman.'

Eva went to cut in but Jimmy got there first. 'She's good at it. And anyway, that's up to her.'

She felt a flash of pride; despite the arguments, here he was defending her.

'And what do *you* say?' Michalis asked her. 'The things she did to Hedy. Why are you helping her?'

'Because there's nobody else,' said Eva. 'And even if she did do it—'

'Oh, she did it alright. The two of them loathed each other by the end. I knew it was a mistake to let her come here but she kept asking and asking – for years.'

'Even if she did do it,' continued Eva, 'she still deserves to understand what's going on. What she's accused of, what will happen, to have someone to speak for her.'

Michalis gave a wry grin.

'Make sure justice is done, eh? Very noble. And what about Hedy? What did *she* deserve? Who'll speak for her?'

There was a silence and then he stood. 'Your food's got cold. Sorry. Listen, you can do something for me actually.'

'Sorry?'

'Are you seeing her in the next few days?'

'Yes. Why?'

'Take a parcel of clothes to her, would you? The prison rang yesterday for them. Would save me a journey – I can bring it to you at work.'

Jimmy shot him a look. 'You've got a nerve, haven't you?'

'It's alright,' said Eva.

'Just thought I'd ask,' said Michalis. 'I'm sorry about your dinner. I'm just... I'm just not myself.'

His eyes looked wet, and in that moment she thought of Zina.

'You know she asks after you,' she said, gently. 'Where you are, why you haven't visited.'

'I can't. Will you take it? Please? As a favour?'

She took a sip of her tea. It had turned cold. 'Alright.'

'Thanks,' he said.

'Can you write to her at least?' she asked.

'No. I've got nothing to say. Tell her to stop sending letters and visiting orders, too. She sent three last week.'

'She's all alone, you know,' she said.

'Well, so am I.' And with that he walked away.

Eva let her head drop towards her plate and everything began to blur.

Jimmy peered at her. 'Hey, Evie, don't cry.'

He put down his fork and reached for her hand but she pulled away.

'I know it's silly,' she said, opening her handbag and taking out her compact, 'but if you saw her, Jimmy.' She swept under her eyes with a hankie. 'If you saw how hopeless she is. She has nobody – not one person. Nobody visits her.'

'Are you surprised?' he asked. 'I mean – what she's done.'

'Accused of.'

'Yes.'

'But even the worst people get visitors – there's always someone who wants to see them. But not her. No family, no friends, no neighbours.' She looked at him. 'And I don't think she's right – in the head.'

'What do you mean?'

'There've been a couple of things she's done. I can't really say, but she gets muddled, calls me by the wrong name, and some of her behaviour isn't just irrational, it's frightening.'

She pictured the red cardigan that had been trampled on the cell floor.

'The wardens have said it, too,' she continued. 'Her defence want her to plead insanity.'

'Really?'

Eva nodded. 'She absolutely refuses. She's even changed her story now, saying there was some man there on the night, though I don't think even she believes that. If someone's not well, should they still go to trial? Maybe she didn't know what she was doing?'

Jimmy took her hand firmly this time.

'That's got nothing to do with you, Evie. You're there just to translate. It's a job. That's all. Don't get involved.'

She nodded, though she knew it was far too late for that.

'Thanks for backing me up just now. I know you're not keen on all of this, but it was nice of you.'

'Of course,' he said. 'I'm not going to let him speak to you like that.'

Picking up her knife and fork, she pushed the fish to one side and started on the chips.

They ate in silence for a while, as all around them friends chattered.

'Hey, this weekend,' he said. 'Shall we go somewhere? Maybe Regent's Park, if the weather holds? Just to get out of that flat. We could take a picnic.'

'I think I have to work,' she said.

'Oh.' He sipped his cold tea. 'Well, that's alright, never mind.'

'Another time?'

'Yes. Another time.'

They carried on eating in silence. After a few minutes he laid his knife and fork neatly on his plate and looked up.

'Evie?'

When he stared at her like this it was impossible to look away. 'Yes?'

He paused, as if weighing up his words.

'What is it?' she asked.

'Evie, you know you can't save her, don't you?'

'What?'

'Zina. You can't save her. You're there to translate, to help her with all the official stuff, but you can't change anything. Not really.'

She stabbed a chip and nodded, but said nothing. She'd had an idea.

CHAPTER EIGHTEEN

Holloway Prison

'One grey skirt… one spectacles case, including spectacles… one green cardigan… two pairs of undergarments… one pair of socks… and… two small wooden icons. Sign here, please.'

Eva bent over the book, looked at the list of Zina's belongings and signed her name.

'Governor wants to see you,' said the warden.

'What about?'

'Don't know. Leave the things, we'll get them to Pavlou. Bennett will take you.' She motioned to another warden next to her. 'She said to send you in as soon as you arrive.'

Eva followed the warden down the echoing corridors, the hard clack of her heels making her self-conscious. She had never met the governor before, let alone visited her office.

'What's it about?' she asked. 'Any idea?'

'None of my business,' muttered Bennett, as she unlocked another gate. They passed through, she locked it behind them and they continued walking.

They reached a part of the prison where some of the cell doors stood open as the women chatted among themselves. Eva looked up. A couple of them leaned over the bannister and stared at her, but mostly they took no notice. There were a few cells where Eva could see the doors were closed, and she thought of the women who didn't want to come out even when they were allowed to. Women like Zina.

Bennett went off down a side corridor and Eva followed her, up some stairs and finally along a quiet, wood-panelled passage with a dark door at the end of it.

The warden knocked and a voice called from inside.

'Come.'

Bennett opened the door, went in.

'Eva Georgiou, ma'am – Pavlou's interpreter. You wanted to see her.'

A tall, wiry-haired woman stood from behind her desk. She was younger than Eva expected.

'Thank you, Bennett. That'll be all. Please sit down, Mrs Georgiou.'

Eva sat but the governor stayed standing.

'There were a couple of things I wanted to discuss with you,' she said.

'There's no problem, I hope?'

The governor took a folder from her desk and flicked through it. Reading upside down, Eva could see 7145, Zina's prisoner number, at the top of every page. She looked up from her notes.

'You know the accused's son, I take it?'

'Sorry?'

'Mr Michalis Pavlou. The victim's husband. I understand you know him?' Her eyes hadn't moved from Eva's face.

'Yes, but I mean, it's not anything. Well, I don't *know* him really, not that well,' she stumbled. Would they take her off the case? Did they know she'd seen him hit that man outside the club and had said nothing? 'He works at the Café de Paris, you see – I have a part-time job there, too. I did tell one of the wardens to inform you, to make sure it was alright. A few weeks ago, in fact.'

'There's nothing to worry about,' said the governor, sitting. 'It may prove beneficial. I want you to convince him to pay his mother a visit.'

Eva shook her head. 'He won't – he's adamant. I even asked him again yesterday when he dropped off her clothes.'

'But she's had no visitors. Is he aware of that?'

'Yes, he's aware,' she replied.

She thought about Michalis clocking off early on the night of the murder. Where had he gone? Perhaps Zina knew, and he was scared she'd say something if he came to see her. No, it was ridiculous. Why would he hurt his own wife?

'He doesn't seem to care,' she added.

'I see. But I do care, Mrs Georgiou. Prisoner Pavlou is relying on your company just a bit too much.'

'Oh, I really don't mind.'

'But strictly speaking you should only be here on prison business – when you need to translate. I gather you're coming most days now?'

Could she stop her visiting? That would mean Zina had nobody.

'Is that against the rules?' she asked, trying to look apologetic. 'I'm sorry – I didn't think. I mean, as she's alone I thought that my visiting might be helpful. Zina – Mrs Pavlou – might say something and I can translate, you see, and she has company, too. It's better than her seeing nobody, surely?'

The governor frowned and, thinking on her feet, Eva blurted: 'I could be a volunteer visitor. To make it official. Would that help?'

'You really have time?' she asked. 'And you'd still be her interpreter?'

'Yes, of course. I'd just pop in every day, make sure she's alright.' As she spoke, Eva realised this could work well for all of them. 'I'm here almost every day anyway, and it would save your wardens constantly calling me to bring things she needs.'

The governor pursed her lips and mulled it over.

'But you'd only get paid if you're undertaking official translation work,' she said, 'letters in and out, visiting orders, any requests. You know that, don't you?'

'Of course.'

The governor pushed the file away and studied her carefully. 'I have to ask you, Mrs Georgiou. If you're not getting paid extra, then why would you want to do it?'

'Well...' Eva stalled. She'd wondered about her fixation a few times herself. It seemed more than trying to help; she felt duty-bound to be there for Zina, whatever happened to her in court. And Jimmy had frequently complained about the time she was spending with her. This would make it worse, for sure.

'Well... you don't have any volunteer visitors who speak Greek, do you?'

'No, that's true.'

'Then it makes sense, ma'am, don't you think? I mean nobody else is visiting her. And even if you were able to get someone other than me to be a volunteer visitor, if they didn't speak Greek I'd still have to be there to translate. What's that expression about killing birds?'

'Two birds with one stone,' replied the governor.

'Exactly. This way you won't have to pay me in an official capacity. And she'll have company.'

'And she does seem to like you,' said the governor, warming to the idea. 'The wardens tell me she calms down when you're there.'

She closed the file.

'Alright, I'll allow it. But if she says anything about the case, or anything at all that you think is significant, you will of course report it immediately. Through the usual channels, write a report that day, get it on my desk for the morning. It has to all stay above board.'

Eva nodded. 'Absolutely.'

'One final piece of advice,' said the governor, and now she held up her index finger and pointed at her. 'Don't get attached – who knows what will happen in court, but it's never a good idea to get too close to the prisoners.'

'You've nothing to worry about there, ma'am.' Eva smiled. 'I've been an interpreter for the Met for five years. I can leave the job at the door.'

The governor looked at her watch and put her hands on her desk as if to get up.

'Ma'am,' said Eva, 'can I ask you something else?'

'Yes.'

'You've seen my reports. Do you think she's in her right mind?'

The governor looked taken aback at the blunt question.

'Well, strictly speaking this isn't…' She hesitated then seemed to reconsider. 'Look, Dr Garrett is compiling a report and from what I can already see here in Pavlou's file—' she patted the folder '—he has reservations about her sanity, too.'

'He has?'

She nodded. 'You may or may not know that, despite her solicitor's advice, Pavlou won't let them defend her on the grounds of insanity. She absolutely refuses. And she's adamant she's innocent.'

'Yes, I know. But if she's mentally unwell,' Eva said, 'would she even *know* what she'd done?'

The governor smiled. 'That's why we have doctors,' she replied. 'All's not lost. In cases like hers, if she's found guilty the judge will consider any medical report submitted by the defence before he sentences. She'll get life in an institution.'

She stood. 'Now, will you come with me? Her trial date is in, and I need to let her know.'

As they walked briskly through the corridors, a succession of wardens quickly unlocked and locked a number of gates, so they hardly had to pause at all. In a few minutes they were outside Zina's cell.

The door swung open and Zina stood up. Her hair was undone and hanging loose over her shoulders, making her look younger. She'd already put on her green cardigan, and the other clothes Eva had brought in were strewn across her bed. She'd just come back from slopping out and looked embarrassed as she pushed the bucket with her foot into the corner.

'Please translate, Mrs Georgiou. Mrs Pavlou, I'm the governor, I'm in charge of this prison.'

Eva did as asked.

'I'm here to let you know that your trial date has been set for 25th October. That's in two weeks' time.'

'Tell her I didn't do it,' said Zina.

'What is it?'

'She says she didn't do it.'

'She needs to save all that for the court. Tell her from me that it's important she tells the court everything she knows if she's to get the most satisfactory conclusion.'

Most satisfactory conclusion, thought Eva. What a way to phrase it.

'You need to tell the court everything,' she explained to Zina. 'If you want to… to save yourself. You need to be honest and tell them everything. Do you understand?'

Zina reached out and stroked Eva's arm. The governor lifted her head a little in surprise.

'Don't worry,' Zina said to Eva, her hand still on her skin. 'You can tell them I've been through this before and I wasn't locked up.'

Eva paused then asked, 'What do you mean you've been through it before?'

'In the end, the court saw I hadn't done it. I'll be alright.'

Eva's face went numb and her fingertips tingled.

'What's she saying?' asked the governor. She stepped in and took Zina's hand away. 'She's not really meant to touch you.' She wagged a finger in Zina's face. 'Mrs Pavlou, *you can't touch your interpreter*.'

Eva ignored the governor.

'What… what do you mean, Zina?' she asked. 'What do you mean you've been through this before?'

'In Cyprus.' She nodded. 'I was young, just a girl. They said I'd killed her, but you know when the court heard my story they saw it was all lies.'

'What's that about Cyprus?' asked the governor. The word in Greek – *Kipros* – was so similar she'd understood.

Eva's mouth felt like it wouldn't work.

'You tell,' said Zina in English.

Time seemed to slow down. Eva swallowed hard and found her voice.

'She... she said in Cyprus.' She took a breath. As she started to speak, she didn't know what she was going to say. 'She has family... in Cyprus and she knows they're all praying for her.'

'Me good,' said Zina in English. Then she patted her chest and looked at the governor. 'Me no do. Me go home.'

'Well,' said the governor, turning, 'we'll see. Goodnight, both of you. And Mrs Georgiou?'

'Yes?'

'Don't forget, please – about the visit?'

The governor said something else before she left the cell, but all Eva could hear was the agitated beat of her own heart.

CHAPTER NINETEEN

To: the Governor
Please find attached a letter translated on behalf of Prisoner 7145, Mrs Zina Pavlou, to her brothers Vasos and Panayi in Cyprus.

Signed
E Georgiou
Interpreter/Translator

12 October 1954

My dear beloved brothers,

The pages of your letter are soaked with my bitter tears.

You say you'd cross the sea for me if you could, but you refuse to spend the £23 for a boat ticket. You could easily raise this money among our village if you wanted to. Am I not worth that much? How many gifts have I sent you since being here? How many times did I go without so you could eat when we were children? How quickly you forget.

Everyone in the family knows how to look after crops, but who will look after me? It seems you don't want to save your sister, and yet I don't know why.

And as for Sophia, she still doesn't come. I wish her health and riches and let's see how far she gets with those. I wrote her many letters when I first arrived, to help her come here too. Every letter I sent cost me two shillings. So much time and money spent and for what? And as for her sons, I've bought presents for them and their wives and children, but now they've cast me aside like a useless rag. They have no manners or sense of what is right. They're all savages.

If you still have any love for me, do this one thing. It may save me.

Take a piece of paper and collect the signatures of all our neighbours in Cyprus, saying what kind of woman I am, whether I'm kind-hearted or if I've ever had enemies.

Ask everyone to sign it. You must sign it, too, as well as all our family and the head priest. I'm a hard-working woman and never did anyone any harm. When they read all the signatures, they'll see they've made a grave error.

Write to Michalis, too. He says I'm no longer his mother. He says I'm guilty, but how could I do such terrible things to him and his children? I think he burns my letters without reading them. Why else would he stay away?

My trial is on 25th October. Hurry.

Always your loving sister,
X (the mark of Zina Pavlou)

CHAPTER TWENTY

The windows of the Royal Café were steamed up, as usual. There was nothing regal about this place. It was a grubby Greek greasy spoon where the coffee was thick and strong and the food shockingly bad. Eva had made the mistake of having a sandwich here once and had never ordered anything again. It had no atmosphere and very few customers.

She came here because it was directly across the road from Holloway Prison. It was the perfect spot to take a breath and gather herself before knocking on those imposing wooden gates.

Shrugging off her coat, she settled into her booth. The owner, a surly man with day-old grey stubble and an unconvincing jet-black hairpiece, shuffled over almost immediately. He nodded at her and placed a *kaffé skétto* in front of her. She thanked him in Greek, he nodded again and walked away. There'd never been any pleasantries – any which-village-are-you-froms? – and that suited her fine.

She pulled the *Mirror* from her bag and glanced at the front page. The electric light on the wall threw a bluish shadow over the newspaper. She scanned the headlines. Nothing there. The only sound was the tick of the clock and the buses that rattled past every now and then, making the door vibrate. She turned the page and continued searching the headlines.

'Well, what do you know – it *is* you!'

She jumped and looked up. She stared for a few seconds at the man in front of her. He'd been wearing a dinner suit the last time she'd seen him. Today he was crumpled, all wrung out. He patted his chest.

'Bert,' he said, and she recognised his American drawl. 'From the other evening. Café de Paris?'

'Of course! John's friend. Sorry, I couldn't place you for a minute.'

He was smiling at her, teacup in one hand, newspaper shoved under armpit, coat thrown over other arm.

'Well, I saw you walk in,' he said, stepping from one foot to the other. 'Wasn't sure if it was you.'

There was a pause.

'It's me,' she said.

He flushed.

'Pardon me, I'm intruding... you look busy.' His hand hovered over the seat back.

'Not at all. Sit down if you like.'

'Well, if you're sure.' He threw his coat across the seat and was now opposite her, arranging his things.

'So what are you doing here?' he asked. 'I mean, do you live nearby.'

She picked up her coffee and blew on it gently. 'I work nearby,' she said. 'Just having this first.'

'Oh, right.' He frowned. 'But you work at the Café de Paris... you have two jobs?'

'Sort of – I just do a bit of translating work. To make some extra cash. What about you?'

He held his hand up. 'First, I should apologise,' he blurted. 'I wasn't on my best behaviour last week, when we met. To be honest, I'm a little embarrassed.' And as if on cue, his cheeks reddened.

She smiled. 'That's alright. It was funny, really.'

'Funny?' He pushed back his hair and it fell over his forehead again, in that way it did. 'I was trying to be debonair. But afterwards John told me I was an obnoxious Yank.'

She laughed.

'And that sister of his – what's her…?'

'Elsie?'

'Elsie, yes. She gave me a real telling-off all the way to the Mapleton.'

'Sounds like Elsie.'

'Apparently, you're a Greek girl, different morals to the rest of us. And I'd never get your attention that way. Or so she says.'

There was a pause.

'Well, more than that,' she said, 'I'm married.'

'Yes, yes – of course.' He stared at her and she looked away. 'So I am sorry if I embarrassed you. What can I say? I'm an idiot.'

'Consider yourself forgiven.' She sipped her coffee. 'You only asked me out dancing. No harm done.'

'Well, that's true. Although I may have had other intentions.' He grinned. Then he held out his hands. 'Sorry. I forget not everybody has a marriage like mine.'

She sat back a little. 'Your wife *knows*…' she said, 'that you… see others?'

'She's back in the States. I stayed after the war. She does too… see others, that is.'

'Really?' She was shocked and intrigued at the same time. She'd be wildly jealous if Jimmy had someone else.

'Oh, sure. We're quite the modern couple, don't you know?' He said it in a mocking voice and she wondered whose idea it had been. 'So no, she doesn't mind. But maybe your husband would?'

She didn't answer. Of course he would, but for how long she wasn't sure. She delved into her bag and pulled out her Craven 'A's. Quick as a flash, he produced a lighter from his pocket and lit her, then accepted one too.

'It's a terrible thing to be rejected by a lovely woman,' he said, blowing smoke to one side. 'Especially when you're keen on her.'

Eva took a drag and turned the page of her newspaper, trying not to smile.

'You know,' he continued, 'most women think I'm a very good catch.'

'Really?' She folded the page over and feigned interest in an article about a new shop opening in Piccadilly. 'You mean like measles?'

He burst out laughing.

'You really are something. I wouldn't mind taking you out one night – dancing,' he said. 'Nothing else. Just a dance or two. Elsie tells me you're an excellent dancer.'

She turned the page again and there was Zina's face staring at her.

'Oh, my,' he said, jabbing at the paper. 'You heard about that?'

She didn't say anything.

'It's dreadful,' he continued. 'Must say, I feel sorry for her.'

'What?'

'The grandmother – that woman. I feel sorry for her. I know what she's done – or meant to have done – is barbaric but, hell, whatever happened to innocent till proven guilty?' Eva stared at him. 'I mean, she *could* be innocent, right?'

Nobody had ever said that about Zina before. Not the police, not Elsie, not even Jimmy.

'Can you imagine,' Bert continued, 'being accused of that and not speaking any English? Not knowing what was going on? Well, I bet she's damn well terrified.' He blew smoke to the side. 'If you excuse my French.'

Eva drained her cup.

'I read somewhere that she's Italian,' he continued. 'How does she get by in prison, do you think?'

'Greek,' said Eva.

'Pardon me?'

'She's Greek-Cypriot.'

He paused. 'Not Italian? You sure?'

'I'm sure.'

'Greek, huh?' Then the penny dropped. 'Hey – like *you*?' He frowned, looked down at the paper and looked at her again. She glanced across the road at the castle-like structure, and he followed her gaze to see what she was looking at.

'Oh, Lord – she's in *there*?' he asked. 'Holloway?'

'That's what I'm doing here,' she said. 'I'm her interpreter.'

His mouth fell open. 'Well, well. Aren't *you* full of surprises?' He paused. 'That must be terrible, right?'

'No, not terrible – but difficult at times, yes.'

'What a job. What do you have to do for her?'

She took a long drag of her cigarette and tapped the filter on the metal ashtray.

'Translate letters in and out, be an interpreter for her.'

'Isn't that the same thing?'

'Translation is written, but interpreting is spoken – I do both. My job's to explain what's happening.'

'That's some responsibility.'

'I try to keep it professional.'

'Of course.'

'But, well, you know… Like I said, it's hard.'

'Must be,' he said. He took a sip of his tea. 'What's she like?'

Eva shrugged. She thought about Zina's comment the other day, that she'd been accused of killing someone years ago, when she was a girl in Cyprus. It must have shown on her face that she was carefully weighing her words.

'Look,' he said, 'don't answer that if you don't want to. It's just sometimes you see these awful stories in the papers, but there's always a human being behind it all, isn't there?'

She sipped her coffee and took her time. He was right, there was a person behind it all and she felt strangely protective of her. Jimmy had never asked her what Zina was like; she'd told him she was worried about her, whether she was in her right mind, but he'd never wanted to know more.

'She's actually quite ordinary,' she said, 'in an old-fashioned Greek way. She comes from a small rural village. I'd say it's about fifty years behind the times if you compare it to here, probably more. But in other ways – her situation – well, she's not ordinary at all.'

'Does she have family here?' he asked. 'Do they visit?'

'She does, but no. Nobody comes. I mean, I can understand her son not wanting to…'

'Of course.'

'But still. She has a sister who's just arrived and nephews. The trial's in about ten days but nobody's come yet. I don't think they will.'

'Nobody? So they've all decided she's guilty?' He put his hand out on the newspaper. 'Though I hear the evidence against her is strong, so maybe they're right. Do you think she stands a chance?'

Eva picked up her cigarettes and dropped them back in her bag.

'I don't know – I hope so.'

'So you don't think she did it?'

She stubbed out her cigarette. 'I'm really not sure, but she's…'

She left it hanging in the air. Should she feel disloyal, discussing Zina? It wasn't as if she'd ever been asked to sign anything or sworn to secrecy in an official way. There was never any paperwork for her interpreting jobs, and Holloway was no different. The governor had more important things on her mind.

'She's what?' he asked. 'You think she's innocent?'

She shrugged. 'I've just got a feeling, well… I think she's not all there. Her mind. She gets confused.'

He leaned in, concern on his face. '*Really?* What do you mean?'

'Never mind – I probably shouldn't say any more.'

He exhaled loudly. 'My grandmother back in South Carolina had problems like that,' he said. 'Towards the end she kept thinking her nurse was a police officer.'

He pulled the paper across the table and read the caption under the photograph. 'Poor Zina Pavlou,' he said. 'Who knows what she's going through, eh? Well, it sure is admirable that you're helping her.'

'Nobody else seems to think so,' she said. 'Her son thinks I should leave her to rot.'

Bert sighed.

'And Jimmy…' Her voice trailed off.

'Jimmy's your husband, right?' he asked. 'What does he say?'

She gave a tight smile. That Zina had taken over their lives.

'It doesn't matter,' she said, and slipped on her coat. 'I've got to go. It was nice seeing you.' She took out her purse but he put his hand out.

'I'll get it. It's on me.'

'Thank you.' She dropped her purse back into her bag.

'Can I come and see you?' he asked. 'At the Café de Paris?'

She hesitated.

'Just to say hello,' he said.

'I'm not going dancing with you. I've told you already.'

He held up his hands. 'I know. Just to say hello that's all. See how you are.'

Where was the harm in that?

'I'd be happy to check your coat for you, sir.' She smiled, and got up. He rose while she slid out of the booth. 'And thank you,' she said.

'What for?'

'For caring.' She motioned across the road. 'Not many people do.'

She turned and walked out of the Royal Café, checked for traffic then sprinted across the road towards the prison. It had been good to talk about Zina. Bert had been kind about her, and even made Eva feel that the hours she was spending in Holloway were worthwhile.

She rarely spoke to Jimmy about her day now. And she'd certainly avoided talking about Zina to him. She didn't want to tell him what she'd said about the incident in Cyprus, because he'd say that she *must* tell the governor. And he'd be right. That was exactly what she should do – still could, in fact. But she didn't want to. Not until she'd found out more. Not until she knew what to think about it herself. So it was easier not to say anything to him at all.

She glanced at her watch, rushed towards the gates and nodded a quick 'morning' to the officer on duty. She felt Bert's eyes on her all the way. If she turned now she knew he'd be watching her. She didn't, of course, but as she stepped through the huge wooden gates, she couldn't help but smile.

CHAPTER TWENTY-ONE

Holloway Prison

19 October 1954

Re: Prisoner 7145, Mrs Zina Pavlou

To the Governor,

Madam, I wish to inform you of something that occurred yesterday and today when I was on duty in Pavlou's cell with her interpreter Mrs Eva Georgiou.

When Mrs Georgiou arrived at 8.30 yesterday morning, Pavlou requested that she write down the full address of the house that is next door to where her son lives. She wanted the address in English.

Mrs Georgiou asked why but she would not say. After she mentioned it to me, we consulted the files and she did as requested. Pavlou then folded the scrap of paper and placed it in her skirt pocket. We thought this harmless enough and nothing more was said.

This morning, I reported for duty at 6.30 a.m. and Pavlou was still asleep. On waking at around eight o'clock, she started crying but would not explain why. She was in a state of extreme agitation.

This continued for perhaps half an hour, until finally Mrs Georgiou arrived. She questioned her and it seems Pavlou's skirt was sent to the laundry last night, and with it the slip of paper.

Pavlou insisted we get it back, but Mrs Georgiou explained that it would take a couple of days, and the paper would have disintegrated on washing. She suggested to Pavlou that she write the address down again.

The prisoner calmed down a little after that and, eventually, after a long conversation with her interpreter, it transpired that Pavlou knew that the house next to her son's stands empty. She stated that she needed the address because she was going to purchase it after the trial, so she might be near her granddaughter. Neither of us made any comment on this.

She said she will now keep the piece of paper in her shoe.

Mrs Georgiou informed me that she has also included this incident in her report to you, but as it is procedure to document anything unusual I am hereby doing so.

Yours respectfully
Officer Hawkins, 0962

CHAPTER TWENTY-TWO

January 1954, six months before the murder

Zina pulled her coat tightly around her and hurriedly walked the half-mile to the school gates. Today was Wednesday, her favourite day; an exquisitely cut gemstone nestled in the middle of her dull, back-breaking week. It was the only day she was allowed to meet Anna from school.

It was the second time she was doing it, and it had all come about because Hedy was now in charge of dressing the window in the boutique.

'I have to work a full day on Wednesdays,' she'd said over dinner one night. 'I'll just ask Mrs Crawford to pick Anna up after school – slip her a couple of bob.'

'Don't be silly,' said Michalis. 'Mamma, will do it.' And before Hedy could say anything he turned to Zina, explained their predicament and asked if she would mind.

Zina was excited at the thought of more time with Anna, but tried to keep her face neutral. She gave a shrug.

'Why pay a stranger when I'm here?' she said. 'Of course I'll get her from school.'

Then she turned to Hedy and used a word she'd recently learned. 'Family.' She patted her chest. 'Me help.'

Hedy gave a tiny, tight grin and shot Michalis a glance. She'd be better off just spitting it out, thought Zina. Whatever she's thinking will eat her up inside.

Zina had asked Michalis a few times now if she could put

baby Georgie in the pram and take him for a stroll – nowhere far, she wouldn't get lost. She'd seen other grandmothers out and about, showing off their grandchildren. But there'd always been a reason why not: Michalis reported back that Hedy thought the weather was about to turn, or that Georgie was looking a bit poorly and she didn't want to risk letting him out of her sight. Last time Zina had asked if she could take him to the shops with her, just for a *peripato*, a walk to get some air, Michalis hadn't even bothered mentioning it to Hedy.

'No – you know what she's like, Mamma. Best not.' But how things have a habit of changing, she thought. Now they needed her. After all the fuss about the oil lamp, and the incense, and the way she mocked her at that wedding.

She reached across the table and put her hand on the girl's sleeve, but directed the words at her son.

'Tell her not to worry,' she said. 'I've had five children. I know how to look after a child.'

Michalis laughed, embarrassed. 'Of course you do.' He turned to Hedy. 'Mamma says she'd be happy to do it – it's decided. She wants to help out and she doesn't need paying either.'

'Well.' Hedy moved her arm to pick up her plate, letting Zina's hand fall off. 'As long as she knows it's just one day a week. I can do the rest.'

'Ask if I can take Georgie, too,' said Zina. 'If you're both working, why don't I take him in the pram on my way?'

Hedy shook her head at mention of Georgie's name.

'I've made an arrangement with Rose,' she said to Michalis.

Michalis translated and Zina nodded. Their loss.

Now, as she cut through the scruffy edge of Camden Gardens, she smiled. Finally, she'd have time with Anna, uninterrupted. And so what if she was being used because it was convenient? It meant Hedy needed her, which was good. As she trudged through the park, Zina wondered if she could make herself indispensable, doing things before they were even needed, to secure her place in the house. She had an uneasy feeling about Hedy. Was certain the girl wanted her to leave, even though she'd said nothing. She had to make sure that never happened, whatever it cost her.

The fog was coming down thick and fast, and as she stood at the kerb she was careful to listen as well as look for traffic. She heard the chug of something approaching and waited till a Vespa went past, before quickly walking across the road.

Just yesterday, she had annoyed Hedy without meaning to. She'd pointed at the net curtains and motioned at scrubbing, to indicate that they needed washing. Hedy had huffed loudly and proclaimed she Didn't Understand A Word. Zina knew the word 'curtain' and had tried to explain in English, using the few words she had; Hedy had just shrugged, although she was sure she had said it right.

These were Hedy's tiny stabs, the cuts too quick, too deep for Michalis to see. Perhaps with time Zina could help her son straighten her out.

The school bell rang as she approached the gates. She loved that sound. Right now she'd forget them both and have a wonderful time. Last week she'd clasped Anna's hand and they'd swung arms home. At the corner, Zina had slipped her a penny and waited while she'd rushed into the newsagent's to buy a bag of bullet-shaped sweets. She'd crunched through them at an impressive rate, then returned the empty bag to her *yiayia*. Zina tipped it into her own mouth and relished the sugardust that cascaded onto her tongue. Since coming here she'd acquired a taste for very sweet things and had even taken to hiding biscuits in her apron, which she ate at night while everyone slept, sucking them till they became putty on the roof of her mouth. Today she had a special plan and knew she could trust Anna not to tell.

Zina could just make her out, her thick, raven-black hair, in a crowd of fair-haired English friends. She shone, even in this fog.

She waved to her and Anna ran over. They kissed, once on each cheek, 'Greek way' as her *yiayia* had taught her.

Crouching down, Zina tucked Anna's red and gold scarf inside her coat and buttoned her up. They started to walk.

'Grandma?'

'Yes, *agape mou.*'

'Grandma, when you were little…'

She looked at her.

Anna motioned with her hand, to show a short person. 'Little.'

Zina nodded.

'What did you want to be?'

Zina frowned.

'When you were *young*, *Yiayia*,' said Anna. 'Like *me*? What job?'

Zina knew what the word 'job' meant, and realised what she was asking. Anna chattered on, and she only caught the occasional word.

They stopped at a crossing. What had she wanted from life when she was Anna's age? *I wanted to stay at school*, she thought, *and learn to read and write. I didn't want to work in the fields to pay off my father's debts, or be married at fourteen to a man so many years older. And I wanted to be loved. To have someone to lie next to at night who didn't smell of another woman.*

'Teacher?' asked Anna. 'Or a nurse or a…'

'Children,' said Zina.

'So a *nanny*?' Anna pointed at the children around them then back at her *yiayia*. 'You wanted to be a *nanny*?'

Zina shrugged. 'She like children?'

'Oh, yes. She takes care of them when their parents can't,' said Anna.

Zina frowned, not understanding.

'Oh, like you. Like today,' said Anna.

Zina crouched down.

'Anna,' she said. 'Today…' What was the word, what was it? She didn't know so she put her finger to her lips.

'It's a secret?' asked Anna. 'What is it? Is it a *surprise*?'

That was the word. Zina nodded.

'*Yiayia* – tell me!'

She laughed, then pulled Anna close for a hug. The curtain of fog that had tumbled over the city would soon shroud everything. Zina looked carefully to one side then the other before she tugged Anna across another road.

She glanced at her watch. They still had time.

'Aren't we going to the sweet shop?' asked Anna, as they walked right past it. '*Yiayia* – sweets?'

'Come.' They dodged past a lamplighter with his long pole, and then came to a stop.

Zina looked up at the curved white building that squatted on the corner like an abandoned wedding cake. The large red letters could just be seen bleeding through the fog.

'PL-A-ZA,' read Anna. 'Cinema? We're going to the *cinema*?'

'Cinema, yes,' laughed Zina.

A group of women pushed through the doors, and Zina and Anna followed them. They crowded around the ticket booth, and Anna started to get anxious.

'You did bring money, didn't you, *Yiayia*? For tickets? And sweets?' Her cheeks were red with excitement.

Finally, they got to the front and Zina motioned to herself and Anna to show what she wanted.

The vendor said something and before Zina had a chance to respond Anna said, 'Downstairs, please.' Then she turned to Zina and said, 'It's expensive upstairs, *Yiayia*.' Zina had, in fact, been here twice before, using her 'pocket money' to watch a film by herself in the afternoon. 'Hurry – we don't want to miss it.'

The man gave them two tickets and they made their way to the stalls. As they were going through the doors, the woman in front of them dropped her handbag and her friends scrabbled to help her retrieve her rolling lipstick and coins. An usher stepped forward and got on his knees, too. Instead of heading to the stalls, Zina pulled Anna to the left and they went through a set of red and gold swing doors.

'But, *Yiayia*, this is the circle!'

Zina bent over to Anna's height and said, 'Mouse.'

Anna put her hand to her mouth as she realised they were sneaking to the expensive seats. She was sharp-witted, thought Zina. More like me than that dullard of a mother. When she'd visited before, Zina's ticket had only been checked in the foyer, not inside the auditorium.

'No laugh!' she warned, and waited while Anna pressed her lips together and composed herself.

They walked up the stairs and as they ascended, a familiar tune swept down to greet them. It was treacle-dark at the top, and Zina blinked several times until her eyes adjusted to the patchwork of greys. Before them was an arched door and she gave it a push to reveal the grand circle of the Plaza. They'd come out at the back of the seats. Several people were already seated but the film was yet to start.

'We haven't even missed the beginning,' whispered Anna, thrilled.

The news reel was playing and, as they walked down the aisle, nobody looked their way. Zina glanced to her right. Scores of people were silhouetted in the dark, staring forward, captivated. She peered around the man on the end of one row to find some seats, but all she could see was a single one right in the middle. At the very end of the row on the other side, an usher held a torch up and directed it in her face.

There were seats right on the other side, but Zina daren't approach her for help; what if she wanted to see their tickets after all?

'There's nowhere,' said Anna, panic in her voice. 'Oh, *Yiayia*, what are we going to do?'

Zina glanced again in the next row, then the next one, till finally she found what she was looking for. Right in the middle, she could see a single seat, and a few seats from the end was another. There was nothing for it. She'd have to speak up.

'Excuse me!' she called, conscious of the weight of her accent.

A long row of people turned to look at her, and she felt the heat rise in her face. 'Move, please. Thank you.'

Nobody shifted.

'Granddaughter,' she said, raising Anna's arm like a trophy. 'Move, please.'

A groan was heard, then a bit of shuffling while the person on the end shifted down a seat and half of the row shifted along too. Zina and Anna then bustled their way through the people who hadn't budged till they reached their seats. Two together. Slap bang in the middle of one of the best sections in the cinema. Zina pushed her to sit down. They looked at each other and grinned.

'No tell,' said Zina.

'Promise,' said Anna and put her arm around Zina's neck and pulled her down for a loud kiss in the dark.

'Coat,' said Zina, and they both unbuttoned themselves, and shrugged off their coats in unison.

Zina opened her handbag, took out a small paper package and handed it across.

'*Sweets as well?*' gasped Anna. She tore open the bag, took one out and shoved it in her mouth. 'Lemon sherbets!'

The music blared, announcing the start of the Norman Wisdom film.

'They're my favourites,' she said. 'Thank you. *Evharisto, Yiayia.*'

'*Barragallo,*' said Zina. She was welcome, with all her heart. For the first time since arriving in this damp, dark city, Zina felt happy. As if she belonged. Right here, sitting in the expensive seats in the Plaza, next to Anna. It had been so many years since she'd loved someone like this and felt it in return.

She focused on the screen, as the silly man in his tight jacket looked straight at her, smiled and the whole cinema erupted in laughter. He hadn't even said a word, and both she and Anna were laughing too. She couldn't remember feeling this happy before. If she had, it must have been a long time ago when she'd been Anna's age perhaps. As he fell over, got up and fell again, she felt the girl's sticky hand reach up to her face.

Anna found her lips in the dark and pushed a lemon sherbet into her grandmother's mouth. Zina sucked hard and the sugary acidic flavour twanged along her jaw. Taking Anna's hand, she kissed it and for the rest of the film kept it in her lap.

CHAPTER TWENTY-THREE

They shared a bag of vinegary chips on the way home, licking the salt off their fingers and tipping their heads back for the crispy bits. Then Anna asked if she could have an ice-cream cone and, despite the cold weather, Zina agreed. That had been a mistake. As they ambled back, Anna's enthusiastic chatter got quieter and, once they were back home she looked pale and sweaty.

Zina put her in the armchair, placed a blanket over her legs and rushed to the kitchen to see if there was any *glykaniso* – dried anise seed – left in the tin for a tea. After a few moments on the chair, she saw it, shoved to the very back. She grabbed it, filled the kettle and went to her room to find a hot-water bottle.

As she was coming back downstairs she heard the front door slam. She stopped on the stairs and waited. Barely ten seconds passed before she heard Hedy yelling her name.

'Zina! Zina!'

She walked to the living room, where Anna was sitting in a pool of vomit.

'What the hell has happened, Zina? What did you give her to eat?'

Zina ran to the kitchen again and got a bowl of water and a rag, and began to clean up the mess.

'Anna, tell me the truth,' said Hedy. 'What have you been eating?'

'I'm sorry, Mummy, I'm sorry.' Anna was bawling now, both frightened of her mother's yells but also trying not to be sick again.

Hedy turned to Zina. 'Leave us alone,' she said.

Zina wasn't sure if she understood. 'I clean.' She started wiping at the lino, but Hedy snatched the cloth and threw it to the floor.

'Get out of this room, Zina,' she shouted. 'I want to speak to my daughter. Alone.'

Zina stared.

'Out!' She pointed to the door, in case Zina was still in any doubt.

An hour later, Anna walked into the bedroom, freshly bathed, eyes red from crying.

'*Agape mou*,' said Zina, and was reaching out to hug her when Michalis' shadow filled the door.

'Mum. Can we talk to you, please?'

Zina stood.

'I'm sorry, *Yiayia*,' whispered Anna as she walked by.

Zina stroked her hair. 'You sleep,' she said.

In the kitchen, there was a smell of disinfectant and Anna's clothes were soaking in a bowl on the floor. Hedy was sitting at the table, holding her elbow as she smoked, her legs crossed and pulled tight under her.

Michalis started to talk but Zina put her hands up. Best to get it over with.

'Sorry,' she said. It was a word the English used a lot. She'd learned it early on. 'Sorry, sorry, Hedy.'

'Mum, it's not working,' said Michalis in English.

Zina shook her head.

'You can bloody understand,' said Hedy. 'We want you out.'

Zina glanced at Michalis.

'You want me to leave?' she asked him in Greek. 'Because I

took my granddaughter to the cinema and bought her chips and an ice cream?'

'No. Because you did it without telling us.'

'Would you have let me if I'd asked?'

'English, Mick,' interrupted Hedy. 'I want to know what's going on.'

He ignored her and continued in Greek.

'That's not the point, Mamma, you know it isn't. You can't just do what you want. She's our daughter. They're our children. We want to raise them our way.'

'But what if it's the wrong way?' said Zina. 'You won't even christen them.'

Grabbing the Woodbines from the table, he lit one, threw the pack down again and turned his back. 'You have to go. You've had a nice holiday, but now it's time to go back to Cyprus.'

Zina pulled at his shirtsleeve. 'Listen to me,' she said. 'It's winter – you can't turn me out like this. And if I return home, you know I'll never have the money to come back. Let's not part like this. It could be the last time we see each other. Please don't send me away.'

He turned around and his cheeks were pink and there were tears in his eyes.

'Oh wonderful!' said Hedy. 'That's all we need, for you to go soft now.'

'Hedy, shut up,' he said.

'What?'

'Just shut up for a minute—'

Zina held her hands up to her shoulders, as if in a stick-up, and they both stopped talking.

'Why don't I leave for a few days,' she suggested. 'A week – or two even. More if you like.'

He hesitated. 'It would have to be more, Mamma. Where will you go?'

'You said your friend in the next street had a room to rent – I could stay there,' said Zina. 'I've hardly spent any of the money you've been giving me. I'll only come back when you're ready.'

'What?' asked Hedy. 'What's she saying?'

'And then what?' Michalis asked.

Hedy stood up. 'Mick, what's she saying?'

'Then we all get a rest,' said Zina. 'And I promise when I come back things will be better. I'll do whatever you want, and I won't take her out again without your permission. I might need some help with the rent for the room, though.'

Michalis bit his bottom lip as he thought it through.

Hedy grabbed his arm. 'I want her out, Mick. We agreed.'

'It'll be difficult, though,' said Zina, 'the cleaning and the cooking and the washing, with the hours you both work. But perhaps Hedy can cut back and do it all herself?'

Michalis nodded. 'Let's say a month – maybe a bit more,' he said. 'I'll pay the rent. He owes me a favour, so it won't cost much. Then if it doesn't work when you come back, that's it.'

Hedy pushed herself between them till they had no choice but to look at her.

'I swear I will scream the place down, Mick, if you don't tell me right now what's going on.'

CHAPTER TWENTY-FOUR

A steady October drizzle was coming down as Eva ran the last few yards to Maison Bertaux. Jimmy had assumed she was going to Holloway, but instead she'd taken the bus towards Soho. She was doing this for Zina.

Inside the café, she slipped out of her soggy coat and patted down her damp hair. There was a silver-haired woman sitting in the corner, slurping tea with a poodle on her lap.

She looked up. 'He's upstairs,' she said.

'Sorry?'

'Tall chap.' She poured some tea in her saucer for the dog. 'Fair hair. Went upstairs five minutes ago.'

'Oh, thank you,' said Eva and pushed past some chairs to the staircase.

The woman said in an exaggerated whisper, 'Good choice, love.'

'What? Oh, no – it's not like that.'

Why was she explaining herself? She trotted up the stairs and entered the room. There was a couple by the window sharing a small round cake. And in the corner sat Dr Garrett.

'Ah, you're here,' he said, and stood, putting out his hand to shake hers.

'Sorry I'm a bit late.'

She started to pull out a chair but he got there first.

'Not at all,' he said as they both sat down.

He looked different. That navy jacket was exquisite, real wool most likely. She'd never seen him out of his white coat and he looked younger, not much older than herself.

She took a deep breath. 'Thank you for coming.'

He smiled. 'Well, it's not every day I find a note on my desk asking me to tea – especially from a pretty girl... woman...'

His words hung in the air then he laughed. 'Forgive me, force of habit.' A light pink glow had appeared under his cheekbones. 'Anyway, I imagine this is work related?'

'Yes, I wasn't sure if you were in yesterday, but hoped you'd see the message. Matron is always hanging around, and I wanted to speak to you in private.'

A surly waitress, no more than sixteen, sloped over with a pad in her hand, pencil poised. They ordered tea for two and the girl sighed at the imposition and walked away.

Eva put on what she hoped was a bright but professional expression. Perhaps this was her only chance to be of real help to Zina.

'So, Dr Garrett—'

'Oh, call me Ted, Mrs Georgiou. We're not at work now.'

'Well, I'm Eva.'

'Not Ava? Sorry, I think I've got that wrong a few times.'

She made a motion with her hand as if to say it didn't matter. 'It's about Zina Pavlou,' she said.

'Yes, I suspected it was.'

'She's becoming increasingly distressed, and I thought if I could understand her case a little better perhaps I could explain it to her? And it might help calm her down?'

He raised his eyebrows and a drop of rain raced down the back of her neck, making her shiver.

'But you're her interpreter,' he said. 'Surely that's her solicitor's job?'

Eva shifted. 'Well, yes, but his Greek is patchy. She doesn't trust him and won't listen to his advice.'

'And you've built up a rapport with her? She trusts you?'

'I suppose so.'

'Tea!' The waitress banged the cups and saucers on the table. 'Sugar's in the spoon,' she called over her shoulder.

He looked down at his empty teaspoon and frowned. 'She's forgotten mine.'

'Here,' Eva offered. 'Have mine.' She tipped the measly smattering of sugar from her teaspoon into his cup, and he stirred.

After a moment, he said, 'So what do you want to know? I'm no legal expert.'

'Well, the governor mentioned you're writing a report about Mrs Pavlou's health.'

He picked up his cup and stared at her over the rim.

'That's right. It's due Wednesday – ready for Monday's trial.' He took a sip and placed it back in its saucer. 'A summary of my observations since she's been at Holloway.'

'But it's not just about her physical health, is it?' she asked. 'You're commenting on how she is mentally, too. If she's – well – if she's troubled.'

He leaned back, a wisp of a smile on his lips.

'Well, there's no doubt she's "troubled", as you put it. I mean the sheer brutality of what she's done... that is, been accused of...' He stopped a moment as if he was picturing the scene. 'And the behaviour I've observed myself. Yes, I'd say she's "troubled".'

'Exactly,' said Eva.

He took out a packet of Embassy cigarettes and offered her one. She accepted and he lit one for himself, too.

'But,' she continued, 'the governor says Zina won't plead insanity. I know I shouldn't really ask, but what are your thoughts? Do you think she's insane?'

'Can't say. I haven't finished the report yet.' He took a puff and blew the smoke into the air above their heads. 'But I can tell you she has a delusional mental disorder. Paranoid episodes that are extreme. All that talk about her granddaughter being taken away, that she was being abandoned.'

'Yes, she talks about Anna constantly,' said Eva. 'She gets frantic at the thought of being apart.'

'From the wardens' reports and what I've seen, she thinks everyone is conspiring against her, punishing her for something or other – God knows what. So, yes, definitely disturbed.'

'And you've seen my reports, I take it?' Eva asked. 'So many incidents.' She started counting them off on her fingers. 'She wanted me to write down the address of the house next to her son's, then got hysterical when her skirt was sent to the laundry with the details in the pocket? She kept talking about buying the house. And she refused to wear the red cardigan, saying it was cursed?'

He nodded.

'Yes, yes – I've seen all that.'

'What about the incident with the book? When she was talking to herself and waving at the drawing in the book?'

He let out an impatient sigh. 'I do get to your reports eventually. I've read all that, and I agree it's disturbing behaviour.'

He stretched in his chair, then glanced at the couple by the window. After a moment's hesitation he leaned in, dropping his voice.

'Listen, her view of the world and her place in it is alarming. So yes, it's a compelling picture of a sick woman. Although my findings haven't been filed yet, *strictly* between us, my opinion is that she *is* insane. That's what I'll say in the report.'

'Good,' said Eva. 'So you can tell them she should plead insanity?'

He laughed in disbelief.

'It doesn't work that way – I can't recommend what plea she puts forward,' he said. 'That's up to her and her team.'

'But you do think she did it?' she blurted.

Garrett's eyes widened.

'Sorry to be so direct,' she said. 'But you more or less said that at the start, didn't you? When you mentioned the brutality of what she's done.' She herself had been so sure of Zina's guilt, but now couldn't shake the feeling that Michalis was hiding something.

The doctor twisted his mouth, then shifted in his chair.

He sighed. 'I never said this,' he said, 'so don't go repeating it, but yes, I think she almost certainly did it. Everyone does.'

Eva nodded. 'So if she's insane, on the night she killed Hedy she couldn't have known what she was doing.'

'Well, not necessarily,' he replied. 'It's probably more complicated than that.'

An elderly man sat down two tables from them. Garrett turned his back slightly.

'Look.' His voice was quieter now. 'Only *she* will ever know what really happened. It's possible she had some sort of an episode – a mental aberration – came to afterwards and realised the enormity of what she'd done. She did try to cover it up, after all.'

'True.'

'Or,' he continued, 'perhaps she *did* know what she was doing all along, but the *reason* she did it was because she's unwell. Because of her fantasies regarding all the terrible things that will happen if her grandchildren aren't cared for properly. Of course, the irony now is that she can't see them anyway.'

'So,' said Eva, 'if that's the case, she can't be fit to stand trial.'

'That's where you're wrong,' said Garrett. 'Very few people are unfit to stand. None that I've ever dealt with. She'd have to be completely delirious – to not understand the charges or even know what a courtroom is, let alone be able to tell the defence how she wants to plead. In Mrs Pavlou's case, that's not true. And she's been very clear she *doesn't* want to be defended on the grounds of insanity.'

Eva's shoulders sank and she looked down at the table. How would Zina fare in a trial? Who knew what she'd say or do in a courtroom? The jury would dislike her instantly.

There was a silence between them as he drained his cup and Eva sat back in her seat.

'But you're her doctor,' she said. 'If you really think she's insane, is there nothing you can do?'

He smiled. 'That's where the report comes in. Her behaviour, my findings, it'll all be there. If she changes her mind and pleads insanity, then her defence can use it in court.'

'But if she doesn't?'

'Well, if she won't let them use it during the actual case, and she's found guilty, the defence will make sure the judge sees it before he passes sentence.'

'*Really?*'

'Absolutely,' he continued. 'After the verdict, her defence is allowed to say something about what kind of sentence she should receive. That's when they'll present it, before the judge passes sentence. I'll either be called to give evidence or it will be read out. Courts *do* listen to doctors, you know.'

'But what if they don't?' she insisted. 'What if they hear the report and disregard your diagnosis?'

He looked startled, as if the notion had never occurred to him.

She stubbed out her cigarette. She tried to take a deep breath, but the air caught in her throat.

'Could they hang her?' she asked.

'What?' He gave an incredulous laugh. 'Heavens, no!'

'But it's a mandatory death sentence for murder.'

'In theory still, but I've sat through dozens of cases at the Old Bailey and have never seen one female murderer sent to the gallows, no matter her crimes. It's thirty years at least since they last hanged a woman at Holloway. The idea that a woman is as cold-blooded as a man doesn't sit well in our courts.'

'Meaning?'

'Well, there's always another reason, according to judges, that a woman kills. She's either not in her right mind, or been pushed to the brink – like that terrible case a few months ago where the woman suffered for years at the hands of her husband and stabbed him while he slept.'

Eva nodded. She remembered reading about it.

'She wasn't even imprisoned,' Garrett continued. 'If Mrs Pavlou is found guilty – and let's face it, she probably will be – the judge will look at my medical report and send her to a hospital. Probably Broadmoor.'

He sounded so sure, but her head had begun to throb and a tumbling anxiety now flipped through her. She remembered feeling this helpless years ago, as she'd sat at her mother's bedside watching her fade away.

'When I spoke to her the other day,' she said, 'she seemed...' Eva could feel her throat tighten and she struggled to keep her voice level. 'Well, she seemed shocked to hear a death penalty even existed, as if nobody had told her.'

He gave a scornful laugh. 'Of course her solicitor has told her! But for whatever reason, her mind won't let her hear it.'

Eva stared at the table as a wave of pity lapped over her. She'd started so calmly, too, had done so well, and now this. Everyone was right; she'd got too involved and now she was surprised at the speed of her growing concern for Zina. For a woman she barely knew. She tried not to blink, but her eyes were welling up fast.

'Look, you're worrying unnecessarily,' he continued. 'I doubt they'll ever hang another woman in this country, let alone one who's so ill. Oh, please! Please don't cry.'

He reached towards her, thought better of it, and handed her a pristine white handkerchief instead. Embarrassed, she tried to dab carefully at the corners of her eyes. She must look a mess. She couldn't leave the café with ruined make-up.

'My advice,' he said, 'is not to get attached to these women. That won't help anyone.'

She sniffed, loudly, and took a few deep breaths, then folded the hankie, stains and all, and handed it back. He looked at his watch and motioned for the bill.

'I have to go.' They stood and he helped her into her coat, leaving his hands on her shoulders for a moment. 'Eva, listen,' he said, with a gentle squeeze, 'stick to your job. It's simply not your responsibility to worry about these things. She has a defence team, my medical report and is lucky enough to be in a country with the best legal system in the world. She'll be alright, you'll see.'

He took the bill from the waitress and left.

Eva opened her bag, looked in her compact mirror and grimaced. Using her finger, she wiped away the mascara smudges, then Max Factored her lips. Moments later, collar up against the rain, she hurried through Soho Square, Dr Garrett's words still in her ears.

Once on the bus, she turned it over in her mind. He seemed so sure, she thought, but the dread had settled into the pit of her stomach and wouldn't shift. And then it came to her. Surely it would be better if Zina didn't *have* to rely on anyone else to save her? What if Eva could convince her that she, Zina Pavlou, could save herself?

CHAPTER TWENTY-FIVE

March 1954, four months before the murder

As soon as she heard the key in the door, Anna rushed and grabbed Hedy by the hand.

'Mummy, come and look!' she cried. 'You'll never believe it.'

Dragging her through to the hallway, she pulled Hedy into the living room. In the corner stood Michalis, and on the small square table was a gramophone sitting in its own case.

Hedy rushed over.

'Mick! Oh, my goodness – it's perfect.' She gave him a hug and he grabbed her waist and laughed at her excitement. Immediately, she knelt down to inspect the record player. 'Oh, thank you! Can we afford it?' she said, as she ran her hands over the burgundy and cream case. 'I can't wait to play all our records again.'

'Don't thank *me*,' he said.

She looked up from her position on the floor and turned to follow his gaze.

'Mamma bought it.'

Zina was sitting in a chair in the opposite corner, a tentative smile on her lips. She got up. 'Hello, Hedy. You like?' she asked, in a small voice.

Hedy stared at Michalis.

'She was outside when we got home,' he said. 'It *has* been six weeks, love.'

'She just turned up... with a gramophone?'

He nodded.

'Says it's a gift, to make it up to you.'

'Where did she get the money?'

'Said she'd saved it – I don't know.'

Zina was watching them both then slowly walked towards Hedy.

'*Baska*,' she said.

'What?'

'She's says it's almost Easter.'

'From me,' said Zina, and she patted her chest.

Mick smiled at his mother and then looked at Hedy, to see what she'd do.

'Come on, Hed,' he said, putting his arm around her shoulder. 'She's trying. Let's make things work, alright? And this place could do with her touch if you want to carry on working.'

Anna took Zina's hand and swung it back and forth. 'Can *Yiayia* come back, Mummy?'

Zina saw Hedy glance to where her coat had been neatly folded and placed on the back of the chair. Next to it was the battered brown suitcase that she'd brought with her from Cyprus.

'Please?' asked Anna.

Zina smiled and Hedy tried to do the same, but her face wouldn't cooperate.

'Looks like she already has, love,' she said.

Zina didn't understand what was being said, but realised from Hedy's tone that it was going to be alright. She leaned in and put a tender kiss on Hedy's cheek, then one on the other.

'*Evharisto*,' she said. 'Thank you.'

Anna pulled her grandmother to the gramophone and turned it on. Her father had already placed a record on the turntable and she carefully lifted the arm and placed the needle on the outer edge of the disc. A loud crackle announced the start and they all waited expectantly. Anna turned the volume up a little more, then the most majestic sweeping aria burst through and filled the room.

Taking Zina's hands, she started swaying one way then the

other. She guided her grandmother around the small room, the two of them holding their arms up and dancing around, laughing.

'They're so happy,' said Michalis, hugging Hedy a little closer. 'Look at them.'

She said nothing.

CHAPTER TWENTY-SIX

October 1954
Holloway Prison

To: the Governor
Please find enclosed a petition sent on behalf of Prisoner
7145, Mrs Zina Pavlou, who is in Holloway Prison, under a
capital offence. It has arrived via her brothers, but with no
letter attached.

From: the family and neighbours of Mrs Pavlou
Spakato, Limassol
Cyprus

*We hereby affirm that Mrs Zina Pavlou, who is now in
London, is of good character and we, her friends and
neighbours, have no complaint against her.*
  There follow 103 signatures.

CHAPTER TWENTY-SEVEN

Holloway Prison

The loud laughs rang down the tiled corridor as Eva approached Zina's cell. She could see that her door was open and there was a crowd outside. A dozen prisoners were elbowing each other towards the entrance, as if daring one another to enter.

On rainy days like today, the doors of D block were often left open, so the women could wander the balconies instead of traipsing outside in bad weather. But Zina never left her cell, and nobody ever looked in on her. So what were they all doing there? Eva pushed into the excited knot of prisoners blocking the entrance.

Peering over their heads, she could see two wardens in the doorway, doing nothing to disperse the crowd.

'What is it? Excuse me.'

A tall prisoner with pitted skin turned in front of her but then turned back, barring her way.

'Move! I'm her interpreter.'

Nothing.

'I said move!'

'Let her through,' shouted an officer.

The tall woman shifted to one side and Eva finally pushed past. She stumbled into the cell.

'What's going on? Is she alright?'

A hush fell as people looked at Eva for her reaction.

'She's fine,' said Mary, the warden. 'In fact, she's ecstatic.' A younger warden next to her tittered.

Zina was in the middle of the cell, her arms held out wide. Her eyes were shut and she was swaying and smiling. She was humming a loud tune and stepped to one side, waited a few beats, then to the other, dancing without a care to music only she could hear. Everyone watched as she spun faster and faster, face raised to the sky. After a final twirl, she came to a stop and someone applauded. Her eyes snapped open and she took an extravagant bow.

The crowd erupted in laughter and cheers and she blew kisses to the left and right, like a diva on stage.

Eva pushed Mary hard. 'Stop this, stop this right now.'

Mary shrugged and turned to the crowd.

'Come on, show's over. Hawkins, move them on.'

The younger warden did as she was told and the women began to disperse.

'Sophia, come!' Zina came and took Eva's hand. 'Don't you like the music? We can put a different record on. What would you like?'

Eva put her arm around her and pulled her away from the doorway, which was now emptying.

'Come and rest, Zina,' she said. 'Let's sit for a while.' She led her to the chair. 'You must be tired.'

'Anna loves the music,' Zina said. 'I bought it for her, not them.'

Then she turned her head, looking for something. 'Where is it?' she asked, getting up again. 'Did they steal it? Sophia, did you see who took it?'

Eva swallowed hard to hide her distress.

'Sit down, rest a little,' she said.

Zina looked at her and then let out a long, painful wail.

'Pavlou!' called Mary, who was leaning against the wall. 'Behave yourself.'

Zina continued to cry, but quieter now.

She's back, thought Eva, from wherever she's been. She's woken up to this nightmare.

She held Zina in her arms and bit her lip to stop her own tears. Her chest was sore as the pity piled up inside, but she couldn't allow herself to fall apart. Not now that Zina needed her more than ever.

Hours later, after filing her report to the governor, Eva scribbled a note for Dr Garrett.

> *Zina Pavlou much worse after an incident today. Please see the attached report filed to the governor.*

She attached it to a carbon copy and placed it on his desk.

As she walked back to Zina's cell, she wondered when he'd read it. It could be days before he was at Holloway again and the trial started on Monday. She wanted to be sure he knew how bad things were. Could he change his mind about Zina being fit to stand trial? Save her from facing a jury? If she knew where he was, she could get in touch. But Matron would never tell her. And she'd already overstepped the line with him. She couldn't make a nuisance of herself, or they might stop her visiting rights altogether.

Back in Zina's cell, the young warden, Hawkins, was dozing in the corner chair. Mary Jenners was nowhere to be seen. Eva sat at the table, where a tin mug of brown, watery liquid stood, and watched as Zina made her bed. She was usually neat and ordered, but after this morning's incident the cell was in disarray. After tugging at the blanket till it was straight and smoothing it down with her hand, Zina rearranged the couple of icons she had on the shelf next to her bed and came and sat at the table with Eva.

'How are you feeling?' Eva asked. 'Has your headache gone?'

Zina frowned as she sipped the tea.

'Don't fuss,' she said, blowing into the cup. 'I'm fine.'

Eva went to say something then stopped herself.

'If you want to be of use,' said Zina, 'you could get me some coffee in this place. Greek coffee, and some *melomacaroona*. I miss those little cakes.'

Eva shifted in her seat. 'I'm not sure the coffee is allowed, but I'll see what I can do about the cakes.'

Zina motioned out of the door. 'The woman down the hall had a birthday cake last week. But maybe they let her because she's English.'

Eva touched her hand. 'Zina.' She knew that she had to say something. 'Zina, do you... do you remember what happened this morning?'

'Of course I remember,' she said. 'I'm not an idiot. I'm tired. I got confused, that's all.'

'I want to ask you something,' Eva said. 'But I'm... well, I don't want you getting cross...'

Zina laughed. 'You're not scared of me too, are you? They either treat me like a child in this place or a monster.'

Eva glanced back at Hawkins. She'd woken but was engrossed in her crossword. Some of the wardens didn't want you whispering in any language. Others didn't care. Hawkins looked young, inexperienced. She probably wouldn't cause a fuss, but Eva took some papers from her bag and her pen, just in case. If asked she could always pretend she was writing letters.

'Listen,' she said to Zina, leaning close. 'I want to be honest with you – talk to you about your trial.'

Zina sat back a little and her smile dropped. 'Go on.'

'You know the evidence against—'

'I didn't do it,' Zina interrupted.

'I know... I know. But what I'm saying is the evidence against you *is* strong.'

Zina put down the metal cup. 'But I didn't do it. I've told you and the police and my solicitor. Why doesn't anyone listen?'

'Let me finish. Will you let me speak and promise not to interrupt till I'm done?'

Zina gave her a sidelong glance. 'Go on.'

Eva watched her as she gripped the cup. The moment was now. She swallowed hard. How was she going to say this? What words did someone use to utter such a thing? The nuances in English just didn't translate when it came to saying them out loud in Greek.

'If you allowed your defence team, they could say you're not *well*, it will help you, you see.'

'What do you mean, not well?'

'In the… in the mind. And,' Eva hurriedly continued, 'you'll still be locked away, yes, but you'll get help. They'll see you as an ill woman, not a criminal. It'll be better for you. You'll be in a hospital rather than a cell.'

She waited for a reaction. Would she shout? Cry? She watched her closely to see if her words had sunk in.

'You…' Zina began, 'you want me to say I'm *trellee*?'

She had used the Greek word for crazy. It was what Greeks called someone who was wild, out of control.

'No, I didn't say that. I said *ill* – there isn't really the right word in Greek. It's more—'

'But it's sick in the head, so it's *trellee*. You think I'm a savage? That I can't control myself? That I did these unspeakable things?'

'That's not what I meant,' Eva said. 'I can't explain it exactly, but in English it doesn't sound as bad, it's… it's…'

Zina laughed. 'But you're the translator. Where are all your words now? Admit it, you want to say I'm *trellee*.'

'Everything alright?' called Hawkins.

'Fine,' Eva replied. Then in a quiet, quick voice, 'Look, I'm trying to help you, Zina. There's still time. You can avoid a big trial. I've looked into it. You could plead "not guilty on the grounds of insanity". I could let them know for you that you want to make a change.'

Zina's face was thunder.

Eva persisted. 'You see, this way you don't even have to say you did it. You weren't well at the time. The doctor's report will help, and you won't go to prison. You'll go to a hospital instead.'

Zina got up and walked to her bed. She plucked the two small wooden icons from the shelf, stretched out on her bed and turned them over in her hands.

'Answer me this,' she said. 'Why is it always the women who are *trellee* but not the men?'

'Sorry?' Eva turned around to look at her.

'They said the same about my mother, years ago.'

'Oh.' Just how many secrets did this woman have? 'Why?'

Zina shrugged. 'She did as she pleased. She didn't care if people liked her. She knew her mind. If you're a woman that's enough.'

Eva wanted to ask so many questions but was afraid Zina would stop talking.

'You know what it's like in the village,' Zina continued. 'They're scared of anyone who's different. People talk. One person said she was *trellee*, then it stuck.'

Eva waited. She knew there was more.

'And do you know what it did to her? Being branded like that?'

'What?'

'It ruined her. Nobody wanted anything to do with us, we lost what little we had and the shame of it seeped through like a terrible stain, all down the years. That's why I had to marry so young. I'll not have the same thing said of me. No.'

Eva came and stood next to her.

'I'm sorry – I didn't mean to insult you, but I don't know what to do. I don't know how to help you.'

'You don't need to do anything,' Zina said, putting the icons back on the shelf. 'I told you. I'm innocent.'

★★★

By the end of the day, Eva's mind was frayed with the frantic thought that had been scratching away for hours. What could she do if Zina wouldn't change her plea? Perhaps there was nothing else.

As she entered the flat, she wondered if she should insist on another meeting with Dr Garrett. But as she slipped out of her coat she thought it through. He'd react badly to being hounded.

'You alright, Evie?'

Jimmy was at the table, gently beating an egg in a bowl to finish off the *avgolemoni* soup. The rice and lemon broth was comforting enough to make most troubles fade away, and he always seemed to serve it when he knew Eva needed it most.

'Evie?'

'Yes – just thinking.'

He tasted the soup to make sure it wasn't too hot before adding the egg; Eva had curdled it so many times because of her impatience. There was no shredded chicken to throw in, but it was still a treat, especially now eggs were finally off ration.

'Come eat,' he said, and nudged the chair out with his foot.

She sat down and he ladled the *avgolemoni* into two bowls and placed one in front of her.

'Hard day?'

She nodded. She didn't want to talk about it: Zina's dancing, the way the others had ridiculed her, and now this, her absolute refusal to change her plea.

'Want to tell me?'

She sighed. 'I wouldn't know where to start.'

He blew on his soup. 'Alright then.' He took a slice of bread from the chopping board. After a few moments he said, 'So, I had an interesting chat with Carlo today. It turns out—'

She got up. 'Sorry, I can't. Not now.'

She went to the bedroom and closed the door. Kicking off her shoes, she slipped under the covers fully dressed and pulled the blanket up to her neck. The world was too difficult a place right now. If she could just stay here, until she knew what to do.

She'd retreated from life twice before, when she'd lost her mother and years later with the baby, and now she wanted to do it again.

The doorknob turned and Jimmy came and sat next to her.

'What is it?' he asked. 'Talk to me.'

'I'm so tired. Please let me sleep.'

'This job's making you ill, Evie.'

'Please.'

He put his hand on her shoulder and gave it a squeeze, but she ignored him. He left it there for a minute or two but she stayed completely still, so he got up and walked to the door.

'You know, Evie,' he said, 'you need to think about others sometimes, how they might be feeling, how they might want to talk. And—'

She half sat up and looked at him. 'I spend my life thinking about others.'

'I meant *me*, not her,' he said, his voice hard. '*Me*. Your husband. This idiot who thinks about you all day and is worried, and wonders when he'll get you back.'

'It's difficult now, you know that. The trial's coming up—'

'Don't use that as an excuse,' he said. 'You were like this before. Do you still want to be married?'

She laughed. 'What kind of question is that?'

'It's an honest question. Do you want to be married? To me?'

He actually meant it.

She didn't speak for a while, and then said in a small voice, 'I can't believe you have to ask me that.'

'I know,' he said. 'Neither can I.'

He walked out, closing the door behind him.

CHAPTER TWENTY-EIGHT

Spakato, Cyprus, 1914

Zina's father stands in the doorway, silent, watching her sweep. His shadow blocks the light coming from the garden and, as she turns, broom in hand, she sees he's not alone.

'Pappa?' She knows to stop what she's doing; he's a man who demands undivided attention.

'Zinoulla *mou*, come here,' he says, and holds out a hand. He hasn't called her 'my Zina' for a long time. 'I want to introduce you to *Kyrieh* Pavlou.'

She leans the broom at the table, wipes her hands down her sides and walks towards the men.

'*Kyrieh* Pavlou, this is my eldest – my Zina,' says her father, and his arm around her shoulders surprises her, because she can't remember him doing this before.

The man nods at her and puts his hand out. In the other he's holding a whole walnut.

'*Herredeh*,' he says in greeting.

She gawps at him and takes his hand, shakes it. He cracks the walnut in his fist and offers her half. She shakes her head and stares, then looks at her father. There's only one reason he would introduce her to a man.

'*Kaffé*, Zina,' he says, and she hurries to the stove while they sit at the table. Standing there, stirring two spoons of the fine, powdery coffee into the *jisve* of water, her mind races. Why so soon? She's too young. He's old – easily ten, fifteen years older than her.

She doesn't want to marry. Not now. Does her mother know? Can she speak for her? Her mother has retreated to bed again, and Zina knows it's useless because nobody listens to her mother anyway, not since neighbours started talking about her weak mind.

Zina carefully pours the coffee into the cups, adds a glass of water for each and carries them on a tray. The walnut shells are strewn on the table and the man has cracked another and now places the meat of the nut on his saucer.

She turns to leave but her father calls her back.

'Zina *mou,* come.' He pats the chair next to him and she sits. '*Kyrieh* Pavlou has the house on the hill. The big one just inside the village.'

She looks at the man. She's wandered past that house so many times, on the way to market.

'Well, it belongs to my parents,' he says, to her father rather than her. 'But it's been promised to me.'

For a moment she imagines what the inside might be like. Running water rather than a well, real tiled floors to sweep instead of this dirt. A house that size will have separate rooms for sleeping and eating too, she's sure.

'When I marry,' the man addresses her now, 'they will give the house to me. As a gift for me and my bride.'

A heavy silence swells around her and she wonders if she's expected to respond. She looks at her father.

'Such a wonderful match for you, Zina. You're blessed.'

They carry on speaking but she doesn't hear the rest.

Last week, she turned fourteen.

Once he has left, she stands and rinses the cups in the bowl of cloudy water. Her father pats her on the shoulder.

'Who'd have thought it, Zina *mou*?' he asks. 'You in a house like that? We'll have a spring wedding. You'll have the sheets your mother kept for you, and we've agreed a gift of the two hens. They insist on paying for everything else.'

She wipes her hands.

'Why, Pappa?' she asks.

'What do you mean?'

'Why are they paying? Isn't that for the bride's family?'

He shrugs. 'He wants a big family. You're so strong and young, Zina. You can start straight away.'

She feels her face get hot and a fist of fear clenches her chest. 'Pappa?'

'What is it?'

'I… I don't want to. I'm scared.'

His face hardens.

'When I'm sixteen?' she asks. 'He seems a good man, Father. Thank you, but please. Sixteen is when girls are ready. I'm not ready.'

'You'll be fine,' he says, his voice brittle.

He's not a man who changes his mind, but she puts her hand out and takes his in hope.

'Please?' she asks. 'For me, Pappa. Please ask him to wait. Just till then.'

He pulls it away as if she has no business touching him. His face is furious but his voice is steady.

'Have some sense, Zina. We will lose him if we delay. Would your father ever mean you harm? Have I ever made a bad decision for you? Have I?'

'No.' Her mouth trembling now. 'But I—'

He suddenly raises his arm as if to hit her and she ducks on cue, but it's more a threat than an actual attempt and they both know it. It means: I can do what I want, so remember that.

He lowers it and talks softly. 'Now no more of this, come. In a few months you'll be married, you'll be in that house on the hill and you'll thank me for taking such good care of you.'

He walks to the door.

'Tidy up in here, and don't forget under the table.' He leaves the room.

Everything around her is blurred now. She stumbles, picks up the broom and starts to sweep again, though she's just moving dirt from side to side. She rubs at her eyes with the back of her hand. She pulls the chair where he sat to one side and, bending over, looks at something by her feet. She hooks it with the broom to bring it closer, and now she can see what it is: the broken pieces of a walnut shell.

CHAPTER TWENTY-NINE

Eva had finished her shift and stood in the shadows of the balcony at the Café de Paris. As she looked down, she wondered which of the dresses worn by the glamorous revellers would suit her best. This spot gave her an excellent view but was tucked away from the bar and supper tables, so she couldn't be seen. There were a few people eating, upstairs and down, but mostly the rich and famous came here for the gaiety and drinking. The dance floor was bursting tonight; every heiress and celebrity in London seemed determined to jostle their way into the small hours.

She gazed at the exquisite evening gowns and wondered, not for the first time, where the fabric had come from. The rest of London was making do with thick cotton skirts and darned woollen jumpers, while spread out before her was a wealth of satin, silk and taffeta.

A vibrant crimson dress came into view. She marvelled at how closely it clung to the hip bones of the very tall woman wearing it – almost as tightly as she was clinging to her dance partner. Too tight for Eva. What about the white dress over there? Elegant, classic. But then the socialite turned around and revealed the outlandish feathers sewn across her chest. No, too flashy for Eva, though she smiled at the woman, whose dance moves now made her look even more like an exotic bird.

She scanned the dance floor and then, there it was. A gown more beautiful than anything she'd seen in weeks. The bodice was a thick French navy with a sheen, possibly a grosgrain satin. From the shoulders it crossed over the front of the blonde's hourglass figure, and slipped seamlessly into the waistband. Then the skirt burst out in a delicate froth of midnight blue taffeta that fell down rather than out, into a stunning zigzag hem. The edges were sprinkled with silver sequins, creating a cloud of winking stars for her to dance on. Now *that* was beautiful.

Eva tried to picture herself in the same gown. She felt a pang of envy; it was the perfect shape for her figure and she knew she'd look a knockout. Jimmy would like it, that was for sure.

'*Bomba!*' he'd say, and let out one of his long, low whistles.

The last time she'd worn a new dress was on her birthday two years ago, when they'd gone out dancing. It had fitted perfectly.

'Is it too much?' she'd asked, as he looked her up and down.

'You're too much,' he'd said, and started to kiss her shoulders. It had taken them an hour to leave the flat.

Now, the band struck up the first notes of the tango, and a wave of excitement swept the crowd. The men set their shoulders back and the women readied themselves for the drama of dips and turns.

The dresses glistened like jewels caught on a current, forced to quickly change direction. One woman leaned away as her dance partner tried to get closer. Eva remembered last night's conversation and Jimmy asking if she still wanted to be married. If the two of them were down there dancing the tango right now, he'd be pulling her towards him, and she'd be pushing him away.

She suddenly felt cold and reached for her coat, draping it over her shoulders. Ever since Zina had told her she'd been accused of murder years ago in Cyprus, she hadn't been able to think of much else. Her world had tipped to one side and nothing would set it right again. Had she *really* killed someone when she was just a girl? Should Eva report it? She'd wanted to talk, to repeat what Zina had said and stop the secret buzzing in her head. But who could she tell? Dr Garrett? The governor? Jimmy?

In the end she'd kept the slippery words to herself. She was worried she'd make things worse, and it sounded like it had been decades ago and perhaps Zina had been mistaken anyway.

In a few days, Zina would be standing in the dock of the Old Bailey. She already had the odds stacked against her, so it would probably make little difference if Eva said something or not. Perhaps Zina had got things confused. Even while Eva was telling herself this, she knew she didn't believe it and couldn't understand why she felt so protective towards her. Why she'd stayed silent.

The music ended and there was a ripple of applause. Some couples waited expectantly for the next number, while others wandered back to their tables. She should probably get home. Her shift had ended half an hour ago and Jimmy would start to wonder where she was. But the thought of leaving this place filled her with dread. Here, caught in this kaleidoscope of joy, it felt like nothing bad could happen.

One more number, she told herself. Just then she glanced across the balcony. There was a couple in the middle leaning over, and beyond that a tall figure raised a hand in greeting. He started to walk towards her, and as he got closer he trailed his fingers along the brass railing. There was no mistaking that hair, the blond flop of it.

'Hey there.' He leaned over the bannister, his arm touching hers.

'Bert. What are you doing here?'

He shrugged. 'I thought I saw you come up here. Why are you skulking in the dark? Why not go downstairs? Have a dance?'

'We're not allowed,' she said, shifting her weight onto her other foot. 'Charlie doesn't like us mixing with the customers.'

'Who's Charlie?'

'The boss. We're not meant to look over the balcony either,

but he's distracted tonight,' she continued. 'There's a rumour we've got royalty in.'

'Really, who?'

'Probably Philip or Margaret – it's usually one or the other. You know there's a staircase round the back?'

He looked to where she pointed.

'It leads straight up to Rupert Street. They sneak in and out.'

There was a clatter downstairs, followed by the sound of glass smashing and loud applause.

'Lively crowd,' he said, laughing. She didn't answer. 'What's the matter?'

'What?'

'You seem preoccupied. Is there something wrong?'

She had an urge to tell him everything – what Zina had said, the fact she hadn't translated it. The dancing in her cell the other day.

'Is it work?' he asked. 'The prison?'

'It's nothing,' she said. 'I thought I could do something to help.' She recalled the conversation with Dr Garrett at Bertaux, then how adamant Zina had been about not pleading insanity. 'But it turns out I can't.'

'What do you mean?'

'It doesn't matter,' she said. 'I can't go into it, not here.'

At that moment, the band struck up again. It was a gentler, slower tune than the tango and Bert put his hand on hers and pulled her towards him.

'May I have this dance?'

'Here?'

'Look,' he pointed to the tall potted palm next to them, 'no one will see.'

She pulled back a little and smiled. 'You're persistent, aren't you?'

'Well, a fella's got to try. Come on.' He placed his hand on the small of her back. 'We'll stay just here. And you don't want to make chit-chat, so what else is there to do?'

She stared into his face. Didn't she deserve a moment for herself? She put her hand on his shoulder and, as the music rose to meet them, she let him lead her towards the dark corner back and forth and around. He was good, light on his feet. Perhaps he held her a little tighter than he needed to, but he was much better than she expected.

He said something but she didn't catch it.

'Sorry?'

He leaned in close. 'I said you're good.'

'Oh, thank you. I was just thinking the same thing.'

'No, but really good,' he said. His breath was hot on her cheek. 'Like an angel, floating...'

She turned and kissed him on the mouth. He seemed startled but quickly returned the kiss and clutched her tightly in an instant. She let him continue. It was like watching herself on stage, trying on a role for size. So this was what it felt like to kiss a man who wasn't your husband. After a few seconds she turned away to catch her breath then stood back at arm's length, knocking into the plant.

He steadied it.

'I shouldn't have done that,' she said. 'I'm sorry – I don't know what I'm doing.'

'Don't be sorry,' he said. 'I've wanted to kiss that pretty mouth of yours since... well, from the moment you humiliated me in front of my friends.'

She laughed. 'I should get home.' She rearranged her dress a little. 'I don't know what got into me.'

He put his fingers to her hair.

'Don't.' She put her hand up and stopped him.

'Sorry.' He leaned in for another kiss but she pulled away. 'Hey, you can't kiss me and leave me like this.'

'Of course I can,' she said. 'Let's pretend it never happened.'

Bert jolted back. 'Hell, why?'

She took her coat from the floor where it had fallen, and picked up her handbag.

'I've had a hard few days,' she said. 'Please don't make anything of it.'

He reached out to touch her arm but she stepped back.

'I was feeling a little blue, that's all.'

'Can't I help?' he said. 'Don't you like me?'

She laughed. 'You need to hear it, don't you? Yes, I like you, but—'

'Why does there have to be a but?'

'—but I'm not interested. Not like that.'

He gave her a nod and a crooked smile.

'Right. I see.' Fishing in his pocket, he pulled out a pack of cigarettes and offered her one. She refused and he lit himself and said, 'Well, for someone who isn't interested, that was one hell of a kiss.' His American confidence was startling; an Englishman would have left by now. Probably after apologising as well, even though he'd done nothing wrong.

'Everything's difficult,' she said. 'Don't make it worse. The trial's soon – and home is awful.'

'Your husband doesn't deserve you.'

'Don't say that,' she snapped. 'You don't know him. He's a good man.'

Bert raised his eyebrows in surprise.

'Anyway, everything is taking its toll right now,' she said. 'On the two of us.' She should stop talking. She didn't need to tell a stranger her problems. She sighed. 'Why is life so complicated?'

He blew smoke away from her.

'It doesn't have to be. Let's keep it simple. Just me, you, my little flat that happens to be a couple of streets away.'

'There's too much at stake.'

'You love him.'

She hesitated then nodded. She'd meant Zina. There was too much at stake with Zina's case. She couldn't lose focus now.

'Yes. And there's work. I can't get distracted.'

He frowned. 'So how's it going, in Holloway? If you don't mind me asking?'

'Not good. It all looks pretty hopeless, to be honest.'

'And how is *she*? Mrs Pavlou?'

'It's hard to tell. I don't think she's at all prepared.'

'What do you mean?'

She felt like crying when she thought of it.

'She's certain she won't be found guilty next week,' she said, 'because she's adamant she didn't do it. Can you believe she was dancing in her cell the other day? Singing, too.'

'What? Are you joking?'

'I wouldn't have believed it either if I hadn't seen her with my own eyes. I actually walked in on it. She was blowing kisses and laughing – it's clear she's not well. She even called me by her sister's name.'

He shook his head.

'And they were all standing around, making fun of her. The officers were as bad as the prisoners.'

'Blowing kisses?' he asked.

'Yes, then suddenly she just burst into tears.'

A look of distress swept over Bert's face.

'But, I don't understand.'

'It's as if she hasn't a care in the world, then suddenly it all comes back to her.'

'She sounds ill – I mean…' Bert pointed to his head.

'Exactly – that's what I've said, but nobody is listening. The doctor says she's fit to stand trial. I've tried to do something, but…' She slipped her coat on. 'It's just awful. Bloody awful,' she said. 'I can barely sleep.' She glanced at her watch. 'And now I'm really late.'

She started walking towards the staff exit.

'Eva, wait!' he called. 'Are you there tomorrow? At Holloway?'

'Yes.'

He strode over to her.

'Can I come and have a coffee with you, before you start?' he asked. 'That same place? The little dive across the road?'

'What for?'

'Company. To see you. To say hello and speak in the daylight.'

She didn't respond but just let out a sigh.

'Come on,' he cajoled, tugging at her coat lapel. 'To cheer you up a little before you have to walk through those gates again.'

Well, it *would* be a nice way to start another long day. Jimmy had never offered, although he had days off.

'Say yes,' said Bert. 'You'll have one cheery thing in your day tomorrow.' He spread out his arms. 'Me.'

She smiled. 'It's early. I'm due at half-past eight.'

'I'll get there for eight.'

She pointed at him. 'Nothing's going to happen.'

'Hey.' He leaned across and kissed her cheek. 'It's just a coffee.'

CHAPTER THIRTY

Later that evening Eva struggled with the key, trying to get into the flat without waking Jimmy. Damn it. It was always getting stuck and tonight she could do without the headache. She'd kissed another man and, although it may have seemed harmless enough, she knew it mattered. It mattered because things were so bad between her and Jimmy. Her head felt heavy with the weight of the secrets she was keeping about Bert and Zina. She was desperate for sleep, to obliterate it all.

She pushed and wriggled the key but it was going to take more than that. Putting her shoulder to the door, she was about to barge through when Jimmy opened it and she practically fell on him.

'Sorry! Sorry.' She steadied herself and he took her key out for her. 'Did I wake you?'

'No, I was reading.' He stopped and looked at her properly. 'What's the matter?'

'What? Nothing.' My God, could he tell? She'd checked her face on the bus home and had fixed her smudged lipstick.

'You look awful,' he said, his eyes searching her face.

She gave a hollow laugh. 'Charmed.'

She could feel his stare.

'It's nothing,' she said. But she could hear the thickness in her voice. She leaned her back against the wall.

She should tell him about Bert – it would make her feel better. Just brush it off as something silly, a tipsy customer chancing his luck. But he hadn't been tipsy, had he? And it was *she* who'd kissed him. That would break his heart. Was half a truth better than none? Would he ever trust her again? She slipped off her coat. Just blurt it out, she thought. Then it will be done.

'Evie?'

She snapped out of her reverie to find him frowning.

'I want to say sorry, about last night,' he said. 'I know your work is really difficult and the last thing you need is me whining when you get home. It's just that—'

'Something happened,' she said.

'Oh.'

'I need to tell you. It's going to kill me if I don't.'

His face dropped.

'Alright.'

He took her coat and pegged it on the back of the door, then led her into the room.

'Sit.'

He pointed to the armchair and she perched on the edge of the seat.

'What is it?'

On the floor next to her feet was a plate with half-eaten toast, and next to that a tumbler with the dregs of amber liquid. She picked it up, swigged it back and pulled a face.

He took the glass from her.

'Stop stalling and tell me.'

'I want to,' she said, sitting back in the chair, gripping hold of the arms, 'but I... I just don't know where to start.'

I kissed someone else... just a man I met... it meant nothing...

'I already know what it's about,' he said.

'You do?'

He nodded.

He got up, went to his jacket and took out his ciggies. He shook two from the pack, offered her one and lit her.

'It's Zina,' he said. 'What else would it be?'

Yes, Zina.

'It's always Zina these days,' he said, not unkindly.

It *was* always Zina, she thought. And it had to stay that way till there was nothing else she could do to help her. She took a deep drag and blew the smoke to one side. Zina was the reason she got up in the mornings and the reason she couldn't sleep at night. All thoughts of Bert and what had happened an hour ago seemed silly.

'It happened a few days ago,' she began.

Jimmy pulled a chair towards her and sat down. 'Go on.'

'I was translating for the governor. She wanted to tell Zina about the trial date. It was something she said.'

'What, the governor?'

She shook her head. 'Zina. It might have been nothing.'

'What was it?' He picked up the plate and flicked the ash onto the side.

'Well,' said Eva, 'she said she'd be alright – at the trial.'

He waited.

'Because she'd done it before.'

'What?' he asked. 'Done what before?'

'Stood before a court,' she said. 'Accused of murder.'

'Whose murder? Hedy's?'

'No, that's just it. She said it had been when she was just a girl, or a young woman, at least. In Cyprus. She said she'd been accused before of a woman's murder but when... how did she put it? "When the court heard my story they saw it was all lies."'

As she repeated Zina's words, a tangle of threads loosened a little in her chest.

'But...' He leaned closer. 'I don't understand. She's been in front of a jury before for *killing* someone?'

Eva nodded. 'I think that's what she meant. It wasn't that clear. She wasn't making complete sense.'

Jimmy held his cigarette very still. The inch of ash threatened to drop onto him.

'Who did she kill?' he asked. 'Or was accused of killing?'

Eva put her hand to her forehead. 'That's just it,' she said. 'I don't know.'

'You didn't ask her?'

'No, I... I didn't want to say anything in front of the governor.'

'Hold on. So you didn't tell the governor what she said?'

Eva was silent.

'Why didn't you say anything?'

'It was a split-second decision and then it was too late.'

He let out a long, low whistle.

'So,' he said, 'they have a double murderer on their hands?'

She shrugged. 'She may have been talking about Hedy. She gets confused. I've told you, I don't think she's all there.'

He didn't speak for a while, but she caught him looking at her, trying to gauge her mood. The unasked question was hanging in the air.

'And no,' she said, 'I don't know what I'm going to do.'

He still didn't speak.

'I mean, I know what I *should* do,' she continued. 'I should say something to the governor. But...'

'But you don't want to?'

'Zina said she'd been acquitted, that she'd been falsely accused. So, do they need to know? Especially if it was years ago.'

'Evie, you've just said yourself that she's not all there. Who knows what she's done? And anyway, she says she doesn't know anything about Hedy's murder and yet the papers say there's so much evidence against her.'

'I know, I know.' She leaned over one side of the chair and buried her face in her arms. 'But she says she wasn't found guilty.'

'But she was mixed up in it enough to be suspected. That's some coincidence, isn't it?'

'But what if I make things worse?' she mumbled. 'By saying something?'

'What if you make things worse by not?' he asked. 'And if they find out, you'll be blamed for keeping it secret. I mean, the woman could have killed twice and you're still protecting her? You don't feel any different about her now?'

'I'm still her translator,' said Eva.

He looked straight at her as he spoke. 'Evie, what if she *does* get let off next week,' he said, 'for Hedy's murder, and then you find out she's done something like this before? And she's free to do it all again?'

'But who was the first woman?' she asked. 'Why did she do it?'

Jimmy laughed, then suddenly stopped, realising she was serious. 'Why does it matter? Murder is murder. Who cares why she did it? Just tell the governor, for heaven's sake, and be done with it.'

'No. It's not black and white, Jimmy.' She stood and walked towards the window with her back to him. 'These things never are.'

'But that's *exactly* what it is,' he said. 'If she killed someone, she killed them. They're dead. It's as black and white as you can get.'

'No', said Eva, not turning. 'I need to know why and who. I need the whole story.'

'And how are you going to get that?' he asked. 'You said yourself that it happened years ago.'

Eva turned around, cigarette held up. She walked across to the table and stubbed it out. 'I'll ask her.'

CHAPTER THIRTY-ONE

7 July 1954, three weeks before the murder

Zina made sure she timed it perfectly. Five minutes before Michalis was due home, she took the kettle off the hob.

Hedy watched, groceries half unpacked on the kitchen table, as she poured the steaming water into the tin bucket.

'What are you doing?'

Zina reached into the cupboard for the tub of Saxa salt and sprinkled it into the water.

'Zina?' Hedy put the can of beans she'd been holding on the table.

'It's good,' Zina replied.

She refilled the kettle with cold and slowly tipped some of it into the mixture, testing it with her fingertips to make sure it wasn't scalding but hadn't cooled too much either. When she was happy that it was the perfect temperature, she pushed up her sleeve and sank her arm in up to her elbow, swishing it around to dissolve the salt.

'Zina, what *on earth*?'

She ignored the girl, pulled out her arm, shook it then wiped it on her apron. Carefully, she lifted the bucket and carried it to the armchair where Michalis always sat. She placed it directly where his feet would be. When he came home from his first job – traipsing the streets all day selling tins of polish and brushes from a suitcase house-to-house – he only had a short break before getting ready for the Café de Paris. She wanted to do something to help.

She could feel Hedy's eyes on her back, so she made a point of plumping up the cushions and straightening the rug, as she was there. Then she turned and smiled. She pointed at her own feet, forgetting the word in English.

'Salt,' she said, 'very good.'

Hedy laughed, incredulous. 'He's meant to put his feet in *that*?'

She nodded. 'For pain.' She leaned over and rubbed her own sinewy calves. 'Make good.'

Hedy rolled her eyes, turned on her heels and started folding laundry.

'He won't want it, that's all,' she said, over her shoulder.

Always with her back to her, bristling with rudeness, showing no respect.

But then Michalis walked in and, after his initial surprise, proclaimed it a wonderful idea, kissed Zina on the head and thanked her twice. He sat down, eagerly rolled up his trousers, threw off his socks and let his feet sink into the cloudy water. It was so relaxing, he said that if he didn't have to get to his other job he could have stayed there all evening. She'd got the temperature just right.

The two women stared at each other as he sat, rubbing at his feet with the towel Zina had placed by his side. He talked about how busy tonight was going to be. It was rumoured Marlene Dietrich was returning with another show, along with secret guests. The crowd was guaranteed to be heaving with celebrities.

As he left for the evening, he leaned across and gave Zina another two kisses, one on each cheek. Hedy was spending ages in the outdoor lavatory, and he hadn't waited to say goodbye, but had called out instead because he'd be late. She'd come back eventually, cheeks flushed pink, and stood in the hallway, mouth half open catching flies.

'Where is he?' she asked.

'Work, busy,' said Zina, picking up the bucket and carrying it to the garden to swill it out. Hedy usually made a big show of kissing him goodbye on the doorstep every evening, in full view of the neighbours. Maybe now she'd know how it felt to be ignored. Zina had been embarrassed when she'd first seen how they carried on, and would watch their goodbyes from behind the living room curtains. But often these days she happened to be tidying the hallway or sweeping the step at the time Michalis was leaving, so his kiss was more hurried.

For the rest of the evening the two women moved around the room in a strange dance of dislike, not speaking as they both tidied away the day's debris. As she walked past Hedy on her way to bed, Zina was shocked to see her eyes glistening.

Silly girl! She reached out to console her, but Hedy shook her off with a move so fast it made Zina jump.

That night, Zina lay in her cold bed and worried. She told herself that she had to control her disapproval of the girl. If she stayed amenable to her, she'd have no cause to throw her out again. But she twisted in the sheets and couldn't sleep.

Her son was weak, she knew this. Occasionally, she'd catch him looking at Hedy the way a hungry man looks at a hot meal. If he was made to choose, he'd choose his wife. And perhaps this time they'd want her gone for good. She couldn't lose him again. She'd tried to be pleasant, she had. But the fact was she didn't trust Hedy. And while she had never actually caught her cheating on her son, she'd seen the way she carried on with that Freddy, laughing and touching his arm when she thought nobody was looking. And that was just as bad, surely.

She closed her eyes and started to drift off to sleep, but could feel the waves of loathing lapping at her feet. She'd been in this place before, and the pain she'd endured so many summers ago swept through the years and washed over her once more. Well, she'd lost someone to a woman like Hedy decades ago and she couldn't let it happen again. As sleep finally wrapped her in its spell, she vowed to push down the hate and do her best to be helpful and kind. She'd give this one no cause to complain, no reason to do her harm, but she'd be sure to watch her carefully, oh yes. She couldn't let her steal the one thing she loved most in the world. She'd spent so many years without her son and now she finally had him back. Nobody would separate them again.

The next morning, after a quick wash and dress, Zina set about making amends. She left Anna sitting up in bed, playing quietly with her rag doll, Maria, as she scrubbed at the sink, trying to get the dirt out of the cracked ceramic. Then she wiped the kitchen cupboard doors, wiped over the stove again – the girl had done it the night before but it needed a better clean than that – and replaced Hedy's grubby pinny with a clean one. The dirty one she added to the pile of washing, which she would tackle later. She did all this quietly, careful not to wake them. They liked their lie-in on Sundays, and strictly speaking it was a sin to do housework on God's day of rest, but she was sure He'd understand in the circumstances.

Zina stood by the back door for her first cigarette of the day and glanced into the yard. The sky promised a crisp, bright day. Perhaps she'd hang the washing outside later.

She looked at her watch. Half-past ten and still not risen. She'd make them tea and take it to them. Hedy was keen on a 'cuppa in bed' as she called it, and had once even had her toast among the sheets, crumbs dropping everywhere.

She stared into the battered tin caddy; there was a scattering of leaves in the bottom, just enough for a small pot. That was mostly down to her. Although she'd never give up her thick Greek coffee, she'd really started to get a taste for tea, just like an *Englessa*. She'd picked up a few vegetables for dinner yesterday, so she'd cook. A family meal eaten elbow-to-elbow around the small table. That would help make the peace. These were the things that mattered.

She tipped the tea into the pot, poured on the boiling water and put on the lid. Then she unfolded one of the pretty napkins that she'd brought with her as a gift from Cyprus and placed it on the tray, setting two cups, saucers and the teapot there too. She finished it all off with the bone-china milk jug she knew was a favourite of Hedy's because it had once belonged to her grandmother.

'You need to be more thoughtful, Mamma,' Michalis always said, especially when the two women argued. Well, today she would be.

With tray in both hands, she climbed the stairs. She was about to give the door a couple of gentle kicks to announce her arrival when she heard the baby start up inside. She cocked her head to one side, listening as the cries got louder. Poor thing. Surely they weren't sleeping through that? Any minute, Hedy would get up to console little Georgie, to whisper and rock him till he fell asleep again.

But no. The screaming continued, his distress clearly escalating. She pictured him trying to catch his breath between cries, choking. Perhaps they'd gone out for a walk before she'd got up? The baby had woken alone and become frantic. Would they have left him without telling her? She couldn't stand it any more.

Balancing the tray in one hand, she quickly put the other hand to the smooth doorknob and turned. The door swung open and she saw the wooden cot in the corner. Little Georgie was clutching the bars, red cheeks soaked in tears. She placed the tray on the floor by her feet and as she lifted her head to stand, she glanced at the wardrobe next to the cot.

The narrow mirror between the two doors reflected the other side of the room. Hedy was kneeling up in bed, straddled over Michalis, naked. He had his hand over her mouth and she was riding him like a cowboy rides a horse in one of those films at the Plaza.

Zina spun round and kicked the tray, sending the milk jug flying. Michalis shouted something and Hedy turned, yelped and fell off him. He shouted again and Hedy dived under the covers, but Zina had already seen the lot.

He leaned up on his elbows and stared at his mother, wild-eyed.

'Sorry,' she blurted in English, then looked down at the mess on the floor. 'Sorry… sorry…' All the other words she knew had seized up inside her head.

'Mum! Get the fuck out!'

She couldn't move. A memory made something in her chest jolt out of place and she unravelled all over again. She knew this wasn't the same scene she'd witnessed years ago, when she'd run so fast out of the house that her sandal had flown off her foot, and yet it felt so familiar. The anger, the violation, the shame brought down on her head. Making her feel as if she were to blame for such a thing.

'*Get out!*'

The baby's screams got louder, and Zina dashed into the room, pulled him out of the cot and covered his eyes with her apron before running out. Her foot kicked the tea things again and she heard crockery break, but she carried on regardless.

'What is it, *Yiayia*?' Anna was in the hallway, doll in hand. 'What's happened?'

'Shhh, shhh,' she said, and jostled her down the stairs to the kitchen. She stood at the table, put her arm around Anna's neck to pull her in and, with the baby whimpering against her chest, she rocked them all from side to side. She was their life raft on this boiling sea. Silently, she started reciting the Lord's Prayer in Greek. God give her strength. She'd been right all along. The children weren't safe.

Cries came from the bedroom as voices rose and fell, then something smashed against a wall.

CHAPTER THIRTY-TWO

14 July 1954, two weeks before the murder

It was a week later and, as Zina walked through the back door into the kitchen, she immediately knew something was very wrong. For a start, Michalis was at the table, in his shirtsleeves, holding Hedy's hand.

'It's gone seven,' said Zina, putting her shopping on the table. 'Won't you be late?'

'I've got tonight off.'

She sniffed the air. 'Dinner not on?'

Hedy stubbed out her cigarette and shifted in her seat. She was wearing that headscarf again, the one she'd barely taken off all week. Zina picked up the full ashtray, placed it in the sink and started unpacking groceries.

'Shall I make some *fasolaki*?' she asked. 'It won't take long. And everyone likes that. Anna was saying—'

'Sit down, Mamma,' said Michalis. 'We need to talk to you.'

'But dinner's not on and I can listen while—'

'Please.' The chair scraped the floor as he pulled it out. 'Sit. It's important.'

She shrugged off her coat and hung it on the back of the door, while she said a silent prayer that they wouldn't mention what had happened that day. The shame she felt, seeing them both like that, acting like animals, weighed heavy on her. She was embarrassed for herself but more for them, being caught. Best if she started, apologised again, headed them off.

189

'Now you know I said I was very sorry,' she said, 'about last week. What happened. But,' she sat down and drew herself up straight, 'if you're going to do that maybe you should lock the door – and the baby shouldn't really see those kind of things. No wonder he was distressed. If you—'

'Mamma.' He put his hand on her arm, to stop her mid-flow. 'It's not about the other day. Let me speak, would you?'

'Oh.'

'We need to tell you something.'

She glanced at Hedy, who had her face turned away as she took another cigarette from the pack and Michalis lit it for her and took one himself. Then he stood behind her chair, a hand on her shoulder.

'We went to the doctor's today,' he said.

'Why? What's wrong?' asked Zina.

'It wasn't for me. It was for Hedy.'

'I'm sorry to hear that,' said Zina. Then, addressing her directly, in English, 'You ill?'

'It's her nerves,' said Michalis, as though Hedy was mute.

'Nerves?' Zina gave a little laugh. 'What do you mean, her nerves?' That girl had such an easy life.

'She's nervous and worried all the time,' said Michalis. He blew smoke to one side. 'The doctor says that's why she can't sleep and isn't eating. It's affecting her health.'

'Tell her she has to eat,' said Zina, smiling at Hedy, and noticing how dull her skin looked. 'Life is full of worries. We all have worries.'

'He says,' cut in Michalis, 'that it *has* to change – we have to do something to help her get better.'

He paused, glancing around the table for the ashtray, and took a saucer instead. He extinguished his cigarette with unnecessary force, although he'd only just lit it, making the saucer spin for a few seconds.

'He says,' he continued, 'that to live like this, always worried, it can be very… damaging.'

Hedy said something to him in English and he nodded. At that moment, she reached up to her headscarf and pulled it off, revealing a patchy scrub, like the feathers on a new-born chick. Zina gasped and instinctively shot out her hand, fascinated.

'Get off!'

Hedy pulled back so violently that the chair almost toppled backwards.

'Sorry... oh... sorry, Hedy.' Then she turned to Michalis and said, 'But how? What happened? Did it just fall out overnight?' She wanted to be kind but tilted her head a little to get a better view. 'Is there a cream? Something she can use?'

Michalis shook his head. Hedy stood and hastily tied the headscarf once more around her hair, but a rough copper tuft poked out at her temple. Poor cow.

'Doctor clever,' said Zina in English, slowly, so she'd understand. 'You young. Medicine? Cream...' And she motioned rubbing something over the top of her own head that might help.

Hedy's lips curled and she pointed at her: 'You!'

'What?'

'You leaving,' she shouted, her voice breaking. 'That's the cure.'

Zina stared at her then at Michalis.

'What did she say?' she asked.

'The doctor says it's because you don't get on,' he explained. 'It's bad for her health, the way you two argue.'

Zina clenched her teeth and felt the familiar ache along her jaw.

'You... you need to leave,' Hedy burst out. '*You've* made me ill.'

Zina shook her head and Michalis translated, though she'd understood. Hedy took a step closer and this time her voice was firm.

'You have to leave this house, our house.' She took a juddering breath. 'Leave us alone and I'll... I'll be better...'

'I go again?' Zina asked. 'A week – two?'

'No,' shouted Hedy. 'Leave the bloody country!'

Zina jumped as if she'd been slapped.

'Hey!' said Michalis. 'That's enough, Hed.'

'And don't you forget what I said.' Hedy turned on him. 'If she doesn't go, I'll do it. You know I will.' She pushed past. 'And you'll never see them or me again.' She slammed the door behind her.

'So now I'm to blame for this?' asked Zina. 'For her hair falling out? *Banayia mou.*' She crossed herself and looked up to the ceiling. 'Mary Mother of God.'

A thick silence filled the room, and after a minute or two he spoke.

'She's right. You have to go.' His voice was tight. 'I told you to try and get on. But it's not working, and she'll leave me if you don't go.'

'Don't be a fool. She'll never leave you. I can move out until she calms down.'

'No, she'll leave me and she'll take the kids, I believe her. It's decided. You have to go. Sorry.'

'But—'

'Look! She's going to Germany in three weeks, taking Anna and Georgie to see her parents. When she gets back, she wants you gone.'

Zina paused. They meant it. He meant it.

She tugged on his shirtsleeve to make him look at her.

'And what do *you* want?' she asked.

He stared down, his face rigid. 'I do too. We both want you gone.'

He prised off her hand and walked to the other side of the room.

'You can still visit, come for a holiday maybe, find a bed and breakfast place… but you can't stay here. This… this arguing and fighting. We can't live like this.'

Her afternoon coffee swirled in her stomach then inched up from her gut to her throat. She swallowed down hard.

'But how can I afford it?' she asked.

'I have some savings. I'll pay for your ticket back to Cyprus.'

'That's not what I meant. If I leave, how can I ever come back? And even if I could get the money for the fare, she'd probably never let me set foot in this house again. If I go, I'm never going to see you again. And Anna. What about my granddaughter? Oh please.' She couldn't lose Anna. She wouldn't allow it.

He started pacing slowly.

'Don't do this,' she pleaded. 'It's not right. Those children need to be brought up properly. Let me stay, I can help you.' She could hear that she was begging now, just words upon words.

'Can't you see you've made it impossible?' he asked. 'You should have tried harder to get on.'

She clutched at her head dramatically and reeled back and forth.

'But I'm your mother,' she whined, 'you can't just throw me out like a dog. I'm not young any more, I—'

'Stop it!'

She let her arms fall.

'You did this yourself,' he said. 'You know you did. You shut her out from the start.'

'What? She shut *me* out.'

'No, she tried. But you're always talking about her, judging her, the way she dresses, the way she cooks and brings up the children. Nothing's ever good enough with you. Do you really think that because she can't understand everything she doesn't know how you feel?'

Zina laughed. 'Listen to yourself. What about *me*? Don't you see, every time you spoke English in front of me, every remark she made when I was in the room. I knew she was talking about me.'

Michalis didn't deny it.

'Did you *see* what she did at that wedding reception?' she asked. 'Mocking me in front of all her friends? Crossing herself over and over, as if my faith is a joke?'

He shook his head. 'She wouldn't do that.'

'She looks at other men, you know.'

'Stop it! She doesn't.'

'If you want to close your eyes to it, it's up to you,' she said. 'You know that all I've ever done is try to help you bring up the children properly, look after the house.'

'You were trying to take over.' His voice was louder now. 'We were doing just fine before you arrived. This was a happy house. We never argued and now we can't stop. And it's always about you.'

She took a deep breath but it broke in her throat. His cheeks had turned scarlet and, as she stared at him, her life collapsed on itself. The sweat on his face, his high pink colour as he abandoned her. Had it been him or his father? Another woman had got the better of her then, too. Either way the shame and the pain were the same.

Michalis handed her a handkerchief and she wiped her face.

'I can't do anything now, Mamma,' he said, gentler. 'It's too late. She's my *wife*.'

She started to fold a napkin as she spoke.

'You know,' she began, 'we could go somewhere. Me, you and Anna. Let her take the baby. When your father left, there were five of you and I did it. With my help, together we can—'

His eyes widened and she knew she'd gone too far. He turned his back and started to clear the draining board.

'The train leaves in three weeks,' he said, his voice as hard as the clattering crockery. 'She'll be away for a fortnight. By the time she gets back, you need to be gone.'

Three weeks. Just three weeks? Three weeks to think of something. Three weeks to bring her round.

'But until then, stay out of her way, will you? Leave her alone.'

Later that evening, Zina leaned back on her pillow, propped against the wall, as the rest of them ate at the kitchen table. She'd ignored Hedy's call that dinner was ready, and when they'd sent Anna up to fetch her, she'd made an excuse about not feeling well. They didn't come to see what the matter was, but instead continued as if it were just another evening, their voices drifting up the stairs.

Zina slipped off her bed and wandered into their bedroom. The sheets were rumpled and there was a half-drunk cup of tea on Hedy's side.

Georgie slept in his cot in the corner, oblivious to the animosity that had been spewed that day. She stepped over the rug to take a look at him. She'd never much cared for him. Anna was the one she loved, the one she couldn't lose. Leaning over the cot railings she looked down at his fair complexion and copperish hair, identical in shade to his mother's. It had crossed her mind more than once that he might not even belong to Michalis. All that rouge and lipstick, the way she squeezed into those skirts, making them pull at the seams; it wouldn't surprise Zina if that was all for another man. The world was full of women like her, who took what they wanted from women like her. The men of course were too stupid to see what was going on until it was too late, until their lives were in shreds.

She stroked the wooden rail that ran across the cot and let her hand drop inside, inches from Georgie. Splaying her fingers, she noticed that her thumbnail had broken and a sharp edge stuck out. She put it to his hot, fat cheek and pressed, watching as he stirred. She pictured pushing it right through his doughy flesh.

They'd turned on the wireless downstairs. She took a chair from the side, slipped her hand in her pinny pocket and took out a large bunch of keys. She walked quickly to the wardrobe, unlocked the door and stood on the chair to fish around on the top shelf. She'd seen Hedy put it here when it had arrived. She pushed her hand right in till her whole arm had practically disappeared, found a corner and pulled hard. The brown paper parcel flew towards her and she just managed to catch it without losing her balance.

She knelt by the side of the bed. If anyone walked in she could shove it underneath and say she was looking for a needle she'd dropped. The address label was written in large, black letters and the stamp was one she'd never seen before.

Unwrapping it, she pulled out the packet of embroidered napkins from Hedy's mother. She tugged one out from the middle of the pile. Their initials, *M & H*, had been chain-stitched in a sky-blue thread, impeccably, in the very corner of the fabric. Underneath, a French knot stitch had been used to create two red roses.

From her apron pocket she took a dainty pair of pointed dressmaking scissors and snipped off the corner of the napkin. Then another and another till they'd all been fixed. There. She wrapped everything up again, stepped up and shoved it to the back of the shelf. Locking it, she placed the chair exactly where it had been and slipped into her room.

Back on her bed, she sat and stared at the tiny linen triangles that she held in her hand. Twelve of them. A dozen pretty roses and letters jumping all over her palm, no order to them whatsoever. She opened her mouth wide, threw the handful of scraps inside, chewed hard and swallowed.

CHAPTER THIRTY-THREE

Eva picked up the espresso cup and took a small sip of her *kaffé skétto*. She was trying to make it last. She was in her usual booth at the Royal Café and Bert hadn't turned up yet. She'd thought of not coming herself, especially after almost telling Jimmy about the kiss the night before. It would be the last time she'd see Bert alone. She'd tell him, if he ever arrived.

Glancing at her watch, she realised that she should be heading off. Zina had asked for five letters today, and it was always a long process, writing them in Greek then translating them for the prison records. She'd promised her they'd all be finished by the time she left.

The bell on the door sang out. Casually, she looked over her shoulder. Not him. She felt relieved. He'd had second thoughts. Good. It had all been a foolish mistake: the jokiness, the chats, the dancing, then that kiss. That stupid kiss. She thought of Jimmy. He was too good for this. She was too good for this.

The owner shuffled past, hairpiece at an angle, and took her cup. She pulled her compact from her bag, reapplied Rose Gold to her lips, and blotted them with a paper serviette from the tarnished holder.

She stared at her eyes in the mirror. She had so many important things to do today, things that people's happiness depended on. Well, Zina's. And yet here she was waiting for some man she barely knew who couldn't even be bothered to arrive on time.

She snapped her compact shut, put some money on the table and left.

Zina sat on her bed, cigarette in hand, sheets of paper all around her. She pointed.

'And this one is for who? Tell me again.'

'That one,' said Eva, picking up the sheet and reading the Greek words she'd translate, 'that's the letter you wrote to your brothers, Vasos and Panayi. Asking again if they'd come here and speak on your behalf.' She had explained to Zina that by the time they arrived, the trial would be over, but she still insisted.

Zina nodded. 'And...' She looked around. 'That?'

Eva tried not to sigh. It had been a long day and she was desperate to leave. 'That's the first one we did this morning.' She picked it up. 'To your other brother, Andreas, and his wife, Maria. These ones here—' she motioned to the pages on her right '—these are all for Cyprus. It's just this one here that's for London...'

'For Michalis. My son.'

'Yes.'

Zina leaned across and took the paper, then flattened it with her hand on the bed.

'Can you take it to him today?' she asked. 'Maybe he'll come and see me tomorrow.'

'I told you, Zina. I'm not allowed.'

Was she forgetting what she'd told her or just not listening? Either way it was starting to grind her down.

'Why not?' Zina stood and walked across to the ashtray. 'They're my letters, why can't you deliver them for me? If I ask

you? You're here to help me, aren't you? That's what you said.'
She crushed the cigarette butt into the metal ashtray.

The warden slouching by the door stood up straight.
'Something wrong?' she asked. This one always checked what
was happening when Zina got agitated.

'No, just explaining I can't personally deliver letters.'

She smirked. 'Thinks it's a hotel.'

Eva turned away.

'Zina, we need to stop now,' she said. 'I need to translate all of
these into English, for the prison records. You know they have
to read everything before it's sent. If you want these to go today,
I need time.'

'Please!' Zina said. 'Just one more – it's important and then
you can go.' Eva glanced at her watch. 'It won't take long. You
did say you'd do this for me.'

She hesitated. What else was she doing?

'Alright.'

She drew herself towards the small table and rolled back her
shoulders to ease the tightness. She took up her pen again in her
ink-stained fingers. She was exhausted. A short letter could take
an hour, as sometimes Zina didn't know what she wanted to say
or would ask her to read it back and rewrite it.

Zina came and sat next to her, and put her hand on Eva's
arm. 'I'll be quick,' she said. 'It's here,' and she pointed to her
head.

'Who's it to?' asked Eva. 'Is it an address we already have?'

'To my husband. In Cyprus.'

Eva stared at her. 'I thought you were separated.'

'We're still husband and wife,' she said. 'He left me years
ago, but he came back. Men always do. Send it to my brother
Andreas' house. He'll pass it on.'

She took a deep breath and began to dictate her letter, as Eva
wrote in Greek.

20 October 1954

My dear Zacharias,

How is your health? Do your legs still pain you? I hope as you read this you will remember what I did for you all those years ago. I was young and did it without question. You promised you would always look after me.

Eva stared at her, but Zina ploughed on, so she hurried to keep up.

Now I'm writing to ask for your help. You must know that I didn't do this vile thing I'm accused of. Your son Michalis has abandoned me. He told lies and the police believe him. This is my great misfortune. I can't speak to defend myself and although I have an interpreter – a good Greek girl who is my only friend now – we're just women here.

Please come to me quickly. Take the train because it's faster and my trial is soon. I don't know the cost but surely with everyone's help you can manage this? Ask Andreas and perhaps he could give you half. If you hurry, there's still time. Your English is good. Come and tell the police that I'm your wife. That you've known me since I was fourteen and know I couldn't do these unspeakable things.

They'll listen to you. You're still my husband and still responsible for me. My time is slipping away and I'm scared. If they find me guilty the scandal will be bad for you, too.

And once you've set me free, perhaps you and I can start again? We may live apart but we'll always be married in God's eyes.

Zina leaned closer to Eva now, her voice tighter.

Zacharias, I risked everything for you. And now I find myself in the same terrible situation as before.

Eva stopped writing but Zina nudged her to continue.

Be sure God will punish you if you don't help your wife. Don't forget me.

May your leg pains disappear.

Your wife,
X (the mark of Zina Pavlou)

'There are words here,' Eva said, 'that…'

'What?'

'You mentioned something the other day,' she said. 'And you've said it again now. Between us…'

Zina's eyes flitted to the warden.

'Between us, Zina. She doesn't understand, you know that. What was the thing you did all those years ago? In Cyprus?'

Zina folded her arms.

'Send the letter,' she said. 'Send it to Andreas. He'll give it to Zacharias.'

'I can't. Not like this. I just told you, I have to translate it into English. They'll ask questions. And they'll cross out anything they don't like, too.'

'So I can't even say what I want to now?'

'Zina, be reasonable.'

'No, *you* be reasonable,' she bit back. 'Everyone has a hold on me, and now you, too.'

'I don't have—'

'You do! More than all of them! You can twist my words if you want to.'

The warden stirred. 'Hey, keep it down. Everything alright, Mrs G?'

Eva nodded.

'You don't understand,' said Zina. 'Even if he doesn't come to help me, I want him to know I remember the things he made me do. I want him to lie awake and think about them the way I do.'

In a gentle voice, Eva asked, 'What happened? What did he make you do?'

Zina didn't reply.

'Did... did you... did you kill someone in Cyprus?'

Still nothing. She wouldn't even look at her.

'When the governor told you your trial date,' said Eva, 'you said you'd been in this situation before and you'd been alright.'

Zina pushed her chair out and walked to the bed.

'Who was it?' asked Eva.

Zina turned her back.

'What happened is between me and God,' she said. 'Send the letter, don't send it. They can't do anything else to me now.'

Even if Zacharias decided to come, he would never make it in time. After writing out all the letters in English, Eva walked to the governor's office to drop them off. She thought about what she was about to do. If she translated the letter word for word, she'd be called into the office, and told to delete whole sections. He'd receive it with some passages blacked out, illegible. And it would go on Zina's record that something had happened before.

What difference did it make to the officials here at Holloway what was in the letter? To Zina, those few sentences meant everything. There was nothing he could do now, but didn't he at least need to know that she blamed him for some of this, that – whatever had happened – in some way he was guilty too?

'Alright, Mrs Georgiou,' said the warden at the governor's door. 'Been keeping you busy, has she?'

'Yes, lots of letters today.'

She handed them over. On the top was the Greek letter in full, with instructions to send it via Zina's brother. Underneath was her English translation in which she'd deleted anything incriminating. They'd never know the difference, probably wouldn't read it for days. By which time Zina would be in court.

CHAPTER THIRTY-FOUR

21 July 1954, one week before the murder

For a couple of days after she'd been asked to leave, Zina went through the same routine of eating alone in the evenings. She placed a piece of bread and a few olives on a plate, sometimes a slice or two of halloumi, and she carried it to her bedroom to sit and eat on the bed. Even when times were difficult, she'd always eaten at a table but this was what life had been reduced to now, picking food off her lap like a peasant.

On the third day, Michalis stopped her at the bottom of the stairs.

'What are you doing?' he asked, looking at the plate in her hand.

'Let me pass.'

'Mamma, don't be like that. Come on, dinner's ready. For Anna's sake.'

But she shook her head, eyes brimming, and continued up the stairs. As she walked into her room, she could hear Anna's voice.

'Why isn't *Yiayia* eating with us again?'

Michalis replied but she couldn't make out the words, just the stern tone. The girl didn't ask anything else.

Zina made a point of not speaking to either of them if they were all in the same room. The only person she spoke to now was Anna.

The following day, Michalis told her again to sit at the table. She didn't answer, but when he put his hand on her arm to stop her going upstairs, she looked him square in the face and said: 'Hedy hasn't asked me. It's her house too. Till then I'll eat upstairs.'

The truth was she wanted to sit with them, to savour every last moment she had with her family around her, but she'd been tricked into a corner and couldn't find her way out.

When Hedy was home, Zina tried to avoid her. She couldn't bear the girl's eyes on her, heard her humming once or twice, and was certain she was gloating.

In the mornings, Zina started rising at half-past six to make sure she missed them all. She was no longer doing all the housework – why would she? She only aired her own bed, pulled the sheets over, then got herself bathed and dressed before preparing a small parcel of food.

Then she left the house in her comfortable shoes, walking the streets in the crisp summer mornings, cardigan and parcel in bag. Sometimes she'd walk around Hampstead for hours, gazing at the delicatessens and watching as women with prams stopped to talk to friends on the pavement. She thought about Georgie and how they hadn't let her near their precious baby. She hadn't minded so much at the time, because she'd had Anna. But now she was losing her, too.

In the afternoons, she often wandered through to Regent's Park, where she'd find a bench before unfolding the wax paper that held her lunch. She loved this park; Cypriots, Jamaicans, Italians, Irish – everyone was here, all making the most of the mild weather, all doing the same as her. Except, of course, they all had friends or family with them.

Today she bit into an olive as she watched a young couple nearby. They'd spread a blue checked tablecloth on the grass and had gently helped an elderly couple lower themselves to the ground. Once settled, they unpacked a wicker basket as a small boy ran round and round the scene. The younger woman served the old lady first, giving her a napkin and a cup of something from a Thermos.

Zina spat out the olive stone and her heart squeezed tight. What had happened? In a mere week, her days had shrunk and her world had collapsed. She'd done so much for them, and look how she was repaid. Feeding on the morsels of other people's joy.

That night, as she lay awake, she heard Anna slip out of bed and come and sit next to her. The child stroked her arm.

'Are you ill, *Yiayia*?' she whispered. 'Why don't you eat with us?'

Zina opened her arms and the girl fell into them.

'No worry,' she said.

Anna wriggled around to face her and pulled up her legs. She burrowed deep till she was comfortable.

'Mummy says you're going to Cyprus,' she said, her breath hot on Zina's face. What could she say to that? She watched as Anna started plucking at the candlewick bedspread between them.

The girl's bottom lip was jutting out in the half-light, and it looked like she was about to cry. Zina took her hand to stop her destroying the bedding and kissed each finger in quick succession. Anna let out a broken sigh and her grandmother rubbed the tears from her cheek and pulled her close. How could she lose her?

The next morning, Zina was making her sandwich when she heard footsteps. She turned and there stood Hedy, bleary-eyed, the headscarf tied on haphazardly.

'Morning,' Hedy said.

Zina didn't speak but stopped what she was doing, bread in one hand, knife in the other. She nodded, waiting. It was the first time Hedy had spoken to her since they'd asked her to leave.

'Will you have dinner with us?' Hedy blurted.

Zina continued staring.

'Dinner?' Hedy repeated, and motioned to the table and cutting food with a knife and fork. 'Tonight? For Mick's sake?'

Zina shrugged.

With an unsure smile on her face, Hedy reached out and touched Zina's shoulder softly.

'Please?'

The warmth of the gesture left her bewildered. Maybe the girl meant well after all. But then she remembered the way she'd mocked her at the wedding reception. Hedy was being civil now because she was leaving.

But it *would* be nice to stop all this, she thought, to sit again like a family. Like the people in the park. She put down the bread and the knife and placed her hand to her chest, to ask something she already knew the answer to.

'Cyprus? Me go?'

Hedy pressed her lips together and nodded, just as Michalis walked in. His face lit up.

'Hey, I thought I heard voices,' he said in Greek. He leaned over and gave his mother a peck. 'Mamma, I've hardly seen you all week. You've shut yourself away for days.'

She was about to reply, but he turned and grabbed Hedy by the waist and kissed her full on the mouth.

'Stop it, Mick,' she laughed, but she pressed her body close to his as Zina watched. Her eyes stayed on them as they made tea together, one nudging the other, always a part of him touching her and vice versa.

When he'd left her in Cyprus, he'd been a sullen young man, a scowl ever-ready on his face, and look at him now. Infatuated. His hand was on the small of Hedy's back as she took the cups from the cupboard, and Zina furrowed her brow and tried to remember if she'd ever felt someone's hand in that place. She doubted it. Her skin and her muscles and her bones would remember it, surely, even if her mind forgot.

'Did you ask?' said Michalis.

Hedy shook her head and looked embarrassed. He smiled indulgently.

'Mamma,' he spoke in Greek again now, 'can you collect Anna today? It's Wednesday. We'll find someone else when they get back from Germany. But just for today – the last time before they go. It would be a real help.'

Zina smiled and nodded.

'Thank you,' said Hedy. '*Evharisto.*'

Now she makes an effort, Zina thought.

'She didn't want to ask,' Michalis continued. 'You know, after everything. Said you'd be furious!'

Zina didn't respond.

'I told her you wouldn't mind.'

He poured boiling water into the pot. Hedy put the teapot onto the table, set three cups out and went to get the milk from the doorstep. Michalis sat and put his arm around his mother.

'Let's have a nice time these last few days, yes?' he continued. 'Eat with us, spend this last week down here. It will be good to have something to remember you by when you're gone.'

'Alright,' she said, taking the lid off the pot and giving the tea a stir.

CHAPTER THIRTY-FIVE

Holloway Prison

It was the day before the trial, a Sunday, and no sooner had Eva stepped up to the reception to sign in than a warden shoved a piece of paper in her hand. She stared at the note:

Come and see me immediately.
The Governor

'What's this?' she asked. 'Is there something wrong with Zina? Prisoner Pavlou?'

The warden shrugged. 'All I know is she's furious,' she said. Then, leaning in: 'Something's going on and it's a real to-do.'

A swarm of awful thoughts buzzed through her mind. Had Zina hurt herself to avoid trial? Or hurt someone else? Eva had never been summoned like this – no niceties, just a command.

'Come on,' said the warden, excitement in her voice. 'I'll take you.'

She signed her in and led the way through the interconnecting gates, locking and unlocking as they went. Finally, a few minutes later, Eva stood outside the governor's office.

'Good luck,' said the warden, and knocked on the door.

'Come!'

Just as she put her hand to the doorknob and turned, a thought crossed Eva's mind. Perhaps the governor had found out about

Zina's previous crime, in Cyprus? And that Eva hadn't translated everything? But how?

She opened the door and was surprised to see another person was already in the governor's office with her.

'Mrs Georgiou, please. Take a seat,' said the governor.

Eva sat and turned. She recognised the warden as one of the women who looked after Zina. Her face was streaked with tears and her breathing erratic.

'What is it?' Eva asked. 'Has something happened?'

The officer rubbed her eyes red but wouldn't look at her.

'So,' began the governor. 'I take it you haven't seen the Sunday papers?'

'No,' said Eva. 'I came straight in. I haven't had time.'

The governor stood and tossed the folded newspaper across her desk and it fell open to show the top half of Zina's face.

'Read that, would you?'

Eva tentatively pulled it towards her.

'Out loud, if you don't mind.' She crossed her arms and didn't sit down. Eva took a deep breath and focused.

'*GRANDMOTHER ACCUSED OF MURDER DANCES IN CELL.*'

Her throat tightened.

'Go on. It gets worse…'

'*Seemingly without a care in the world, Zina Pavlou, fifty-three, from Hampstead, London, was seen dancing in her cell last week – despite the fact that she's due at the Old Bailey tomorrow.*'

Eva paused and swallowed. She looked up and the governor nodded for her to continue.

'*You'd think that most prisoners accused of a terrible crime would spend their days in quiet contemplation, but not so for…*' she faltered, '*not so for the illiterate Cypriot grandmother, Pavlou, who is accused of strangling her daughter-in-law and setting her body on fire.*'

'*She is so confident she'll be released that she's celebrating already…*'

Eva stopped and looked up.

'Well?' asked the governor, hands on hips. 'Do you know anything about this fiasco getting into the papers?'

'No… I, er…'

'From your report that day I know you were angry, and I realise it's unlikely to be you, Mrs Georgiou, but I have to ask.' She tapped the newspaper several times as if trying to pierce it with her nail. 'Is this your doing?'

'Absolutely not,' said Eva, almost before the governor had stopped speaking.

She hadn't even told Jimmy about Zina's dancing. And definitely hadn't mentioned it to Elsie, because that girl couldn't keep a thing to herself. There was only one person she'd told.

'Well, the prisoners don't have that kind of access and Hawkins here assures me it wasn't her.'

'I didn't do it, madam,' Hawkins blurted, then blew her nose. 'I promise you. I never would.'

'Alright, Hawkins, stop your fussing.' The governor sighed. 'I believe you.' Finally, she sat.

Eva glanced at the newspaper again. Zina's eyes stared at her. She still had time to say something. To come clean. The governor straightened a blotter and pen on her desk.

'Well, I'm sorry to get heavy-handed, Mrs Georgiou. I didn't think it was you. I know you take this case too seriously to sell salacious information to the papers, but you understand I had to check.'

'Yes, of course.'

'Because we can't have this happening here.' Her voice was getting louder. 'The women still have rights despite being prisoners.'

'Of course, madam.'

'And anyone who doesn't respect that will be dismissed. The

very thought that someone sold this tittle-tattle to the gutter press, and profited from it – well, it makes my blood boil.'

'I'd never do such a thing,' said Eva.

But she knew who would. How could he? After all that talk about feeling sorry for her.

Hawkins gave an embarrassing snort, and the governor shoved a box of paper tissues her way.

'Your job is safe, Hawkins. Please try and control yourself.'

'Sorry, madam.'

'It seems our theory was right after all,' said the governor. Then to Eva she said, 'It appears the blame lies with Jenners.'

'Who?'

'Mary. She was on duty with me,' said Hawkins.

The governor sighed. 'It wouldn't be the first time an unscrupulous warden has sold stories to the press.'

Mary *had* been horrible to Zina that day. Was Eva really going to let her shoulder the blame?

'You're sure?' she asked.

'Who else?' said the governor.

'What… what will happen to her? To Jenners?'

'Nothing. Luckily for her, she left last week.'

A rush of relief surged through her.

'In fact, I think it was just after this incident. Is that right, Hawkins?'

Hawkins sniffed loudly and nodded. 'Yes, madam. She said she couldn't stomach the job any more. "Cooped up all day" she said.'

'Yes, well, it's not for everyone. You, however, Hawkins, are very good at it.'

'Thank you, madam.' For some reason her tears restarted.

'Aren't there rules,' asked Eva, 'forbidding them printing something like this before a case even starts?'

'Whether there are or not, it's irreparable damage and it's already been done, I'm afraid.' The governor reached across and took the newspaper.

Eva felt her mouth tremble. 'What do you mean?'

'Well, if a juror reads or even hears about this sensationalised story – *GRANDMOTHER ACCUSED OF MURDER DANCES IN CELL* – what are they going to think of her?'

'She was crying as well – do they say that?'

'Of course they don't. It doesn't fit their story. What would *you* think, if you read this report, Mrs Georgiou?'

Eva sat up a little straighter in her chair and pushed her shoulders back. 'I'd think the prisoner – Mrs Pavlou – is unwell. And that's why she's behaving like that in the face of such a serious charge.'

The governor walked to the door. 'Yes, yes, well I think you're far more charitable than most people,' she said, indicating the exit.

Eva gathered her things. 'What do you mean?'

'Well, most will assume these are the actions of a woman who simply doesn't care. Has no remorse. And even if she didn't do it, as she's been saying all this time, it shows a total disregard for the law, and a lack of respect for her dead daughter-in-law. As if it's all just a game she thinks she'll win. Confident she'll walk away scot-free. But we know that's not going to happen, don't we?'

Eva bought a copy of the paper on her way to the Café de Paris. Sunday evenings were a quiet affair, and she'd agreed to a shift because she was taking the following week off for the trial. As she stood behind the coat-check, she hurriedly flicked through the pages then stopped at the article to drink it all in. The source of the story wasn't named, just referred to as an 'eyewitness', and she supposed that was her.

Something heavy landed on the counter.

'My feet are killing me,' said Elsie. Her tray was in disarray, and she rummaged around separating the cigarettes, cigarillos and gold-tipped Sobranies. 'You alright?'

Eva nodded. 'Did you see this?' She showed her the article.

Elsie scanned it. 'Bloody hell. That's not going to do her any favours, is it?'

'It's terrible. And the trial starts tomorrow.' Eva went to pull away the paper but Elsie put her hand on it and drew it closer.

'Dancing?' she asked. 'She was really dancing? Were you there? Did you see it?'

Eva shifted her feet. 'Can I ask you something? About that man? John's friend?'

Elsie frowned. 'Who?'

'The American. The one who was fooling around that night? When you were all going to the Mapleton and he asked me along?'

'Oh, Bert. What about him?'

'Did he ask anything about me? On the way. Did you tell him about... about me translating for Zina?'

She blushed and put her hand to her hair. 'Well, maybe I did, but it's not a state secret, is it? He was asking all kinds that night. He was smitten with you.' Then she looked down at the paper. 'No!'

Eva nodded. 'This is his doing.'

'But I didn't tell him anything about dancing,' protested Elsie. 'I didn't even know, honestly.' Then she paused for a few seconds. 'You saw him again?'

Eva didn't say anything.

Two red rosettes burst onto Elsie's cheeks.

'Oh, Eva!' Her eyes were bright as she waited for details. When none came, she asked, 'Have you been seeing him all this time? I mean, did anything happen?'

Eva folded the paper in half.

'I bumped into him, and then he turned up here and – well, stupid me.' She gave a tight smile. 'I thought he was taken with me. But it wasn't me at all, was it? It was Zina he was interested in.' She waved the paper. 'Or the money, I suppose, that he got from selling the story. He pretended to feel sorry for her and that made me say more than I should have.'

Elsie nodded sympathetically.

'He'd probably thought about selling the story as soon as he knew my connection,' said Eva. 'That's why he pretended to like me.'

Elsie's mouth dropped. 'Oh, hell.'

'I know. It's bloody awful, isn't it?'

'No,' said Elsie. 'It's not like that. He didn't sell it.'

'What do you mean?'

'He wrote it,' she said. 'He works there, with John, my brother. I thought I told you? He's a journalist.'

Eva let out a long sigh. 'Right. Well. That makes it even worse. He must have planned the whole thing.' Suddenly she realised that bumping into him by chance that day in the café opposite Holloway hadn't been a coincidence after all.

'Oh God, Eva. I'm sorry. I didn't think...'

She reached out and held Elsie's hand.

'It's not your fault. I should have been careful. I assumed he was a snapper, like John – you know, film stars and the like, for *Picture Post*. He didn't put me straight.'

'Bloody men,' Elsie said. She shifted her tray of cigarettes and played with the silver chain on her shoulder, straightening it out. Then she chewed on her lip and finally said, 'Eva?'

'Yes?'

'Are you and Jimmy alright?'

'What?'

'I mean, did you and Bert...? It wasn't, you know, serious, was it?'

Eva took the newspaper and dropped it in the bin.

'Nothing happened,' she replied. 'It was never going to.'

CHAPTER THIRTY-SIX

Day one, Old Bailey

It's just before ten o'clock when they come for Zina. It's only October now but an icy chill in the air promises a brutal winter.

Last night, at Holloway, her dreams had been full of foaming green waves thrashing against the cell walls, as the Thames tried to sweep her away.

Then in the early hours, the wardens had dragged her awake and brought her to this new cell beneath the court. She'd paced and shouted because she thought they were going to start her trial without Eva. What if they didn't wait for her to arrive? What if they did it while everyone slept? But they gave her a frayed blanket and locked the door, so she'd understood that she was to wait.

Of course Eva will be with her. Now she remembers. The girl has told her she'll be in the court next to her throughout, and she's not let her down yet. Eva knows what she's doing. She doesn't make mistakes.

Now it's time, and Zina leaves the cell at the Old Bailey with a female officer on either side, and walks hesitantly along the brightly lit corridor.

She stops at the bottom of a dark wooden staircase and sniffs at her sleeve before starting the climb. There was a sour smell in the cell and she hopes it hasn't clung to her.

Her stockings are twisted around one ankle and she wants to stop and pull them straight but is wearing handcuffs. She slows down and leans against the bannister, but the prison officer behind her pokes her fingers into her back, shoving her on.

Just before she reaches the top of the stairs, the other officer uncuffs her and beckons her forward. 'Come on, hurry up.'

She walks upstairs and finds that she's risen from the floor into a room within a room. She had no idea she'd enter the court this way, coming up like an animal through a trapdoor, now standing on a platform for all to inspect her, as if she's being sold at market. She's surrounded by a railing on all four sides. She's been in a courtroom, years ago – well, a courtroom of sorts. It had been hastily arranged, with sawdust on the floor, upturned crates for sitting and the sun slicing through the open slats of the shutters.

Now, here, a forest of dark wood encloses her. There are a few men in robes milling around. Straight ahead is a large throne with a leather padded backrest and fancy scrolls carved around the top. It's empty.

Everywhere she looks is heavy oak; the benches, the chairs, and even the walls are lined with the wood. The clock to her right that's set in the balcony on high is the same dark brown. Oh, this place would burn in a moment!

She stares at the ceiling and is reminded of the imposing church she visited once when she'd gone into Limassol.

An old man in a scarlet robe walks in and everyone has to stand while he takes a seat on the throne. He's wearing a pale wig and she remembers Eva telling her the men of the court dress like this. His sleeves are wide and trimmed with a thick fur. Eva sketched a drawing for her of what the room would look like, but she's forgotten the detail of it and now she feels lost in this sea of faces. Where *is* Eva? She promised she'd be here.

'You can sit for now,' says the prison officer who poked her, and nudges her to the chair.

She hears a door open and turns to see that Eva has entered the dock.

'Hello, Zina.' A chair appears and she sits next to her, notebook in hand. The prison officers sit right behind them.

'Look how high those ceilings are!' says Zina.

'I know,' says Eva. 'Look, I'll tell you everything they say, and when you're questioned I'll translate everything back to them. Alright? I have to whisper it into your ear. And remember to only speak when they ask you something.'

Zina nods absentmindedly. There's a rumble of chatter and she's distracted because it occurs to her that everyone is here because of her. A woman in a tweed hat and matching coat whispers to her friend and points down at her. A few others lean over to get a good look. Suddenly a thirst takes hold of Zina and she licks her lips then rubs her mouth with the back of her hand.

Her mind feels tired today, and when a man of the court starts talking she loses the thread of what Eva is saying, and is uncertain what's expected. Eva explains that she needs to respond to the charges, so she tells them again she isn't guilty.

The door opens and she sees several people dressed in ordinary clothes walk in. They make a point of not looking at her and sit on benches to her left. Are these the people who will judge her?

She can hear shuffling upstairs and turns to look up at the balcony. It's filled fast and people openly stare back at her. They're wearing outdoor coats; have people come in off the street to see her? She leans down and tugs at her stocking, trying to straighten it, but it's still twisted and grasps her ankle. She tries again and considers asking if she can visit the lavatory to straighten up, but doesn't want everyone watching her as she stands.

There's the noise of scraping chairs and the officers stand. With a hand under each of her armpits, they pull her up in one swift move. Everyone turns towards the judge as he bows to a few of the men in the well of the court, then sits back on the throne.

The judge says something to Eva and she stands to reply. Zina watches her serious face and feels a flicker of pride; she's the only woman working here who isn't a police or prison officer. Just an ordinary Greek girl – and look at her.

While the judge is speaking, Zina stares at the jury. She wants to get a measure of their nature, check how they hold themselves. The man nearest her has turned his shoulders away.

An officer's hand grabs her shoulder and pulls her back, and it's only then that she realises she's been leaning right over the railing.

Eva gives her a warning glance, so she smiles at her broadly, as if to say that she shouldn't worry, she knows how to behave herself. After all, she's a respectable woman with truth on her side.

Above her is a murmur, and as she looks up, still smiling, there's a shout, 'She has no shame!' followed by loud hissing.

Grasping the wooden bannister, Zina lunges forward and hisses back. The court erupts and the judge bangs his palm on his desk to silence the calls.

He says a few harsh words to Eva.

'Zina.' She leans and translates into her ear, softly. 'You must behave properly. Stop leaning over the railings, and don't speak unless you're asked a question. The judge won't have it, do you understand?'

'Yes.'

'The gallery, the prosecution – they'll try to make you angry. Ignore them. Stay calm. Remember we spoke about this?'

'Yes, yes, alright.' Zina nods but remembers no such conversation.

CHAPTER THIRTY-SEVEN

E va sits inches from Zina. She has to be close enough to whisper the words to her, so as not to disrupt the rest of the court. There's a faint acrid smell and she wonders if it's risen from the staircase behind her that plummets down to the underground cells.

It's her first time inside Court Number One, and she's never attended a murder trial. She pushes back her shoulders a little to take a deep breath, tries not to let her nerves take charge. Sliding a finger inside the back of her blouse collar, she pulls it away from her neck for a moment's cool relief.

She's interpreted in court several times and isn't usually fazed by being stared at by the wigged men, having to think quickly and work accurately. But as her stomach clenches she knows this couldn't be more different to the other times.

She glances up at the gallery and notices Dr Garrett, sitting at the end of a row. He licks his finger as he flicks through a folder of papers. How many times has he sat there, she wonders, waiting for his moment? To give his expert opinion on someone's state of mind? Dozens, perhaps hundreds. Imagine wielding that power.

She looks across at the men sitting near her and spots Mr Carrington, the senior barrister defending Zina, and his junior behind him. Mr Ellis, Zina's solicitor, left a note a couple of days ago at Holloway. He informed her that, with the defence team, he'd brief Zina in her cell every morning and Eva's presence wasn't required. He has never asked for her help to date, never even met her despite Zina telling her that his Greek is terrible. He's said he won't attend the trial itself, but his clerk will be there in his place.

Eva had replied last night and asked if he might change his mind, what with this being a capital crime. But a terse response mentioned how busy he was, and that he doubted he could be of any further use. And, while his clerk didn't speak Greek, Mr Ellis was certain Eva was capable of translating anything necessary for the record.

Now she glances at Zina and worries she'll do something unpredictable. Every so often, her head jerks from one side to the other, as her eyes dart from corner to corner. And that shapeless navy blue dress, thinks Eva, it looks ready to swallow her. Zina looks unsettled, bewildered, as she pulls at a handkerchief between her fingers. Can she really have done the things they say she has?

Eva's gaze falls on a man sitting on the press benches. His face is turned away, but she knows that light brown hair with the blond strands. Before she can look away, Bert turns and catches her eye. He doesn't nod or acknowledge her, just looks straight past.

A heavy air of anticipation hangs over the court, and the judge gives Mr Stanford, the barrister for the Crown Prosecution, the nod to begin. He stands to launch into his opening address. He is a thin man, with a look of disdain on his face.

Eva will quietly, quickly translate into Zina's ear, but also has her pad and pencil to hand. The trial will go at a fair pace, and she's expected to keep up. It's her responsibility to tell Zina everything that's essential.

'Ladies and gentlemen of the jury,' Mr Stanford says. 'This is a most terrible case and I ask you to steady yourselves. You will hear how a young woman, Hedy Pavlou, just thirty-seven years old, a loving wife and mother, was killed in her own home in the most brutal of ways by the accused, her mother-in-law, Zina Pavlou.'

He points to Zina. 'You will hear how the accused hit her on the head with an ash pan, then strangled her with a scarf.' He's relishing every word and pauses so Zina can get the full effect as Eva explains. 'The accused then dragged the victim's body to the garden, where she placed it on a bonfire, poured paraffin over her and set it all alight.'

The court erupts and the judge quickly issues a warning: 'This trial will be conducted in an orderly manner,' he says to the gallery. 'Silence, please.'

Zina looks at Eva, puzzled at the chatter above.

Now Mr Stanford looks at the jury one by one before he continues. 'You will hear how this woman, the victim's mother-in-law, had both motive and opportunity to do this, and how evidence collected at the scene—' he sweeps his arm to show the array of labelled items on the prosecution table '—shows she is most definitely the culprit of this heinous crime.'

'What's he saying?' says Zina, loudly.

Mr Stanford nods, pausing again.

Does Zina really need to hear this? With everyone's eyes on her, Eva decides to give her a condensed version.

'He's summing up what you are accused of,' she explains in Greek. 'The detail of how Hedy died.'

Zina baulks and motions to the gallery, who stare down.

'How can they be against me already then? If all they're hearing is *that*?'

'Because he's saying he has evidence that he'll show. To prove your guilt.'

'May I resume?' Mr Stanford asks. Eva nods.

'You will hear how the accused tried to cover her tracks. But, unfortunately for her and thankfully for us, she is not... how can I put this, ladies and gentlemen?' He turns to Zina and puts his index finger to his temple and taps. 'She's not very bright, shall we say?'

There's laughter upstairs. Zina glares at him, understanding the gist of what he's said. Eva waits for Zina's barrister to jump up and protest, but nothing.

'In fact,' the prosecution continues, 'as you can see, she has an interpreter here. This woman's job is to tell her everything said in this court because she understands none of it. She reads and writes no English, *nor* can she read or write her own language, which I believe is…' he consults a piece of paper, 'Greek.'

'Mr Stanford,' the judge interrupts. 'Can we stick to the *relevant* information, please.'

He bows slightly. 'Apologies, My Lord.'

Zina rolls her shoulders back as though bracing herself. She might not understand every word, thinks Eva, but anyone can tell from the tone of his voice that there's worse to come; he's building up to something.

'We will show the jury the trail of *solid* evidence against her, and untangle the *wicked* lies she has told.' He breathes, and now he speaks slowly for emphasis: 'And we will undoubtedly prove that on the night of 28th July 1954, Zina Pavlou did murder her daughter-in-law, Hedy Pavlou.'

He holds up a finger to indicate he isn't quite finished. He's promised them a gruesome spectacle, thinks Eva, and the crowd is loving every moment.

'I'm certain by the end of this trial you will find Zina Pavlou guilty of this capital crime. And I am confident of this because of the witnesses we will call and all the evidence against her.'

Eva hurriedly tells Zina what's been said.

He returns to his seat, but before sitting turns, stretches out his arm and points right at Zina's face.

'This was a stupid murder,' he proclaims, 'by a stupid woman of the illiterate peasant type. The one you see before you.'

There's a bubble of excited chatter in the gallery.

Can he say that? Eva looks to Zina's barrister. Surely he'll object?

Mr Carrington half gets up then thinks again and stays in his seat. His junior barrister leans forward and says something, and he shakes his head. Won't one of them stand and speak for Zina? Have they decided it's not even worth trying?

Zina frowns at the gallery, then she turns her head to Eva expectantly, waiting for a translation.

She knows, Eva thinks. She knows they've said something awful.

So Eva leans across and tells her word for word. She can't save her feelings – not now. She has a right to know what's being said. As she tells her all of it, she's just inches from her face and she searches for a flicker of emotion. Nothing. Not a twitch, not a frown. Zina soaks up the words and then looks down into her lap, where she is still holding the handkerchief.

Zina sits obediently as the man talks about her. She recognises her name and Hedy's. But what little English she's learned has started to fail her, and she's not sure if it's the worry of it all or some trick God plays, as He unpicks everything towards the end. She trusts that Eva will look after her. Who'd have thought she'd lean so heavily on this girl, who she didn't even know six months ago.

When the man's finished speaking there's a buzz in the room and she knows he has said something terrible. He must have started repeating lies about the unspeakable acts from that terrible night, when her life came unfastened. Spewing lies again that have tarred her for months.

He's pleased with himself, she can tell. She glares at him now as he sits, flicking through his papers, streams of words appearing and disappearing on the pages he turns. Eva is talking calmly, telling her everything he said. She listens and the words get jumbled, but there was one word that he spoke that needs no translation. She understood it straight away.

Stupid. He called her stupid.

CHAPTER THIRTY-EIGHT

That afternoon, after Sergeant Parks has given his account of what had happened and the evidence against Zina, the prosecution calls Stanley Collins to the witness stand. Eva has no idea who he is, and she watches Zina as he puts his hat on the chair, places one hand on the Bible and swears to tell the truth. Zina looks puzzled too.

He's a tall, rangy man, in his forties or thereabouts. His three-piece suit is impeccably pressed and he stands, rocking slightly, with his thumbs in his waistcoat pocket as he speaks.

'Can you explain how you know the accused?' asks Mr Stanford.

'Yes, I'm her neighbour,' he says. 'I live two houses away. At number seventy-five.'

Eva explains and Zina looks surprised, as if she's never seen him before.

'And please, in your own words, tell us what happened on the night in question.'

'It was about quarter to midnight, and I noticed some flames coming out from Mrs Pavlou's garden.' He leans back a little on his heels and turns towards the jury. As the story unfolds, Eva relates it to Zina, who sits, frowning.

'And how can you be certain of the time?' asks Stanford.

'It was the light programme on the radio,' he replies. 'I listen to it every evening and go to bed when it's over. It finishes at ten minutes to midnight and it hadn't ended yet.'

'Thank you, continue.'

'Well, like I said, I saw some flames coming from the garden at number seventy-one. So I crossed next door's garden – we share a gate – and looked over the Pavlous' fence, to check everything was alright.'

'And what did you see, sir, when you looked over the fence?'

There's a pause and Zina leans forward.

'I saw a fire,' Collins says, 'and what I took to be a wax model half lying on top of it.'

Stanford glances at the jury, then up at the gallery, but says nothing. He nods at Collins to continue.

'It was surrounded by flames. And I took it to be one of those models you see in shop windows.'

A murmur sweeps through the court. Stanford raises his hand and silence falls.

'And?' he asks. 'Did anything else strike you in that moment?'

'The smell. There was a very strong smell of wax.'

'When you say wax, what do you mean? Describe the smell, please.'

'Paraffin wax,' he says, without hesitation. 'Now, of course, I realise it may have been paraffin, but I didn't think of that at the time because I just assumed it was a dummy.'

'Could you make out this figure? Anything remarkable?'

'It... she... was wearing just a pair of briefs.'

Someone tuts and Zina crosses herself when Eva explains.

'So what happened next?' asks Stanford.

'I saw a light on in the kitchen. I could see straight through the French windows.'

'And?'

'I could see her—' he points at Zina '—the accused, Mrs Pavlou, move around the table and then come into the garden.'

'Was she rushing?'

'No, she was very calm.'

227

Chatter floods through the court, and as soon as Eva has whispered the words, Zina shouts in English: 'He liar!'

Eva jumps and the judge taps the desk with his hand.

'Can the defendant please control herself,' he says. Then, looking up, 'And if members of the public cannot do the same, I shall not hesitate in clearing the gallery.'

'Please tell us,' Mr Stanford continues, 'what you saw next. Tell it exactly as you remember.'

'Well,' says Collins, swallowing, aware he has everyone's complete attention, 'she came out – Mrs Pavlou – bent over the body with a large stick and began to stir the fire.'

Zina shoots a glance from Eva to Collins and back.

'And did that shock you, sir?'

'Well, no – because I thought it was a dummy.'

'You thought it was a dummy. So what did you do then?'

Collins shifts. 'Well…' A wash of pink comes over his cheeks. 'I left when I saw her because I recognised her. I thought all was in order and I returned to my house.'

A chair scrapes. Someone coughs.

'And, Mr Collins, can I ask you when it was you first realised that everything wasn't, as you put it, *in order*? And that it was anything but?'

'An hour or so later, I heard the commotion outside. I came to the door and someone said something about a fire. About someone being dead. That's when the penny dropped. That's when I realised what I had seen.'

'And by then the police had arrived and you spoke to an officer at the scene?'

'Yes, sir.'

'Thank you – that is all.'

Mr Stanford has barely sat down when Mr Carrington, Zina's barrister, gets up to cross-examine. He's small and stocky and his gown hangs at an angle as if thrown on in a hurry.

'Mr Collins,' he says, 'I notice you're wearing spectacles. Are those reading glasses?'

'No, I'm short-sighted.'

'I see. Were you wearing them on the evening in question?'

'Er… yes. I think so.'

'You're not certain?'

'Well, I sometimes take them off when I'm listening to the radio, but I'm fairly sure I had them on.'

'*Fairly* sure, sir? Is that as sure as you can be?'

Mr Collins purses his mouth, obviously offended. 'Well, I suppose I might not have had them on. But it's unlikely.'

'Mr Collins, do you understand how serious this case is? A woman is being tried for murder.'

'Of course I do,' he bristles. 'I'm sure I was wearing them.'

Eva can almost hear his confidence wash away.

Collins turns to the jury. 'I saw what I saw.'

Carrington smiles. 'Very well, let's assume you were wearing your spectacles and you did see what you say you did…'

Collins shifts a little.

'Can I ask you *why* you would think the body on the fire was a wax dummy? If I saw a body on a bonfire, I would think it's just that – a body.'

There are a few nods in the gallery.

'There was the smell, for a start. And, well, our youngest daughter, Lucy, plays with Anna, Mick and Hedy's little girl. She told me there was a tailor's dummy in the house when she was there once. The mother did dressmaking on the side. I suppose I assumed it was connected to that.'

'I see,' says Mr Carrington. 'Well, let me ask you this. Why did you go to bed? Weren't you worried about the fire? It was two doors away from you. Weren't you concerned it might spread? Didn't it occur to you to *do* something, sir?'

Stanford gets up. 'I must object, My Lord. It's not Mr Collins who's on trial here.'

'I'm sorry, My Lord,' Carrington concedes, bowing to the judge. 'I'll rephrase that. Mr Collins, let me ask you why you went to bed knowing there was a fire two doors away.'

Zina puts her head to one side, listening, as if she too wants to know the answer.

A snigger escapes Collins' lips. 'Well, that's easy,' he says. 'It's because *she* was there, Mrs Pavlou.' He points at Zina. 'I thought it was all under control. I had no idea what kind of person she is. I mean, she looks so harmless.'

CHAPTER THIRTY-NINE

At the end of the first day, Eva is crouching in the foyer, pushing her notes into her bag, when she's practically knocked over. She gets up, shaken.

'Oh my, I'm so sorry!'

'*You.*'

It's Bert.

'Hello, Eva.' A woman behind him turns at the sound of his accent. 'How are you? Not mad at me, I hope?'

'Get out of my sight,' she says, quietly. 'Or I might just slap you.'

'Hey! Come on. It's not like I used your name.'

'It's not about me, you idiot.' Putting her things down, she shoves her arms through her coat. 'You had no right – no right to repeat what I'd told you. That was private.'

He gives an exaggerated shrug and in an instant his face hardens. 'So private that you described it in detail?'

She laughs in disbelief. 'I didn't know you were a *reporter*.'

'Actually,' he says, pushing his shoulders back, 'I'm Crime Correspondent for the *Daily*—'

'Honestly? I couldn't give a damn what they call you.'

'Charmed.'

'The point is you didn't tell me about your job, and there must be rules or something about that. Using information you get from people when they don't know you're a journalist? I'm sure your editor wouldn't be happy.' Her voice is louder now, and a few people have slowed down to watch from a distance.

'Hey, come on, lady—'

'*Excuse me?*'

'Come on – I'm hardly a spy or something. You said something you shouldn't have and you got into trouble, maybe, but you're here, aren't you? They didn't fire you, did they?'

Hands on her hips, she looks him up and down.

'What?' he asks. 'You need to calm down. I'm just doing my job.'

'You don't understand, do you?' she says. 'Your job – whatever you call it. It could have cost her the trial.'

'Come on,' he scoffs. 'Like she stands a chance! Everyone knows she did it – the police, the jury. This whole trial is just a formality. Even *you* know she's guilty.'

She slaps him, hard. Just the once, right across his stupid, pretty face. His hand flies to his cheek in disbelief and then he tries to laugh it off, turning to the people watching.

'Someone's got a temper,' he says, as if he's in a play or something.

She leans towards him.

'You use anything else you know,' she whispers, 'and I will have you banned from the court. You won't be able to walk up those stairs let alone report on this trial. Or any trial in the future.'

'You're a bitch,' he mutters.

'And you're a liar. And I know which I'd rather be.'

Her head is humming with hatred as she walks to the door. Of course, she can't have him banned, but he doesn't know that.

'*Evie?*'

No. She freezes on the spot.

'Evie!'

Only one person calls her that. She turns.

'Jimmy.' He runs towards her. 'Jimmy, what are you doing here?'

His face is white.

'What the hell was that?'

'What are you doing here?' she asks. 'Aren't you working?'

'I got off early. To come and meet you. What... what was that?'

She opens her mouth to speak but doesn't know what to say.

'Why did you hit that man?' he asks. 'Who is he? What's going on?'

On the bus home she begins to tell Jimmy about Bert.

'I didn't know he was a reporter,' she explains. 'He's a friend of Elsie's brother. Just hung around the Café de P, then I bumped into him one day near the prison. In a coffee shop I sometimes visit.' Her mind is racing ahead, wondering how much to say, what to leave out. 'I stop off there most days, because it's hard to go straight in to Holloway. It's just across the road.' She's stalling now and they both know it.

'He was waiting for you? Was he following you?'

She shrugs. 'He made out it was a coincidence. But thinking about it now...'

'You talked to him about Zina?'

She gives a slow nod. 'He noticed the newspapers. The story was everywhere. Said he felt sorry for her.'

'I see.' Jimmy's voice is flat. 'Then what?'

'Nothing,' she says. 'I went to work. But then he turned up again at the Café de Paris, and we talked and...' The words turn to dust in her mouth and she falters.

She feels his hand on her arm, and she looks at him.

'Did something happen?' he asks. 'Between you?'

It was just a kiss because I was lonely. And it meant nothing.

'Evie, did something happen?'

'I did something stupid.'

His hand falls away.

'We just talked, that's all,' she says, hurriedly. 'But I didn't think, and I said something about the way Zina was behaving – in prison.'

Suddenly, the bus takes a sharp corner and Jimmy grabs the rail.

'Was it him?' he asks. 'I read something in the paper about Zina singing and dancing in her cell. Did he write that?'

She nods.

He winces, not bothering to hide his disapproval. 'And that came from *you*?'

Putting her hands over her face, she mumbles, 'I'm so ashamed.' After a few moments he pulls her hands down so he can look at her. 'It's just sheer luck I didn't lose my job,' she continues. 'But there was this warden, you see, who—'

'It doesn't make sense,' he interrupts. 'Why would you slap him? What did he do?'

'I was angry,' she says. 'He could have ruined Zina's chances – well, any chance she might have. Made people think she doesn't care about the charges.' He doesn't speak. 'The woman's ill, Jimmy.'

Now her throat aches and she wants to cry.

A couple come upstairs, laughing and chatting, dressed for a night out. The woman's emerald-green netted skirt pokes out from under her coat. The man is wearing an immaculate deep navy suit with a white silk evening scarf draped around his neck. What she wouldn't give to swap places.

'Evie? Evie, look at me.' Jimmy's voice is muffled, as if he's holding something back.

'Yes?'

'Did he – this man, what's his name?'

'Bert.'

'Bert – did he… try anything? Did something happen with the two of you?'

She shakes her head.

'Nothing,' she says. 'Nothing happened.' And now she gives in and starts to cry.

He stares straight ahead and says, 'Did… did you want it to?'

She can't answer, but finally says, 'I was upset because – well, I suppose I just felt tricked by him, that's all.' With the heel of her hands, she rubs at her eyes.

'You felt tricked?'

'Yes.'

Taking a handkerchief from his pocket, he gives it to her.

'But you're the cleverest person I know.'

She looks at him. He knows there'd been something.

After a juddering breath, she asks: 'Is my mascara smudged?'

'Yes.'

'Do I look awful?'

'Yes.'

She smiles weakly, and he returns the smile then looks away. They sit in silence for the rest of the journey.

CHAPTER FORTY

The London Post, Tuesday, 26th October 1954

JURY'S NIGHT-TIME VISIT TO MURDER HOUSE

In the freezing rain, an Old Bailey jury last night was driven in a police coach to an unkempt garden where a terrible murder is alleged to have been committed on 28th July.

Pushing through overgrown weeds, they stared at a ditch where the body of 37-year-old Mrs Hedy Margarethe Pavlou was found at her home at 71 Cedar Hill, Hampstead NW3.

The person accused of murder is her mother-in-law, Mrs Zina Pavlou, a 53-year-old Cypriot who is illiterate in her own language and speaks very little English. She is alleged to have bludgeoned the victim, then strangled her and finally set fire to her body in this very backyard.

The ten men and two women of the jury were visibly moved at the scene, pointing at the burned ground. It was the defence's counsel, Mr Michael Carrington QC, who requested this visit. A neighbour two houses away, Mr Collins, had that day told the court that he'd peered over his garden wall and seen Mrs Zina Pavlou setting fire to the victim's body.

Once they'd inspected the garden of the deceased woman,

the men and women of the jury then walked to Mr Collins'
house to examine what could be seen from that vantage
point.

After returning, the jury went inside the victim's house,
where they stayed for half an hour. Tables and chairs had
been brought from the court and arranged in the same
manner as the furniture had been on the night of the alleged
murder.

The jury members then left in the police coach. They
walked past a board that was standing in the garden, to
which they did not give a second glance. On the sign were
the words: house for sale.

CHAPTER FORTY-ONE

Day two, Old Bailey

The next morning, as Zina listens to the white-haired man in the witness box, she thinks of her father. His hair looked like that towards the end: a slate grey that turned snow white by the time he died. She recalls a photo she'd seen of him once, when he was younger. His hair slicked back, a glistening cockroach black, as polished and impenetrable a shell as his heart.

The man speaking now doesn't look like her father – he's richer, smarter, taller – but something in his manner, the way he gesticulates with his plump hands, brings him to mind. Men are all powerful in their various ways.

Eva's words seep into her ear, but she stopped paying attention a while ago. She doesn't need to hear about the tonic this man gave Hedy or the girl's hair falling out, and all the medical issues she had. It seems to go on for ever.

Who'll speak of *her* complaints? Who'll stand and tell her side of the story?

It's late afternoon now. There's a tightness in Eva's back and she wishes she could bend over and stretch right here. They've all sat through hours of testimony so, by the time Blanche Harris takes the stand, there's a restlessness in court. She watches Mrs Harris stare at her audience while fidgeting with the white lace collar of her violet dress. Her cheeks are flushed and at her throat sits a single row of pearls.

'Mrs Harris,' begins Stanford, 'can you tell us what happened in the early hours of 29th July and how you encountered the accused?'

She nods and gulps.

'May I have some water, please?' she asks, her voice tight and high.

The judge agrees and a glass is brought to her.

Her hand shakes a little as she drinks it, then quickly hands it back. A drop has fallen and stained the front of her dress.

'Take your time, Mrs Harris.'

She nods again, gives a nervous smile and then catches Zina's eye and quickly looks away.

'I was driving back from work with my husband. We own a little restaurant in Holborn, you see. Wholesome English fare – nothing foreign, nothing fancy.'

'What time was this?' asks Stanford.

'Around 1 a.m.'

'And what happened as you were approaching Cedar Hill?'

'Well, we were driving along, listening to the radio and enjoying the breeze. It was hot that night, so we opened the windows.'

For someone who's started out jittery, she now seems to be hitting her stride.

'And then all of a sudden a woman – that woman – appeared in the middle of the road, as if out of nowhere, waving her arms about.'

Zina listens to Eva's words as if she's hearing this all for the first time.

'And by that woman you mean?'

'The prisoner, Mrs Pavlou.'

'We call her the accused or the defendant, but thank you. Then what happened?'

Mrs Harris glances at the jury, enjoying the attention now,

and continues as if confiding a story over cocktails. 'We slowed down. Bernard, my husband, thought there'd been an accident or something. When she ran right up to the car we stopped completely.'

'And what did she say?'

'Well…' she pauses, touching the pearls at her neck, 'to begin with we couldn't make head or tail of it because her English was very bad.' She gives another glance at the jury and Eva notices a couple of them nod. Zina bristles at the mention of her poor English. 'But then she said the words "fire" and "children sleeping" and, well, you can imagine we were startled.'

'And what happened next?' Stanford asks.

'She continued running up the hill,' says Mrs Harris, 'so we followed in the car, slowly. As we approached the top we could see the smoke for ourselves.'

'Then what?' asks Stanford.

'We parked and ran through the house with her, to the back – through the French windows, where the fire was.' Her voice is shaky. 'I'll never forget it.' She looks down into her lap and sighs.

There's a hush in the court. Zina shifts in her chair and folds her arms as Eva relays all this to her.

'Please carry on,' asks Stanford. 'Why do you say you will never forget it?'

'It was horrible. I still see it.' Mrs Harris' voice breaks, and her self-assurance falls away. 'When I close my eyes at night.'

'I'm sorry to hear that,' says Stanford. 'What was it? What did you see there?'

'I… I saw the body – Mrs Pavlou. Although I didn't know who she was at the time, of course.'

As Eva whispers into Zina's ear, her head drops a little.

'And by Mrs Pavlou you mean the *young* Mrs Pavlou? The victim? The deceased?'

'Yes. Hedy Pavlou. Poor girl.'

Stanford sighs loudly and softens his voice.

'Tell us what you saw. I know it's distressing, but please describe it.'

'Well,' she begins, 'she – the younger Mrs Pavlou – was lying with her head a couple of feet from the back step and the rest of her was in the fire. Her legs were sticking up, God help her. She was more smouldering than burning by this point. I'm afraid I screamed. I really felt quite faint with the horror of it.'

'Well, as anyone in their right mind might. It must have been a shock to you and your husband. Tell us, what did *this* Mrs Pavlou do? The accused who stands before you?'

Zina looks up, stares straight at her and waits for her response.

'She said, "Sssh. Children sleeping."'

There's a mutter around the court and someone laughs.

'Now,' says Stanford, 'let's get this clear, shall we? There was a body in her garden that had been horribly burned and, as you rightly suspected, the person was dead. But Mrs Zina Pavlou told you not to scream because of the children?'

'That's right. That's when I knew something wasn't right.'

Carrington shoots up. 'My Lord, this is speculation.'

'Agreed,' says the judge. 'Will the witness please refrain from offering opinions.'

Mrs Harris blushes.

'Let me ask you,' says Stanford. 'Was the accused still frantic? Waving her arms. Crying or shouting? Was she in a state of panic?'

'Oh, no. Far from it. She was very calm.'

'I see. Tell us what happened next.'

'Well, we called the fire brigade and they said they'd call the police. She didn't know the address to tell them, so she went and got a letter and showed us the address on the front.'

'And then what happened?'

'I had to stand somewhere I couldn't see her – the poor girl. While we waited, I asked the accused who the woman was – if she knew her. I asked her a few times in different ways and then she finally understood and said it was her son's wife. Then she said the oddest thing.'

Stanford waits longer than necessary for Eva to catch up, building the suspense till it's at breaking point.

'What?' he asks. 'Please tell the court what the accused said when faced with the half-burned body of her daughter-in-law.'

'She said...' Mrs Harris swallows hard, 'she said, "Girl plenty shoes, plenty dresses. German girl go Germany, take children." Just like that.'

Zina nods. 'It's true,' she says to Eva. 'She was taking them away from me.'

'Will the defendant please refrain from speaking,' says the judge. 'What did she say, Mrs Georgiou?'

Does she have to tell them? Everyone's eyes are on her, and she isn't quick enough to think of something else.

'She said it's true.'

'And?'

'And she said, "She was taking them away from me."'

There's a murmur around court.

Stanford continues. 'So, Mrs Harris, let's go over this one more time, please. Mrs Pavlou – the accused – said, "Girl plenty shoes, plenty dresses. German girl go Germany, take children." Is that correct?'

Nodding, Mrs Harris puts her hand over her heart. 'Word for word. I'm certain of it. I'll never forget those words coming from her mouth.'

'And why is that, may I ask?'

'Well, she was so calm, so cold and heartless. It was such a horrific scene. And yet she didn't seem at all shocked or upset.'

'That's all,' says Stanford. 'Thank you, Mrs Harris.'

As Stanford sits, Carrington rises to cross-examine.

'Mrs Harris,' he begins, 'would you consider yourself a level-headed person?'

'Yes, I like to think so.'

'Not hysterical? Not highly strung in any way?'

She frowns, affronted at the notion.

'Not at all,' she says. 'I think I'm as calm as the next person.'

Mr Carrington nods.

Where's this going? wonders Eva. She'd seen barristers try to discredit witnesses before, but there's nothing about this woman's statement that doesn't tally with Zina's.

'I see,' says Carrington. He pauses. 'And yet, in the heat of the moment, faced with the events as they unfolded on the night in question, you said…' he looks down at his notes, '"I'm afraid I screamed. I really felt quite faint with the horror of it."'

'Well, yes,' she says. 'It was a truly awful sight.'

'Agreed, Mrs Harris. But you said you're a level-headed woman, not highly strung and "as calm as the next person".'

Her cheeks flush and her hands go to her pearls again. Eva pictures them scattering around the courtroom.

'It was the worst thing I've seen in my life,' she says, in a quieter voice now. 'So when I said I'm as calm as the next person, well, I am *usually*, but these were very unusual circumstances.'

'And?'

'And,' she replies, affronted now, 'I'd never seen a burning body before, so pardon me for reacting the way I did!'

Carrington holds his hands out.

'Mrs Harris, I'm simply trying to show that in unusual circumstances, under great stress, when faced with horrors like these, well, who knows how we'd all behave? We might behave in *any* way at all. Would you agree?'

Her mouth trembles. 'Yes, yes, I suppose so.'

'So a woman like yourself – usually calm and collected – might scream and feel as if she could faint. Even though she's not, how shall we put it, the screaming or fainting type.'

'I truly am not.'

'And it would be unfair to judge you in that one extreme moment.'

Stanford gets up. 'My Lord, can my learned friend get to the point?'

'Yes, Mr Carrington,' says the judge, 'please do.'

Carrington nods. 'Very well, let's turn to Mrs Pavlou here,' he says, motioning to Zina. 'When faced with the awful scene before her, she started talking about the clothes her daughter-in-law had bought and how she was taking the children on holiday.'

There is silence in the court.

'Mrs Pavlou was hysterical in the street when she flagged you down. You said so yourself. But back at the house, you screamed and her mind turned to practical matters; she was worried you'd wake the children. Isn't that so?'

Blanche Harris doesn't respond.

'Isn't that so, Mrs Harris?'

'Yes.'

'Can you tell me, please,' Carrington continues, 'what is cold and heartless about her not wanting the children to see this horrific sight? The smouldering body of their mother?'

'Oh, well, I…'

'You'd already decided Mrs Pavlou was not trustworthy because you couldn't understand what she was saying. Because she wasn't like *you*.'

'Well, no, I didn't say—'

'A woman trying to protect her grandchildren at a terrible moment in their lives. A guest in this country who has few words, and yet is mocked for not finding the right ones at a time of great emotional turmoil.'

'I wasn't mocking anyone.'

'At a moment that you, a complete stranger, said was the worst sight you'd ever seen, isn't that so?'

'Yes, but…'

'Imagine if the person who lay dead in the garden was someone you knew? How would you react? I put it to you, Mrs Harris, that the defendant was trying to *calm you down*, while all the time thinking of those poor children upstairs who had just become motherless.'

'I ask, does that sound like a cold, heartless person to you, Mrs Harris? Or is that what any loving grandmother would do? No more questions, My Lord.'

CHAPTER FORTY-TWO

Day three, Old Bailey

Eva sits in the dock and watches as Zina rises from the stairs below. She's wearing her green cardigan today, the only one she'll wear now. Eva's pleased to see she's got a different dress on – a black shift that follows the line of her strong, square shoulders more closely and skims her hips, showing off her small but strong physique. The dark cotton is harsh against her sallow skin, but at least it fits.

What does she really understand? Eva wonders. She's done her best to translate everything she can, but at times Zina turns away as if someone has called her name and Eva doesn't know how much attention she's really giving the proceedings. In those moments, Zina doesn't seem to be in the dock of Court Number One at all, but in a different place entirely.

Zina says something to an officer and appears to get cross and starts gesticulating. The officer barks: 'Pavlou, you need to calm down.'

'Can I help?' asks Eva. Then she turns to Zina. 'What is it? What's wrong?'

She can see in her face that she's been told Michalis is testifying today.

'I feel sick,' says Zina. 'I need water.'

Eva tells the officer, who calls over an usher and they bring her a small glass. Zina drains it immediately and repeatedly wipes her mouth roughly with the back of her hand, as if trying to rub herself out.

'Zina, try and calm yourself.' She reaches and touches her sleeve. The officer gives her a look but doesn't say anything. 'Are you well enough to continue?'

'What difference does it make?' Zina snaps, handing back the glass. 'Nobody cares how I am. My son, my family, everyone's deserted me.' Her eyes begin to tear over. 'I've got nobody.'

'That's not true, Zina. You've got me.'

She nods. 'For now, but you'll turn too. They'll tell you lies and you'll stop coming to see me too. Just like the rest of them.'

'No,' Eva whispers. 'I'll always come and see you.'

'And if they stop paying you?' she asks with a smirk. Eva doesn't mention the fact that she's been visiting her for weeks now, unpaid.

There's a shuffling behind her and a call for everyone to stand, but Zina tugs her sleeve.

'What is it?' Eva whispers.

'I want to know it all,' she says, motioning to the witness box that stands empty. 'Tell me everything. Don't leave anything out.'

A low buzz of voices floats around the gallery as Michalis walks up to the witness box. With one hand raised and the other on the Bible, he takes the oath then casts his eyes down. The slight chubbiness of his cheeks has disappeared, and a tuft of hair on his crown is sticking up. He has nobody to tell him, Eva thinks. To check him before he goes out.

Could he have killed Hedy? Despite all the evidence pointing to his mother? She can't imagine his motive, yet she's sure he's hiding something about that night. He'd left work half an hour early, and she'd never found out why. But apart from asking a few questions early on, the police hadn't seemed to consider him a suspect. So they'd obviously believed whatever story he'd spun. Unless they'd already decided on the murderer.

Michalis is allowed to take a seat and his answers come in a slow, monotonous voice. The judge has to ask him to repeat things once or twice. An usher moves the microphone a little closer and he stoops towards it to give his responses. Zina cocks her head and listens with more attention than she's given anything up to now.

'Mr Pavlou,' starts Mr Stanford for the prosecution. 'We realise how difficult this must be for you. Not just because the victim is of course your wife of ten years and the mother of your two children, but because the accused is your mother.'

There is a tut in the gallery and the judge throws a warning glance at the balcony.

'Tell the court, please, how your mother first came to London.'

'I sent for her. That is, I sent her a ticket,' he says.

'You'd left Cyprus, what, twelve years before, is that correct?' asks Stanford.

'That's right.'

'And during that time you never wanted to return to Cyprus to see her? Or ask her over before that? Why is that?'

Michalis hesitates. 'Well, to begin with I couldn't afford it, but then I got together with Hedy and I – well – I didn't want my mother to ruin it.'

'What do you mean by that?'

'We didn't always get on that well in Cyprus,' says Michalis. 'She was… How can I put it? She liked taking over.'

'Can you give us some examples?'

'She would try and run my life, choose who my friends were, decide what job I did. That kind of thing.'

'But you're a grown man now, married with your own family? Surely you could stand up to your mother, sir?' says Stanford.

Michalis pulls a face. 'You don't know Greek mothers. I was worried she might ruin things, with me and Hedy. Especially as Hedy wasn't Greek, I knew she wouldn't approve.'

There's a murmur in court.

'But, after several years, you did finally agree and your mother arrived in July 1953, is that correct?'

'Yes.'

'And what made you change your mind?'

'She kept asking, and we thought perhaps she should see the grandchildren. It was Hedy who convinced me in the end. Said Mum wasn't getting any younger and I'd regret it.'

'I see. Can you describe the relationship between the two women? Your mother and your wife. Did they get on?'

Michalis pauses. 'For the first day or so but, well, they had their differences,' he says. 'They didn't speak the same language so there was that.'

'But it was more than a language barrier, wasn't it?' Stanford asks. 'Your mother's statement says that she actually left the family home because of the situation. The disharmony, shall we call it?'

'That's right, she stayed with a neighbour. But she'd been back a few months before... before it happened. And things seemed to be better for a while... until...' Michalis' voice falters and he lifts his head and looks at the barrister now, as if searching for the words.

'Go on, please. Things seemed better, but then what happened?'

'Well, we'd argue over how the children were being brought up, the fact they didn't speak Greek and didn't go to Greek church. Things like that.'

'And these things mattered to your mother, did they? But not to you and your wife. Is it fair to say that?'

'Yes. She also wanted us to christen Georgie, our son, but we didn't want to.'

'Tell us about the christening,' says the barrister.

'She wouldn't listen. She was adamant. She even made an appointment with the priest, but she had to cancel it when we refused to go.'

Zina makes a sudden twist in her seat as though Michalis' words have prodded her.

'How did she react when you refused?'

'Well, she talked about it all the time. We said it wasn't important to us. But she kept saying it was a terrible sin not to christen the children and we'd be punished for it.'

Zina puts her hand on the rail and leans forward, but is pulled back by one of the officers, who holds her shoulders for a few seconds.

'By who, sir?' asks Stanford. 'Who was going to punish you?'

Michalis shrugs. 'God, I imagine. She was – is – very religious and doesn't listen to anyone on matters like this.'

'Would you say, Mr Pavlou, that your mother is a woman used to getting her own way? One who doesn't like to be crossed?'

'Well, I don't know,' says Michalis. 'I mean I hadn't seen her for years, but she often said we ignored her, said it showed a lack of respect.'

The barrister pauses, letting the words hang in the air. When he speaks again, his voice is harsher, more clipped.

'Is your mother hot-headed, Mr Pavlou? Is she likely to lash out if something angers her? Is she *violent*?'

Zina's barrister, Carrington, shoots up. 'My Lord, my learned friend knows that these are leading questions!'

'Yes, please choose your words more carefully, Mr Stanford.'

'I apologise, My Lord. Let me rephrase that. Have you ever seen your mother in a temper?'

Michalis stares at his hands and Eva recalls him leaning over that man outside the Café de P., repeatedly punching his face. She can hardly believe this is the same person; he seems depleted, a whisper of who he was. Now, for the first time, he looks up at Zina, and Eva senses her stiffen.

'Sometimes she flies off the handle,' he says.

Zina shakes her head repeatedly.

'She would shout at times,' he continues, 'and once both Hedy and I came home and there were broken plates in the sink. I think she'd thrown them in a fit of temper, though she said they'd fallen off the draining board. We'd argued that morning.'

'Anything else?'

He pauses.

'Any other examples of her temper, Mr Pavlou?'

'We have a set of napkins,' he says, looking at the jury now. 'That Hedy's mum gave us as a wedding present. They have our initials embroidered on them and we keep them for best, in the wardrobe.'

'Yes? Continue.'

'I've moved out of the house now – where we used to live. And, well… I came upon them a few days ago.'

The whole court is hanging on his every word. He leans too close to the microphone and his words distort as they buzz around the courtroom.

'All of our initials had been cut out.'

A gasp fills the room.

'I'm sure she'd done it,' he says.

'Now,' says Stanford, 'unless you saw her yourself, how do you know your mother was responsible?'

'But who else could it have been?' says Michalis. 'My daughter has no reason to go through the wardrobe, whereas my mother was always putting bed linen away or taking napkins out.'

'But it's not an impossibility it was your daughter, is it?'

'No, but the key to the wardrobe is on a set that my mother carried around. Both she and Hedy had a set. If it was Anna, she would have had to get the keys without either of them noticing.'

'Alright then. Now, tell us about your wife, Mr Pavlou. What was she like?'

Michalis smiles. 'You know those people who light up a room? That's Hedy. Everyone loved her. Well, everyone apart from my mother.' He shifts his weight. 'She called me her better half, but it was the other way around.' His eyes well up. 'She made me a better person. We were very happy – before it all came apart.'

'I'm sorry to put you through this,' says Stanford. 'We've already heard from your wife's GP, Dr Bates, but can you describe in your own words Hedy's health in the weeks preceding her death?'

Michalis takes a deep breath and exhales with a judder. 'She'd become very nervous, on edge the whole time. That's why I took her to see him, to see what he could do.'

'What were her symptoms?'

'She couldn't sleep, stopped eating, and… and her hair was coming out in patches.' He points to an area at the side of his head.

Eva feels a stab of pity for her, this woman she's never met and who is only referred to in regard to her awful death.

'She started wearing a headscarf to cover it up.'

'Tell us for the record what happened when you took your wife to the doctor,' says Stanford.

'I told him about the situation at home, about them not getting along.'

'Did he say why a thirty-seven-year-old woman, who'd previously been in the best of health, would suddenly become unwell?'

'He said it was nerves. Because of my mother and the animosity.'

'Now we know from the doctor's testimony this morning that he gave her a tonic. Is that right?'

'Yes.'

'What other advice did he give – if any?' asks Stanford.

'He said the best thing for Hedy was not to be in the same house as my mother. He said the two women should not be under the same roof.'

There's a mutter around the court.

'What happened when you got home that day?' asks Stanford.

'We told my mother she had to leave. Hedy made arrangements to see her parents in Germany in three weeks' time, with the children, and when she came back she wanted – *we* wanted – my mother gone'

'How did your mother take this news?'

'Badly. She argued with us – said she'd never have the money to come here again if we sent her back. Kept talking about losing Anna, her granddaughter. But she saw our minds were made up.'

'So, did life carry on as normal while you were waiting for the day to come?'

'No, to begin with she kept to her room. She wouldn't eat with us. But then eventually she came down and we made up. Or so I thought.'

'And two days later?'

Michalis sighs and for the first time his voice breaks.

'And two days later I came home from work and... and I found the police there and the house full of people and...'

'Yes?'

'And Hedy lying dead in the garden. She'd been murdered.'

A wave of chatter spreads throughout the court and a male voice booms out: 'The bitch did it!'

'If you continue to disrupt proceedings,' says the judge, raising his voice for the first time, 'I will remove you from the court.'

Everyone settles down, and like an actor waiting for undivided attention from his audience, Mr Stanford pauses a little longer. Now the only sound is the ticking of the large clock.

'Mr Pavlou, can I ask you to look at something?' He turns to an usher. 'Can we revisit evidence P2, please?'

A ring is produced from an envelope, shown to the judge then passed to Michalis.

'This court has already heard from Sergeant Parks on this matter, but can *you* tell us, please, what this is?'

'It's Hedy's wedding ring,' says Michalis. 'I gave it to her.'

'There's an inscription on the inside. What does it say?'

'It says Michalis – my name – and the date, 1944. That's when we married. I have her name inside mine.' He lifts his hand up to show his ring. A woman on the jury pushes a handkerchief to her mouth, but her sob still escapes.

'This ring was found on the mantelpiece in your mother's

room. It was wrapped in paper and hidden behind the clock. Who put it there?'

'She must have taken it off Hedy's finger.'

'Speculation, My Lord,' says Carrington.

'Please stick to the facts, Mr Stanford, and stop asking the witness to imagine what may have happened.'

'Of course, My Lord. Mr Pavlou, was your wife's wedding ring loose? Did she ever take it off?'

'No, it wasn't, and no, she never did. If anything, it was tight.'

'Your mother insists she found it on the stairs and thought it was a curtain ring, and put it there for safekeeping.'

There's a pause, then Michalis says, 'She must have taken it off after Hedy was dead.'

'Again, speculation,' says Carrington, his voice weary.

A wave of tutting goes around the court.

The judge shifts in his seat. 'Mr Pavlou, stick to the facts, please.'

Stanford nods as though he agrees, as though he hasn't led Michalis to exactly where he is.

'I know this has been most difficult, Mr Pavlou,' he says. 'My final question. Please look at your mother, the defendant.'

Michalis lifts his head and looks straight at Zina. She stares back without a flicker of emotion.

'Do you think Mrs Pavlou – the accused – do you think she would be capable of doing such a thing? Of killing your wife?'

Eva waits for Carrington to protest, to say this is leading the witness and shouldn't be allowed, but nothing. The judge is silent, too.

Michalis says something, but it's lost in the general chatter.

'I'm sorry, you'll have to speak up,' says Stanford.

He clears his throat and leans forwards. With his eyes still on his mother, he says: 'I have no doubt that she is capable, and that she did it.'

* * *

At the end of the session, Eva asks permission to follow Zina down to the cells. The warden is about to say no but then waves her through.

Once in the cell, Eva offers Zina a Craven 'A', and they both light up. They perch on a bench and wait for the van that will take Zina back to Holloway. It's cold and damp down here, and there's an awful smell of sewers.

'Are you alright?' asks Eva.

Zina shrugs.

'I never thought he'd do it – go on the stand and say those things. And yet he can't come and visit me.' A tear races down her cheek and she swipes it with the heel of her hand. 'He couldn't look me in the eye, could he?'

Eva doesn't respond. Zina had stared at him throughout his testimony; was it any wonder he wouldn't look at her? She'd felt sorry for Michalis, the centre of attention as he'd gazed at the wedding ring and talked about Hedy.

'Will they ask him more questions tomorrow?' asks Zina. 'The other side? The man who's working for me?'

'Your solicitor will tell you first thing,' says Eva, 'but probably not.'

'Why?'

'Well…' How could she put this? 'The jury, they might feel sorry for him. Your barrister probably wants him out of the courtroom as quickly as possible.'

'Hmmph,' Zina snorts. 'So he can say what he wants and walk away and have everyone believe him?'

'Let's wait and see, shall we? They know what they're doing.'

What a ridiculous thing to say, Eva thinks. So far, the defence's lethargic efforts have chilled her to the bone.

CHAPTER FORTY-THREE

Holloway Prison / Spakato, Cyprus, 1920

Z ina wakes with her arm over her eyes. For a moment she doesn't know where she is, and then she does. She turns over and sighs.

Tonight her mind reels back to years ago. At times, her past feels so close it is just there, over her shoulder.

She sees Zacharias, tall and broad in his youth, not wizened as he is now. It's morning and she's picking her way over the rocks to go to the stream, bucket in hand because there's no running water after all. His parents still live in the house on the hill, and Zina, her husband and their five children squeeze into the ramshackle farmhouse on the edge of the valley.

She's only twenty years old and her bones are tired with it all, but she says nothing. Zacharias hates to hear her complaining and tells her with his fists. Silence is less painful.

She shifts in her bed and suddenly she's there again, back in the dusty barn, the day it was first mentioned. The smell of the animals and the earth fills her nostrils.

Zacharias is there. He's told her to come at sundown. His two brothers and their wives are already waiting. She pushes the wooden door and knows by the way they stare that they've been discussing her. It's a coming together for something that's already been decided.

He walks towards her and pulls her into the group. For a moment she wonders what he wants – he wants something, that much she knows – then he starts talking about the fact that she's the youngest one here. And that's why she's the perfect choice.

He wants her to do what he won't dare. And with five children tugging at her all day, she has nowhere to go even if her heart were brave enough to consider such a thing.

He comes and holds her shoulders now and she is not sure what he'll do next.

'It makes sense,' he says, smiling. 'It has to be you.'

She doesn't say anything, knows better than to argue, especially in front of others.

'Don't worry,' he says, stroking her hair. 'I'm hardly going to let my wife go to prison, am I? And we know the judge. He's a friend.'

The others nod in reassurance and the water is at her shoulders now and her head is about to go under.

She takes a breath and dares a question: 'Why?'

He reveals what his mother has done to them, to their family – to his father.

'It's the worst possible sin, Zina, don't you agree? To go with another man when you're married?'

All eyes are on her now. Everyone knows that her husband is the least faithful of all. But how can she not agree? So she nods.

'Good girl,' he says. He puts his arm over her shoulder and walks around the barn with her, as if they're strolling by the beach, just the two of them.

'So you agree it's a terrible sin? So the punishment needs to be harsh. It needs to be handed out by one of us, to show everyone in the village that our family won't tolerate it.' He stops walking and looks straight at her. 'Do you understand?'

'To reclaim our good name?' she asks, knowing this is what he wants her to say. Knowing it might help her later, when the drinking starts, if he's in a better mood.

'Exactly.' He kisses her forehead.

With his arm hooked again around her shoulder, they continue to walk.

'Tomorrow,' he says, louder now, 'they'll help you.' And he points at her sisters-in-law, who give sly smiles because they're only helping. Then he tells her in detail how she is to do it. She can feel the blood drain from her head and the barn is reeling. She stands still and bends over, breathes deeply to steady herself.

'But... I... I don't think I can,' she says, still upside down. 'Not like that.'

'You have to.' He pulls her up and stares into her face. 'It has to be the worst punishment, for the worst crime. To show we won't tolerate this. You said you understood.'

She hesitates, then gives a little nod.

'It will be quick,' he says. 'She won't be able to fight back. There'll be three of you.'

She looks down and kicks the sawdust on the barn floor.

'Zina?'

'Yes?'

'It will be alright. I promise.'

She nods, but she has bruises that show what his promises are like.

'Look,' he says, quietly now, so the others can't hear. 'I didn't want to say anything, but once it's done Father says the house will finally be mine – ours. I'm the eldest, so it comes to me. He'll go to the farmhouse. All of it ours, everything.'

Living in the house on the hill is what she's dreamed of for six years now. It was promised to her, wasn't it? And what choice does she really have? Who knows what his temper is capable of. She has always had to bend to the will of men. First her father, now her husband. Women bend or they snap.

She turns again in her cold prison cell, pulls the blanket over her head and thinks: this is where I came undone.

CHAPTER FORTY-FOUR

Day four, Old Bailey

Zina clasps a metal cup in her palms, sips tea and waits. She's perched on the bench in her cell in the pit of the Old Bailey.

'Please? Sugar?'

The warden snorts. 'Not a chance.'

She gives her a sidelong glance and takes another sip. She won't let it upset her, not today. Her trial is almost at an end. Her solicitor has said that this morning she'll take the stand. The man who's on her side will question her first. Then the other one. They told her she didn't have to testify if she didn't want to, but how else will she save herself if she doesn't say a word? And she's spent her life not speaking.

Her stomach twists at the thought of everyone watching her, as she has to deliver her words through the girl. What if she can't find the right ones? If she can't say the things that are in her head?

They'll think her stupid. If she can just keep her mind quiet, concentrate on what's being asked, perhaps she can show them that she's a decent woman, that all she's ever wanted is to make a good life for her family.

Footsteps reverberate in the corridor outside and stop at her door.

'Get up, it's time,' says the warden.

She wants to leave, to go home, but where is that now? Where is she safe? Where is she happy? She thinks of a dark cinema, blaring music and a warm sticky hand pushing a lemon sherbet into her mouth.

The warden takes the cup from her hand. Zina gets up and smooths down her dress. A thought pushes into her head. How much does it cost for an adult and a child to get into London Zoo? She's never been but has heard of it and would love to take Anna. She nudges the idea into a corner of her mind, ready to examine later when she's in bed. She likes to have something joyful to consider when she can't sleep. It would be a wonderful day out.

Eva's surprised at how calm Zina looks as she slips into the witness box. It's a small, raised box, too small for both of them, so she places herself as close as she can beneath it. Zina stands very still, her face expressionless as she's sworn in. Upstairs, the wooden benches in the gallery sigh with the weight of people who sit elbow-to-elbow, jostling for a better view. The judge is having no nonsense today, and has told them all as much. The slightest call or eruption from the public and they'll be ejected from court.

'Mrs Pavlou, I'd like to ask you about your life while living with your son and his wife,' begins Mr Carrington. 'Your son told us you looked after the house, is that correct?'

Eva translates everything Zina says back into English and has to speak louder now that she's not whispering into her ear.

'Yes,' says Zina. 'I wanted to get a job. That's why I was here. I wanted to make money to take home.'

Carrington pushes his glasses up his nose. 'What did that involve?'

'Everything. Cooking, cleaning, ironing. I usually got up early, before everyone, and washed some clothes or tidied up from the night before. Then I would make breakfast and help Anna get ready for school.'

'Your granddaughter?'

'Yes. Hedy didn't let me walk with her, but once a week I was allowed to collect her.'

'Why only once a week?' he asks. Zina likes this man – he's asking all the right questions.

'On Wednesdays they had other things to do,' she says. 'They were both working so they needed me.'

'Is it fair to say that you were used a bit like a servant?' he asks. It's a word she's used herself in letters back home, when she's spoken of how Michalis treated her.

'Yes, but I was happy to do it. We're family.'

'But didn't it sometimes get too much for you?' he asks. 'You're how old – fifty-three? You've had a hard life working the land in Cyprus. I understand you're not in the best of health.'

'I have a few aches and pains but I'm stronger than I look.' Here Zina touches her bicep as if to prove a point. Eva hesitates to translate.

'Mrs Georgiou,' says the judge, 'please tell us what the accused has said.'

'She says she has aches and pains, My Lord,' says Eva. 'But...'

'Yes?'

'But is stronger than she looks.'

As soon as the words are out of her mouth people are chattering across each other, and one of the women in the gallery leans over to get a closer look at Zina.

'Order! Mr Carrington, please continue.'

'But it was hard work?' asks Carrington.

'Yes,' replies Zina. 'I felt like a skivvy.'

She instinctively holds her hands out and examines them, to see the rough skin that has washed hundreds of dishes and scrubbed numerous collars.

'Tell us why Mrs Pavlou – the deceased – couldn't do all of this cooking and cleaning and housework herself. She was the woman of the house, and you were the guest. Wasn't it her job?'

Zina shrugs. 'She went to work. She'd got a second job when I arrived, to make more money.'

He nods and then immediately frowns. 'So she left her children to be looked after by you?'

'Only when it suited her, when they couldn't find someone else. They didn't like me being with the children. I don't know why.'

'Did they have debt, to your knowledge? Did they *need* more money?'

'No, I don't think so. My son works two jobs too, so they have enough. He told me her family have land, in Germany, so they weren't ever going to go hungry.'

'I see.' He looks through some papers but doesn't seem to find what he's searching for and looks up again. 'What did she do with this extra money she earned? From the second job? Did she buy you a gift, perhaps, or thank you with a night out, something like this?'

Zina laughs uninhibitedly and looks around to include everyone in the joke. She stops when she notices the jury staring at her.

'That amuses you? Why?'

'She didn't buy me one thing,' she says, her voice harsh now. 'She bought herself plenty, though. Plenty clothes, plenty shoes. She went out with friends sometimes when the children were asleep. When Michalis was working nights.'

'So she didn't mind you looking after the children while they slept?' Carrington asks. 'Did she tell you why she didn't want you with them when they were awake?'

Zina shrugs. 'She didn't like me speaking to them in Greek. Maybe she thought they'd pick up my good manners.'

'Anything else?'

'She didn't like me giving Anna sweets or playing with her. I took her to the cinema once and Hedy got very cross.'

'So she didn't want her children to feel close to you – their grandmother – but still used you as a safety net. As an unpaid nanny when she went out without her husband? Did she have male friends?'

Eva's translation is cut off as Mr Stanford shoots up. 'My Lord, my learned friend knows better. I don't see that casting aspersions on the deceased woman's character has any bearing on this case.'

'Yes, do get to the point, Mr Carrington.'

'Very well, My Lord,' he says. He squares his shoulders now and pauses for effect. 'Mrs Pavlou, did you or did you not kill Hedy Pavlou?'

'No! I did not.'

'Tell us then what happened that night.'

'It was the man downstairs. The man I saw on the doorstep.'

'But who was this man? You didn't see his face, you didn't know him.'

'Perhaps he was someone she met on one of her nights out. Maybe they'd argued and he came back. It might have been Freddy. By the time I'd gone down the stairs he'd run away.'

'My Lord,' says Stanford. 'This is all speculation. It should not be allowed.'

'Agreed,' says the judge. 'Please stick to facts, Mrs Pavlou. Who is this Freddy?'

'Freddy is a friend of the family, My Lord,' says Stanford. 'And it's been ascertained that he was actually in the Royal Free Hospital with his new-born son that evening, who was poorly.'

'Mr Carrington, you may continue,' says the judge.

'Well, Mrs Pavlou,' says Carrington. 'The prosecution will say you're making all of this up. You didn't mention this man on the night of the murder, when you were first questioned by the police, did you? You said you saw the door open, but you didn't mention there was a man there.' He turns to look at the jury, even though his words are still addressed to Zina. 'On your first questioning, why didn't you tell the police about this man? Surely you could have said something about him?'

'I didn't say anything because I didn't want my interpreter to know.'

'I see. But why keep it from Mrs Georgiou, here. Surely she's here to help you?'

'Mrs Georgiou wasn't my interpreter the first time I was questioned,' says Zina.

'So who was your interpreter that very first time you were questioned by the police, Mrs Pavlou? On the night your daughter-in-law died? And why didn't you say anything about this man then?'

Zina puts her head to one side.

'The interpreter was my son, Michalis.'

There's a buzz of voices in the gallery. The judge points to the crowd up there, and the voices subside.

'What do you mean? Explain, please,' says Carrington.

'When Michalis came back from work, they asked him to translate,' she says. 'Well, I didn't want to say anything because his wife was dead. If I'd said there was a man here he would have got angry with me. He has a temper.'

Two men on the front bench of the jury turn and look at each other.

'Are you telling this court, Mrs Pavlou, that the police asked the victim's husband to question you – his own mother, your own son? And that's why you didn't speak of this man on the doorstep?'

'Yes.'

'No more questions, My Lord.'

The judge orders a break and Zina sits in the holding cell and waits. She twists her hands in her lap. The man who called her 'stupid' on the first day will be asking the next questions.

Funny, she thinks, she has no recollection of whole hours of this trial, as if she wasn't even here, and yet she can still see the smirk on his face so clearly.

Sometimes the days and years fold into themselves, slip and cascade. Time disintegrates. Only a few things feel certain as the events of her life shift beneath her feet. Two things she is sure of. There was a woman once who took what was hers. And a man who was going to protect her if she'd do one thing for him. Of course she'd be blamed, he said, mothers and wives always were, but they'd never punish her. They didn't punish women, not in the same way. But if he did it, he'd hang, of that he was sure.

Zina, just a girl really, would be acquitted. He'd slip some money into the right hands to guarantee the case was dismissed. And people would forget – they'd forgive.

Only they never did, did they? And here she is again, waiting to see how her days will unfurl. For the second time in her life, waiting to learn if she'll be convicted of murder.

CHAPTER FORTY-FIVE

After an hour's break, Eva makes her way back to court. Zina launches into complaints about her aching back, and she tries to calm her, saying that day four of her trial is almost over. She just has to get through this final part – being questioned by the prosecution.

Mr Stanford gets up, chin raised, ready for a fight. He speaks quickly and Eva does her utmost to translate as fully as she can. She owes Zina that. Occasionally he has to wait for her to catch up.

'Mrs Pavlou, did you like your daughter-in-law?'

'I had nothing against her,' says Zina. 'I tried very hard to get on with her. We just had our differences.'

'Now you make it sound like something minor – just skirmishes. But isn't it true you argued? About the children? About the way she kept the house? The cooking?'

'Yes, we did argue sometimes.'

'The truth is it came to a head and you couldn't get along at all, could you?' he asks. 'Didn't you have to leave the family home for several weeks because of the problems between you?'

'Yes... I left but then I came back and we were getting on much better.' Zina looks up at the gallery. 'We even cooked together and I helped with the children.'

'What was your relationship like with Hedy Pavlou before she died?'

'We were getting on very well,' says Zina.

'But we've heard and seen evidence that shows that's not true. Are you really going to stand there and say you got on? When we know for a fact that your son took his wife to the doctor because the situation had become insufferable. The two of you couldn't be under the same roof, isn't that so?'

She twists away, as if someone's poked her in the back. 'No, that's not true.'

'So Dr Bates, who gave evidence yesterday, has lied, has he? And your son, too? He lied when he said Hedy wasn't sleeping or eating and her hair had started to fall out? And she was advised *for her health* to get you out? Are these *all* lies, Mrs Pavlou? Are we to believe you're the only person telling the truth here, madam?'

As Eva translates, Zina clutches the rail of the witness box and leans forward.

'No, her hair *was* falling out but that had nothing to do with me,' she says. 'You're making it sound worse than it was. Making me look bad.'

'Mrs Pavlou, let's turn to the night of the murder. Let me read you what you told the police the night Hedy died.' He takes a folder from the table and opens it.

'You said, "Around 1 a.m. I woke to go to the bathroom. From the top of the stairs I could see that the street door was open. Smoke was coming from downstairs." Is that correct? Are these your words?'

Zina nods.

'You have to speak, Mrs Pavlou, for the court's records.'

She leans into the microphone. 'Yes.'

'And afterwards, weeks later, in fact, you added to your statement to say that "there was a man on the doorstep".'

'Yes.'

'But you didn't mention him before. You only mentioned him weeks later. Why is that?'

'I told the court – my son was the translator. I was worried he'd get angry if I said something about another man at the house.'

'But according to you, this "man" you speak of is another person at the scene of the crime. A potential suspect when you're accused of a terrible deed. Do you expect us to believe that you're more worried about your son getting cross than being found guilty of murder?'

He doesn't wait for an answer.

'Tell us, Mrs Pavlou, are you certain you saw the open door from the top of the stairs?'

'Yes, yes – I saw it. And that man, standing there.'

'I put it to you that you are lying.'

'No!'

'You *didn't* see the open door from the staircase. And you *didn't* see a man. I know this for a fact.'

There's a murmur in the court as Eva frantically tries to catch up, and when she tells Zina what he's said, she jolts back a little.

Mr Stanford takes his time, surveying the court as he speaks. 'Mrs Pavlou, it is physically *impossible* to see the front door from the top of the stairs.'

Silence.

'The police have checked and double-checked this. Sergeant Parks has already stated that fact when he took the stand at the start of this trial. Did you not hear him?'

Zina frowns at Eva as if she has no recollection of the policeman saying this or even taking the stand.

'We have photos and measurements that have been submitted as evidence on day one of this trial. And yet you still are adamant, madam, that you're telling the truth.' He sighs and waves two pieces of paper. 'These are two copies of the same photograph again, madam.' He turns to an usher. 'Please pass one to the defendant and one to the judge and jury – to refresh everyone's memory.'

Zina stares at the picture.

'You saw these photographs three days ago, yet you want us to believe you don't remember? I put it to you there was no man.'

'There was.'

'You then go on to say, "I went downstairs and saw that there was a bonfire in the garden and... and Hedy was lying there... on top of the fire." Correct?'

Zina nods, then leans into the microphone. 'Yes.'

'You tell us you tried to save Hedy. That you frantically threw a bucket of water over her – twice, in fact – but, in your words, "the fire was strong".'

Zina's eyes dart towards Eva, then around the court. She goes to speak, hesitates, then a flat 'Yes.'

'Well, the police have already stated there was no bucket near Hedy. The bucket was in a cupboard under the sink. It had a box of detergent in it and some cloths.' He pauses for effect, then says, 'It was *dry* inside, Mrs Pavlou. It had not been used. There was no sign you'd tried to put out any fire. And according to your neighbour's testimony you actually *started* the fire.' Zina shakes her head slowly.

'And even though you say you didn't enter the garden, Mr Collins swore under oath that he saw you stoking the fire. Making it *stronger*.'

'No!'

'Making sure that the body burned. That your daughter-in-law burned.'

'Mr Stanford, please,' says the judge. 'Less of the amateur dramatics.'

There's a titter in the gallery and Eva glances up to see enraptured faces, row upon row, staring down.

'I apologise, My Lord.'

Eva glares at Carrington. Why is he letting Stanford speak to her like this?

Stanford turns back to Zina. 'We also heard evidence that your shoes were soaked in paraffin. Why was that? You told the police that you didn't enter the garden, but stood on the step throwing water over your daughter-in-law.'

'I've explained it already,' she says. 'I spilled paraffin, filling the heater.'

'Let's say, for one moment, that you're telling the truth.' He waves his hand around, to show his benevolence. 'And that you *did* spill paraffin on your shoes filling a heater on a very warm July night. How do you explain the *blood*?'

Zina frowns in confusion.

'Did you not hear the evidence at the start of this trial, madam, that stated blood was found on the kitchen lino? Because I distinctly remember your translator telling you.' He pauses. 'Tests proved it to be Hedy's blood, and it's clear that someone had tried to wash it away. You can't have *forgotten* these details, madam? Or are you choosing not to remember?'

One of the women on the jury whispers to the man next to her.

'I... I had a toothache,' stutters Zina. 'I pulled a tooth out. That's why there was blood.'

As Eva translates, there are titters of laughter. Realising they're laughing at her, Zina erupts.

'Make him stop!' she shouts. 'He's making a fool of me – he's lying.'

'Control yourself, Mrs Pavlou,' says the judge.

In a quieter voice, Zina says, 'He told me to kill her. I've held it inside me all these years. He promised he'd stay.'

What? Eva hesitates. Her mind is racing. Is Zina talking about her husband? Has she got this trial confused with the one she'd mentioned before? The one that had happened in Cyprus? Everyone is staring, waiting for Eva to tell the court what Zina has said.

Stanford raises an eyebrow. 'Well, are you going to translate, Mrs Georgiou? Or is this all just chit-chat between the two of you?'

'Sorry... yes. She just asked me to help her, to make you stop your questioning. She says that you're lying.'

'And that's it?'

Eva nods. She should interpret the rest, she knows that. But every instinct tells her otherwise. How could she even begin? To say that Zina has been accused of murder once before?

'Mrs Georgiou?'

Eva jumps.

'Sorry, yes, that's everything,' she confirms.

Stanford is speaking again and Eva's trying to keep track but her heart is racing. Should she have said something? Explained exactly what Zina had said? She opens her mouth to speak, but she's already left it too late. She's wrapped herself tight in the sticky lies.

She catches up and, as the questioning continues and the court is shown Anna's faded red and gold scarf again, Eva wills Zina to stay calm. But she's started to fidget and scratch at her hands. Her cool demeanour from the beginning of the day has disappeared entirely.

'Mrs Pavlou, what were you wearing when the police arrived?'

'My clothes – a skirt and a blouse.'

'Not nightclothes?'

Zina hesitates.

'I got changed. Before they came.'

'While trying to put out a fire and make sure your grandchildren were safe you had the presence of mind to dry the bucket, put it away and change your clothes?'

Zina says nothing.

'I put it to you,' he continues, thumbs under lapels, 'that you were wearing your day clothes because you hadn't gone to bed at all. Your bed hadn't been slept in – or did you have time to make the bed, too, before running into the street to flag down a car?'

Laughter bubbles up in the gallery.

'I spoke the truth,' she says, and Eva translates, but nobody seems to be listening.

'I will have order in my courtroom!' says the judge.

The ring is brought forward and given to Zina to look at.

'We've all seen this before in this courtroom,' Stanford says.

Zina shrugs.

'Do you know this ring?'

'Yes, I found it on the stairs. I thought it was a curtain ring.'

'It's a wedding ring. I think anyone can see that.' He shows it to the jury and a couple of people nod. 'Now I know you can't read,' he says. Zina blushes and a fury crosses her face. 'But you know what it says, don't you? You heard your son say this ring was always on his wife's finger. And just to be certain, let's ask your interpreter to read the inscription.'

He passes it to Eva and she reads it out loud in English then Greek.

'It says "Michalis, July 1944",' she tells her.

'It's the wedding ring your son gave Hedy,' he says. 'He told us she never took it off, and it was in fact too tight to have fallen off. Did you steal this ring? Because you were jealous of their happiness?'

'No.'

'Perhaps you wanted to sell it or throw it away?'

'No.'

'But we know she wouldn't have taken it off herself, and she had it on when her husband saw her for the last time.'

'I didn't dislike her,' bursts Zina.

'You were jealous of the loving relationship she had with your son. You're right, you didn't dislike her.' Stanford pauses. 'I think you despised her.' He waits, making sure Eva has time to translate the detail.

Zina shouts two words in English: 'No! Lying.'

'You didn't like the way she was bringing up the children, and in fact you've admitted many times that you wanted them to speak Greek, go to church – you even arranged a baptism without the parents' permission.'

'It's a sin not to be baptised,' she explains in Greek. 'I was trying to help.'

Stanford barely waits for Eva's translation before ploughing on.

'Hedy was young, she was pretty and she had the love and devotion of your son,' he says.

Zina bristles as Eva tells her what he's said.

'In fact,' he continues, 'she was loved by all her friends and neighbours too. A fact that you have used to cast aspersions on her good character.'

Zina raises her chin as if waiting for the final blow.

'And not just that – she was educated. She had a future…'

Eva hates translating these words. She knows there's more to come.

'Let's just state the facts – she was everything you are not.' And here he counts on his fingers. 'Young, pretty, popular, educated and – most of all – loved.'

Eva pauses, can't believe the cruelty of his words.

'She'd made an effort. She could speak the language and she liked our English way of life here. She was happy. *She was one of us.*'

Slowly, he leans towards Zina. 'She had everything that you didn't. That you still don't. So you took it all away.'

Eva says it all, as dispassionately as she can. Zina leans forward and places her head on the rail.

'And when you did that, you also took it all away from her husband, your son. And his children. And all for what? Because of your jealousy and your resentment.'

Eva can hear her crying, takes a handkerchief from her pocket and looks at the judge, who nods. She passes it to Zina and she hurriedly rubs under her eyes.

'No more questions, My Lord.'

The day has finally ended and Zina is led down to the cell. Eva glances at the warden and she nods to let her through. She watches Zina's hands shake as she washes her face, rubs her cheeks dry with paper towels and slumps down onto the bench. There's a warden in a chair by the wall, reading a magazine.

'I'm sorry I got cross,' says Zina. 'I know you told me not to, but all those questions… he twisted it all.'

Eva reaches out and takes her hand. 'I know. It's been a long day. They'll take you to Holloway now.'

As she goes to leave, Zina calls her back.

'He won't question me again, will he?'

'No.' Eva smiles. 'He won't.'

'Good,' says Zina. 'Then the worst of it is over.'

Eva hesitates, wants to say something about the sentencing, but the raw devastation on Zina's face makes her stop.

'I'll see you tomorrow, Zina,' she says, already dreading what's to come.

CHAPTER FORTY-SIX

The trial was almost at an end. As Eva leaned on the bus window, her mind hummed with the day's events, and she was already worried about not sleeping that night. She settled in for the long journey home to Camden. Behind her, a noisy group of friends was fooling around, jostling for space with each other.

Was it possible they'd find Zina not guilty? Unlikely. The past few days had brought out the worst in prisoner Pavlou, showing her as volatile, unpredictable and shifty. But if she *was* found guilty, Garrett would be able to throw light on her state of mind, before the judge passed sentence. After watching her for months in Holloway, his medical report would reveal what Zina was really like. And once the judge heard of her paranoia, crying and delusions – all that unnerving behaviour – he couldn't ignore it. The doctor had said so himself.

Eva stared out of the window and mulled over her own actions that day. Lord knows she'd tried to keep up, to translate what she could, but there were moments when she'd let things slip, when she hadn't told Zina everything. But that wasn't what was bothering her; it was the tangle of lies she'd got trapped in. The words she hadn't told the court and that now couldn't be said. Was she a dishonest person? Should she even be working in the court if she couldn't tell the truth? She'd raised her hand and taken an oath like any other witness at the start of the trial and yet she'd broken that as if it had meant nothing.

A double decker pulled up on the opposite side of the road and the two buses lined up next to each other. For a moment she stared at a man on the top deck, who looked directly at her. He grinned and licked his lips, then tilted his head to get a better look. As her bus moved on, she turned away.

Why did men do these things to women? Because they had the upper hand? Elsie reckoned all men were animals, but if you thought that then they'd always have an excuse. It was like saying they had no choice in the matter. Her Jimmy wasn't like that.

She took a deep breath and when she exhaled it came out jagged, the anger rising to the top. She'd felt the deep dislike of men all day long, the way the prosecution had spoken to Zina, the looks Eva had received when she translated for her. Even poor Hedy had been discussed in a disparaging way. For going to work and buying nice things. Poor, dead Hedy. She tried not to think about Hedy too much, because if she did she might never be able to look Zina in the eye again.

As the bus juddered and turned a corner, she pictured Jimmy instead, stretched out on the sofa at home, reading or listening to the comedy programmes on the wireless. She had hoped he might come to meet her at the court again, but since that first day when he'd seen her with Bert, he hadn't returned.

She wanted to tell him what Zina had said today, but would he think less of her for not translating everything to the court? What was it Zina had said?

'He told me to kill her. I've held it inside me all these years. He promised he'd stay.' She *had* to be talking about the first killing, in Cyprus. Surely? Because if she wasn't... well... then she was talking about Hedy's murder. And who, wondered Eva, was the man who'd told Zina to kill Hedy? After the police photos and measurements, it was clear she hadn't seen someone on the doorstep that night. Who else could have put her up to it? Michalis? No, that was unthinkable.

Opening her handbag, she took out her Craven 'A's.

'Go on!' whispered a woman behind her.

Suddenly there was a man by her side, offering a light. She looked around and saw that he was one of the noisy group sitting a few rows back.

'May I?' he asked

She accepted.

'My friends and I were wondering, miss...'

As she stared into his face she realised what was about to happen and was determined not to make it easy. She pulled on the cigarette, blew smoke to the side and said nothing.

'Well, it's you, isn't it? From the Old Bailey? The interpreter?'

She didn't say yes or no, but blinked slowly and looked towards the window.

'It *is* her,' he called back, an excited note in his voice. The others came and sat behind her.

'We've been there every day,' he said, sitting down. 'What's she really like? The murderer.'

Eva turned to them, her voice tight as she spat out the words like bullets: 'She's *not* a murderer. She's on trial and is innocent until proven guilty.'

'Well, we know that, but she's obviously done it, right? Surely you think she's done it?'

'Of course she has,' chipped in his friend, a woman in a black furry hat. 'I mean, did you see the way she was fidgeting?'

Eva was silent.

'Can you imagine standing so close to her?' continued the woman. 'I wouldn't do your job for the world.'

'Guilty as sin, I say,' said the man. 'All that playing the innocent, staring around the court.'

'Well.' Eva stood suddenly, making him get up. 'It's just as well *you're* not on the jury then, isn't it?'

Furry-hat woman opened her mouth and pulled back a little.

'Everyone in the gallery was staring around,' said Eva. 'Including you, sitting there gawping.'

She grabbed her bag and knocked his knees as she pushed towards the stairs. Then she turned back: 'Maybe we should hang the bloody lot of you!'

She could hear their laughter chase her as she rushed down the stairs. Taking a seat at the front, as far away from them as possible, she wondered what had happened to her.

Three months ago she didn't even know Zina. Today she'd protected her, lied for her and had almost thumped a complete stranger on her behalf.

And yet, Zina was a stranger too. Who knew what she'd done in that terrible house in Hampstead, just a few miles from Eva's own? Who knew what she'd done years ago in Cyprus?

Despite all the questions she had, there was one thing Eva woke every morning absolutely certain of. Zina had taken Hedy's life; the evidence was just too overwhelming for that not to be true. And she'd killed her in the most brutal, horrific way.

Eva stared down at her gloved hands and wondered how a person lived with themselves after doing something like that. Perhaps it was easier to tell yourself it hadn't happened, and that was why Zina had denied it all along.

She opened her bag, pulled out her compact, fixed her make-up then checked her hair. She didn't understand why she felt such raw pity for the woman. Even when she was working at the Café de Paris, hanging up the velvets and furs of the famous, even then Zina slid into her mind. She'd become her compulsion.

The bus lurched. She knew Garrett's report would make everything alright, so why did she feel sick with worry? Was it because she could do nothing herself? She'd felt this helpless once before, sat next to her mother's hospital bed. It had been years since Eva had stepped inside a church, but now, clasping her hands tightly, she closed her eyes and prayed for Zina.

CHAPTER FORTY-SEVEN

The final day, Old Bailey

As Eva stands in the dock of Court Number One on the final day, she scans the faces in the gallery. She can't see the awful people from the bus the evening before, but they've probably squeezed onto a bench somewhere. They won't want to miss this for anything.

Zina enters and Eva tries to read her mood. Today her shoulders are rounded and her head dipped as if she's being pulled to the earth. A thick strand of hair has escaped from her plait and hangs down the side of her neck. Eva would like to clip it back for her.

The prison transport arrived late this morning, and she hasn't had a chance to speak to her. She'll be found guilty, Eva's sure, but spending the rest of her life in hospital means at least she'll be looked after.

There's a noise in the gallery. She glances up and there, where he's sat every day of the trial, is Dr Garrett. Eva smiles, pleased he's here and ready. He nods down a hello and waves a brown folder. It must be Zina's medical report. Once the jury returns a verdict, if Zina is found guilty, it will be his turn to speak. She knows he's just doing his job – he's done this for dozens of defendants over the years – but right now it feels like Zina has an ally.

There are no further witnesses to call, so both sides give their closing statements, followed by the judge. Their droning voices are interminable, and Eva does her best to summarise for Zina. Why do they have to go through all this again before the jury is sent out to reach a verdict? After all, how many times does a woman have to hear all the things men say she's done? All the things they say she is?

The judge suddenly stops speaking and there's a buzz of excitement running through the gallery. Everyone realises they're near the end of this spectacle. There's some whispering and shuffling above, and he shoots the gallery a warning glance, before addressing the jury:

'You must reach a unanimous decision. But before I send you to reach your verdict, consider this.' He pauses. 'If the defence has shown that there is some reasonable possibility – *not* some figment of the imagination – that Mrs Hedy Pavlou was murdered by someone else, you must find the accused not guilty.'

Eva whispers it all to Zina – it's the least she can do for her now.

'However—' and here he stares along the jury for emphasis '—if there is no reasonable doubt that she did in fact kill her daughter-in-law, it is your duty to find Mrs Zina Pavlou guilty.'

Soon, thinks Eva, they will all see just how unwell Zina is. They will hear the doctor's report and perhaps there will be a little compassion for the woman who's been ridiculed throughout this trial. The jury stands and files out to decide Zina's fate. The chatter in the courtroom is deafening.

CHAPTER FORTY-EIGHT

Zina is expecting a long wait for the verdict; Eva told her it might even be overnight. So she's surprised when after just two hours they're all called back into court.

She sits now in the dock, Eva next to her. The girl's got skinnier, thinks Zina, and it doesn't suit her. At that moment, Eva turns and asks, 'Are you alright?'

Zina wants to hug her, to reassure her, and she can't remember the last time she felt the urge to hug anyone. It must have been Anna.

She's told the truth throughout, she wants to say, and really doesn't know how Hedy died, or what happened that evening all those months ago. She is almost certain she had nothing to do with it.

Now, every sound in the court is amplified, like a wireless turned to ten. She gazes at the dozens of people, all here to see what happens to her. Yesterday she was so tired, had been sick of it all. But today she feels hopeful. How can they lock up a woman like her? Someone who's helped so many people in her life, who does endless chores for others and never complains? That petition from Spakato has over one hundred signatures. They can't ignore that.

She aches to see Anna. Will Michalis let her visit? She heard him say they've moved to a new home. Perhaps she can sew some curtains for him, or if there's a garden she can plant some vegetables. She misses the cool earth on her hands. There may even be a room for her, to stay over occasionally, something small with cheery yellow flowers on the curtains. As long as it isn't damp she doesn't mind.

The jury files in. None of them look at her and a silence sweeps across the court. The judge says something.

'We need to stand,' says Eva.

'Is it now?' Zina asks, getting up.

The officers around her readjust their position so they can reach out and touch her whichever way she turns.

'Yes.'

One member of the jury stands and the judge asks him something.

'In the case of the Queen and Pavlou, have you reached a verdict upon which you are all agreed?' translates Eva into her ear.

'Yes, My Lord, we have.'

'What say you? Is the defendant guilty or not guilty.'

Zina presses her lips together, waiting. Eva went through it all with her, but now that she's mired in this moment that seems to stretch forever, she cannot remember if it's two words or one that means she can go home. She'd learned them but has forgotten; one of them means freedom and the other not. Did Eva say they'd take her to a hospital? Her mind has lost its grip on everything now.

Eva is flushed and staring at the foreman, so Zina stares too. He speaks and a wave of whispers travels the courtroom. Eva turns to face her and Zina shakes her head, to show she hasn't understood, the last in the room to learn her fate.

'Guilty,' says Eva, her mouth trembling. 'They've found you guilty.'

'I will have silence in my court,' says the judge.

Zina wonders how old she will be when they let her out.

Sixty? Seventy? Perhaps they'll never release her? And what about Anna? Will she see her again?

Eva's neck is cold and she holds her own hand to stop it shaking.

Guilty.

Why is she so shocked? She knew in her heart it would be like this. There's no recess. The sentencing hearing has begun straight away – each side will have their say. She takes a breath. *It will be alright*, she tells herself. *The medical report will make it alright.* She glances at Dr Garrett, who's sitting straight-backed, alert, ready. *Any moment now*, thinks Eva.

Stanford is speaking first, giving his reasons why Zina deserves a harsh sentence.

'I urge My Lord to take into account that Mrs Pavlou has shown no remorse or taken any responsibility for her actions.' Murmurs of agreement can be heard in the gallery. 'Her callous, senseless crime has had a devastating impact not only on her son – who's lost his wife – but on his children. Two children who will grow up without the love of a mother, because Zina Pavlou decided to kill her. In the most brutal, horrific way.' He goes on for a while about Zina's evil nature, but Eva doesn't bother whispering any more into Zina's ear.

Finally, he sits and Mr Carrington rises. Eva turns to look at Dr Garrett. He's leaning forward now, ready to spring up when called.

'My Lord,' begins Mr Carrington, 'Mrs Pavlou maintains she's not responsible for this crime, therefore she cannot be remorseful for something she didn't do.'

'Does Mrs Pavlou want to add anything?' asks the judge.

'I want to go back in the witness box,' says Zina. 'Tell them I want to speak.'

Eva translates but the judge refuses, dismissing it with his hand, not even bothering with words.

'We will adjourn for fifteen minutes,' he says, 'then I will pass sentence.'

What?

Eva gasps and turns to the gallery.

The report. What about the report? Why hasn't Carrington asked for the report?

Garrett jumps up.

The judge must *hear Garrett's opinion. That Zina is insane.*

'Excuse me, My Lord!' The doctor's voice is broken, weak. 'There's been an error.' He waves the folder, desperately. Someone near him laughs.

'Dr Garrett, you are not new to this court, are you?' asks the judge.

'No, My Lord, but—'

'Then you know not to interrupt.'

'I do beg your pardon, My Lord, but I have the medical report right here. The defence team need to call me in evidence or submit it to the court.' There's a deadly silence. 'Before you pass sentence, My Lord.'

Eva can hear the blood pumping in her ears.

'Mr Carrington,' says the judge, with a weary sigh. 'Has an error been made? Did you mean to call on this report before we proceed with sentencing?'

Carrington stands. 'No, My Lord,' he says briskly. 'No error. Everything's in order.' Then sits again.

'But,' starts Garrett again, 'I'm always—'

'Sir!' The judge's raised voice makes a clerk jump. Throughout this trial he's never shouted. 'You have heard it from the defence counsel himself. You are not required. Desist or I shall have you removed. We will have a fifteen-minute recess, as I said. Then I will pass sentence.'

Dr Garrett sinks back into his seat, distraught, as people nearby get up and nudge past him. A crack in Eva's chest cleaves wide open.

★ ★ ★

Eva rushes out of the court and runs up the stairs that lead to the public gallery. She scans the crowd. Where is he? She turns and comes back down, stumbling in her hurry. She looks around the heaving foyer, then towards the door of the Gents' lavatories to see if Dr Garrett might be there, but she can't see him anywhere. She stands on the staircase again so she can get a better view and stares at the entrance to the building, in case he's leaving or coming back in from somewhere. Where *is* he? Perhaps he's speaking to the defence team or the judge, trying to fix it.

'Eva!' He grabs her arm.

'Ted! What's happening? Why didn't they call you?'

He runs his hand through his hair.

'I've no idea,' he says as they rush towards the court doors. 'It doesn't make sense. I'll protest it – I'll do what I can.'

'But it'll be too late,' she says.

'I know.'

'You said they'd call you.'

'I know.' His face is crumpled, his confidence dust.

An usher announces that the court will now reconvene.

'They're sentencing her *now*, Ted,' Eva says. 'Right now. *Do something.*'

Zina twists a handkerchief and gazes around the court for the last time as it fills up. It'll be over soon, she thinks. Whatever her punishment, she will take it. She always has. Her life will now be spent locked away, waiting for the years to pass. Fleetingly, she thinks of Anna, then pushes the image away. When she's by herself at night she'll allow it, but now she must be composed. She cannot weep in front of them. She won't show them her sorrow.

The judge is speaking and the girl is translating, though Zina stopped listening a while ago. Then he stops talking and she swallows hard and watches for a clue as to what might happen next.

A man approaches the judge and she hears a gasp. What? Why are people whispering? What's that in his hands? The man holds something out, lifts it and she sees it's a square of black cloth. He gently places it on top of the judge's wig, letting one of the corners hang over the front.

Eva grasps the side of the dock to steady herself. She watches a court official adjust the black cap on the judge's head. She can see Zina out of the corner of her eye, looking from her to the judge and back again, waiting to hear what's been said.

His voice is solemn and he's speaking slowly, allowing Eva time to translate every phrase. She chooses to summarise. She speaks the Greek words gently, less formally than the judge does, tells Zina only what she needs to know for now, revealing the details as softly as she can.

'They've found you guilty of murder,' she explains. 'You'll go back to the prison and, after a while, to a place of execution where... where you'll be hanged.'

Zina's face blanches and she says nothing.

'I'm so sorry, Zina.'

Eva doesn't translate 'from the neck until you're dead' or that she'll be buried in the prison grounds. That can wait. But she does repeat the final line that the judge utters: 'May the Lord have mercy on your soul. Amen.'

Eva is devastated. The woman is insane, Dr Garrett said so. The medical report would have saved her.

The judge gets up, everyone rises and he leaves the court. Eva waits for Zina's reaction, but there are no tears, no shouts. There's just an emptiness behind her eyes that's heartbreaking.

A warden puts her hand on Zina's shoulder and Eva watches as she begins her descent to the cells.

A voice from the gallery yells, 'You murdering bitch!' And there's an almighty cheer, as others join in with laughs and claps.

Zina glances up, places a handkerchief to her lips and walks down to the basement.

Twenty minutes later, Eva is still in the dock as she looks onto the empty court. She hears the door swing open and Dr Garrett bursts in.

'You're here!' he gasps. 'I've been outside looking for you.'

'What just happened, Ted?' The anger is making her head fizz. 'Why didn't they call you?'

He leans against the dock and catches his breath, the tatty manila folder in his hand.

'It's highly irregular,' he says. 'But I just collared Carrington and he insists Pavlou wouldn't let them use it.'

'Well, of course not,' says Eva, 'because she thinks she's sane! So they just left it at that? Because they didn't want to make the effort?'

He shrugs. 'I do think the defence put on a poor show,' he says. 'They called no witnesses. As if it were a foregone conclusion.'

A wet shiver runs down her back.

'As if they'd given up before they'd even begun,' she says.

Could they know about the previous case? Even if they did, they'd want to defend her, surely, if only as a matter of professional pride? To win the case? She folds her arms and stares at him, this man who she'd pinned all her hopes on. Zina's hopes.

'You have to fix it,' she says. 'You have to *make* it right.'

He gives an incredulous laugh.

'I almost got thrown out of court trying to make it right. The judge passed sentence, you heard him. I can't turn back time.'

'Well what *can* you do?' She leans towards him. 'What can you do to save her from the gallows? Because it seems to me that we relied on you and this report and now – what? We give up?'

He baulks at her outburst and his face hardens.

'Look, didn't I tell you not to get attached?' he says, coldly.

'But you said they never hang women at Holloway. That they hadn't done that in – what – thirty years?'

'And they haven't. But it seems for Mrs Pavlou they're going to make an exception.'

Eva shakes her head. 'There has to be something you can do. She's insane – you said so yourself. Lock her up in hospital, yes. Or even a prison. But hanging? It's too cruel.'

'I know,' he says quietly.

Then he lets out a sigh and explains what he will do as soon as he leaves the court. It's the only thing he can do now.

CHAPTER FORTY-NINE

Holloway Prison
29 October 1954
Reg. No: 7145 (Zina Pavlou), age 53
Central Criminal Court, 25 / 29.10.54
<u>Murder. Sentenced to death</u>
<u>After Trial Report</u>

To the Governor:

I beg to report that I have attended the five-day trial of the above named woman at the Central Criminal Court.

Please note that I was not called in evidence. I had written an extensive medical report, as you know, on Pavlou's physical and mental health but this was not referred to once.

In fact, the defence informed me that – taking Rex v. Ley *as precedent – as I had passed this woman fit to plead, he would take instructions from her. Pavlou's instructions were that he should not proceed on the grounds of insanity.*

This means that all medical evidence was ignored and she was therefore defended in the ordinary way. <u>The question of her mental state was not at any time raised at the trial.</u>

I beg to note that since my report was written, following further extensive observation, reading the translator's reports of her behaviour and the reports of the prison officers whose care she was under, and bearing in mind her appearance at the trial, my opinion regarding her remains unchanged.

As detailed in my report to the court, it is my professional opinion that Pavlou without doubt suffers mental delusions and is insane. Therefore I strongly recommend she should not be sentenced to death but sent to an institution, where she can be cared for.

With respect, I feel I need to insist that a Statutory Inquiry be held in this case, and that she be examined by three other doctors as is usual procedure in these matters. It's my opinion that this is a matter of great urgency.

Signed
Dr Edward Garrett
Principal Medical Officer

CHAPTER FIFTY

As Eva made her way home, she pictured Zina returning to Holloway, but this time to the condemned cell. She wished she could have gone with her, but she'd visit her first thing.

It was only three in the afternoon as she stepped off the bus, but the light was already fading. She wandered back, imagining the long afternoon and evening ahead.

Hours spent in that flat, sitting alone, her mind spiralling as she reflected on Zina's sentence, with nobody to talk to as Jimmy was working late. She considered stopping in her tracks, jumping on another bus and going into town. Anything to avoid being by herself. But she was exhausted.

She turned into her road. The newspaper vendor was packing up his kiosk, and fluttering under the grille where the front page was displayed were the headlines from earlier that day: *Grandmother Accused of Murder, Verdict Today*. Tomorrow the headlines would scream out Zina's sentence. A grandmother, convicted of murder and sentenced to hang.

Pushing her key into the flat door, she tried to unlock the latch but it wouldn't move. She tried again – nothing. She turned the other way and it slipped open. Jimmy had forgotten to lock up. That was unlike him. She wouldn't mention it; there'd been such an atmosphere between them lately, it would only make it worse.

She closed the door behind her and jumped as she saw him rush in from the bedroom, concern on his face.

'You're home!' she said, relief flooding through her. She wouldn't have to sit with her thoughts after all. 'Did you hear?'

He nodded and walked towards her. 'It was on the wireless. I told Carlo I needed to leave early.'

He hugged her, and she put her arms around him too. Despite everything, here he was at precisely the right moment.

'I'm so sorry,' he said, into her hair. 'Are you alright?'

'They're going to hang her, Jimmy. They didn't even look at the doctor's report. It would have saved her. They would have seen she's not well.'

He held her at arm's length and looked her square in the face.

'You did everything you could,' he said. 'Come on, let's have a drink. Tea, or something stronger?'

She slumped into the armchair.

'Tea,' she said. 'If I have a proper drink now that'll be the end of me.'

He boiled the kettle, filled the pot and brought the tea things on a tray to the table, along with a plate of biscuits.

'Thanks,' she said.

'That's alright.' He handed her the shortbread. 'They're from work. A day old, but still good.'

'I mean for coming home.' She took a biscuit and bit into it, letting the sugar dance on her tongue. He sat next to her and neither of them spoke for a while.

'She loves sweet things,' she said. 'The first day I met her she asked me for biscuits.'

He squeezed her hand.

'What happens now?' he asked.

'The defence will appeal, but I don't know what her chances are. I just saw her doctor – he's asking for a statutory inquiry.'

He stirred the pot. 'What does that do?'

'Three doctors examine her to see if she's sane. Psychiatrists.'

He looked up.

'Well, that's good, isn't it?' His voice was hopeful. 'I mean, from what you've said any doctor would see she's not all there.'

Eva shrugged.

'I don't know. They seem to hate her. I mean what she *did* was hateful and shocking, but they really seem to loathe her. The doctor said it was as if they'd already decided on the sentence.'

He motioned to the newspaper that was on the chair. He'd underlined some of the words and had a dictionary on the floor.

'I've been reading about it,' he said. 'The way they spoke about her, saying it was a "stupid crime by a stupid woman".'

She nodded. 'And the fact she doesn't speak English... they mentioned it time and again – as if that's a crime in itself.'

He poured her a cup of tea.

'Maybe it is,' he said. 'They say they want us to come here but they don't really want *us* with our food and our language and our ideas. They just want obedient workers. People who'll try to be English, who want to *be* like them.'

'But I've never felt like that here,' she said, picking up her cup. 'Have you?'

He nodded. 'Sometimes. When a supplier speaks quickly on the phone, or I have to ask a customer to repeat an order. I can sense their impatience. It's as if they're tolerating me, but it wouldn't take much for them to turn.'

'What?'

'You know, change their minds, tell us we can't be here after all.'

'Zina said something like that,' said Eva.

'Really?'

'We were talking before the trial and she said, "They hate you too – don't be fooled. Just because you sound like them and look like them doesn't mean you really belong."'

'And yet look at us,' said Jimmy. 'Drinking *chai*, trying to fit in.'

She smiled.

'What about the appeal?' he asked. 'When will you know?'

'It could take a month – and in the meantime she's waiting to find out if she's going to be hanged. Can you imagine?'

He shook his head. 'I can't.'

Eva got up and walked to the window. She looked outside.

'I can't help feeling I should have done something else,' she said. 'Did I miss something? Should I have done more?'

'Don't be daft, Evie. You did so much. She was lucky to have you.'

She turned around.

'I want to keeping visiting her, now it's so near the end.'

She'd hardly been home the past few months, but she couldn't abandon Zina now.

'Of course,' he said. 'Just cut back on the Café de P. Don't run yourself ragged. We'll manage.'

She turned back to the window and stared outside. Would she tell him? The words whined like agitated wasps in her throat. But if she parted her lips and let them escape, what would he think of her?

'There's something else,' she blurted.

'What?'

She hesitated.

'You'll think I'm terrible. I didn't plan it.'

He came and stood next to her, then took her arm, making her face him.

'I'd never think you're terrible. What is it?'

She'd confided so easily in Bert all those weeks ago, and all the time Jimmy had been here, ready to listen. Perhaps he'd always been on her side and she just hadn't noticed.

'Zina said something in court yesterday. I didn't translate it and I… I just feel awful.'

'Go on.'

'If there'd been anyone there who'd understood Greek… Well, I'd be prosecuted, I'm sure.'

'Evie, just tell me.'

She swallowed hard.

'When they were questioning her about Hedy, she said, "He told me to kill her. I've held it inside me all these years." Something about him "promising to stay".'

'What? Did she say who?'

'For a moment I thought she meant her son, Michalis, told her to kill Hedy. But that doesn't make sense. She said it was years ago.'

'So it's the thing she spoke about before? In Cyprus? When she was tried for murder?'

'I think so. And I didn't translate any of it. I just sort of brushed it aside and made out she'd said something else. I can't believe I did that in court.'

'Look.' He tried to bring her towards him but she pulled away. 'Will you look at me?' So she did.

'Listen. You were shocked, that's why you didn't say anything. And whatever it is, whatever happened, it doesn't matter now. It was years ago, like she said.'

'I know, but—'

'No, look. They've sentenced her to hang, for heaven's sake. They can't do any more to her.'

She could feel her throat tensing. 'But I took an oath that I'd translate it all.'

He took her hand. 'Worse things have happened in that courtroom. You said it yourself they were against her from the start. It would have been even more ammunition for them. You're a good person, Evie. You've done all you can. Don't be so hard on yourself. You have to forget it now.'

'Alright,' she said. 'I'll try.'

And she attempted a smile, but her mind was scrambling, wondering if there was anything she'd missed. If there was anything else she could do to save Zina.

CHAPTER FIFTY-ONE

Urgent minutes to Head Office
HM PRISON HOLLOWAY

13 November 1954

SUBJECT
CAPITAL CASE
7145 Zina PAVLOU
Criminal Central Court 29.10.54

Charge: Murder
Sentence: Death

I beg to forward herewith a copy of the petition received
from the acquaintances in Cyprus of the above-mentioned
woman, asking that she be spared.

Two copies have been sent to the Home Office by hand
this day.

The Governor
Holloway Prison

* * *

To: His Excellency, the Minister of State, London

From: Limassol, Cyprus

1 November 1954

Your Excellency

We the undersigned, priests, dignitaries and esteemed members of the community of Spakato, Limassol, wish to beg Your Excellency to recommend that the life of Zina Pavlou is spared.

She was condemned to death in London and she is kept in Holloway Prison No 7145.

When we knew her she was a woman of good character. We trust that, moved by your philanthropic feelings, you will consider her case favourably.

We remain Your Excellency's Obedient Servants

Thirty-seven signatures follow

CHAPTER FIFTY-TWO

Holloway Prison, condemned cell

It's mid-November, two weeks after her sentencing, and Zina has finally had word that Michalis is visiting. She has dressed early, taking particular care with her hair. She stares into the tiny mirror they've given her and tries to pat it flat with her damp hand. She's always liked her hair – thick, black, it's obedient enough to tie back quickly, and in her younger, happier days she'd let it hang loose when she wasn't picking fruit in the orchards. But since coming to this damp place, her hair has turned wiry, and wisps now stand away from her scalp, painting a halo of darkness around her face. She pats it again. It will have to do.

After the trial, they brought her to a different cell where two female wardens stay with her, day and night. It's bigger here, with a large table, chairs and a corner for the bed that feels more private. There's a proper lavatory in a room next door, along with a basin. They never turn off the light, even at night, but have given her a dark cloth which she uses to cover her eyes. The women come and go, swapping over twice a day, and they watch her more carefully now.

The rules say she's to wear a prison uniform now she's been convicted, but the governor sent word with Eva that she makes a special case occasionally, and she thought Zina might like to continue wearing her own clothes. These glimmers of kindness that seep out of dark places make everything harder.

The only prison clothing she wears is the short cape that every inmate is given when they step outdoors. The daily walks still take place, but now it's just her and the two wardens. They pass her the cape and she slips it over her shoulders and ties it at her neck as they set off for an hour. She never sees any of the other prisoners; the path they take is in a separate part of the grounds.

When the time for her visit arrives, they take her to a room along the corridor where there's a table and two chairs. She sits and the officers stand. After a few minutes the door opens and the girl walks in.

'What are you doing here?' Zina asks, standing up and looking behind Eva. 'Where's Michalis?'

'I'm sorry,' she says. 'He hasn't turned up.'

'Perhaps he's late?' says Zina.

'No. He rang to say he'd changed his mind. I'm so sorry, Zina. I wanted to tell you myself.'

She's been a fool to think he'd come. She grabs the chair and sits down again.

Eva's face is red. 'I can stay for a while,' she says. 'I can be your visitor if you like.' She takes a seat. 'I don't know why—'

Zina puts her hand up to stop her words. 'He's betrayed me, that's why, and can't face me. The things he said in court. Why would he come now?' She puts her hand in her pocket and pulls out her cigarettes. The warden comes over and lights one for her, and points to the metal ashtray that's on the table. She takes a long drag, exhales and stares at the wall.

'He was always a cowardly child. When I leave this place I'll deal with him then.'

Eva shifts in her seat and coughs.

'You don't think I'll get out?' Zina asks.

It seems the girl wasn't expecting such a direct question. 'Well, the appeal should come through soon,' Eva says. 'Any day now.'

Zina nods. 'Yes, the appeal. When they see it's been just one lie on top of another,' she flicks ash to the floor, 'then they'll let me go. They have to. Like they did before.'

'When?' asks Eva.

'In Cyprus.'

Eva takes a breath and her voice quivers.

'Zina?'

'Hmmm?'

'What happened before? In Cyprus?'

Zina shakes her head. 'No, they'll tell them,' she says, her eyes glancing at the wardens.

'But neither of them speak Greek,' says Eva. 'And I'm writing up these visits but they're not going to know what we really said.'

'No. They'll use my words against me, like they did in court. I won't speak of it.'

Zina sits back for a moment, but then leans forward and whispers, 'You know, Michalis told the police everything on the first night, before you arrived. He told them all about it.' She reaches towards the ashtray and taps her ciggie inside. 'Why do you think they were all against me from the start?'

Eva frowns.

'I don't understand,' she says. '*What* did he tell them?'

Zina presses her lips together.

'Look,' the girl continues, 'there was nothing like that in his statement to the police, the night it happened. He didn't say anything.'

Zina can feel her temper rise. 'I was there, I know what happened.'

'I don't know what you're talking about,' Eva says, 'but they didn't say anything in court, either, about any other case. I don't think they're allowed to. It wouldn't be fair.'

Zina jumps up and the chair crashes to the floor. 'You're not listening to me!'

Both wardens' hands are on her in a flash.

'Sit down or the visit's over!' shouts one, pressing her into the chair. Zina's lip curls but she does as she's told.

There's a silence, then she leans towards Eva. '*They knew.*

Just because it's not written down doesn't mean it didn't happen. That night he fed the police lies about me and they ate them up.'

Eva frowns as if trying to make head or tail of the beast.

'Your problem,' says Zina, impatiently, 'is that you think everyone's as honest as you are.'

'But *what* did he tell them, Zina? What happened all those years ago? And what's it got to do with this – this thing you're accused of now?'

Zina hesitates and considers telling her about the promises made and broken in that dusty barn. 'I can't speak of it,' she says.

'I wish you would. Maybe I can help.'

Zina glares down. 'First my husband betrays me, then my son.' She picks up the cigarette from the floor where it's fallen and smiles to herself. 'I write letters every day, and my children in Cyprus sit and read them and do nothing. And yet,' she looks up at Eva, 'and yet you're a stranger and you care. I should have had a daughter like you.'

Eva looks like she's going to cry. What's the matter with the girl?

'You really won't tell me?' she asks.

Zina glances away. 'If you knew, you'd turn against me too,' she says.

They sit in silence for a while, then Eva asks, 'Well, what can I do for you? Is there anything you need? I'm seeing the governor later.'

'Biscuits,' says Zina. 'There's nothing sweet here. And all of my clothes. Bring them or he'll probably sell them or put a match to them. They're mine. I paid for them. They've only given me a few of my things.'

Eva nods, takes out a notebook and writes something down.

'And my book,' Zina says.

'Sorry?'

'There was a book, under my pillow in the other cell. I need it.'

Zina can see that she wants to say something but stops herself.

'It's just pictures,' she explains. 'They gave it to me when I arrived and I like it. I need it.'

'Oh, alright.'

'You'll get it back for me?'

'I'll try.'

'They might be angry – I've had it a long time, but I've taken care,' she says. 'I always wipe my hands before looking at it, and there's a tear on the back page, but you tell them that wasn't me.'

Eva nods and writes again.

'Time's up,' says a warden and comes towards Zina. 'Let's go.'

Zina stands and without saying goodbye walks to the door.

'Zina?' Eva says.

'Yes?'

'Do you mind if I carry on coming every day?'

She shrugs.

'I'll ask about your clothes,' says Eva.

'The book,' says Zina, pointing at her. 'Don't forget.'

CHAPTER FIFTY-THREE

The following day, Eva arrived with something in her bag.

'Is it my book?' Zina asked, as she peered inside.

'Not yet. I've put a request in with the governor. But it *is* a book.'

She pulled out a small hardback. It had a yellowing cover and Greek writing on the front, and the picture was of a girl in a blue checked dress by a stream, looking at a hare next to her.

'What's this?' said Zina, sitting down. 'This isn't what I asked for.'

'It's called *Little House on the Prairie*. It's translated into Greek – about a girl who lives on a farm with her family. It's about their adventures and hardships.'

Zina took the book in her hand and turned it over, examining it like a piece of fruit at market.

'I thought you might like it,' said Eva, 'what with you growing up on a farm too. I could read it to you.'

Zina put the book on the table and looked up at her. 'Really? What for?'

Eva laughed. 'Well, to pass the time. Books help you escape... I mean...' She stumbled, kicking herself for her choice of words.

'Is this book yours?' Zina asked, carefully touching the cover.

'No, it's from Camden Library.'

'You stole it?'

'I borrowed it,' Eva explained, 'the way you did your book, the one you're waiting for. When I've read it I'll return it and get something else.'

'How do they know you'll take it back?'

She'd never thought of that. 'Well, I suppose they trust me. It's meant to be a very good story.'

'Does it have pictures?'

'Some, look.' She opened the book and flicked through till she found a sketch of a girl on a horse, all muted yellows and greens. 'It's set in America – based on a true story. The writer had a hard rural life. Fighting nature, poverty...'

'Like me.'

'Maybe. Shall I begin?

Zina sat on her bed, pulled her legs up to her chest and nodded. 'Let's hear it.'

Eva brought the chair closer, cleared her throat and began: '*A long time ago...*' As she started the story about Laura, her sister Mary, Ma and Pa, and their adventures in the American Midwest, Zina closed her eyes and rested her head on her knees. Occasionally she'd look up and ask for an explanation or she'd glance at Eva and smile at a phrase, but mostly she sat very still.

And so began their reading sessions. Every day, as they delved into the world between the pages, Zina became increasingly absorbed. Within a few days they'd finished the first book, and Eva went to the library and borrowed the next one in the series. When she showed her the new cover, Zina gave a little clap. Then she settled down with her tea and cigarette.

'Let's see what's happening to those unlucky fools now,' she said, laughing.

Eva laughed too. She's happy, she thought, even for these few hours every day she's genuinely happy. And while she was here, so was Eva. Together they tumbled into the story, and Hedy and Michalis and what had happened that night at 71 Cedar Hill fell away.

But once Eva walked out of Zina's cell, down the tiled corridors and through those prison gates, she was overwhelmed with the enormity of what lay ahead. There was the appeal, of course. There was always a *chance* it would go Zina's way, but in her heart she knew that was very unlikely. And even as she rushed to her shift at the Café de Paris, she could feel her grief steadily rising inch by inch and, like a ship taking on water, the outcome was inevitable. The grief wasn't just for Zina.

Reading out loud resurrected the memories Eva had buried long ago. Once, when she was eight, maybe nine, she'd woken from a nightmare and couldn't get back to sleep. Her mother had sat by her bed and read aloud the only book she had to hand, an old notebook full of recipes.

'Listen to this, Eva. It sounds delicious. *Take a cup of sugar, two fresh eggs…*' Her memory of the words had faded long ago but she could still hear the lull of her mother's voice as she turned those pages, and Eva fought against the pull of sleep.

Zina didn't often speak about the appeal, so Eva didn't mention it either, although she wanted to many times. She wanted to be sure that Zina was prepared, but how do you prepare a woman for her own hanging?

Over the weeks, as the pages became chapters and the chapters became books, Eva realised that she loved reading aloud as much as Zina did listening.

'Would you like some Greek stories?' she asked one day. 'There's a bookshop I know, in Soho. They have books from Cyprus, Greece too. I could easily get you something. Greek stories about home.'

Zina blew cigarette smoke out of the side of her mouth. 'What for? No. I've had enough of home.'

'Oh.' Eva was surprised.

Zina shuffled down the bed. 'I like these ones about adventure. Different worlds. Home is always in my head.'

'Of course,' said Eva. What was she thinking? Why would she want reminding of a place where nobody cared?

She turned the page. 'Alright then,' Eva said, settling down. 'Let's catch up with these fools, shall we?'

Zina nodded. 'And I figured it out,' she said.

'What?'

'Who Nellie Oleson reminds me of.'

Nellie was the vain girl in the *Prairie* books; the heroine's nemesis.

'Really?' asked Eva. 'Who?'

'*Her*,' she said, leaning in. 'With her fancy clothes and her curls and the way she thinks she's better than everyone.'

Eva didn't speak.

'*Hedy*,' Zina whispered. 'It's her.'

CHAPTER FIFTY-FOUR

Eva opened her eyes and watched Jimmy as he picked up her skirt from the floor, put it on a hanger and hooked it around the handle of the wardrobe. Then he took the whisky glass he'd left on the bedside table and walked to the kitchen. She could hear him washing the dishes.

Yesterday, she'd grabbed her uniform in the morning and gone straight to work at the Café de Paris. She'd forgotten to tell him she wasn't coming home first.

When she'd finally got back after midnight they'd argued about why she was still working there if Holloway was taking up so much time.

'We can always use the extra money…' she'd begun, but even as she said it, she knew that wasn't the point.

'Imagine if I didn't come home,' he asked. 'If I just didn't turn up and you were here worrying.'

She flopped into the armchair. 'For heaven's sake, Jimmy. You know if I'm not here or at Holloway I'm at the Café. Where else would I be?'

He shrugged. 'I don't know,' he said. 'I have no idea.'

The past few days it had felt like something had lifted between them, and here she was dragging everything down again. She slipped out of bed, put on her robe and walked into the kitchen.

'Good morning,' she said. He glanced up but didn't speak. 'Can we make up? I'm sorry.'

He shook his head.

'It's me, I was being stupid,' he said. 'I was excited because I had something to tell you, then you weren't here and, well.' He put his hands on her shoulders. 'Oh, my hands are wet.'

She didn't pull away. 'So we're friends again?'

'More than that, I hope.' He smiled.

'I'm really sorry – of course I should have said that I wasn't coming home first.'

He picked up the tea towel.

'So, what did you want to tell me?' she asked.

'It's Carlo at work,' he said, drying between his fingers. 'He wants to try a whole new range. He's asked me to come up with some recipes.'

'Really?'

He nodded. 'He wants everything from breads to cakes and biscuits.'

'And you kept that to *yourself*? Jimmy, that's wonderful news!' She felt a surge of pride. 'It's what you wanted, isn't it? Getting more involved in that side of things.'

He hooked the tea towel back on the cupboard and grinned. 'He liked my ideas – for making Greek and Italian biscuits. I'm doing some testers today.'

She took his hands.

'I'm so pleased,' she said. 'You deserve this. Who knows, he's not far off retirement – maybe he wants you to take over eventually.'

'One step at a time. I need to show him I can do this first. And if I improve my English, it can only help.'

'You've worked so hard there. You'll be a huge success. People will be coming to Soho from all over London for your biscuits.'

He laughed, then his smile dropped.

'So have you heard anything about the appeal?'

'No, but any day now, I think. It's been almost a month.'

'Look, I know it's probably the last thing you feel like doing, but I thought maybe we could have a few drinks later? Remember the one o'clock club? To celebrate my new job?'

It was the least she could do after last night.

'That's a wonderful idea.' She grabbed her wash things and glanced at the time. 'I'm not at the Café this evening. I'll be back around six. Let's make it dinner, too.'

He leaned in. She didn't offer her cheek like she usually did. He hesitated, then kissed her on the lips.

'And a dance?' he asked, gesturing with the sweep of his arm to the gramophone in the corner. 'We haven't had a Friday dance for ages.'

Her heart lifted at the expectation in his eyes. She'd missed having his arms around her as they swayed to and fro in their tiny flat.

'A Friday dance?' she asked, in mock horror. 'On a Wednesday?'

He kissed her again, taking his time with it. 'I'll get some gin in, you pick up the fish and chips?'

'Lovely.'

Eva walked to Zina's cell, a box of her clothes in her arms. A warden accompanied her and opened and closed the gates as they wound their way through the prison.

'Condemned cells are always the worst,' said the warden. 'They give me the willies.'

Eva didn't reply.

'You know they had to call extra wardens in from Manchester. We didn't have enough here,' she continued. Then she stopped and ran her fingers through the keys, finding the right one. 'If you ask me,' she said, 'it's because nobody wants the job.'

They carried on down the corridor, Eva's heels click-clacking all the way.

'Some of the women get to know them well – the condemned prisoners, that is,' the warden said.

'They spend so much time with them,' said Eva, wishing she would stop talking.

'Well not this one,' said the warden. 'She doesn't speak a word. Can you imagine being shut up with her all day long?'

Eva wanted to chastise her, make her feel ashamed. But where to begin? If she started, she'd never stop.

'Here we are.'

The door clanked open and Eva walked in.

One of the wardens was puzzling over a crossword in the newspaper and the other was standing by the wall.

Zina was lying on her bed.

'I have permission to give the prisoner her belongings,' said Eva, showing them the box with the form on top. Before they'd said yes, Zina stood and started rifling through the box.

'Hello, Zina.'

She nodded and took out the items one by one, laying them neatly on the bed as they all watched. A bottle-green skirt. A navy-blue short-sleeved blouse. Some undergarments that looked like they'd seen better days. A long nightdress with sprigs of lilac flowers around the edges. And a pair of men's slippers that she immediately pushed her feet into.

The door opened again and the governor stood on the threshold.

'Hello, Mrs Georgiou. They said you'd arrived. Can I speak to you a moment?'

Zina hadn't looked up, she was rearranging the items on the bed as Eva stepped out into the corridor. The door locked behind them again.

The governor was clutching a brown envelope. 'Let's do this here,' she said. 'No point going back to my office.'

No, not like this.

'I'm afraid her appeal has been dismissed.'

Eva felt her legs jolt and she pressed firmly into her shoes to steady herself.

'But... but that's not possible,' she said. 'Doesn't she have to be present? Surely I'd be called, too?'

'No, not necessarily. Are you alright?'

'Yes – but how can it all happen without her even there?'

'They decided not to call her up. It's not uncommon. They said she wasn't needed. Apparently they only took four minutes to decide.'

'But why? Is that allowed?'

'Of course,' said the governor. 'If they think the case is cut and dried. She appealed against her conviction – insisting she was innocent – and I think we all knew she wouldn't receive an acquittal.'

'That's it then? There's nothing else that can be done?'

The governor gave Eva a long, hard stare.

'I did tell you not to get attached, didn't I?' she said. 'There's still the medical inquiry. Three doctors will examine her and check her mental health. But the appeal isn't upheld.'

And all so matter-of-fact. Eva closed her eyes and tried to gather her thoughts.

'Mrs Georgiou.' The governor's voice had an edge of impatience now. 'Are you alright?'

'Yes... yes, of course.'

'Come on, you need to translate for me. I need to be sure she understands.'

Inside the cell, Zina had piled all her belongings into a corner of her bed and was staring at them.

'Mrs Pavlou,' began the governor, not bothering to sit down. 'Do you remember me? I'm the governor. I'm in charge of this prison.'

Eva swallowed hard and translated, her voice rough.

'I know you,' said Zina.

'It's my painful duty to tell you that your appeal has been dismissed.'

Eva spoke the words and Zina frowned.

'What does that mean?' she asked her.

Eva looked at the governor, at a loss. 'She asks what that means. What shall I say?'

'It means,' said the governor, 'that her sentence of the death penalty stands, and the date for her execution is now 14th December.' She paused and nodded to Eva, who repeated the words. Zina tilted her head to one side.

'Tell her about the statutory inquiry. That three doctors will examine her. If they recommend it, she may still be granted a commuted sentence, so instead of execution she spends her time in an institution.'

Eva considered her words carefully, the responsibility of getting it just right weighing heavily.

'Doctors?' said Zina. 'I'm not ill.'

'They'll decide,' said Eva. 'It's a chance – you never know.'

'Do you need anything?' said the governor. 'Tell her I'll do my best if there's something she wants.'

Eva explained and Zina replied, getting agitated.

'What is it?'

'She wants to see the Greek priest,' said Eva. 'And she wants to see her son. She's insisting on it.'

'I can do one,' said the governor. 'The other I'll have to leave to you. I've written to him three times but no response. Perhaps now he knows there's very little chance of a change in sentence he may relent.'

Then she leaned in towards Zina and said in a loud voice, slowly, as though addressing a toddler, 'Don't give up hope, Mrs Pavlou. You must stay strong.'

Zina stared at her with thunder in her eyes.

'Oh, I almost forgot.' The governor opened the envelope and pulled out some tatty cardboard. 'Your book.'

Zina snatched it from her hands and walked to the bed. Sitting down, she turned her back on them and started to pore over the pages.

CHAPTER FIFTY-FIVE

It was after seven o'clock that evening when Eva finally walked past the turrets of Holloway Prison and out of the gates. Zina hadn't wanted her to leave, and she'd filled her day with translating several letters to her children in Cyprus, telling them that her appeal had failed. In the past few weeks, the tone in her letters had changed; rather than repeatedly proclaiming her innocence, she'd taken to reminding them of everything she'd done for them as she criticised their abandonment.

Eva boarded the number 29 to Camden, determined to try Michalis one final time. The governor had given her his new address and, as the traffic stuttered along Parkway, Eva stared out of the window. The Christmas lights had been left on in a toyshop across the road. Would Christmas really come around again as if nothing had changed? Last year still felt so close. She'd spent the day crying. On Christmas Eve, at half-past six in the morning, she'd woken to a sticky, wet puddle between her thighs. She'd sat up and stared as the red bloom spread out on the white sheet. Her crying had woken Jimmy.

She'd stayed in bed for weeks after that, and then for months her grief had threatened to drown her. But slowly she had lifted her head out of the water. Zina had helped with that; her case, the translations, the court appearances – it had been exhausting and yet she'd gained a strange energy from it too. What would happen once Zina had gone? Would she grieve for her too, knowing what she'd done?

She stepped off the bus and walked towards the Victorian tenement block. As she made her way, she suddenly remembered that she'd dreamed of her mother last night – not the usual bedside visions of her shrinking before her, but a laughing, chatty woman she didn't recognise but knew to be her, straightening the seams on her stockings as she dressed for an evening out.

Taking the steps quickly, Eva trotted up the winding brick staircase, round and round until she reached the fifth floor. She caught her breath, and as she exhaled, a vapour hung in the frosty night air. The scrap of paper in her hand said she needed number 53. She walked down the long corridor, and a warm glow seeped from behind several curtains. From one house she could hear a television blaring.

Here it was. A scruffy red door, no Christmas lights, no sounds coming from inside. But there was a light on in the hallway. She knocked three times and waited. She was about to raise her hand again when the door swung open and an olive-skinned girl with long black hair stood before her.

'Hello,' said the girl. 'Who are you?'

Eva stuttered. The resemblance was uncanny.

'I'm – I'm Eva… Is your daddy home?'

Michalis called down the hallway. 'Anna, I've told you – don't open the door unless I'm here.' Then to Eva, 'What are you doing here? How did you know where to find me?'

'The…' She glanced at the girl, who was staring at her, and continued in Greek. 'The governor told me. I just need a few minutes, if that's alright?'

He nodded and showed her through, Anna close behind him.

'I'd offer you something,' he said, walking her into the living room, 'but I've run out of coffee.'

He gestured to a seat and she sat down.

'I won't stay long.'

He turned to Anna.

'Can you go to your room, love?' he said in English. 'Daddy won't be long.'

She nodded then said to Eva, 'My mummy died.'

Eva's mouth dropped open.

'Did you know my mummy?'

'No, no, I didn't. But I heard she was a lovely person.'

Anna turned and walked out, then Michalis got up and closed the door behind her.

'She thinks Hedy had an accident,' he explained, switching back to Greek. 'In the kitchen. I can't tell her the truth... she'll hear about it soon enough.'

Eva hadn't even thought about that. How do you tell a child what had happened that night, while they were sleeping upstairs?

'I've not brought a newspaper home...' His voice tapered off and he wandered to the sideboard. 'She keeps asking after her grandmother.'

'What have you said?'

'That she's gone away. Won't be coming back. Brandy?'

She hesitated. 'Alright.' It had been a long day.

He poured the amber liquid into two tumblers and handed one to her, then perched on the side of the armchair.

'I have some news,' she began. 'The governor asked me to—'

'Her appeal's been dismissed. I know.'

'Oh.'

'Sergeant Parks rang and told me this morning,' he said. 'Thought I'd want to know before the papers get hold of it.'

'Of course.' She took a swig and the warmth of the brandy burned its way down her throat.

'Sorry,' he said. 'You've had a wasted journey if that's what you're here for.'

'I know you had second thoughts the other day – about coming. She was expecting you.'

He shrugged.

'Well...' she continued, 'I thought I'd come to see if you'd visit her now... now there's...'

'Now there's no hope?' he asked.

Eva turned the tumbler in her hands.

'There's still an inquiry to come,' she said. 'Three doctors will examine her to decide if her sentence should be changed.'

'Yes, I heard about that,' he said. He knocked back his brandy, got up for another and showed her the bottle. She declined. 'So what are they looking for?' he asked. 'Are they trying to decide – what did they say in the papers – if she's mad or just bad?'

He slumped back in the chair. She watched as he took a large gulp then coughed, his eyes watering. He rubbed at them with the back of his hands.

'Well, she's both,' he said. Then his voice broke. 'It's Hedy's birthday tomorrow. She's thirty-eight. Even when I dream about her, I know it's not real. I know when I wake she'll still be gone.'

She recognised that feeling. Those awful dreams in which the person you're aching to see again is *right there*, and yet in that very same moment you know they've left you forever.

There was a sound in the hall and he shot up and went to the door. Eva could hear him talking to Anna and her door closing again. Had she been listening?

'Look, I won't keep you,' she said, when he came back in, 'but I just wanted to let you know that she asked for you today. When we told her about the appeal, she asked for a visit from the priest and from you.'

'I'm not sure a priest will do much good now.'

'She hasn't stopped asking for you, from that first night. Will you come?'

He shook his head. 'Probably not. I don't know.' Then he put his hand through his hair. 'I mean, why would I?'

'Because she's your mum, because she's not well – you know that, don't you? And because in a couple of weeks she may not be here any more.'

'Will they really hang her?' he asked, eyes wet.

Eva walked to the sideboard and placed her tumbler next to the brandy bottle, which was almost empty.

'December 14th at nine in the morning. Unless the doctors say not to. So, if even a small part of you wants to come...'

She'd run out of words. What else could she say to convince him? She'd done so much for Zina, but this one thing that she wanted more than any other, she hadn't managed.

'Look,' she said. 'I just had to try – one last time.' She stood at the door. She'd never see him again, so she just blurted it out: 'Why did you clock off early? That night at the Café de Paris? The night she died?'

The question had taken him by surprise and he hesitated. Then he gave a smirk. 'So, after all this time and all that evidence, you still don't want to believe she could do it? You'd rather it was me.'

'No, it's just—'

'It's none of your business,' he interrupted. 'But if you must know, I was meeting a man to pay off a debt. That's why I didn't say anything – I didn't want Hedy or my mum knowing.' He took another swig of his drink. 'I'd lost it on the horses, you see. He's not the sort you want to cross and I'd been paying him for weeks, a pound here, a few shillings there. If I didn't make the last payment that night he was going to double the debt.' He smiled. 'Hedy would've been furious. We were meant to be saving.'

'Why didn't you just tell the police?' she asked.

'I panicked. I said I'd skived off early for a quick half before I headed home. I could tell they didn't believe me. But if they knew I had money problems they would have seen me differently. Hedy had money coming to her – well, her parents hinted she did. They had land and were going to give it to her. Maybe they'd think that was a motive to kill her? I don't know.' He shrugged. 'I wasn't thinking straight. Of course I'd never get the money without her! The truth is I would never have hurt Hedy. I was besotted with her.'

She believed him. She put her hand on the door handle to leave.

'You know I blame myself,' he said. 'I should have gone with my instincts – never let her come here. But we thought it would help us save money, have her look after the house. Hedy was all for it. I tried to tell her what she was like.' He laughed. 'Well, she soon got the measure of her. Within a week we both realised we'd made a terrible mistake.'

Eva nodded. 'I know, Michalis. You said it all during the trial. You can't change any of that now.'

'Did she tell you that she's killed before?' he said. 'Years ago? In Cyprus.'

She froze. A wave of panic swept over her. Should she admit to knowing? And did it even matter now?

'I... er...'

A puzzled look crossed his face, followed by realisation.

'Oh,' he said. 'You *knew*? You knew about it? Well, well.' He gave her an up-down flick with his eyes.

She didn't speak.

'Did she ask you to keep it a secret?' he said.

'No, not exactly. But she... she mentioned something, about a long time ago, but didn't say anything else. I... I didn't know if it was true. She gets so confused.'

'So you didn't check?' He gave a crooked smile. 'You didn't say anything to anyone?'

She didn't respond.

He folded his arms and his face hardened. 'You really *are* on her side, aren't you?'

She felt the heat rise in her face.

'No – I mean...' She faltered. 'Well, I didn't say anything because I just didn't know what to say.'

'Well, you can stop worrying,' he said. 'I'm not going to report you or anything.' He swigged his brandy again. 'The police know.'

The police know?

'What do you mean?' she asked. 'How?'

'I told them.'

He put his glass down and took a pack of Woodbines from

his pocket and lit one. 'The night it happened and I came home to find what she'd done to Hedy, I told them they needn't look elsewhere. She's done it before, I said, and I know it's her.'

She stared at him, could hardly believe what he'd said. Finally, she said, 'But it didn't come up in court.'

He shrugged. 'She got away with it – she was only ever put on trial in Cyprus, never found guilty. The whole village knew what was going on, they just decided it didn't matter. The police here got in touch with the police in Limassol. They know the whole story.'

'So *everyone* knew?' she asked. And all this time she'd thought it was just her carrying the secret.

He nodded. 'The judge and both legal teams, but they're not allowed to mention it, are they? They said I was forbidden to say anything in the witness box, in case it "prejudiced the jury".'

He laughed.

'It wouldn't have made a difference, though,' he said. 'That evidence was damning. Any fool could see she'd killed Hedy.'

Eva let out a deep breath. This secret had gnawed at her day and night, and it turned out that everyone knew all along.

'So,' she said, 'that explains why the prosecution were allowed to talk about her the way they did, and why the defence team said nothing.'

Suddenly she understood the defence's half-heartedness. If they thought she'd escaped punishment for murder in the past, why would they bother believing her now? Yes, she'd been acquitted all those years ago, but once her past had been discovered, Zina hadn't stood a chance.

'Can I ask you…' she said, 'what she did in Cyprus? If you don't mind telling me.' She'd wanted to know for so long.

He shrugged. 'I was only five, so I don't remember, but there were always rumours growing up. People would whisper, but I thought they were just stories or I'd never have let her come. I only found out the details after Hedy died – when the police looked into it.'

She nodded for him to go on.

'She was probably – what? – twenty, maybe twenty-one. Her mother-in-law had been caught with another man, so the sons – including my father – took the law into their own hands.'

A chill ran through her. Suddenly she wanted him to stop speaking.

Instead, she asked, 'What did they do?'

'*They* didn't do anything. The story goes they were too smart for that. They forced the women to do it.'

'What? How?'

'They set the sisters-in-law to holding her down while my mum...' he swallowed and let out a heavy sigh, 'while my mum put a lit torch down the woman's throat.'

Her hand flew to her mouth. 'My God, that's horrific.'

There was a silence, then Michalis said, 'Goes without saying, my grandmother didn't survive. But they say she fought hard, even though it was three against one. My mum's got a scar.' He pointed just under his shoulder.

Eva remembered Dr Garrett asking Zina about the burn mark.

'Then what happened?' she asked.

'Nothing. There was a murder trial, but it was just for show and none of them was found guilty.'

'What do you mean, for show?'

'The whole village was in on it – that's what the police think now. It seems they all thought what they'd done was justified. Reasonable punishment. This was years ago – it's a lawless place.'

'That's terrible.'

'She never talked about it, but I heard snippets because she often complained about my father. He'd made her all these promises, you see. His mother was wealthy, but we lived in squalor. My mum and dad should have inherited it all. But you know what he did?'

'What?'

'Eventually, he inherited the lot, but then he left her anyway.

Went off with someone else and spent every shilling. Came back and forth for years but she never forgave him.'

As Eva hurried along Camden High Street she thought about everything she'd just heard. Could Zina have killed her mother-in-law with such brutality? She'd been young, scared. From the story Michalis had told her, it sounded as if she'd been forced into it. Could she have refused her husband if she'd even wanted to? She waited at the crossing and imagined what it would have been like to be married off at fourteen, in such a poor village, to an older man. She thought of all the choices she'd had in her own life and realised Zina had probably never had much say in anything that happened to her. Even here, halfway across the world, she was powerless.

As she quickly walked home, she noticed she was trying to cast her in a better light, despite the horrific story Michalis had told. If someone kills once and gets away with it, what makes them think they can't do it again? Was Zina that calculating?

She turned a corner, looked left and right for traffic, and ran across the road. And then there was the way Michalis had described his grandmother's murder. Such brutality – such violence. And even if Zina *had* been forced to do it, she'd still had the ruthlessness to carry it out.

While he'd been speaking, a piece of the puzzle had fallen into place. Although the two murders were separated by thirty-five years or so and thousands of miles – there was something about both killings that mirrored each other.

As a young woman, Zina was accused of killing her mother-in-law; years later, a mother-in-law herself, she was convicted of killing her own daughter-in-law. Both murders were shockingly brutal, and involved fire. Eva still didn't know *why* Zina had killed Hedy. Maybe she never would. Perhaps the first murder had stirred up something in Zina years later? She shivered and started to walk faster.

After all these months, she was no closer to knowing if the woman who lay in that cold condemned cell was a ruthless killer or a victim herself. Perhaps it was possible to be both. In two weeks a rope would be placed around Zina's neck either way. All Eva could do was be there till the very end.

It was ten o'clock by the time she walked towards her flat. Exhausted, she wondered if she could risk a hot bath, or if the rattle of the water in the pipes would wake the whole house.

She opened the door and saw Jimmy slumped in the chair, asleep. His hair was slicked back and he had on his only suit, now crumpled. The gramophone had been pulled out and the turntable was going round and round, the record crackling, finished long ago. She suddenly remembered the plans they'd made that morning.

Next to his feet was an opened bottle of gin, an empty glass and what looked like the remnants of a couple of small iced cakes on a plate. She was meant to be bringing dinner. The dancing. The drinks. All of their chances, passed hours ago.

'Jimmy, I'm so—'

He woke up with a jump, looked at her and his watch, then ran his fingers through his hair.

'I'm so sorry,' she started. 'I can't begin to—'

'Don't.'

He put out his hand to stop her, then got up. He grabbed his coat from the rack and walked to the door.

'Jimmy, please – where are you going?'

'I need some air.'

Then he turned back.

'That's for her,' he said, and pointed at a paper bag on the table.

Before she had a chance to say anything, he slammed out of the flat, making everything shake behind him.

At the table she picked up the brown paper bag. There was

a large *CB* on the front and under it the words *Carlo's Bakery*. She opened it and peered inside. A piece of card had been carefully inserted into the bottom and on it sat half a dozen *melomacaroona*. The golden honey cakes were all exactly the same oval shape, and sprinkled with crushed walnuts and a dusting of cinnamon.

They were perfect, and Eva had no idea why six small cakes would make her cry like this.

CHAPTER FIFTY-SIX

Holloway Prison, Hospital Ward

Three men are standing around Zina as she sits up in bed in the stuffy room that's separated from the rest of the ward. They've brought her here to 'check her health and mind'. That's what Eva told her. She is furious. She has shouted, *then eemeh trellee, I am not mad*, so many times at Eva before today and feels ashamed and humiliated that these men are now here to see for themselves. Did someone gossip about her mother? Do they think she's mad too?

She has now decided not to make a fuss, because if she lets her anger out they will think there is something wrong with her after all, and the shame will be too much.

Two of them are giving each other looks and then the third one says something, as he starts writing on a piece of paper. 'What are you doing?' she asks. Eva steps forward and translates for her.

'Just a check-up, Pavlou,' says one of the men. 'Calm down.'

They pull her around, listening to this, looking at that, getting her to open her mouth wide as if she's hiding something inside. She remembers the day she was examined by the other doctor. The good-looking one who liked Eva. He hasn't come to see her since the trial. Her gaze slides over to Eva now and she wonders what she knows that she's not telling. She keeps things to herself, that one.

The doctor who hasn't spoken yet sits on the side of the bed, and motions for her to lean back. The others write in their folders.

'He wants to ask you a few questions,' says Eva.

'Are they court men?' She looks from one of them to the other. 'I've answered everything about that day.'

'No, they're doctors. Just reporting on how you are. Be patient, Zina, it will be over soon.'

The men look at Eva and she says something, then the one who's on the bed starts talking and Eva explains.

'How are you feeling in yourself?' he asks.

'I'm strong.' She thumps her chest.

'Good – and what about your mind?' He taps his temple.

'What questions are these?' she says to Eva. 'My mind is not sick.'

Eva repeats her words.

'Are you sleeping? Are you worried?' asks the doctor.

'They're going to hang me, of course I'm worried. Tell him nobody comes for me, nobody is helping me.'

They listen and nod.

'Tell him I have a son and a sister,' she's counting on her fingers now, 'and nephews in London, but they've abandoned me. I have four children in Cyprus. None of them has made the journey. Brothers, too.'

Eva translates and the doctor on the bed shifts, making the sheet pull and pin Zina in. She wriggles free. He starts to ask her about Cyprus, says he heard she married very young. *Tell us about your life there, your husband, are you still with him?*

'Why do they want to know?' she asks Eva.

They say they want to hear what kind of life she had, to see what kind of a woman she was before all this happened. They're testing her, she thinks. To see if she will mention her mother or talk of the thing Zacharias made her do. They must know.

'I grew up poor and hard-working,' she tells them, 'and was married too young – just fourteen – with no choice in the matter. I have worked every day of my life. I had five children by the time I was twenty.'

Everyone stares at her.

'That's the kind of woman I am, tell them.'

One of them glances at the others, but his face shows no emotion.

'Where's your husband now?' one of them asks. 'Are you still married?'

'These questions,' says Eva, 'have nothing to do with Mrs Pavlou's health. They're private.'

'I think you'll find, miss,' says the doctor by the door, 'that whether these question are relevant is for us to decide.'

'It doesn't matter,' says Zina. 'Let them ask. You want to know about my husband?' she asks calmly. 'After I gave him five children I found him with another woman, in our bed. And that's the kind of man he is.' Her jaw tightens at the thought but she wills herself not to get angry.

Eva translates and her words are followed by a silence.

'Nothing else to ask?' says Eva.

'So he left you,' one of them says.

'He left,' says Zina, 'came back, did it again and over again. He went from her to someone else then someone else. The women were a sickness with him. He couldn't be cured.'

Eva looks at her.

'But he was weak. Men always are. Tell them that. They drink to be brave. He used to…' And here she shows with her arm how he would whack her around the head.

The men pass a look between themselves, and the one furthest away comments and the others laugh. Eva doesn't laugh.

'Why laugh?' Zina asks in English, and they seem taken aback by her challenge.

Eva says something to them, and her words come out fast. Her cheeks are pink and her voice trembles, but they take no notice of the girl and scribble some more on their papers. Damning Zina with their words.

Words are weapons here and she has so few.

CHAPTER FIFTY-SEVEN

Home Office
Whitehall
London SW1
11th December 1954

From the Office of the Under Secretary of State
To: The Secretary
Prison Commission
Horseferry House
Dean Ryle Street
London
SW1P 2AW

Regarding: Mrs Zina Pavlou
Prisoner number 7145

Sir,

I am directed to inform you of the results of the recent special medical inquiry into the above-named prisoner's mental condition, now lying under sentence of death in Holloway Prison.

The examination and interview was conducted by Dr

Nicholson, Dr Martin and Dr Twomey, under Section 2(4) of the Criminal Lunatics Act, 1884.

Having carefully considered all the circumstances of this case, the Secretary of State has been unable to find any sufficient ground to justify him in advising Her Majesty to interfere with the due course of law.

Therefore the sentence stands.

I am, Sir,
Your obedient Servant,
G R Andrews

CHAPTER FIFTY-EIGHT

Holloway Prison, condemned cell

Zina's hair has been compliant today, and she takes that as a good sign. The thick braid nestles between her shoulder blades as she's led down the damp corridor to the visiting room. She wipes her mouth again to make sure there are no crumbs from the honey cakes she's been eating.

Eva has told her he's coming early this morning, but she's waited so long that it feels absurd that he should visit now, so near the end. Perhaps the girl made a mistake? She digs her nails into her palms as she walks, trying to hold onto her hope tightly.

They stop and the warden opens the door and prods her towards the tatty table and chairs in the middle of the room, where another warden is waiting. Zina takes a seat, gets up again, smooths down the back of her skirt and sits once more, fanning the fabric carefully so there are no creases.

She puts her hands in her lap and waits, holding her trembling fingers to keep them still. The two wardens lean against the wall and feign boredom, but Zina can feel them gawping. The women who work here seem to be staring more openly now, and the two who were guarding her last night were quite brazen about it even when she was changing her undergarments. How did it come to this?

She closes her eyes and pictures the room she shared with Anna, remembering the lumpy mattress and the pathetically thin pillow. What a luxury they'd be now. After a back-breaking day shopping and cleaning for her son and his wife, she'd fall into bed, turn her back to the world and sleep facing her granddaughter as the rheumatic house creaked around them.

A key scrapes in the lock and Zina stands quickly. Eva enters, followed by Michalis. She goes to rush towards him and he flinches, she's sure of it. One of the wardens holds out her arm, stopping her.

'No touching,' she says.

'I need to stay,' says Eva. 'To report back to the governor, but please…' She backs away and stands in a corner, leaving the two of them just feet apart, notepad in hand. Always with that notepad in hand.

Zina tilts her head and looks at her son. 'You look terrible,' she says.

'You're surprised?'

'I'm surprised you came.' She takes a seat.

He edges to the table, pulls out a chair and does the same.

She waits for him to say something but he doesn't.

'What took you so long?' she asks.

He sits back as if she's slapped him.

'I've been rotting in here,' she continues, her voice agitated now. 'I've been writing every day, asking you to come, but nothing. And now you're here – now it's too late. In three days I'll be gone.'

He looks at the floor then purses his lips in that ungrateful way he has, but still he says nothing.

'You were quick to stand up in court and tell stories about me,' says Zina, 'yet you can't come and visit? Do you know how much I've done for you? I've broken my back cleaning your house, looking after your children, cooking and—'

He holds his palm out towards her face, the way Greeks do when they want to curse someone.

'How dare you show me your hand!' she yells. 'You're cursing me now?'

The wardens look at each other but do nothing.

'I'm not cursing you,' he says, reddening. 'I'm trying to get you to shut up for one minute.'

Zina folds her arms and raises her chin a little. 'Go on then,' she says. 'Speak – tell me what you want to say. After ignoring my letters for months, not thinking about me at all—'

'I'm grieving, for God's sake!' His fist bangs the table. 'My wife is dead. My children don't have a mother. I've had to move from the house. *These* are the things I'm thinking about. Not coming here to make you feel better.'

She takes a packet of cigarettes from her pocket and irritably waves them in the air until a warden walks over and lights her. She blows the smoke out and says, 'I don't know anything about that situation.'

He turns to Eva. 'You see? You wonder why I don't want to come? I knew she'd be like this.'

'Boy!' Zina scolds, making him jump. 'Don't talk about me as if I'm not here – I am *sick* of people doing that.'

There's a silence during which her mind wanders. Her gaze falls on Eva.

'Look at her.' She smiles. 'Always scribbling, getting it all down. What for, my love? They don't believe anything I say.'

Eva doesn't respond, but keeps writing as Zina turns back to him.

'Anyway, this situation—'

He leans forward suddenly, making his chair scrape. 'Will you stop calling it a "situation"'?

'Well, these unspeakable acts they accuse me of.'

'You've never even said the word, have you? It's *murder* you committed. A brutal killing.'

She shakes her head. 'I know nothing about it,' she says, though her voice falters a little. 'I'm innocent. You lied to them and they don't believe me. I'm just a poor woman and I can't speak their language. You're to blame for this.'

He gets up. 'I've had enough.'

'It's *you* who's brought me to this place,' she says, standing too. She's much shorter than him and looks up into his face as she accuses him. 'You told them about that case all those years ago. You betrayed your mother.'

Eva stops writing.

'I told them I'd heard rumours you'd killed my grandmother – yes,' he says. 'Everyone talked of it – you know that. But I was a child when that happened. I didn't *know* the details. If I'd known do you think I would have let you come here? To live in my house? The police told *me* what you'd done. They wrote to the court in Limassol. Imagine that – the police telling me such a thing!'

'But I was acquitted!' she says. 'They shouldn't have talked of it in court.'

He smirks. 'Oh, they didn't have to. They knew about it alright – the defence, prosecution and the judge. But why would they need to even mention it when the evidence...' his voice breaks now, 'was so bloody damning.'

'Innocent!' she says, banging her chest. He backs away from her. Her voice strengthens. 'Innocent,' thump, 'innocent,' thump, 'innocent,' thump.

And so she carries on now, repeating it, repeating it, thrilled that nobody is stopping her. With each utterance she's more certain that it's true and she spits the word out, again and again, till it rings against the damp bricks and presses deep into the crevices of the walls.

He turns to leave and she suddenly stops shouting. As he looks back from the door, she points at him.

'You abandoned your mother,' she says. 'We will both take that to our graves.'

CHAPTER FIFTY-NINE

There are just two days now until Zina's execution. Eva glances up at the menacing lilac clouds as she hurries through the gates of Holloway. What mood will she find her in today? Since her son's visit, Zina's been much quieter, calm almost. As if the rage she'd been hoarding for these past six months has all been spent now on poor Michalis. And Eva had been so pleased that he'd agreed to visit his mother, but within a minute of them being together, she'd realised it had been a terrible mistake. He'd been right all along. And now Zina's accusations and rantings will probably stay with him for the rest of his life.

Late yesterday afternoon, Father Dimitri, the Greek priest, finally sent a message that he could spare time today to visit Zina. As Eva walks into reception, he's there, waiting for her. He's foreboding in his formal soot-black over-cassock and chimneypot hat, and she suddenly feels nervous.

She reaches out to shake his hand, but instead he offers it like royalty expecting a kiss. His fingers are warm and plump, and coarse hair sprouts across his knuckles. It's been so long, she's forgotten this is how they like to be greeted. Hesitating, she takes a moment then dips her head and brushes her lips on his ring, forgiving herself the insincerity.

'I don't know you, my child,' he says, as they follow a warden through the corridors to the condemned cell. 'Perhaps I know your parents?'

'I don't go to church, Father,' she replies.

He stops and turns, surprised at her brazen honesty. 'But you must, you must. It's a sin not to attend.'

'I used to,' she says, as another gate is locked behind them.

They continue down the corridor and she remembers how she would kneel in the Camden Town church several times a week, her mother by her side. A coin was slipped into Eva's palm and she'd place it on the silver plate, and take a tall taper candle. As she lit it from one of the other candles and pressed it into the sand-filled candle tray, she'd make silent bargains with whoever was in charge.

'What stopped you going?' he asks.

'My mother died.'

He crosses himself. 'God bless her soul.' He rests his hand on his chest, just under his wiry, greying beard. 'Your father still lives?'

'I never knew him. He died when I was a baby.'

'God bless both of their souls,' he says. 'Who took care of you?'

'My auntie was here. She did everything.'

He gives her a glance. 'And this auntie wasn't a churchgoer? What a terrible shame.'

She doesn't bother answering.

The warden now leads them through E Wing and they continue down another corridor towards the condemned cells. The officer's rubber soles squeak and Eva's heels ring out, but Father Dimitri's footsteps are as quiet as a whispered prayer.

'Do you attend all of Mrs Pavlou's visits?' he asks. 'Even when she doesn't need an interpreter?' He seems put out, as if she's intruding.

'Yes, the governor wants to know if anything important is said.'

'It's all important.' He smiles. 'It's God's work.'

The warden raises her key to unlock the cell, but he puts out his hand.

'One moment, please,' he says in English. Then to Eva, 'Before we enter, there's the matter of the small contribution.'

She frowns. 'Sorry?'

'Well, this visit will take up much of my morning, and then of course I will be with Mrs Pavlou on the day itself.'

'You want money.' It's a bald fact, not a question. She knows this is the way they do things in the Greek Church; some priests ask for small, nominal amounts, while others take advantage. Funerals, weddings, blessings, you always give a little something. But surely this is different?

She squares her shoulders and raises her chin a little.

'And how much do you charge for visiting a condemned woman?' she asks.

He jolts. 'The money's not for me, madam. It's for our Church. How much is completely up to you. But please keep in mind that I took a taxi here and I'll need one to return. It's my morning gone, really.'

A fury sweeps through her and she wants to refuse, just to see what he will do. But she won't, for Zina's sake.

'If you don't have the money,' he says, 'perhaps there's a member of Mrs Pavlou's family—'

'No, there's no one.' She can't ask Michalis. 'I have the money,' she says. 'I'll bring it to the church tomorrow, and leave it in an envelope for you.'

The warden lets out an irritated sigh. 'Can we go in now?'

In her cell, Zina touches the hem of Father Dimitri's robe and marvels at how thick the cotton feels. That cost a good few shillings. She would have liked to have seen him in the resplendent ivory robes woven with gold and silver threads, but she supposes those are kept for church days. Not for prison visits. He's saying a prayer and to begin with she is reciting it too, but the words now crash against each other and she's not sure she knows what comes next. Best to stop – she wouldn't want to get it wrong.

Head bowed, hands clasped, she shifts on her knees, and thinks of all the hours of her life that she's spent kneeling in church. As a girl, scraping wax from the wooden benches. As a young woman, cleaning the stone floors and carefully dusting the icons.

And all those Easters, when she stayed up late weaving wild flowers into the epitaph, before everyone carried it through Spakato at night.

She hears a clank and raises her head now, to see him waving incense over her, blessing her. This is her church now. He helps her up and sits at the table. Eva's there too, with her notebook.

'Do you have anything on your mind?' he asks.

'I need you to help me,' she says. 'Get them to see I'm a good woman.'

'But you've received two petitions from Cyprus, haven't you?' He looks at Eva and she nods. 'One from your village and family and the other from officials who spoke up on your behalf.'

'But it hasn't worked,' she says.

He holds out his palms. 'I can't do anything else.'

'I'm frightened,' she says.

'Of death?'

'Of course. But of the pain too.'

He smiles and puts out his hand for her. She takes it with both of hers. How warm it is. What life he has running through him. Her fingers have been cold for days.

'*Kyriah* Pavlou, you mustn't fear death,' he says. 'It is a natural part of life.'

'Not a death like this, it isn't.'

'This is true and—'

'I won't see my grandchildren grow up,' she interrupts. 'I won't be with my loved ones. I'll be dust.' Her eyes begin to fill and she promised herself she would stay calm so she could ask the questions she needs answers to.

'No, you won't be dust,' he says. 'Your soul lives on. You know that.'

Doesn't he understand that the fear has grasped her throat these past few days and she can barely breathe? Eva passes her a handkerchief and she rubs at her eyes and blows her nose. It's clear he understands nothing of her distress. A rage rises inside her and she must speak to him the way nobody speaks to a priest.

'Is God here?' she asks, her voice loud, tinged with anger. The two wardens exchange looks. 'Or has He abandoned me? I did so much for Him.'

Father Dimitri raises a finger, as if to silence her.

'God doesn't abandon us,' he admonishes. 'It is we who abandon Him. Now the best thing you can do is pray for your soul – I will too – and you will be at peace.'

A laugh bursts out of her and he looks shocked.

'Do you hear him?' she asks Eva. 'I've never had a *moment's* peace in my life, and he says I'll have it now.'

Eva sits there, dumb. She's written nothing down. Why doesn't she write this? This is the truth of it.

'Father Dimitri,' says Zina. 'Do you *know* what they're going to do to me?'

He doesn't reply but swallows hard. She lifts her hand and puts it to her own throat to show a choking motion.

'Could you be at peace with that?'

He rises.

'I have some church business I need to attend to. Did you want to say a prayer together before I go?'

'No.'

'Would you like me to come and pray with you on the day?' he asks. 'Before you go through? It's the day after tomorrow, isn't it?'

She considers it for a moment then turns to Eva.

'Will *you* visit me instead?' she asks. 'On the morning?'

'I... I can't. It's not allowed. I've asked. But I'll come tomorrow. I promise.'

Father Dimitri coughs.

'The governor says the chaplain is usually present,' he says. 'But as you speak no English, she's given permission for me to come instead. If that suits you.'

She wants to say that she can face it alone, but knows the loneliness will be terrible.

'Please come,' she says.

'Very well.' He walks to the door. 'God is with you, *Kyriah* Pavlou.' Then to Eva, 'Is there a cross? In the... room itself?'

'I'll ask,' says Eva. 'Would you like one if there isn't?'

Zina hesitates, then nods. She may as well.

CHAPTER SIXTY

Holloway Prison, condemned cell

Eva's last visit

It's three in the afternoon when Eva arrives. She watches Zina cup her hand around the flame as the warden lights her cigarette. She exhales, long and hard, as if she's been holding her breath.

'I have...' Zina glances in the cigarette box, 'four left. I'll have another tonight and...' counting on her fingers, 'one when I wake and one just before they take me. So... one left.' She draws one out of the pack. 'Take it.'

Eva hesitates.

'Go on,' she coaxes. 'I'm not leaving the bastards a thing.'

Eva takes the cigarette and the warden lights her, too. It tastes harsher than her Craven 'A's, and she swallows the smoke as a kind of penance. After everything, she's been of no use to Zina. She wants to get up and walk out. Jimmy told her not to come, but she couldn't refuse this last visit.

Zina takes a sticky paper bag from her skirt pocket and opens it.

'Your husband's a good baker,' she says. 'Want one?'

Eva shakes her head.

Zina pushes her fingers inside and brings out a honey cake.

'I'll save the other one for tomorrow, too.'

She licks her fingers and puts the bag back in her pocket.

'I've told them I want you to have my things,' she says.

'What things?' Eva looks around. There's very little here.

'Two skirts, some blouses, these shoes, a coat.'

'Oh.' This is too awful. 'But... are you sure?'

'Of course – who else am I going to leave them to?' Then she points at her feet. 'I'd give you my good shoes but the police took them, remember? They never gave them back.'

Eva recalls Sergeant Parks sniffing at the soles and making Zina do the same.

Is she meant to keep these things? Like she's kept the baby clothes, shoving them to the back of a drawer? She can't.

'But what shall I do with it all?' she asks.

'Sell it, take the money, give it to the Church if you want.' She shrugs. 'If I were you I'd spend it on myself. If there's any left over, you can put some flowers on my grave. That would be nice.'

Zina hasn't asked where she will be buried so Eva hasn't told her. She must already know, she thinks. An unmarked grave within the grounds of the prison, alongside other women executed long ago.

She sighs. 'I'd like to give something to Anna but I know he won't allow it.'

She flicks ash onto the floor and one of the wardens snaps her fingers and points to the metal ashtray. Zina gives the woman a sideways look, takes another puff and blows smoke towards her.

'Thank you,' says Eva, 'for the things.'

'Don't look so sad – it doesn't matter about me now.'

She has been doing so well till this point.

'I'm sorry...' She dabs at her eyes with her finger. 'I'm sorry I couldn't help.'

'You've helped me plenty, my girl – I hope they paid you well. Make sure they pay you.'

Eva shifts.

'Is there anything you need?' she asks Zina. 'Anything I can get for you?'

'No. I have everything now. Just one more evening, then bed

and then...' Zina gets up and wanders across the cell. She looks up at the lengthening shadow of the window on the wall. 'They brought the cross for me.'

'That's good.'

'They showed me it. They've put it in the room where they're taking me.'

Eva tries not to look at the wardrobe. Everyone who works here knows that it hides a door to an empty room, and in that room is a second door that leads to the execution chamber. The wardens call the wardrobe Narnia.

'Would you like me to read to you today?' she asks. 'I've got a book with me.'

'I was going to ask you to write a final letter to Michalis,' Zina says. 'To let him know I forgive him. But I doubt he'd read it. Did he read the other letters, do you think? I asked him to come and see me one last time.'

'I don't know,' Eva replies. He's read them all because he's complained to her about their content. Has said nothing could drag him there again.

'You're not even family,' Zina says, emphasising her point with a wagging finger, 'and yet you believed me all along. Nobody else.'

Eva feels the blood rise in her cheeks.

Zina places her hands on the table and leans close to her.

'You *know* I'm a good woman, don't you?' she whispers. 'That I'd never do those unspeakable things?'

Eva's hesitation is a mere split second. What good would it do to be honest now, so late in the day?

Zina leans closer. 'You *do* believe me, don't you?'

'Of *course*, Zina,' she says emphatically. 'I've always believed you.'

Zina smiles, but she knows. She takes two long drags from her cigarette until there is hardly anything left but the filter.

'It was good of you to come today,' she says. She turns away from Eva. 'You should go now. Get home to your husband. He must feel neglected after all these months.'

A mixture of relief and misery sweep over Eva; she'd imagined she would spend that final evening with her, but she's both thankful and upset to be dismissed like this. Her mind scrambles for a way to say goodbye. A way to show her what she's meant to her.

'And your husband,' says Zina, 'thank him for these.' She pats the cakes in her skirt pocket.

Eva stands. She wants to embrace her and kiss her goodbye, but doesn't trust herself not to bawl.

'I'm... I'm glad to have known you, Zina,' she says. It sounds feeble to her ears and she regrets it immediately.

Zina turns to her and smiles, but her gaze is vacant. Then she takes her chair and places it in the corner of the cell. She sits down, moves her body to one side and takes a final puff. Her head is swathed in a cloud of cigarette smoke. Once at the cell door, Eva looks back. Zina is in exactly the same position she'd sat in five months ago, in Hampstead police station. The day she'd first met her.

'Goodbye then,' says Eva.

Zina flicks the cigarette butt to the floor.

CHAPTER SIXTY-ONE

Eva spent the half-hour bus journey crying. The tears dripped off her chin and she rubbed at her eyes. She didn't bother trying to fix her face. What was the point? She blew her nose loudly and a well-dressed woman who was leaving the top deck gave her a look of disdain.

'What's the matter?' called Eva. 'Haven't you seen anyone cry before?' Her voice was louder than she'd intended, and the woman hurriedly clip-clopped downstairs. Exhaling with some effort, she stared out of the window.

Once off the bus she walked very slowly towards the flat. The roads were busy and she wandered home in the fading light, past several houses where open curtains showed off tinsel-strewn Christmas trees. Eventually, she reached home and, as she pushed her key into the lock and the door swung open, Jimmy looked up from his newspaper.

She burst out crying again, and he came and wrapped his arms around her.

'You shouldn't have gone,' he said. 'I knew it would upset you.'

She cried into his shoulder for a minute or so.

'Come on. Come and wash your face.'

He walked her over to the sink and she leaned over while he ran the cold water and splashed her cheeks and eyelids.

She breathed deeply, trying to calm herself. As she lifted her head, he passed her a clean face towel from the dresser. She wiped herself and he held her at arm's length, looking at her, then dragged a thumb under her eye to wipe away a remaining smudge of mascara. She walked across the room and slumped into the armchair.

'Tea?'

'Whisky,' she replied.

He poured one for her and one for him, too, and handed her the tumbler. She took a gulp, coughed, and drank another sip.

Kneeling next to her, he said, 'Was she hysterical?'

She turned the glass in her hand. 'She was calm. Almost cold. As if she's accepted what's going to happen.'

'Probably best. Are you alright?'

'No.' She turned the tumbler in her hands. 'I know I was just the interpreter,' she began, 'but there was still that stupid spark of hope.' She smiled and could feel her mouth wobble. 'I thought I might be able to help her.'

He took the glass from her hands and put it on the floor, then wrapped his fingers around hers. His skin was warm and rough and familiar.

'You *did* help her,' he said.

'How? At nine tomorrow she's going to hang.'

'You couldn't do anything about the evidence, Evie. But you helped her every day from the moment you met her. What would she have done without you?'

She shrugged.

'They'd have found another interpreter, I'm sure. I'm not the only one who could have done that job.'

He sat on the floor but kept hold of one of her hands. 'Well, that's true – but you're the only one who could have done it the way you did.'

She didn't say anything.

'She would have chopped and changed interpreters and it would have been worse for her. And you were *kind*, Evie. You were so kind to her, even though you thought she'd probably done it – hell, it was clear from the outset, wasn't it?'

She nodded. 'I suppose it was.'

'But you still treated her like a human being. Who else did that?'

She didn't speak. She let go of his hand and unbuttoned her mac, then rested her head on the side of the chair.

'I know you're right, but in the end what good did it do?' she said. 'Visiting her every day? Writing those letters, reading books... trying to get Dr Garrett and the governor to *do* something.'

He put his hand on her leg to make her look at him.

'But it was never your job to save her,' he said. 'If she'd agreed to plead insanity she may have had a chance, but she was adamant, wasn't she?'

Eva nodded.

'You helped her in court,' he continued, 'making sure she knew what was happening. Then you translated all those letters she wrote to her family in Cyprus, as well as their replies. It's plenty, Evie.'

She began to say something then stopped herself. She could feel him watching her face as they sat in silence. The clock ticked loudly and the faint sound of the radio seeped down from the upstairs flat.

Finally, in a very quiet voice, she said, 'I tried so hard – I really did. But she still died.'

'What?'

She looked at him now. 'I tried to tell the doctors that she wasn't well, but I was so young. They brushed us off, said it was nothing. But she knew. She *knew*.'

Jimmy came closer and took her hand. The sadness that had shored up against her heart these past few months wasn't just for her mother or Zina; it was for all the lost women everywhere. Including herself.

'By the time they listened,' she continued, 'it was too late.'

'You were a child,' he said. 'You did all that you could for her.

And now you've done what you can here, with Zina. You were a friend to her when she had nobody.'

Eva swigged back her whisky and put the tumbler out for a refill. He took it and poured another shot.

As he went to hand it to her, he pulled back so she'd look at him. 'You have to stop punishing yourself,' he said. 'For your sake, Evie, and for ours. Stop tormenting yourself about your mother... and... Zina... and...' He stopped.

'And what?'

'And stop tormenting yourself about the baby. *Our* baby. It wasn't your fault. It wasn't mine, or anyone's.'

He kissed her wet face.

CHAPTER SIXTY-TWO

Holloway Prison, condemned cell

Zina's final evening

Zina rummages in the paper bag and breaks off another piece of honey cake. She pushes it into her mouth and uses her tongue to press the sticky delicacy to the top of her palate, revelling in its yielding nature. A glorious sweetness floods through her and she surrenders to it, letting it coat the bitterness she's felt for so long. It's a simple gift from Eva but she's grateful; only happy thoughts seem possible with a headful of honey. In this moment, she feels a calmness. The fear has dissolved and she knows she has the strength to face what's coming. She hopes she won't feel differently in the morning.

Before getting into bed, she kneels on the cold, hard lino to say her prayers, hands clasped at her chest. She'd stopped praying months ago, but started again last week. And now there's only one more night, so she may as well. She screws her eyes tight and thinks of all the things she's asked Him for over the years and how He didn't really give her any of them. None of it matters any more; all she needs now is courage.

She thinks about the priest, who is due tomorrow, before they take her away. Her thoughts unspool as she envisages his sermon in her honour, after she's died. He's in the pulpit of the Greek church in Camden Town, resplendent in his ivory gown, intricately woven with gold thread. The heaving congregation hang onto his words, as he talks of her many good deeds over the years and how she was done a great disservice in this country of wet windowsills and dark, unfriendly corners.

And then, just as she thinks about getting up from the floor, she feels a hand touch her lightly on the shoulder. She turns. It's Anna. Standing next to her, smiling, in her pretty blue birthday dress.

She grabs the girl into a tight embrace.

'What's happening?' she asks into her hair. 'Are they letting me go? Did they send you to come and tell me?'

Anna climbs into Zina's lap but doesn't reply. Instead, she reaches behind her *yiayia*'s head and starts to play with her plait, swishing it a little then pulling the braid apart. She unfurls her grandmother's hair completely and lays it along Zina's shoulders, patting it down.

Letting her head fall, Zina puts her nose into the crook of the girl's neck, sniffing deeply. Oranges, bay leaves and sun-scorched earth. Home. She takes another deep breath.

'Look,' says Anna, and pulls something from her dress pocket. It's Maria, the small rag doll with yellow wool hair that Zina gave her on her first night in London. 'I still have her.'

Anna pushes the doll into her *yiayia*'s hands and places Zina's fingers tight around Maria's body, so she won't drop her. Then she kisses her grandmother once on each cheek, 'Greek way', and Zina's heart lifts. Their faces are so close, her tears are falling fast.

She must control herself. She rubs at her eyes and, still holding the doll, quietly pulls Anna onto the bed, and they curl up facing each other, the way they used to at Cedar Hill, both of them clutching Maria between them.

A little later, half asleep, Zina feels the cold crawl up her legs. She shifts and, without opening her eyes, uses her right hand to search the blanket next to her, pat-patting. She pushes herself up and looks around. There's an ache in her neck and she reaches back to rub it; she has slept awkwardly on her thick black plait, which is still tightly braided. Her left hand is gripping something firmly and her fingers ache. Slowly, she drops her head and glances at her familiar rough-skinned knuckles. She's holding a fistful of blanket and nothing else.

CHAPTER SIXTY-THREE

The London Post, 13 December 1954

MRS PAVLOU SENSATION – ARE THEY RIGHT TO
HANG HER?
Prison doctor says she is 'insane'

*Four MPs are tonight trying desperately to get a reprieve for
Mrs Zina Pavlou, the 53-year-old Cypriot grandmother who
is due to be hanged tomorrow at Holloway Prison at nine in
the morning.*

*A furore has arisen because it's been revealed that a medical
report on Mrs Pavlou, by Dr Edward Garrett, the Principal
Medical Officer at Holloway, was never called for during her
trial. Dr Garrett has observed Mrs Pavlou for several months
and he reported that she was insane. His report stated that
when she bludgeoned her daughter-in-law, Mrs Hedy Pavlou,
then strangled her and tried to set her body alight, Mrs
Pavlou was not aware that what she was doing was wrong.*

*But this evidence was not used during Mrs Pavlou's trial
because she instructed her counsel not to do so. Had the
court known the details, Mrs Pavlou may have been found*

guilty but insane – in which case she would not be facing the noose tomorrow, but rather a lifelong incarceration at a hospital.

The four MPs, led by Mr Hugh Brackley, say they have not been able to secure an urgent appointment with the Home Secretary for this matter. Although Dr Garrett's report has only just been made public, they say the Home Secretary will have been aware of it, and also of Mrs Pavlou's continuing erratic behaviour. The Home Secretary has used his power to recommend reprieves in many other cases, and in fact no woman has been executed at Holloway since Mrs Edith Thompson in 1923, thirty-one years ago.

CHAPTER SIXTY-FOUR

Holloway Prison, condemned cell

Zina's final evening

Hours pass and she's in bed again. She has refused the injection they say will help her sleep.

Instead, she places the dark cloth over her eyes to block out the light and watches the young woman before her. Only the happy scenes of her life come to her tonight. There is one beautiful memory she has saved for today, a carefree day with her children around her, and now she relishes watching it play out in her mind. Reliving the joy, so many years later.

She hears the cell door open and wakes as the wardens enter to swap shifts. She's surprised she has managed to sleep tonight of all nights.

So it must be six o'clock in the morning, although the dark December sky would have you believe it's still night. Three hours left.

One of the wardens who's off home walks over and squeezes her shoulder by way of goodbye.

'Stay strong, Pavlou,' she says.

Her kindness surprises Zina and, although she does nothing but stare, she wonders if she's misjudged her. Perhaps others, too.

Slowly, Zina rises. Just three hours. She wishes it were three minutes. She's ready.

CHAPTER SIXTY-FIVE

The following morning, Eva opens her eyes and is facing him. He has his arm draped around her waist in an easy intimacy. She had woken in the early hours to find him half awake too, and they'd talked about their baby and what kind of a girl she might have been. And although she's felt melancholic, in among the sadness now is a speck of something she hasn't felt for months. Hope.

She turns and looks at the clock, surprised to see it is already eight. Just one hour. She's almost overslept. She gently takes his arm and lifts it away, trying not to wake him on his day off. She slides out of bed, splashes her face and hurriedly dresses. She considers not bothering with her hair but decides Zina deserves that she make an effort. Quickly, she slicks on some lipstick, brushes on mascara, slips on her shoes and takes her bag. She glances at him, walks across and kisses his lips before grabbing her warm coat and dashing out

The bus comes quickly and she finds herself across the road from Holloway Prison with fifteen minutes to spare. A few people have already gathered outside the gates. They're the ghouls who love an execution, who wait for the notice to go up immediately after a hanging, declaring that the punishment has been served.

She recalls a grainy photo she saw in the *Daily Mirror* a year or so ago. It showed a crowd of onlookers just like this, outside

Pentonville Prison on the day of an execution. A few yards from them stood a ragged knot of people dressed in black, holding each other. Friends and family of the condemned, the caption had said. But today nobody has pulled on their dark clothes to come and stand at a distance.

She enters the Royal Café, orders a *kaffé skétto* and stands at the counter to sip it as she faces the road. She can do nothing for Zina now. She pictures her being readied behind those walls. She looks at the tall red-brick monstrosity and hopes, somewhere in that building, Zina knows that she isn't alone. She glances at her watch. In five minutes it will be nine o'clock.

CHAPTER SIXTY-SIX

Wednesday, 28th July 1954, the night of the murder,
71 Cedar Hill, Hampstead

The house is quiet, save for the tinny ticking of the clock. Zina sits in the kitchen, alone with Hedy. It's just gone eleven and Michalis won't be back from the Café de Paris for a few hours yet. There's no sound coming from upstairs, so Anna and the baby must be fast asleep.

As she finishes mending a hole in Anna's sock, she knots the thread and cuts it with the tiny sharp scissors that she keeps in her apron pocket. She winds the cotton back on the spool, drops it into her sewing box and gets up to return it to the dresser.

Hedy stands at the sink, ignoring her again. Earlier, she'd made a cup of tea for herself without asking Zina if she'd like one, and now she has her back turned as she bends over and rummages for the soap powder under the sink. *How many times has Hedy turned her back to her?* Zina wonders. They've both told her she should have learned some English by now, but what about Hedy? Can't the girl learn this one simple courtesy?

She tries to take a calming breath. The pounding in her head has been there all day, and now her stomach swirls with acid, too, as the familiar panic ripples and rises. There are only two days left before Hedy and the children go, and she's tried everything. She'd abandoned all the housework when they'd first asked her to leave, but as the days have crept closer she's frantically started doing everything again. She's cooked and cleaned and undertaken chores before they've needed doing. She's even weeded and raked the garden, although nothing will grow there. And for what? To stop Hedy taking Anna away from her. To stop Hedy kicking her out. To stop Hedy. She searches her mind for what else she can do, but is drowning in her fear of abandonment.

Now it's so close, the girl has given up on all niceties, all pretences. Zina has been cast aside; they've tired of her and she's served her purpose. All that remains is for her to be discarded.

She coughs a little to make Hedy turn, to say goodnight. But the girl continues pouring boiling water from the kettle into the tin bath, ready to soak some clothes. Zina's head rattles with indignation and she stomps upstairs. Halfway up, she stops and calls her name sharply, to test her more than anything, to see if she will acknowledge her. Hedy looks up.

'Goodnight, Hedy,' Zina says in English, emphasising both words in suppressed anger.

Hedy nods and carries on, not bothering to speak.

Zina walks to her bedroom and sees the large ugly suitcase again, squatting outside their door, taunting her. It's sat there for two days. Hedy opens it often, feeding clothes and shoes into its mouth every time she thinks of something else they might need. Just two days, then Anna will be gone, and by the time she's returned, Zina will be in Cyprus. Michalis gave her the one-way ticket today.

Her head feels worse and she lies on top of the covers, trying to be quiet so as not to wake Anna. Rubbing at her forehead, the terrible images she sees in front of her are clearer now. The two of them laughing and twisting naked in her sheets. That's how she found them on that hot, dusty day. Zacharias had promised to keep his filthy comings and goings out of their house. But his promises blew away on the dust. And today, when she'd taken the children to the beach, she returned to find them together again.

Despite what she'd done for him, she said, that thing nobody else would do – this was her reward? She shouted, he hit. He was pink-cheeked with anger, as if it were *he* who'd been betrayed, *he* who'd been humiliated. He said he'd leave her, to see how she'd like it. And he'd left her alright, with all those mouths to feed. When he finally returned weeks later, she was actually grateful. There would be no more scrabbling for food.

After a while, Zina sits up in the dark, still fully clothed despite the late hour. She can hear her splashing about downstairs. She's back. Washing clothes in the tub, as if *she* were the woman of the house. She has dared to return when she knows Zacharias is at work, when she knows full well that Zina is upstairs.

There's a suitcase in the hall, a ticket in her drawer. He has told her that this time it is she, Zina, who must leave.

That woman downstairs has taken her husband once before and now she wants her house and children too.

No. She won't allow it. She can't steal her life from her again. She clasps her hands in her lap and thinks hard. She will scare her off. Yes. Chase her away for good. She's a slight thing and Zina's strong. By the time he's home it will all be done.

Zina gets up and looks towards the corner at the sleeping mound under the covers. She can't remember which child is there, but it hardly matters. They rarely wake. She creeps across the room, steps onto the landing and closes the door silently behind her.

She can hear her humming as she pours water into a tin bowl. She must be washing herself. Zina slinks down the stairs and stoops to get a good, long look. First she sees her bare feet then, as she descends further, her sturdy legs, her briefs and finally her torso. Well, look at the hips on her. She's filled out plenty. And that new hair colour doesn't suit her one bit. Zina's at the bottom of the stairs now and stands unseen in the kitchen doorway to watch the intruder. The woman lifts one arm and washes her armpit as the water sloshes onto Zina's floor.

All the injustices and slurs that Zina has endured throughout her life now rise like bile inside her. The mess is intolerable. *She* is intolerable. Zina swiftly takes the ash pan from the corner of the kitchen and whacks her on the head. There's a loud crack, the same sound a good, ripe watermelon makes when you split it open with a knife.

She drops like a sack of flour, and her blood quickly pools by Zina's feet. She warned them both. When will people start listening to her? There. She squeezes her throat then finishes her off with whatever is to hand.

Zina grabs her calves and drags her to the garden, marvelling at how well fed she is when she remembers her as a runt of a thing. Back in the kitchen, she grabs the paraffin can. It slips from her hands and spills onto the floor. She wipes at the swirl of blood and paraffin and water and wonders where this floor covering has come from, when it's always been dirt here.

Never mind. She takes everything she needs outside. As she's about to strike a match, something glints before her eyes. She reaches forward, pulls hard and finally the ring loosens. She slips it in her pocket and sets about her work.

CHAPTER SIXTY-SEVEN

14th December 1954

Inside Holloway Prison, 8.40 a.m., the day of the execution

Some time later, Zina is told to ready herself and Father Dimitri enters. He's bleary-eyed, tall ivory candle in hand, and he seems distracted. He sets the candle on the table and the warden pushes it into a brass holder and lights it. From his pocket he takes a small Bible; she kneels, and he says a short prayer in his monotonous voice. She isn't offered communion. In ten minutes he's crossed himself and left.

She doesn't eat but sips a cup of hot, sweet tea, and it strikes her that it's delicious. Has it always tasted this good? She looks around the cell and notices cracks in the bricks that she'd never seen before, hears the sound of the podgy warden breathing, and there's the musty smell of damp that she'd got used to, but now seems so sharp, as if she's experiencing it for the first time.

After visiting the lavatory, she folds her nightclothes and places them neatly on a chair. She starts to make the bed then stops herself and strips it while the wardens stare at her practicality. The dirty sheets are placed in a pile on the floor and she puts the pillow in the middle of the mattress. She puts on her shoes and places her slippers next to each other by the bed.

There are footsteps outside and Zina quickly turns her back, slips her hand in her pocket and places the final piece of honey cake in her mouth. She will suck at it slowly and let it melt. By the time it's gone, she will be too.

The young warden looks at her watch and glances at her colleague. A key scrapes in the lock and the governor stands in the doorway with two men behind her.

The governor speaks but Zina doesn't respond. She'll keep her words to herself now. The two men each take one side of the wardrobe and slide it across the wall, revealing a door with no handle. The governor steps forward, unlocks it and the door swings wide.

One of the wardens goes to take Zina's arm but she doesn't need leading. She walks in by herself. What's that music? It's so familiar. She carries on walking as the sound sweeps through the treacle-dark room. She blinks and her eyes adjust to the patchwork of greys. Look – there's the staircase. At the top is an arched door, and beyond it is the grand circle of the Plaza. She hears Anna's laugh and feels a sticky hand reach to her mouth and push in a sweet. The sugary lemon sherbet twangs along her jaw.

CHAPTER SIXTY-EIGHT

Outside Holloway Prison, 8.55 a.m., the day of the execution

Eva takes a few coins from her purse, pays for the *kaffé* and walks out of the door. She can't cross the road. She can't stand near the people who've come to read the execution notice. Instead, she stays where she is and watches from a distance, like family might.

She looks again. Two minutes to nine. She takes a deep breath and closes her eyes. An image of Zina comes to mind – sitting in her cell, cigarette in hand the way she'd left her. But this time she's smiling, and leaning towards her, laughing at something that Eva has read from a book.

Suddenly, a warm, rough hand takes hers and, startled, she turns to see Jimmy there, breathing hard.

'You came,' she says.

'I ran. I didn't want you to be by yourself.'

Just then there's a commotion up ahead and the crowd across the road pushes forward as a guard pins a notice on the gate. A moment later, a cheer rises and one person starts to applaud. Others join in.

Eva turns into Jimmy's shoulder.

EPILOGUE

December 1955, one year later

The old woman pulls at Eva's sleeve and points at the Ladybird book.

'Why is he always sawing wood?' she asks in Greek. She's jabbing at a drawing of a man on the page. 'Doesn't he work? Hasn't he got anything better to do?'

Eva laughs. 'They're just showing you the different things the family do around the house,' she says. 'Though he does make a lot of furniture, doesn't he?'

This woman, Despina, is the oldest one in the group of six that Eva has been teaching, and she's taken to the new alphabet and words faster than the rest. Eva has watched her follow the sentences with her finger, then try them out as she looks up at her to see if she's got them right.

'That's it for today, ladies,' she says in English. 'Thank you, and see you next week.'

One by one the women get up and tidy away their books, and the cups and plates that they've eaten cake from. They make a point of straightening the chairs in the church hall, and wiping the table down though it's already spotless. The English vicar stands and nods and they nod back and say thank you, and cross themselves and try to take his hand and kiss it though he sometimes manages to pull away just in time.

As they walk out chatting in Greek, they each say goodbye and thank you to Eva in English. A couple of them still think it's funny, and make a point of trying on a posh accent for a laugh, but the others have taken to it quite naturally.

These classes on a Saturday are the best two hours of Eva's week and she relishes them.

Once they've left, she exits the English church and, three streets away enters another. High ceilings, icons, the smell of incense – it couldn't be more different than the draughty, sparse place she's just left. This won't be a regular visit and she's pleased to see that Father Dimitri is nowhere to be seen.

She places a coin on the silver tray near the entrance, takes a beeswax taper and walks to the sand tray. She puts the candle's wick to another that's already lit and then presses it into the tray. The taper stands tall next to all the others, row upon row of prayers and hopes.

She doesn't want to kneel or pray or kiss an icon, but instead she closes her eyes for a few moments and thinks of those she's lost. It's been almost a year to the day since Zina died. And longer for the others – her mother, her baby. How quickly it's all gone. Those who've left her are always still there, she knows that now. She's no longer swept up in sadness when she thinks of them. She opens her eyes and turns away, pleased to have marked the occasion.

She exits the church and she smiles when she sees that snow is now tumbling down fast. It's settling in drifts against shop windows and in the cracks along the paving stones. She's wrapped up against the cold, and she has time, so decides to walk.

As she wanders towards Charing Cross, crowds of Christmas shoppers hurry past, the weather putting everyone in a holiday mood.

She sees Jimmy before he sees her. He's standing, collar up, hands deep in pockets, looking for her. In the past year they've gradually made their way back to each other; she no longer feels lost when she's with him, but found. She waits and suddenly he spots her and rushes over.

They kiss and then trudge along the Strand, arms linked.

'Whose idea was this?' she laughs, shivering and brushing the snow from her shoulders.

'Yours. I'm sure it was yours.' He pulls her in closer as the snow flurries whip around them.

They stop at the traffic lights at the junction of Trafalgar Square and wait for them to change.

'God, it's freezing,' she says. 'We should be home now.'

'In our cold little flat?'

'I can keep you warm,' she says, and he grins and pulls her across the road.

As the crowds thicken up ahead, they slow their pace to enter Trafalgar Square.

'Oh, look how lovely it is,' she says.

'I told you it was worth coming.'

They both stare at the huge Christmas tree in the middle of the square.

After a few minutes he asks, 'How was it today? Your women behaving themselves?'

She laughs. 'Of course not. That's why I love them. One of them told me she has three friends who want to come, so I'm thinking of holding another class in the week.'

'And the vicar won't start charging you a fortune?' he asks.

'Nothing like that Greek priest wanted to. The hall's not being used, anyway. I think he loves the attention.'

'And all the food they bring him, no doubt.'

'Yes, that too.'

She's still at the Café de Paris, but hasn't worked for the Met Police since Zina. She can't bring herself to – even though they've asked her a few times. She told them last week to take her off their books.

Arm in arm, they weave their way through the crowds and walk towards the fountain. The snow is coming down heavily and for a moment they stand and hold onto each other's lapels.

'How are *you*?' she asks. 'Work alright?'

'Great,' he says, and kisses her. 'Carlo is very happy... I think he has plans.'

'Really? Like what?'

'He was hinting that he's getting on, might like to step back a bit. Come in just a day or two a week, and reckons I can handle the rest.'

'I knew it!' she says, hitting him lightly on the chest. 'He's going to get you to run the whole thing.'

He laughs. 'Steady – he hasn't quite said that yet.'

'Yet. But he'd be a fool not to.'

A bustle of families and friends have gathered. The air is full of wild joy, as children dash around, aware that the light is fading and it will soon be time to go home.

Jimmy brushes the snow from the ledge and they both perch there, looking out on the scene. He puts his arm around her and they don't speak for a while, just sit watching as the sky turns lavender-pink.

Two children run in front of them shrieking, throwing snowballs at each other and ducking. Suddenly, a snowball smacks Eva's foot, hard.

'Ow!' She jumps up and shakes it off her boots, but it hasn't hurt her, it's more the shock.

'Sorry!' A young girl runs up. 'Sorry, miss!'

'That's al—'

Her words won't come out.

The girl smiles, turns and dashes off, a thick black braid bumping up and down between her shoulder blades. The likeness is unsettling.

'You alright?' asks Jimmy.

She nods and looks around, searching the square. Then she sees him. A figure in a long dark coat, carrying a toddler in one arm and waving Anna over.

The girl runs up to him and he bends down and says something. She nods, puts her arms around his neck and pulls him in for a kiss on one cheek, then does the same on the other.

Jimmy looks to where she's staring. 'What is it? What are you looking at?'

'It's him. It's Zina's son.'

Jimmy squints then opens his eyes wide. 'So it is. Who's that with him?'

'That's her granddaughter. Anna.'

'No, the other one.'

Michalis has stood up now and next to him is a woman Eva doesn't know. She holds her hand out and Anna clasps it, and Michalis reaches for the other.

'It's a bit soon, isn't it?' says Jimmy.

She shrugs. 'It's been a year, I suppose.'

He looks different, she thinks. From here, in the fading light, she might not even have recognised him had it not been for Anna. Then she realises what it is. He's smiling. She's never seen him smile before. And it seems right that he has this now. That he's happy.

'You alright?' Jimmy asks.

She turns up her collar.

'Of course. It was just a shock. She looks so much like her.'

She watches Anna let go of the woman's hand and run ahead, twirling in the snow, arms out wide. Dancing without a care. They stand and watch her as she spins faster and faster, face raised to the sky.

'Come on,' she says to Jimmy. 'Let's go home.'

The sun scorches the earth outside, but here in the mud-walled kitchen it is damp and cool. She pummels the dough on the scarred wooden table, covers it with a clean cloth and, while she waits for it to rise, scrubs some of the children's clothes in the sink. Once it's ready she takes a knife, slashes a cross in the top and carries it to the stone oven in the yard. Here she slides it in on a wooden palette.

It's Tuesday, always a good day, and the children play carefree. He's at market today; town is far, so he stays overnight. Her youngest, Michalis, catches a whiff of the baking and runs to tell the others. They have to wait for it to cool, and their shouts of impatience fill her with happiness.

Finally it's time and she pulls off chunks and hands one to each of them – three boys, two girls – and a last handful for herself. She sits on the ground under the fig tree and they fall around her, moulding themselves to her shape, eating in hungry, contented silence. She gives Michalis the biggest piece of the loaf, the *psisha*, its soft, crustless soul. He knows she favours him and yet the others don't seem to notice. He hugs her, takes another bite and looks up at her, opening his mouth wide as he chews, making her laugh. She pushes this moment of pure bright joy into a pocket of her mind, for safekeeping. It will always be there whenever she needs it.

She glances at him again. He is her most-loved thing and she his. It will always be like this, she thinks. It's the way everything else can be endured. She puts her hand in his hair and ruffles it, and he moves in even closer.

AUTHOR'S NOTE

The true story of Hella and Styllou

CONTAINS SPOILERS

The Unspeakable Acts of Zina Pavlou is a work of fiction. It was inspired by the true story of Hella Dorothea Christofis (née Bleicher), who was murdered by her mother-in-law, Styllou Pantopiou Christofi, on 28 July 1954.

In 1941, Styllou's son, Stavros, emigrated from Cyprus to London, where he met German-born Hella and got married. They had three children. When his mother came to visit in 1953, there were tensions between the two women. At one point, Styllou left for a few weeks, and things calmed down. But on her return the situation worsened.

Styllou criticised Hella constantly, especially regarding the children's upbringing. Hella's health deteriorated, and Stavros took her to see a doctor, whose advice was that the two women shouldn't be living under the same roof. The couple decided Styllou had to leave. They told her that Hella would take the children to Germany, to visit her parents, and by the time she returned they wanted her gone. Days later, Stavros returned home after working at the Café de Paris to find that Hella had been murdered.

Styllou spoke very little English and read and wrote no Greek. From the night of Hella's death to her own execution five months later, she needed an interpreter/translator. Unlike today, in the 1950s there was a very relaxed approach to employing police translators; a list was kept of people who spoke various languages and they'd be called on when needed. Translators were paid by the hour and would chop and change according to who was available. Sometimes the police had to improvise (like the night of Hella's death, when, yes, they *did* ask Stavros to translate for his mother). In fact, Styllou had at least three other translators throughout the next few months, one of whom was a petty criminal himself. All her translators were men (though female translators existed, as this was one of the few clerical jobs open to married women).

Styllou was found guilty of bludgeoning Hella, strangling her and setting her body alight. Her version of events just didn't add up, and the evidence against her was damning (petrol-soaked shoes, traces of Hella's blood on the kitchen floor, a neighbour who saw her burning what he assumed was a tailor's dummy, a stolen wedding ring). And yet, she maintained her innocence.

Her son, Stavros, urged her to plead insanity but she refused. The Chief Medical Officer at Holloway Prison, Dr Thomas Christie, who observed her over a number of months, declared her insane (though medically fit to stand trial). His report, detailing his findings, was never presented in court, and once Styllou was sentenced to hang, he protested and insisted on a medical inquiry. Three other doctors then examined Styllou and determined that she was not insane and there was no reason not to allow the death penalty to stand. A woman had not been hanged at Holloway Prison for over thirty years.

The night before her execution, with the medical report now public, a handful of MPs requested an urgent appointment with the Home Secretary, to ask for a reprieve. They were convinced she was insane and should be locked up rather than executed. An appointment was not granted, and Styllou Christofi was hanged the following morning.

This is a relatively unknown case and received little publicity at the time, especially considering its gruesome nature. Seven months after Styllou's execution, there was a huge public outcry when Ruth Ellis was hanged for the murder of her abusive lover, David Blakely. In his autobiography, the executioner to both women, Albert Pierrepoint, noted the lack of press interest in Styllou's fate. He said, 'One wonders if it was because she was middle-aged, unattractive and foreign?'

It wasn't until after the sentencing, of course, that the jury and public discovered something that the police, legal teams and medical officer already knew: that decades earlier, in Cyprus, Styllou, along with two neighbours, had been put on trial for the murder of her own mother-in-law. There are scant facts about this, but the story goes that her accomplices held the woman down while Styllou rammed a burning torch down her throat. She was acquitted.

What's fact and what's fiction?

Although a work of fiction, I've tried to keep to the facts as much as possible where the crime and evidence are concerned. Styllou Christofi's treatment in court and the disparaging language used about her was reported by the press and is reflected in Zina's court scenes.

The actual trial transcripts are not available, so general impressions of the proceedings inside Court Number One at the Old Bailey are from press cuttings and from an interview with Robbie Lancaster. Aged just twenty-three in 1954, she was one of the first female officers in the City of London Police and was in court during Styllou Christofi's trial. Now in her nineties, Robbie still remembers Styllou clearly as a 'very small, wizened lady with dark hair and darting eyes'. She also recalls how pleased the public gallery was when her death sentence was announced.

Police and medical reports often noted Styllou's rough peasant nature and press reports focused on her lack of education, poverty, foreignness and age. The prosecution called this 'a stupid crime by a stupid woman of the peasant sort'. A deep jealousy of Hella was presented as the motive.

In this novel, Zina's police statement from the night of the murder, and statements by her son and neighbour, are largely based on fact, though dramatised. The characterisation of everyone involved is a work of fiction and bears no resemblance to the actual people who were involved. Mick, Hedy and Anna are works of my imagination and not in any way connected to Stavros, Hella and their children.

The memos and petitions in the book are informed by actual documents, as are the letters in and out of prison, apart from the letter to Zina's estranged husband, which is not based on any truth. In reality, Styllou did write to him just days before her execution, but the backstory I have created about how the first murder in Cyprus came about is fiction. In fact, it seems Styllou's husband left her after she was acquitted of killing his mother. The scenes set in Cyprus are pure fiction, as is the village of Spakato, though it's true that Styllou was married to an older man at the age of just fourteen.

In my book, Zina's disturbing behaviour in prison and the unnerving incidents that take place in her cell are informed by Styllou's actions, as documented by wardens who were obliged to report anything unusual.

I've taken some liberties with the legal process, allowing Eva more access than a translator would have had, and adding a few dramatic touches to the Old Bailey, like microphones to amplify voices rather than just record.

ACKNOWLEDGEMENTS

My first thanks are to Kate Wheeler, Marianne Holmes and Liz Ottosson, my writing group, who were instrumental in helping me discover where the story was. Without their ongoing support, I may not have persevered.

A huge thanks to my agent, Abi Fellows, who always understood what I was trying to achieve and why it mattered so much. Her positivity and belief in Zina and Eva kept me going. And thank you to everyone at the Good Literary Agency for their constant backing.

And, of course, thank you Laura Palmer, Peyton Stableford and Polly Grice at Head of Zeus for seeing the potential in this story and making it happen. To Jessie Price and Ben Prior for creating the cover. To Jo Liddiard, Andrew Knowles, and Zoe Giles in marketing; and Karen Dobbs, Vicki Eddison, and Dan Groenewald in sales. And thank you to everyone else at Head of Zeus and Bloomsbury who has worked on this book.

To Sam Baker for being an enthusiastic early reader and supporter.

To author and former criminal barrister Victoria Dowd, who read a very early draft and patiently explained why I couldn't just write a court scene however I liked. And to author, former detective and crime fiction adviser Graham Bartlett, who was instrumental in helping me tackle the trial scenes. Any errors are my own.

To Dr Yvonne Fowler, who has trained hundreds of interpreters and is an expert in her field. Her insight into the profession now, and how it may have been in the 1950s, was essential in creating Eva's character. And to Dr Stephanie Carty, whose Psychology of Character course was invaluable in getting to grips with themes of loss and mental health.

To the librarians and archivists at: the National Archives; the British Library; the London Metropolitan Archives; the Museum of London, and the Howard League Archive (via Warwick University).

To Robbie Lancaster for agreeing to an interview. In 1954, she was a twenty-three-year-old police officer who was present at the Christofi trial (see Author's Note). Thank you to Robbie's son, Robert, and his partner, my good friend Vicky Mayer, for putting me in touch – the connection was a sheer coincidence and I still can't quite believe it.

To the Curtis Brown Creative gang of 2015, especially Caroline Hodges for her friendship and book chat.

To my writing pals, who make me laugh on a weekly basis, and share their triumphs, failures and wisdom on our Friday Zooms. With a special shout-out to Charlotte Levin, whose insight regarding this book was like striking gold at a crucial moment. Similarly, Sophie Hannah for her sage advice.

To constant good friends, Nicole Carmichael, Helen Gent, Rosalind Lowe, Alison Lusuardi, Angela Martin, Gillian Mosely and Sat Wilks. To my sister Kaytrina Jons. And my cousin Anna Kioufi, who was almost as obsessed with this story as I was.

To Andrew, for his love, confidence and uncanny ability to solve plot issues. And last here, but always first, Ryan and Aaron.

READING GROUP QUESTIONS

1. Eva's job as an interpreter is to 'speak for a murderer', but Eva doesn't translate crucial information about the first murder to the governor and, later, omits information in court.
   a. Why does she do this? In her position, what would you have done?
   b. Why do you think Eva feels drawn to Zina, and is determined to help her?
   c. What other jobs in today's world present moral dilemmas like this? Could you do any of them?
2. Eva contemplates whether Zina is a victim or a ruthless killer, and wonders if it's possible to be both.
   a. What do you think? Why?
   b. How did you feel about Zina at the start of the book? Did that change and why?
3. Compare the experiences of the characters who are all immigrants – Eva, Jimmy, Michalis and Hedy.
   a. To what extent has each one assimilated and how? Is there any personal cost?
4. Zina's illiteracy is constantly referred to in court – and the power of language is a huge theme throughout the novel.
   a. Why is Zina's illiteracy mentioned in court? How does her lack of education impact what happens to her?
   b. Why does language matter so much?
   c. How would Zina be treated in court today? Have things changed?
5. Although a work of fiction, this novel is inspired by the true story of Styllou Christofi, who killed her daughter-in-law, Hella. How does that affect the way you feel about the book?

ABOUT THE AUTHOR

ELENI KYRIACOU is an award-winning editor and journalist. Her writing has appeared in the *Guardian*, the *Observer*, *Grazia*, and *Red*, among others. She's the daughter of Greek Cypriot immigrant parents, and her debut novel, *She Came To Stay*, was published in 2020. Her latest novel, *The Unspeakable Acts of Zina Pavlou*, is inspired by the true-crime story of the penultimate woman to be executed in Britain.

Follow her on @EleniKWriter and
www.elenikwriter.com.